HAMAMA

SARIT GRADWOHL

ISBN-13: 978-0-9888782-9-7

DEDICATION

This book is dedicated to the memory of my grandmother Yonah (Hamama) Vazif and my grandfather Yefet (Hassan) Vazif, may they rest in peace, for their tale, for my wonderful childhood, and for the love of stories that they instilled in me.

CONTENTS

ACKNOWLEDGMENTS

I would like to thank my dear husband, Ronen Gradwohl, who, in addition to his support and encouragement, also translated this book and everything associated with it (including this acknowledgement). I am also grateful to my mother for helping with the family research and to my sister Hani for designing the cover, my website, and promotional materials. Many thanks also to my father and my sister Talia for running around Israel selling and promoting this book – the book was born of this family and receives its constant help and support, which I truly appreciate.

Many thanks to all those who helped edit the book, including Manya Treece and Patricia Zick. A special thanks to my agent Jonathan Agin, who believed in the book and greatly improved it. I'm not sure which one of us is Don Quixote and which is Sancho Panza, but I believe that our journey together is not yet over!

Finally, I am eternally grateful to my grandmother Yonah (Hamama) Vazif and my grandfather Yefet (Hassan) Vazif, may they rest in peace, for their tale, for my wonderful childhood, and for the love of stories that they instilled in me. This book is dedicated to their memory.

[The Poet:] Tell me, pure and perfect one, tell me so that we may rejoice here in Taima[1]—O wise princess, tell me, where do you make your home?

The dove answered: 'Sa'adiah, there is a high chamber reserved for me in the Palace[2].

סַפְּרִי תַמָּה תְמִימָה   סַפְּרִי נָגִיל בְּתֵימָא

בַּת מְלָכִים הַחֲכָמָה   אָן מְקוֹמֵךְ סַפְּרִי לִי

עָנְתָה יוֹנָה סְעַדְיָה   לִי בְּפַלְטֵרִין עֲלִיָּה

Sa'adiah ben Amram
Yemen, the 17th century

Translated by T.Carmi
The Penguin Book of Hebrew Verse

ר' סעדיה בן עמרם
תימן, המאה ה-17

1. A province in North Arabia.
2. The land of Israel.

2007

When I was a little girl, Grandpa was already old. But back then, he was a mischievous kind of old, and he would talk, laugh and sing, peel oranges for us, and poison our noses with tobacco. He's grown much older. He hardly speaks and is constantly in pain. Grandma worries, and even though she repeatedly says that they've already lived their lives, and she's not afraid of death, I know that she's terrified of remaining alone.

This house was once my second home. I would go there every day after school. Mom worked shifts, so she was either at work or resting after a night of work, and Dad didn't come home until five. Grandma would cut me a slice of bread with sour cream and cucumbers. Sometimes there were homemade pitas, the kind you couldn't find anywhere else.

When I was little, I complained about the thick pita that I couldn't cut open straight. The ones from the store were pre-cut. When I cut Grandma's pita, the knife always poked out of one of the sides, and when I spread the sour cream, it would ooze out of the holes and get all over my clothes.

Grandma always laughed at me while she cooked our dinner: steamed vegetables, Yemenite chicken soup, or green-yellow lentil soup. But I lived for dessert. I'll always fondly remember those days when she served us a huge slice of yeast cake, hot and dripping with date spread and cocoa, saying, "Just don't tell your mom."

Grandpa would arrive at the meal in a blue robe—his work robe—straight from the garden or the yard. Sometimes, he would come on

1

his motorized bicycle, riding on the trail that meandered from the center of town. When I was really little I could sit on the white basket in the back. I always proudly told people that my grandpa built the bicycle and its motor. That's how he was—building, constructing, planting, and picking. He was a born craftsman. He had golden hands, gray and cracked hands, with fingers that could crush my nape with affection, and, in the winter, warm my own.

I grew up and left our little town of Pardes Hanna, drawn to the intellectual life of Tel Aviv.

A year ago, Dad called me at work and said that Grandpa was in the hospital. He urged me to come—Grandpa might be nearing his last moments, he said.

"You have to understand that it's going to happen. He's old and sick. This is it, it's going to happen."

But it didn't. Grandpa left the hospital, and the oxygen mask in the bedroom became a permanent fixture. Grandma started sleeping in the living room.

I knew I should visit then more than ever, but it was so hard to see Grandpa like this. My sister encouraged me, and we went together. After our visit, we walked behind the house.

My favorite childhood hiding spot—a hollow tree surrounded by mushrooms where I read books and learned to dream—was gone. I looked for old photographs to show my husband the dear place where I grew up—the room where Grandpa slept and studied Torah; the pecan grove behind the house; the spot where the loquat, apricot, and pomegranate trees stood; the myrtle bush at the entrance to the yard, whose round, purple fruits I picked each year during the holiday of Sukkot, and from which Grandpa would make laxatives; the old mailbox that housed the hornets who ruined two of my birthdays.

"You write, no?" My sister said. "Why don't you write Grandpa and Grandma's story? Before it's too late."

I started coming to Pardes Hanna once a week to hear my grandparents' life story. Grandma was thrilled, as if she had waited all this time to finally share her biography. And even Grandpa would sometimes join in. They reminisced. I heard new stories and listened to the old ones in a new light. And this is what they shared.

CHAPTER 1

"I met your grandfather when we were little kids in Yemen," my grandmother began. "He came to live with us after his mother died. His mother—Nadra—that was her name. In Hebrew, it means *kokhava*, or star. She was the sister of my father, David. I didn't know about Nadra or her son, until one day Father came home with him."

Grandma sits across from my camera, with Grandpa at her side. He listens to the story of his life. I drown in his green-gray eyes and see Nadra, his mother.

Nadra, a light-skinned girl with green eyes. The little princess in her family. The only daughter amongst many brothers. Many marriage proposals, yet time was running out. They might see, they might desire; her beauty might expose her to one of the soldiers. And then she met Salem Salem.

And what did she see in Salem Salem? No one really knew. The smell that emanated from him scared everyone away. He was a fish merchant, from a small distant village on the coast of the Red Sea. Salem Salem bought the little fish from the Arab fishermen, packed them well, and went off to sell them in the villages far from the sea. The merchandise was high-quality, but the smell very strong, and since it stuck to his body, it stuck to his life, and he was renamed Vazif, the name of that small smelly fish. He would wander great distances and enjoyed the journey and the encounters with the different people. But when he glanced into Nadra's eyes as she bought his merchandise, he couldn't help but say to her, "Your eyes remind me of the sea."

And as he spoke his eyes welled up with tears, and the ocean of love she saw within him moved her greatly.

The wedding was held in Nadra's home village. David, Nadra's favorite brother, had a hard time letting go of his sister, and even though he was married and a father of three, and his work was strenuous, he insisted on accompanying the couple a long distance until he himself saw the sea.

Nadra and Salem Vazif's great love warmed the hearts of all those around them. Jews and Arabs alike treated them well, and Salem's business flourished. But right around when Nadra became pregnant, Salem grew ill. And soon after baby Hassan was born, the father died. The joy turned to grief, and David and his brothers were quick to organize the shiva for the fish merchant, the first of the Vazif dynasty.

At the end of the shiva, they celebrated the *brith*—the Jewish ceremony of circumcision—and David tried to convince his sister to return home:

"Nadra, you don't have anything keeping you here anymore," he said.

"This is my home," she answered.

"And how will you support yourself?"

"And what will I do at home? You'll want to marry me off again?"

"I didn't say that."

"This is my home, and Hassan's. Here, by the sea," she said.

David understood that because of her grief, his sister wouldn't leave, so for the time being, he didn't persist in his attempts to convince her. At the end of the *shloshim,* the thirty-day period of mourning, David and his brothers left, leaving Nadra behind.

Nadra wove baskets, laundered other people's clothes, and helped the local midwife in order to support herself and little Hassan. Occasionally, David came to visit, and every time, he suggested that she return home, but every time she refused. At night, she sat facing the sea and yearned for Salem. When Hassan turned two, he came and sat beside her on the sand and asked her why she was crying.

Her tremendous grief was clear for all to see, but that didn't stop the Arab neighbors from gossiping about Hassan. Whenever tragedy struck, Yemenites would accuse the demons of the house, demons who usually lived peacefully with their human landlord. Now the neighbors whispered to each other that, because of a lack of myrrh incense, the child Hassan was transformed into a demon by *Albada and* had eaten his father. They conjured prophesies about the father's revenge that would strike at the birth of a grandson.

Years later, when Hassan would jokingly recall the prophesies to his pregnant wife, she always refused to laugh. And even though by then they lived in the Land of Israel, where the evil spirits hold no sway, Hamama's heart was always struck by the fear of her husband's death.

Nadra lived with her son for nine years, during which time she taught him a variety of skills: weaving baskets, fixing jags, and laundering clothes. Despite his young age, he too took on work, and his golden hands eventually gained fame throughout the village. He was a strange child—he was very serious did not laugh much. He watched his mother, who watched the sea. He watched as she slowly deteriorated, and there was nothing he could do about it.

"I'm not worried about you, *ya ibn*, my son. You have strength and courage like your father, may he rest in peace."

"Tell me more about my father!" demanded the child. But she couldn't. Instead, she told him stories of a different land, a land where everything was good, the Land of Israel; stories that she had heard in her childhood, from her father.

Hassan's green-gray eyes sailed into the distance with his mother's stories.

One day, David came to visit his sister. But as he approached the entrance to the village, the Arab neighbors came running toward him with bitter cries. "Your sister is dead! Your sister is dead!"

David ran to the little house and found her as beautiful as he remembered her, lying on a mat with her eyes closed, with little Hassan Salem Vazif sitting quietly at her feet. David hugged his nephew tightly. They sat together, their feelings caught up in the whirlwind of a great storm, and not a word had to be spoken.

After an hour, David channeled his grief into small chores, and eventually went to gather a *minyan*—a quorum of ten Jews for the traditional public worship—from the adjacent town and started to plan the burial. The whole time, Hassan stayed in the house, sitting by the empty mat, steeped in uncertainty about his future. He was too young to decide his own fate and too distraught to even consider what might happen next.

5

He was not permitted to attend the funeral, and in any case, didn't want to go. They had to transfer the body to the neighboring town where there was a Jewish cemetery, but Hassan couldn't imagine going on such a frightful journey. The only thing he could think about was the smell of her decaying body.

After the *shiva*, David helped him pack his few possessions. Hassan parted from the sea and headed inland to Tholet.

"Our village was in the county of Shar'ab, and its name was Tholet," Grandma tells me.

I try to pronounce the name correctly, with an emphasis on the first syllable. Both of my grandparents smile at my pathetic attempts—the Yemenite accent did not pass on to the third generation, and I'm butchering it.

"Tholet means 'third,'" Grandpa translates. I'm happy that he's participating and encourage him to continue.

"Your grandmother tells it very well," he says and smiles at her lovingly.

"Come on, Hassan, you tell the story. Here, to the camera." Grandma also tries to encourage him, but he waves her off tiredly.

"Hamama, tell her about your childhood. About the monkeys!" He winks at her and she laughs.

The village of Tholet was a small Arab village that was spread out over the center of one of Yemen's mountains. The Sekaya River flowed at the foot of the mountains, and at its peak, the village residents tended to terraced fields where they grew various fruit trees and legumes. The tallest house in the village naturally belonged to the governor, who liked watching out over his subjects from his porch, whereas the shortest and smallest house belonged to David.

At the time, Jews were protected people, *dhimmah,* and were granted religious freedom and assurances of personal security and property in exchange for their acknowledgment of Muslim political and social supremacy. This acknowledgment was expressed by the payment of the *jizya,* the poll tax, and obedience to a collection of discriminatory restrictions as detailed in the Shari'a laws. For example, Jews were required to wear distinguishing clothes; they could only ride a donkey side-saddle and were not allowed to ride horses at all; they were prohibited from carrying weapons; and their homes could not be taller than those of their Muslim neighbors.

David and his family were the only Jews in the village. Their house, three stories tall, was made of clay and mud mixed with cow dung. In reality, it was inferior to those of their Arab neighbors because of the family's financial situation, and not because of the Imam's discriminatory laws, which their governor did not strictly enforce.

The first floor consisted of a pen occupied by a cow named Yamima and two elderly goats. The chicken coop and small vegetable garden were also found on that floor, but Yamima considered the whole area her home and the others as mere guests. Luckily, she was a welcoming host. All who passed through the door were greeted with a blessing and a lick of affection on the hand. Nevertheless, Sa'adia, David's son, built a ladder that led straight from the outside up to the second floor.

Ahuva, David's wife, loved her friendly cow, but had to chastise her daily to keep her from the family's main sources of food—a variety of vegetables and legumes. Some say that her strict disciplining of Yamima came at the expense of her children's upbringing.

Ahuva herself was quiet and pleasant. She learned to keep her many worries about the house's upkeep to herself, and there they stayed, plowing wrinkles into her young face.

On the second floor, Ahuva cooked the family's meals. She ground the wheat with a smooth stone, and sometimes also ground the legumes—this way she thickened the modest dishes to better satisfy her small children's hungry bellies. Sometimes, she dragged the stone to the little terrace and was comforted by the sun's caressing rays. The dishes sometimes turned out a bit salty because of her sweat.

On the third floor, four children shared cots. Sa'adia and Sarah spread themselves out over most of the space. Little Kadya didn't care—she would simply curl up into a little ball—but Hamama always felt suffocated.

During the nights —and all day, really—she had difficulty finding her place. She would often go down to the second floor and crawl in between her parents, who slept on the terrace. In the morning, David would wake her up, so she could run up to the cots upstairs and avoid getting chastised by Ahuva. Those were little moments of grace, clean air, and a blanket of stars. But on stormy, rainy nights they all cuddled together on the third floor, and if it was very cold, they would go down to the second floor and sleep in the kitchen next to the large clay ovens.

These were the days of drought, and David's livelihood suffered, but his pleasant character and creative solutions saved his family from starvation. David peddled haberdashery tools and chunks of turmeric with which the Arabs colored their faces. Every day, David went door to door, stood in the souks, or bazaars, and sold his wares for money or food. Sometimes, Hamama awoke early in the morning and followed her father, trying to keep up with his quick pace, and after the first successful sale, she would return home with a jug of milk or bag of flour.

Hamama was chosen to accompany her father for a reason. She was innocent and hardworking, and most of all—honest. Little Kadya was only three years old and couldn't lift a jug without breaking it. The oldest child, Rivka, was already married and lived with her husband, Shumuel, in the village of El Be'aden. And Sa'adia and Sarah were little rascals. Ahuva knew that if she were to ask them to carry any foodstuff, they would undoubtedly extract a tax. They already ate from the flour and chewed the wheat seeds, and even the stomach pains they had to endure afterwards didn't cause them to change their ways.

But Hamama didn't like to help her father. Not because she was lazy, but because of her two mischievous siblings who would harass her every time she returned, trying to grab her jug or bag the moment she entered the house. She had to endure getting pinched all over and was forced to call out to her mother for help.

One Friday, David came back from his journey to earn his family's keep.

"I forgot to bring the *dugra*," he said with drooping shoulders from his long journey.

The *dugra* was a sort of bean used in the lassis, a hot, steaming dish topped with cumin. The dish was served on a large plate, which Ahuva placed on the mats. The family members would sit in a circle around the plate and eat together. This family lassis meal was held only on Shabbat and was undertaken ceremoniously. The children sat and waited for David to partake first, before charging at the plate.

The strongest ate the most. Sarah would hold her dress folded close to her chest, so she could take a large amount of lassis and pretend to eat it, but instead she would throw it onto her dress. That way she grabbed more lassis than what she managed to eat, and later, she would go outside to eat the rest. Everybody already accepted this habit of hers, but Sa'adia didn't like to give in and followed her out every time to argue with her. Ahuva always complained about the dress getting soiled and filled with lice, but David just smiled silently and kept on feeding little Kadya.

"The kids will be so disappointed if there's no lassis for Shabbat!" Ahuva said to David as she cooked the chicken soup. A moment later, she smiled and called for Hamama.

"Hamama! Grab one of the large jugs for me, please!"

Hamama went to the shelves on the wall and chose a suitable jug.

"I'll give you a jug of soup for Grandma. I'm sure she has lassis. Tell her that we'll trade this time."

"But—" Hamama tried to object.

"No 'but.' You know you're the only one I can trust with this."

"Ya, Ahuva, leave the girl alone, I'll go," David suggested.

"That's all right, Father, I'll go," Hamama said, feeling embarrassed that she had caused her father, who worked hard all day, to suggest something like that. Hamama grabbed the jug of soup before David could get up, and she ran outside. At least Sarah and Sa'adia weren't around to follow her.

The day was hot and dry and the walk to Grandma's house took about two hours. Hamama left Tholet and made her way to the next village. She headed down the mountain on which Tholet was situated and crossed the Sekaya River. She looked up tiredly at the top of the mountain and saw Hassabyein, the adjacent village. Her father walked there every Shabbat to go to the synagogue. Except he didn't carry a jug full of chicken soup on his head. Her small, bare feet led her skillfully between the rocks in her way, and her skinny body was strong enough to carry such a large jug. She was only five years old.

Her grandma, who was standing outside the house, recognized the little girl with the jug on her head from afar. She quickly prepared a jug of lassis, and when Hamama finally showed up at her door, she gave her granddaughter water to drink, and two dates and a bag of nuts to reenergize her for the walk back to her village. Hamama adored her grandmother for the way she spoiled her.

"Now go back home. *Yalla!* Come on! It's almost Shabbat!" her grandma warned as she placed the jug of lassis on Hamama's head. Hamama y raised her hands to grab it, and reluctantly started the march back.

If only I could stay here a little longer! It's always nicer at Grandma's. Quieter.

The heat started to bother her more, and droplets of sweat covered her little body. The appetizing smell of the lassis on her head gave her the strength to continue walking. Her stomach was grumbling, as if it too smelled the lassis and demanded its share. Only then did Hamama realize that she hadn't really eaten anything that day.

The thoughts with her conscience began. *What's a little taste? No one would notice. But then, will I be any better than Sa'adia and Sarah? Mother and Father trust me!* Her mind was engaged in a heated debate. The sun's rays beat down on her, her stomach grumbled, her feet marched, and then, up ahead, she saw Tholet. *So close, I'll definitely make it!* Hamama was filled with pride for overcoming this trial, and the pride gave her additional strength to quicken her pace. She approached her house with a smile and glistening eyes, only to find her brother and sister staring at her furiously:

"You thief! You ate from the lassis!" Sarah yelled.

"No, I didn't!" Hamama retorted, as her joy, shattered into pieces, had disappeared amongst the little rocks by her feet.

"I see it in your eyes!" Sarah insisted.

"And where did you get all that strength? You practically skipped all the way to the house," Sa'adia added.

"She definitely ate," Sarah said to Sa'adia as she approached Hamama. Hamama slowly stepped back.

"Leave the girl alone!" Ahuva yelled from the top floor.

But her intervention came too late. Hamama placed the jug of lassis on the ground and started running, her eyes burning with tears of affront.

She ran between her neighbors' houses, as their kids watched her, puzzled. She ran between the vendors' stands in the souk at the center of town, oblivious to the colors and smells that usually brought her joy. She rounded the governor's enormous yard, not noticing the policemen standing guard. She continued to run between the rocks and boulders, ascending the mountain. She ran all the way out of the village, up to the terraced fields. She avoided the guard's gaze and skipped up the steps, one by one. Her heart raced, and her thoughts focused on revenge.

Mother and Father will be so mad at them! I won't come back home! And Sa'adia and Sarah will get in so much trouble!

The sun no longer bothered her, nor did her hunger. But as her courage grew and her pride recovered, Hamama unknowingly crossed the border of the town's jurisdiction, where an unpleasant surprise awaited her.

A group of large monkeys with red butts congregated at the peak of the mountain. They were busy discussing matters of the day when a little barefooted girl invaded their territory. The instant Hamama noticed the monkeys, and their gaze met hers, a momentary silence pervaded the air. Hamama froze, taken aback by these enormous creatures that she had never before encountered. The monkeys too were curious, and the largest of the pack slowly and carefully approached the little creature in front of him. He stopped twenty paces from the girl, examined her from head to toe, and then pierced the silence with a loud shout. It's possible that he only wished to greet her, in his way, but the frightened girl responded with a terrified shriek of her own and raced down the mountain. The other monkeys recognized this as disrespect and started yelling loudly.

The largest monkey took off after the intruder. Hamama's little heart thumped and thumped, and every time her foot landed on the ground, her heart leaped up and threatened to escape through her throat. She ran through the terraced fields, the monkey close behind; ran past the guard, the monkey still close behind her. The guard, who saw it all, quickly fired a shot into the air. The shot frightened the monkey off, but Hamama kept running, as if possessed by a demon.

The impetus for her flight down the mountain was consigned to oblivion the moment Hamama arrived at the doorstep of her house, where she fainted. Ahuva and David quickly helped her regain consciousness, but she was still gripped by such great fear that David pronounced, "She needs *machva*."

The machva was a white-hot metal rod that was placed next to the patient's head to treat various illnesses and fears. Everybody knew that only an expert could treat with a *machva*. And those who didn't know learned it the hard way.

When Hamama heard the verdict, she nearly fainted again. Had she escaped from a vicious gang of moneys only to face a white-hot rod?

David took Hamama to the village expert. They walked slowly, hand in hand. David felt Hamama's little hand trembling in his own.

He lifted her in his arms, and she wrapped her arms around his rugged, tanned neck.

The Arab looked at her with gentle eyes as he held the rod over the fire. Hamama shut her eyes and swore to herself to be brave. She glanced at the Arab, and then at the heating rod changing color in the flames. She shut her eyes again and swore never to agree to any more errands for food, so she wouldn't have to think about stealing and wouldn't have any more rendezvous with red-butted monkeys and *machvas*.

"Ready?" the Arab asked, and without waiting for an answer he placed the tip of the white-hot rod above her right ear. It felt like a dagger, and Hamama lost consciousness.

She woke up to the beat of her father's footsteps and found herself being carried home. All the neighbors, their kids, and their animals, stood outside their respective houses and looked on with mercy in their eyes. Even the chickens. She buried her face in David's chest as he walked peacefully home. That day was the only time she could remember her father raising his hands against Sa'adia and Sarah.

The ill-behaved siblings didn't bother Hamama anymore, and one time even invited her to play with them. This was a big deal for Hamama, who up until then had only Kadya to play with because, after all, the Arab and Jewish children did not play together. The three siblings went down to the Sekaya River and dangled their feet in the water. Sarah helped Hamama tie her pants above the knee, so her clothes wouldn't get wet. Hamama didn't really care if her clothes got wet in the desert heat, but her older sister's caring touch was so rare that Hamama would have been fine had her sister wanted to tie all the ends of her clothes into flowers and butterfly knots.

"Shh…they're coming!" Sa'adia cried.

Sarah shoved Hamama behind a boulder and hid beside her.

"What's going on?" Hamama asked.

"Shh…shut up, or I'll poke your eyes out," Sarah whispered.

Two Arab merchants came to the edge of the river, carrying heavy bags on their backs.

"*As-salamu 'alaykum,*" Sa'adia greeted them. Peace be with you.

"*Wa'alaykumu s-salam!*" the merchants answered as they folded up their gowns. And peace upon you.

Hamama peeked out from behind a boulder. When she wanted to ask Sarah again what was going on, she noticed that Sarah had disappeared. Hamama stayed hidden, watching.

"Where are you going to sell?" Sa'adia asked. One merchant was already crossing the river while the other stayed back to converse. In the meantime, Sarah hopped quickly and quietly behind that merchant, and with a short blade she cut a small hole in the sack on his back. White yams fell from the sack, and she caught them in her dress and ran off.

"What's this?" The merchant was baffled by the sound of yams falling behind him, but before he could figure out what was going on, Sa'adia also started running away. Hamama froze for a moment, but then took off after the two, so that the merchant's rage wouldn't land on her.

"Thieves! Thieves! I'll tell your father!" the merchant yelled as the kids disappeared into the distance. When out of sight, Sa'adia and Sarah fell on the ground, and Hamama joined her siblings, panting from running. Sarah handed Sa'adia a yam and also cut a piece for Hamama.

"I'm not touching that," Hamama declared. "You stole it."

"Shut up. I won't offer again. Here," Sarah said and handed her the yam. But Hamama knew that if she partook of the bounty, she would be implicated, and that one of these days her siblings would want her to be the one to cut the poor merchants' sacks.

"I don't want it!" she said and stood up.

"You better not tattle. I'll rip your ears off," Sarah said as Sa'adia grinned.

But Hamama didn't have to tell her father. The merchant, who knew David, did. David quickly paid the Arab with food to cover the cost of the damage. Ahuva scolded the children and said that because of what they did, they wouldn't get dinner or breakfast. Hamama was sure that they had more yams, so how would this punishment help? But David's disappointed look hurt her more than the hunger and anger. She untied the knots in her pants and went to bed, upset by her siblings' indifference and convinced that her life was destined to boredom and loneliness.

A week later, Hassan arrived.

They didn't expect him, and even Ahuva was surprised. Making a living was still difficult, and David was forced to wander for long periods of time. Sometimes, he didn't even return for Shabbat. Ahuva had known that David planned to visit Nadra, but there had no news of her death. When David entered the house with the boy, she understood. David smiled despite his grief as he gathered his family.

"Everyone, this is Hassan, the son of my sister, may she rest in peace. He'll live with us now." David rested his hand on the boy's shoulder.

"He's so white," Sa'adia whispered.

"And he has green eyes!" Sarah whispered.

"No, they're gray!" Hamama whispered, but then a moment later she wasn't sure anymore. It looked like the boy's eyes kept changing colors.

Kadya was the first to hug Hassan. Then Sa'adia shook his hand.

"Welcome," Ahuva said as she pushed Sarah forward, but David already knew his children's nature and didn't want the introductions to drag out too long.

"Okay, *t'fadel*," he said in welcome and led Hassan into the house. "Is dinner ready?"

Kadya quickly took Hassan's hand and led him to the mats. When he passed by her, Hamama took advantage of the moment and said in a near whisper, "*As-salamu 'alaykum.*"

"*Wa'alaykumu s-salam,*" Hassan replied, smiling at her.

Hassan was different from anyone Hamama had ever known. He wasn't bigger than Sarah and Sa'adia, but he was more capable than them. Already on the first day, he helped Ahuva fix one of the cooking wares. Ahuva was ready to give up on the cracked jug, but she had a heavy heart. David's livelihood was difficult, and the large jugs were expensive. Hassan came, mixed some mud and dried it on the crack. An hour later he told her, "Now fill it with water."

"Won't it be a waste of water if the jug breaks, and it spills all over the floor?" Ahuva worried.

"Let's do it over the vegetable garden, or over Yamima's water trough," Hassan suggested.

The two went down to the ground floor with two water jugs, and Hamama followed from behind to watch. Hassan raised the jug over his head to prevent Yamima from breaking it in her excitement. When Yamima saw that Hassan's hand was not available she settled for a lick of his armpit. Hassan wasn't ready for this. The tickling sensation shook his whole body, and he almost dropped the jug.

"Yamima!" Ahuva shouted. But the friendly cow was enjoying the game.

Hamama who observed them from afar, quickly ran over and restrained the animal.

"Thanks, Hamama!" Ahuva said. She walked over to the water trough and held the repaired jug over it. Yamima, who thought that her water supply was about to be replenished, used all her strength to try and get out of the five-year-old girl's grip.

"Hold on tight," Hassan encouraged Hamama, and smiled at her. He spilled the water from his jug directly into the repaired jug. Ahuva held on to the jug tightly, but not a drop of water spilled out of the repaired jug.

"You did it! Good job!" she cried happily.

"It was very easy. Easier than what Hamama is doing right now," Hassan replied. He quickly carried the jug of water upstairs, and Ahuva followed him. Hamama released the cow, and the beast bellowed angrily.

"I'll bring you some water, Yamima" Hamama panted and filled the cow's water trough from the carafe on the wall. She then ran upstairs to keep a close eye on the magical feats performed by the boy with the green-gray eyes.

She found him in the yard, of all places, digging small holes and dropping seeds of alb—a fruit that resembles a cherry.

"They won't grow here, Hassan Salem. You have to put them in *hamra* or loam," she said hesitantly.

"I'm not trying to plant them. It's a game I'd see my neighbors playing. Do you want me to teach you?"

Hamama sat down on the ground next to him. Hassan dug a row of four small holes followed by one large hole, and across from them another identical row but in the opposite order. He placed four seeds in each hole.

"You have four holes and a 'home' hole, and I have four holes and a 'home' hole. Each one, in turn, takes the seeds from the first hole and splits the seeds in his hand into the other holes, in order. If you finish the seeds in your row, you get another turn. If you finish the seeds in my row, it's my turn. The goal is to leave your small holes empty and to have the most seeds in your 'home' hole."

Hassan picked up the four seeds from the first hole and handed them to Hamama. She took them with some hesitation, afraid Hassan would realize that she was just a little girl, and that he would run off to play with the older kids. Hassan looked at her expectantly, and she played. They played for almost an hour. And she even won a few times. Had he let her win? It didn't matter. She looked up at Hassan. Maybe he was the answer to her prayers. Maybe she wouldn't be bored and lonely anymore.

Hamama liked to watch her new friend eat. He would eat slowly, confidently, as if he knew he would always have food in front of him, or as perhaps as if the little he ate would always suffice.

Hassan didn't seem to like Sarah and Sa'adia, and when he wasn't playing with Hamama, he occupied himself with his own tasks. He fixed the taboun at home and organized the vegetable garden. He made up games with sticks and built furniture from wood and stone. Within a week of showing up at their home, he had already found a job in the village. He walked from door to door and offered repairs and home improvement ideas. He built wooden shelves in stores to complement the nooks in the walls; for the women, he wove baskets from long, narrow leaves; and he emptied squashes, dried them, and sold them as carafes.

It looked as if this wasn't the first time he had worked for a living, and this pained Hamama. Here she had just sworn not to help her father anymore—and already the new member of the household was providing food for the home.

"Mother, can I eat with Hassan when he comes home from work?" Hamama asked.

"Mother, me, too?" Kadya joined in on the request.

"Of course. That way he won't eat alone," Ahuva said. She knew that the little girls wanted to dine with Hassan, so they wouldn't have to battle over the food with their siblings. Sarah also knew this and grew angry.

"They get more food than me and Sa'adia!" she complained.

"No, sweetie. It only looks that way to you. That's because they don't eat as fast."

Hamama was grateful to Hassan for the way he treated her and Kadya, and she helped him at every opportunity. She was forbidden from walking with him in the village, but when he was responsible for the laundry, she would hang the clothes with him. Ahuva laundered the clothes with boiling water over the *taboun*, adding *ragrag*, a plant they would crush and that would foam and remove stains. She would then hang the clothes on the *hilfa*, a high bush with many thin, dry branches, to which the wet clothes would stick. Whoever was on duty had to sit and guard the laundry until it dried, otherwise the wind would blow it off and mix it with the neighbors' clothes, rendering it impossible to distinguish what belonged to whom.

"Ahuva, let me hang the laundry, I'll go farther, and the clothes won't get lost," Hassan offered, and from then on, that became the custom. Ahuva laundered and Hassan hung. Hamama would go with him to hang the clothes on the high, far *hilfa*. When they finished hanging the laundry, Hassan carved strings from sticks and tied the laundry to the *hilfa*.

"Who'd you learn that from?" Hamama asked.

"My mother," he answered, and his face grew sad for a moment.

"Tell me about your mother," Hamama demanded.

But Hassan couldn't. Instead, he told her tales of the Land of Israel.

He told her of the sacred bond between the Jewish people and their promised land, of how the love in that bond is said to make the earth fertile and its fruits ripe. He told her the story of a turnip that was so large that a fox used it as its lair, and of an enormous peach that comfortably housed three sages and their horses. There was the legend of Rabbi Shimon ben Tachilifa's cabbage, a vegetable so tall that the wise man needed a ladder to climb up and pick its upper leaves.

"When the people of Israel do the will of the Holy One, blessed be He, their land is blessed with fertility and goodness. A sage named Rami ben Yehezkel visited the city of Bnei Brak. One day he walked around a field and noticed fig trees whose fruits were ripe and sweet. The figs were so sweet that their honey poured out to the ground. Goats who were grazing nearby ate the fallen figs as their swollen udders dripped milk, mixing with the fig honey. Rami ben Yehezkel exclaimed, 'This is what God promised us—a land flowing with milk and honey!'"

Hamama listened intently and wide-eyed, her stomach growling, and Hassan smiled at her and felt an overwhelming sense of comfort, of home.

The following week there was a wedding in the village, and David had lots of work, so he didn't have to wander far. Everyone was happy, and even Sarah and Sa'adia behaved exceptionally well at dinner.

"Maybe Hassan will tell us a story?" Hamama asked.

"I didn't know you tell stories," David said.

"They're just stories I heard from Mother, may she rest in peace," Hassan whispered.

Everyone grew silent in Hassan's sorrow. Hassan hadn't planned on telling a story, but he couldn't stand the look of anticipation on everyone's faces, and he began:

"They say that in the Land of Israel, the Holy Land, springs of milk and honey flow there. And Jerusalem is made entirely of gold. There is no land more beautiful, and it grows more beautiful as more Jews come to it. Just like a loving couple, in which the woman becomes more beautiful and fertile and brings children after the man comes to her."

Hassan's eyes shone. For a moment, everyone forgot he was only a boy. The language that emerged from his mouth was an ancient language, and David recognized his own father's words in it. He had also heard these stories as a child, but he had grown wiser, more pragmatic and realistic with age. His sister, he knew, never stopped dreaming in this language.

"The Land of Israel?" David finally interrupted his nephew. "You're trying to speed up the Redemption. The Jewish people of Yemen never learn. Have you heard of the Kamaran Exile? Of Shabtai Tzvi? Of the Mawza Exile? You talk of a Land of Israel that awaits us, but every time we've tried to go there, no good comes of it."

"David, he's only a child," Ahuva intervened.

"I'm not a child anymore," Hassan said.

Everybody had heard whispers of the "Kamaran Exile" and the "Mawza Exile," but the children had never heard the tales in their entirety. Hamama looked up at her parents and hoped that tonight, with all its intimacy, they would tell the tale that everybody wanted to hear, but nobody wanted to tell.

"The Land of Israel might be as wondrous as the Garden of Eden but getting there—" David sighed. "That's about as hard as getting to the actual Garden of Eden. Lots of death. For centuries, we've been waiting for the Redemption, for the Messiah, wanting to go to the Land of Israel. Even if our lives here are not bad, we're still inferior to the Muslims. But we are under the patronage of the monarchy, and we shouldn't take that for granted. There were those who tried—our entire people began selling their property and preparing to go to the Land of Israel. This was around the holiday of Passover. About three hundred years ago. There were rumors of a messiah, Shabtai Tzvi, and everybody sold their possessions and prepared for the journey. They waited for a loud signal that would reverse the powers, so the Jews could overpower the Muslims. When the signal didn't come, the Muslims attacked the Jews out of fear, then robbed and pillaged them."

Hassan couldn't contain himself. "But we're not waiting for the Messiah or rebelling against the monarchy! We just want to go to the Land of Israel!"

"And this journey, this is the rebellion against the monarchy," David retorted. "Otherwise, you could go during the daylight instead of hiding in the desert and traveling only by night!"

Hamama didn't want her two favorite people to fight, so she tried to change the subject:

"Father, keep telling what happened," she said.

David looked over at Hassan, as if asking permission. It appeared as if the boy also wanted to hear the tale of his ancestors. David took a deep breath and continued:

"When the Jews of Yemen believed in the messiah Shabtai Tzvi, the Muslims told the Imam that the Jews had crowned their own king. And, of course, they saw all the preparations for the journey; they saw that the Jews were trying to leave. The Imam, Almahadi Asma'il, called the heads of the Jewish people in Yemen and accused them of rebelling against the monarchy. To 'repent' for their betrayal he offered them to convert to Islam, but they refused. You know what he did to them? For three days, they were hanged in a slaughterhouse in the sun—without any clothes—"

Ahuva interrupted David: "David! The kids won't sleep tonight!"

"We'll sleep!" said Sa'adia. He had been silent this whole time. He was engrossed.

"Whoever doesn't want to hear it can go to sleep!" Sarah declared.

Ahuva picked Kadya up and parted from everyone with a smile. "But David—don't exaggerate with the graphic descriptions."

19

"So, where were we?" David asked. "Oh yes, after that, he imprisoned them for three months, in a dark, filthy place. But he still wasn't satisfied. He was very evil. He exiled the leaders of our people to Kamaran, which is an island in the Red Sea, and imprisoned many Jews in fortresses. What he did to Rabbi Shlomo Jamal was terrible. *Alav Ha-Shalom,* may he rest in peace."

"And who was Rabbi Shlomo Jamal?" Sa'adia asked with keen interest.

"Rabbi Shlomo Jamal was a *nagid,* a Jewish community elder. The ruler took him and offered him to convert to Islam. After he refused, one of the ministers killed him and cut off his head."

Hamama trembled. David noticed and started to wrap his arm around her. She evaded him so as to see his eyes as he told the tale, and he smiled and continued in a whisper, so Ahuva wouldn't hear him.

"The ruler's servants took the dead nagid's clothes, so he remained naked. After they kicked his cut-off head around, they hung it in the street. To mortify all the people. The Jews had to bribe the guards with a lot of money to get the head and body back, so that he could be buried in the way of Israel."

This time even Sarah trembled in shock from her father's description.

"Well, I think that's enough for today," David said.

"But you didn't tell us about the Mawza Exile!" Hassan objected.

"All these stories are very sad. I don't want you to be sad."

"But we're not sad, Father," Hamama cried. "All this happened a long time ago."

"Fine. So just about the Mawza Exile, and that's it. And don't think, Hassan, that I'm trying to diminish your love for the Land of Israel. On the contrary. I just want you to know where dreams can lead you."

"That's all right, Uncle David. There's no story you can tell that will stop me from getting there." Hassan smiled.

"In that case, I'll go on. The Jews are a stubborn people. Just like Hassan," David smiled, too. "After all, they knew that before the coming of the Messiah there would be hardships. Before the good, there's always some bad. Ten years after the Kamaran Exile, a different Imam by the name of Ahmed ben Hassan decided to punish the Jews some more. He claimed that this entire obsession with the Messiah caused them to rightfully lose the patronage of the monarchy, and so he destroyed all the synagogues. He exiled the Jews to Mawza, which was a plane on the bank of the Red Sea. A hot, harsh land. After the Imam died the edict was cancelled. The Jews could go back, but many had already died of hunger and disease. Rabbi Shalom Shabazi was there, and he describes it all in his songs."

David quietly started singing a well-known song of Rabbi Shalom Shabazi. The children lay down on the mats and enjoyed his soft, gentle voice. Ahuva brought Kadya in to sleep by Hamama and left with David to the porch.

"Hassan," Hamama whispered, "I also want to go to the Land of Israel."

"Don't worry, we'll all get there," Hassan promised.

Hamama shut her eyes but couldn't fall asleep. In her mind, she saw images of the Land of Israel, the land of dreams, and she tried to get rid of them. Her father's reaction bothered her. Her life here was good. But then again, she couldn't play with the neighbors' kids…what did that mean? *And Father's job was hard, and he had to work at that because it was a Jew's job. What did that mean?*

She remembered Shmuel, Rivka's husband, talking about this. He was a goldsmith, which was a well-respected profession. But he had this job because Muslims were forbidden from being goldsmiths, and Jews had to work at those jobs that were forbidden for Muslims, and those were considered dishonorable. How could a job be well-respected *and* dishonorable?

Her father's cousin was responsible for collecting feces and burning it as a means of heating. At home, he was mocked. "Mister shit," they called him, all the while knowing there was no other option. A livelihood is a livelihood. In fact, because of the drought, he would sometimes earn even more than the Yemenite farmers.

Hamama sighed and rolled from side to side. *Why did Father disagree with Hassan?* Hassan said that in Israel they could work the land, and here they were forbidden from doing that. What were the Jewish occupations here? Cobblers, blacksmiths, butchers, and tanners. They provided services to the Muslim farmers, the farmers needed them! And they, the Jews, depended on the farmers. She could not imagine her life differently. There was always respect between neighbors, as well as mutual help. The Arabs liked them. So, what was so bad here? Hamama opened her eyes, and the thought came to her. *Everything*. Soon she would turn six, and they would have to find her a husband.

In Yemen, marriage at such an early age arose out of a fear for the Jewish children's lives. Imam Yahya's orphan decree forced Jewish orphans to convert to Islam. People's livelihood was difficult because of the long drought, and because of this—as well as the diseases and other disasters—the number of orphans increased, and the fear for their lives grew. That's why children were married off at a young age— that way they would have somewhere to belong, in case their parents died, and the rulers found out about the helpless children. Not only that, there was always the possibility that wicked Yemenis would take advantage of that law.

Hamama didn't want to get married, but remembered the story of her pretty cousin, Rachel, who had yet to find a match. Her looks were so striking that some Yemenite man coveted her and kidnapped her. He tried to force her to convert to Islam, so he could marry her, but she refused. She screamed that she was not an orphan and would never convert, but he refused to listen. At first, he tried to get his way gently:

"All you have to say is, '*Ash hadu an la ilaha ill Allah wa ash hadu anna Muhammadar Rasul Allah*' Say that." She refused to declare there was no god but Allah and that Muhammad was the Messenger of Allah.

After that he tortured her, but she still didn't agree to marry him:

"I'll die a Jew." She remained steadfast.

He was furious and continued to torture her. He tortured her with metal rods, and she still didn't agree. When her body was covered with bruises and burns, he didn't want her anymore, and so he sent her home. She barely made it to her parents' house alive. They took care of her and revived her, but she was never pretty again.

And so, in the throngs of these debates, Hamama drifted off to sleep.

The following morning, David and Hamama walked through the village together, oblivious to the internal conflicts that the day's events will inflame. Hamama had long changed her mind about helping David with his work and did so at every opportunity. Her jealousy of her new brother's abilities outweighed her fear of Sarah and Sa'adia. She wanted to help the family, too.

"These are twenty chunks of turmeric," David said to the cloth merchant. The latter's wife smiled and handed Hamama a jug full of milk.

"Thank you," David said.

"Shar'abi!" roared the cloth merchant in order to direct David's attention. A Yemenite soldier rode into the center of the village.

"Hamama, run away quickly. Go home," David commanded.

"I'm staying with you," Hamama insisted.

"It's safer for the girl to stay with us," said the cloth merchant's wife, and without waiting for his approval, she took the jug of milk from Hamama and dragged her into the store. In the meantime, the soldier noticed David's sidelocks and Jewish garb and rode over.

In those days of harsh drought, the soldiers took advantage of their power. Because of the famine, they tended to go to the Jews, cursing and hitting, to demand additional *jizya*, taxes. Just the past Saturday at the synagogue, David had heard horrifying stories from the neighboring village. The soldiers sat in the Jews' homes, and the Jews had to slaughter a lamb and cook it for them. The soldiers sat there as long as they wanted, and the Jews couldn't say anything out of fear of the Imam. David already guessed what was about to happen, and he knew that the food situation at his house was dire and that he didn't have anything to offer the soldier.

"Jew, *ya mal'un ibn mal'un*, you son of a scoundrel, where are the taxes you're supposed to pay?" yelled the soldier.

"I already paid my taxes for the year," David said as calmly as he could. The cloth merchant slowly backed into his store.

"What's that?" the soldier asked, surprised by David's reply.

"I already paid my taxes for the year," David repeated himself quietly.

The soldier angrily spurred his horse on, and the horse ran over David and pushed him to the ground. The soldier stepped down from his horse and pulled out his weapon:

"You're still not interested in giving me your taxes?"

"I already paid my taxes for the year," David answered, regretting the fact that Hamama was probably watching all this and hoping that she would understand that he couldn't defend himself from the soldier for fear he would interpret it as aggression and kill him. The soldier started kicking David, and Hamama, her body trembling, tried to run and help him, but the merchant's wife held her so tightly that her fingernails lefts marks that lasted a whole week.

This entire time the governor, Abdullah, observed all that was happening in the street from his terrace. Without hesitation, he sent his guards to arrest the menacing soldier. David shut his eyes in pain, imagining Ahuva's face when the kicking stopped. He waited quietly for the sound of a rifle's bolt action, but instead the governor's guards helped him to his feet. He stared with confusion at the soldier, who was struggling with the guards and kicking into the air furiously.

"You'll regret this!" the soldier screamed.

Hamama finally freed herself from the merchant's wife and ran into her father's arms.

"You also have to come to the governor," one of the guards said.

"Go home, Hamama," David instructed his daughter. Hamama took the jug of milk and hurried to tell her frightened mother what had happened. In the meantime, the guards brought the soldier and David to face the governor.

"How dare you arrest me? I'm a soldier in your Imam's army!" the soldier shouted.

"And I'm a subject of your Imam, operating under his laws. This Jew is under my protection, and everything that you demand from him, you have to come to me and demand from me."

David tried to hide his smile, which wasn't particularly difficult given his injuries.

"Well? What's your deal with the Jew?" the governor asked.

"I came to collect taxes," the soldier answered.

"Well, I already collected taxes this year, and this Jew paid me his obligations. Are there new taxes I should be aware of?"

The soldier stood in silence. The governor continued in anger:

"You should have known to come to me about this first rather than acting violently. Because you injured a man under my protection, I am punishing you with thirty lashes and two days in jail."

The soldier was shocked by the severity of the punishment and blushed with shame and fury. David felt his heart drop.

"You'll regret this!" he yelled toward David as the guards took him from the room.

"An unpleasant situation. Are you all right?" the governor asked David.

"Yes. If possible, I'll go home to calm my wife." David sighed in pain.

"Of course. I'm sorry about all this," the governor said.

"You're a good man, sir. Thank you."

David bowed before him and left. Ahuva was already waiting for him at the governor's door. She came with Hassan and Sa'adia, and they held David and helped him walk home. Ahuva held her tears back.

"What's going to happen to us, ya David?" she asked.

"It'll be fine. Have trust in God," he answered.

David's broken ribs healed, but Ahuva's angst did not subside. She tried to perform the household chores as usual, but her heart was heavy. The soldier's pride was injured, and this was dangerous. The governor probably didn't think about that. He just wanted to show his strength. He didn't worry about the Jewish family who now lived in fear of the Yemenite army's vengeance. News of the event passed from mouth to mouth amongst all the people in the village, and the village, which usually lay in an eternal stupor, was brimming with rustles of worry and whispers of gossip. David embarked on a new business journey and left his family behind. Ahuva knew that David wanted to stay with them, with her, to calm her, but how would he bring food for his children?

Ahuva tried to toughen up and have faith in God. That day the children played a new game with sticks that Hassan had invented. Ahuva started to launder their clothes. The sight of her children both relaxed her and frightened her at the same time. Then Omar, their neighbor, showed up at their door.

"They're here! My son was sitting on the roof and saw them coming!"

"God help us! What'll we do?" Ahuva was alarmed, her heart about to burst.

Omar's wife and children pushed through the door behind him.

"Little Fatima will take you to one of the rooms in our house. There are some closets there where you can hide. My wife and children will trade places with you. Quickly, Ahuva, quickly!"

Ahuva collected the children, and they ran after Fatima to Omar's house.

"You'll hide in the cabinet. The children can play here with me."

Sarah helped Ahuva hide in the closet. The children exchanged their clothes with ones that Fatima had brought. In the meantime, at David and Ahuva's house, Omar's wife continued to launder the clothes. The children collected the sticks and played a different game with them, and Omar sat on one of the large mats, one hand holding prayer beads and the other a book he kept in his pocket.

Not five minutes passed when loud knocks were heard at the door: "Jew, *ya mal'un! Eftah el bab!*" cried the shamed soldier, demanding the door be opened. His friends stood behind him with their weapons drawn.

Omar opened the door looking furious. "Who are you calling a 'mal'un Jew?'"

"What are you doing here? Where's the Jew who lives here?" the soldier asked, pushing Omar aside and entering the house. He looked at the family in the middle of their daily routine.

"They all went to *al Kuds*, the Holy Land. They even left some of their belongings here." Omar lifted a hand-washing bowl that was noticeable to the eye. "Just like that, in the middle of the night, they left. Quickly. I asked the governor to take the house."

The soldier inspected Omar and his family. He then walked around to look in the other rooms. Finally, he came back to the door:

"*Al Kuds*, eh?" he growled. "Rebelling against the monarchy. We'll catch them on the way."

The soldier instructed his friends to leave, and they rode out of the village, to search for their prey in the desert, on the way to the Land of Israel.

Omar sighed with relief and went to call Ahuva and her children. Ahuva couldn't stop thanking him. When David returned from his journey, he slaughtered a sheep and held a celebration of gratefulness for Omar and his family.

Because of his unwavering faith and trust in the Creator of the Universe, David went about his life with a tranquil confidence. He faced every obstacle with the underlying conviction that as long as he does his best, God will do his. Perhaps for this reason, he didn't notice the dread eating Ahuva from within, her body succumbing to her angst.

2007

"All right, it's time to give Grandpa his shot. And I have to heat his food." Grandma gets up, with some difficulty, from the white plastic chair on the patio. I take a deep breath and snap back to reality. Grandma hesitates for a second and looks at Grandpa, who has fallen asleep on the chair. "We had a beautiful life. You know? We have already lived our lives."

The nurse gently wakes Grandpa and measures his blood pressure and sugar level. Grandpa looks at me and smiles.

"I'll go now," I say. "You're going to eat lunch, and then you'll probably go to sleep."

Grandpa nods in agreement. I part from them, but before I head to the car, I decide to look around behind the house. Grandpa's room, the grass, and fruit trees are already destroyed, but the room in the back is still there, and so is the storage area with the taboun where we made matzos for Passover. For several years now, we've made them only on the grill. Nobody has the strength to work the taboun. But this year, my uncle promised that we'd do it, like we used to. I guess everybody wants to hold on to something.

Something captures my sight. A dusty wooden board. I open it, smiling, and immediately recognize it. This is the Mancala game, the game my grandfather and grandmother played in their childhood with alb seeds. I clean it off and stuff it into my bag. I'll ask for permission later.

I come back a week later. Grandpa is in the shower with the nurse. After Grandma finishes her telephone conversation with her friend Miriam, we go sit on the cement outside. The sun is good, and we want Grandpa to join us in its warmth.

"He's always inside," Grandma tells me. "Always wants to sleep. Yesterday, I didn't sleep all night. He screams that he's hurting and asks God why he doesn't take him already."

I feel like a knife is twisting in my heart. Grandma is silent for a moment:

"That morning I lectured him. I told him, 'Look at all the people around us—we see them on the news—old people at home alone. There are workers who take advantage of them. And us—we have Yossi, the nurse, who's okay, except that he drinks too much. And we have the kids, the family. We have each other. Aren't you ashamed to ask to die?"

She's silent again, and I want to flee. I don't want to hear this. I don't want to know. Grandma sees my despair and smiles.

"That's life, *ya binti*. But come on, you came especially from Tel Aviv—what else do you want to hear about?"

"We stopped when Grandpa came to live with you. You were already good friends. So, when did you get married?"

Grandma laughs. "Slow down, slow down. Your grandfather was actually planning on marrying someone else. And lots of other things happened before that…"

CHAPTER 2

Hamama was excited. Soon it would be Passover. Every Passover her family left the house for a week and traveled to Hasabyein; there they celebrated the holiday with their extended family. This year Rivka and Shmuel also planned to come, all the way from El Be'aden—and Rivka was pregnant! She missed her older sister so much and wanted her and Shmuel to meet Hassan. She couldn't stop jumping around with joy, despite her futile attempts to pack for the journey. Sarah grew annoyed and pinched her younger sister.

"Oy!" Hamama yelled.

"You're driving me crazy!" Sarah said with a sharp tone.

Hamama pinched her back and ran off.

"Just wait until I catch you, you little leech!" Sarah called out.

"You're just trying to find a way to take your anger out at me because they'll probably offer you a marriage proposal there!"

Sarah blushed, dropped the holiday clothes she was packing, and started chasing Hamama around the house. Hamama was quick, but Sarah was quicker, and Hamama's teasing cost her a few bruises.

"Stop it already!" called Ahuva. "Why do you always have to fight?"

"She started it!" Sarah yelled.

"You pinched me!" Hamama retorted angrily.

"You drive me crazy with all your jumping around," Sarah continued.

"Shut up already," Sa'adia interrupted. "Can't you see that you're giving Mother a headache?"

Sa'adia had matured since the incident with the soldier and tried to help his mother with everything. Hamama thought about that. Maybe that's why Sarah was a bit quick to anger? Her partner in crime had retired.

The next day the family embarked. David and Ahuva led, and Hassan was the rear guard. David borrowed a donkey from Omar to assist Ahuva, but she preferred to hang the heavy dishes from the animal and to march slowly on foot. When they arrived at the Sekaya River, David announced a short break, and the children took advantage of the reprieve to splash around in the water.

"Don't spray water over here," Ahuva ordered, "so you won't leaven the Passover flour."

The children swam a bit further downriver.

"How are you feeling, Ahuva?" David asked suddenly.

"Tired. Why?"

"You've been looking tired for a long while now."

"I thought you didn't notice."

"All will be well, my dear—have faith in God."

"You always say that," Ahuva told her husband, "but we need to marry Sa'adia off already, and find a husband for Sarah, and with what? What dowry?"

"We'll be all right. The Lord will protect us."

"Only Hassan works. I told him, 'Put some of your salary aside, save for your future.' So instead of giving me his money, he goes out to buy food which he then brings home."

"Don't worry about Hassan. He's like a chameleon: He blends into his surroundings. He'll always find some work."

"We also need to find a match for Hamama."

"Ahuva, let's start with the oldest ones. Why are you so worried?"

"Because I'm tired, ya David, and don't know how long I'll still be with you."

David held her hand and tried to lift her spirits, as well as his own:

"Don't talk like that. It'll be fine. Have faith."

They both grew silent and returned their gaze onto the children, jumping around in the river.

The commotion could be heard from far away. When they arrived at Hasabyein, the men unloaded the baggage from the donkey, and the women gathered the bundles of clothing, trying to find the sleeping area.

"Here's Rivka!" Hamama called out. A short young woman with a large belly ran toward them from behind one of the houses. Hamama dropped the bundle of clothing from her arms and ran toward Rivka, with Kadya at her rear. They hugged, and Hamama touched Rivka's belly.

"Such a large belly!" Hamama laughed.

Rivka alternated tickling and hugging them until Ahuva and Sarah came closer.

"Mother!" Rivka called excitedly as she hugged Ahuva.

"My Rivka! You're so beautiful. What a belly," Ahuva said with excitement in her voice.

Sarah hugged Rivka warmly, and Hamama watched with jealousy. The men kept their distance and waited patiently for the female excitement to pass. Sa'adia started to joke with his father about the sounds of laughing and crying that emanated from the reunion but saw that his father's eyes also welled up with tears, and so he kept his silence.

"And this is Hassan. The son of Nadra, Father's sister," Hamama explained as she pulled Hassan to Rivka.

"Yes, I've heard a lot about you," Rivka said with a smile.

At that moment, Shmuel appeared. He was a young, handsome man, with the look of a scholar.

"You ran so fast, I almost lost you in all the commotion," Shmuel said, laughing.

"Shmuel!" David shook his hand. Shmuel kissed David's hand and smiled at the whole family.

"Come, Grandma Shar'abi has already prepared your room," Shmuel said as he hoisted the lion's share of the baggage onto his back. "David and Sa'adia, we will sleep with the rest of the men in Madvil's big dewan."

"Leave something for us to carry," Sa'adia said.

"I haven't seen you in so long. You're already a man," Shmuel answered.

"Yes. I finished learning. After Passover, Garfi promised he'll take me to his smithy here."

"You must be Hassan." Shmuel smiled toward the young man. "Do you already know what you're going to do?"

"I get by. I fix things," Hassan answered.

"You haven't found a profession yet?" Shmuel asked.

"He wants to go to the Land of Israel," Sa'adia answered for Hassan. David looked at Hassan to gauge his reaction, but the latter was entranced by the commotion.

The village of Hassabyein was neither big nor important, and there was usually only one minyan for Shabbat prayers. But now, as Jews from all over the region came together to celebrate the holiday, there were at least four. Hassan had never seen so many Jews in his life.

The women followed Rivka. Hamama's gaze was transfixed on Rivka's belly, and she touched it at every opportunity. Rivka laughed.

"Not long ago you were also this little," Rivka told Hamama. "When did you grow so big?"

"When you weren't around…" Hamama cast her eyes to her feet. She had missed her sister.

"It's good to finally be together," Ahuva said.

The women went up to the guest rooms in Grandma Shar'abi's house. There they met Grandma Shar'abi and the other women. Hamama longed to spend time with the only person in the world who spoiled her every time they were together.

"I want to sleep by Grandma!"

"You'll sleep here with everyone," Ahuva said, which ended the discussion.

Hamama stayed close to her grandma until the latter slipped two dried figs into her granddaughter's pocket and sent her to eat outside. Hamama called Kadya and shared the booty with her. Later, she tried to teach Rivka some of the games Hassan had invented.

"I'm happy that you at least get along with Hassan." Rivka smiled.

"He's great! He builds things and fixes all whatever is broken, and he's so nice to me! He's also very smart and tells stories and everything is so much better when he's around!" Hamama exclaimed.

"She gets along with me, too," Kadya chimed.

"True," Hamama agreed and tickled her little sister, who laughed and ran upstairs. The girls came up after her, and Rivka led them to three mats she put aside for them. After a short rest, Ahuva joined the family gathering together with Sarah, Rivka, and Kadya. Hamama managed to slip off to the porch for a moment before the inevitable onslaught of her aunts' coddling and pinching.

It was noon on the day before Passover eve, and the *chametz*--the leavened foods—were only permitted to be eaten outside in the yard. Soon the ceremony to destroy the chametz before Passover, the *bi'ur chametz*, would start, along with the traditional baking of the matzos. After a brief respite from the journey, the women busied themselves with cooking the holiday meals.

There was no need to prepare any food in advance since twenty families were gathered together in the village for the holiday, and the women divided themselves into twelve kitchens in twelve houses. One made the salads and legumes, and the other boiled eggs and made the *ducha*, a Yeminite *charoset* made from sweet date paste and spices eaten during Passover. Each according to her expertise.

Others prepared the *j'ala*—a mix of roasted nuts and cereal—cakes, potatoes, and chicken soup. The next day, the men would slaughter a sheep to commemorate the Passover offering, and then roast it on the fire in a big celebration. In the meantime, the women would bathe and get ready for the holiday, and after the men finished with the meat, the women would take it from them, cut it up, and prepare the Seder table. Then the men would bathe, put on their holiday garments, and go to the synagogue.

"Are you coming to see them bake the matzos?" Kadya asked, waking Hamama from her thoughts. "What are you dreaming about?"

"I'm not dreaming. That's the thing. It's all real," Hamama answered and twirled around.

Suddenly, the sounds of the men singing the "Hallel" erupted. Hamama and Kadya quickly ran downstairs and joined the matzos-baking ritual. The village rabbi was already kneading the dough, and the singing of the "Hallel" was meant to set a rhythm to the process— the baking of a matzo must take no more than eighteen minutes. In due time, the clay ovens that were used only on Passover were lit with fire, and the men took their positions between the rabbi and the man in charge of the *taboun*.

"Hallelujah! Praise the servants of the Lord," sang the cantor.

"Hallelujah!" answered the entire congregation after every line of the "Hallel."

"Praise the name of the Lord!"

"Hallelujah!"

Hamama pushed herself in between Shmuel and David, who had volunteered to take part in the matzo baking this year. While singing, the rabbi skillfully broke off balls of dough with his finger and threw them toward the men. Each man, in turn, caught a ball, and kneaded it into the shape of a round, thin pita. When he finished, he placed the pita on a special pillow that was sewn onto a dry gourd or an implement made of woven straw. The man in charge of the *taboun* took the pillow and the matzo covering it and stuck it onto the walls of the taboun.

"As Israel left Egypt…"

"Hallelujah!"

"The house of Jacob from a foreign land…"

"Hallelujah!"

The dough glued to the *taboun's* walls hardened quickly and rose a bit. The man in charge of the *taboun* immediately took the matzo out and placed it on a mat. Another man sat across from the taboun, and he checked whether the matzo was damaged. If he believed it was, he placed it on a basket of *chametz*; the undamaged ones were kept for the holiday meal.

Hamama never saw her father cook, except on Passover. It was as if his gaunt but powerful figure grew larger and stronger in front of her eyes. His eyes shone of faith and inner peace, and his hands moved in unison with the crowd. Suddenly, she noticed Hassan, who also looked at her father with pride and joy. Her admiration and fondness for the boy swelled. Hamama shut her eyes, listened to the melodious singing, smelled the fresh matzos, and smiled.

Hamama missed the slaughtering of the sheep and the burning of the last *chametz*. She was sent, along with fifteen other girls, to pump water from the well. The water was meant to last the guests throughout the entire holiday. Hamama was exhausted from pumping the water and carrying the jugs, and the ensuing bath did not help. Ahuva scrubbed her daughter's small, gaunt body, and Hamama tried hard not to scream.

"Mother, I'm not *chametz*!" she complained.

"Be quiet and help me!" Ahuva retorted.

Sarah, who sat next to her, scrubbed herself carefully and then bathed Kadya.

"I want Sarah to bathe me!" Hamama continued.

"You know what'll happen if you get under my loofa," Sarah said with an evil smile.

"Come on, Hamama," her mother cajoled. "Just a little bit more. I'd let Sarah do this, but I can already see how you two would start a fight over it."

"And how Hamama would run off naked right into the center of town," Sarah said, and laughed.

"That's not funny." Hamama was annoyed but tried not to let her sister disrupt her peace.

After the special pre-Passover scrubbing, each girl washed her hair. Hamama loved the smell of the *doum* fruit. She didn't wash her hair often, and actually liked this part. From an early age, she would help Ahuva crush the *doum* fruit while it was still unripe, and then they would soak it in water overnight. The following day her mother would then whip the resulting mash into a fragrant foam.

This time, Rivka and two other pregnant women were in charge of whipping the hair-washing soap, and their hands were bruised from the whipping. When the women in charge of cooking suggested that the pregnant women could sit and rest, and just crush the peppers for the spicy sauce, *s'hug*, the three insisted that they would prefer to cook while standing.

The women put on their holiday clothes and combed their hair. The older ones even put some *samneh*—refined butter—into their hair, and the sight of the wasted food surprised Hamama.

"Here, they're better off," Rivka explained, aware of her family's relative indigence.

"They also know that they'll be checked out tonight for a possible match," Sarah said jealously.

"But in any case, we all cover our heads! So, what does it matter?" Hamama asked.

"You're still a little girl." Sarah shook her head with a frown and covered her hair.

Hamama wasn't offended. She felt sorry for her sister. One of the women had offered to rub *samneh* into her hair, but Sarah had refused. Despite their many differences, Hamama greatly respected her sister's hard-headedness.

The evening of the Seder had arrived. The families were divided into four different houses. There wasn't enough room for everyone together, not even in the synagogue's main hall. Hamama and her family were at the same meal as Grandma Shar'abi, Rivka, and Shmuel, and the rest of their extended family. Following the evening prayer, they sat down on mats and pillows around a long table made of wooden planks and covered with white cloths. The table was filled with many savory foods: bitter herbs, celery, hardboiled eggs, roasted meat, sweet *ducha* made of dates and *hawaij*, radishes, and fresh matzos from the *taboun*. Hamama was tempted by the vast amounts of food, the many strong scents, but after she tasted a bit of wine and celery her stomach relaxed, and she started to doze off.

The sounds of the reading of *Haggadah*, the Jewish text that sets forth the order of the Passover Seder, reached her through the fog of her dreams. She still managed to hear her father recite The Four Questions—the children's favorite part in the *Haggadah*, and which was designed to pique their curiosity—immediately followed by Hassan's Hebrew translation.

"Ma kabar hade alaila min gami alaili." David sang the Yemenite tune.

"How is this night different from all other nights," Hassan translated slowly. The translation wasn't necessary, since all in the audience understood Yemenite, and in fact, most did not understand Hebrew. But, regardless, David insisted on teaching him, and Hassan did not object. They both knew that if Hassan's dream were to become a reality, he'd need to practice his Hebrew.

"Karagu gdudana va'abayana, min mitzar bait alabudia."

"We, our elders and our forefathers, left Egypt, home of the slaves."

"Ma kanu ifalu?"

"What did they do there?"

"Kanu ikaltu atibn filibn, va'libn fitibn."

"They would mix the straw with the clay, the clay with the straw."

"L'man?"

"For whom?"

"L'Par'o alrasha algamur, aladi raso sa atzim'ur, ufumo sa manak atanur."

"For the evil Pharaoh, whose head is like that of a monster, and his mouth like the eye of an oven."

Sounds of laughter erupted from the direction of the children. This was their favorite part. David waited a bit for them to calm down and then continued:

"V a'vrad Allah al almitzriun."

"And God brought upon the Egyptians," Hassan said, and all the diners held the matzos on the table and lifted them every time David and Hassan named one of the Ten Plagues.

"Aldam. Vatafadia. Valkaml. Valkumal. Valvkush. Valfana. Valgarab. Valbarad. Valgarad. Vatalam. Umavt alabkar."

"The blood, and the frogs, and the lice, and the wild animals, and the diseased livestock, and the boils, and the thunderstorm of hail and fire, and the locusts, and the darkness, and the death of the firstborns."

Hamama was now fast asleep. And here in her dream she was also leaving Egypt. But no, she wasn't leaving Egypt, but rather Yemen. And Hassan was marching ahead of her, with determination in his eye. She was surrounded by many people whom she didn't recognize. She glanced back, searching; there was Rivka and Shmuel…but what had happened to their hair? For some reason it had fallen out. And from afar, she saw her father, Sa'adia, and Sarah carrying bundles on their backs, walking with the convoy. Hamama kept searching. What was she looking for? She didn't know. Suddenly, her foot hit a rock, and the pain stirred her from her dream.

"What, are you sleeping?" Sarah whispered angrily.

"You kicked my foot?" Hamama asked, trying to kick Sarah back. But her sister managed to avoid her little legs.

"Shhh…that's not nice! Let them finish!" Ahuva scolded.

Hamama then knew that she had been looking for her mother and for Kadya. She wanted to tell her mother about her dream, but Ahuva was listening intently to David and Hassan.

"And so, it was said, that there was no house without death," Hassan said with a grave expression.

"V'gurku al mitzriun fi bakr alkulzum, v'karagu bani Israil min vasta."

"And the Egyptians drowned in the Red Sea, and the children of Israel walked out of it."

"V'kalozhum Allah byad shadida udra mamduda, v'akhkam atima, v'ayan ubarahin, by Moses, may peace be upon him."

"And God brought them out of Egypt with a strong hand and outstretched arm and miracles and wonders, by Moses, may peace be upon him:"

"V'hada algavab," David said.

"And that's the answer," Hassan concluded.

The men congratulated Hassan and praised the two for their recitation. Hamama took advantage of the brief lull.

"Mother!" she called.

"Yes, Hamama?"

"I dreamt a dream!"

"Yes, I noticed you fell asleep." Ahuva frowned at her daughter.

"In the dream, we were leaving Yemen—we went to the Land of Israel—like this, like the exodus from Egypt. Me and Hassan, Rivka and Shmuel and Father and Sarah and Sa'adia. Mother, you weren't there. Neither you nor Kadya."

Ahuva looked at her young daughter intently and caressed her hair. She sensed the anxiety shining in Hamama's eyes.

"It's only a dream, my daughter." Ahuva tried to calm Hamama, but when she noticed her daughter's distress, she added, "I'll always be with you, my love."

At that moment, an old, wrinkled man stood up. Hamama could never remember his name, but she remembered his annual Passover task. He bundled some food around his cane and went outside. A few seconds later, several knocks came from the door, and all the children yelled loudly, "*T'fadel!*"

The old man walked in, smiling.

"Where did you come from?" the children asked.

"From Egypt," he answered.

"And where are you going?"

"To Jerusalem!"

"Why don't you sit down and dine with us? And tell us about the wonders?" The children surrounded him.

The old man sat down and started telling the story of the exodus from Egypt. The men joined in, and each, in turn, read from the *Haggadah*, and when they finally completed the *Maggid* part of the Seder, they washed their hands once more and ate the bitter herbs and matzo. Then the feast began. Hamama was already wide-awake and helped serve the meats and vegetables. Then they all sat down to dine, and she smiled at Rivka. But Rivka didn't smile. Hamama followed Rivka's gaze and realized she was staring at their mother. Hamama also looked over at Ahuva, and only then noticed how tired she appeared.

After the Seder, Hamama went out to the yard and played with the other children, which allowed her to forget her worrisome dream. In Tholet, they were the only Jewish family, so she never had the chance to play with as many other kids as in Hassabyein.

Even Hassan joined, and taught them his new game with sticks. The children jumped over five sticks with roaring laughter, and Hassan kept moving the sticks farther apart. Hamama tripped early on but still enjoyed sitting and watching the other children. Sarah also played and was even one of the last ones remaining in the competition. Hamama hoped that someone would see how talented her sister was, and maybe they would forget about the lack of *samneh* in her hair. A girl so successful at long distance jumping would surely succeed at starting a family.

"Ya Hassan, come here a minute," Shmuel said.

Hassan left the game and ran toward Shmuel and David, who were sitting together.

"Hassan," David began. "Shmuel and I have spoken quite a bit, and it appears that Shmuel has a proposition for you."

"Look, Hassan, I need a helper in my workshop," Shmuel said. "Being a goldsmith is a good job, it pays well, and you'd have time to study Torah."

"I really like you, Hassan," David added, "and you're my sister's flesh and blood. But what future can you have in our village? And you have dreams..."

"But I work there. I help fix things," Hassan answered. He was hesitant to leave the family alone, steeped in poverty.

"That's true," Shmuel said. "But in El Be'aden people are wealthier and will pay you more for the work you do."

Hassan stayed quiet. His body screamed out for a change, for adventure, and Shmuel's offer tempted him. But it was hard for him to leave the family that had adopted him, especially since he knew their livelihood was so difficult. Hassan looked at David questioningly, and David, as if reading his mind, answered the unspoken question.

"We'll be fine. It's time for you to take care of yourself. I don't have a good occupation to pass on to you. Here in Hassabyein, Sa'adiah has already found work with Garfi, and you go with Shmuel." He looked as his nephew with love. "Just don't forget us..." he said with a smile.

"How could I forget you? You all are my family," Hassan said.

The holiday came to an end. Hassan helped Sa'adia and David pack their belongings and loaded them onto the donkey. The whole family crowded around Rivka's belly.

"Well, by next Passover then?" Shmuel joked.

"I hope to see you before then," David said.

"Yes. You can bring the rest of Hassan's belongings then." Shmuel patted Hassan on the shoulder. Hamama stared at them, perplexed.

"What?" she asked.

"Sarah? You didn't tell her?" Ahuva asked.

"Me? I told Kadya. Kadya was supposed to tell Hamama."

"Tell me what?" Hamama asked and looked at Hassan.

"Hassan is coming to live with us," Shmuel said. "He'll be an apprentice in my workshop."

Hamama blushed with anger. He had taken Rivka, and now Hassan, too? She was furious. Without thinking twice, she flexed her foot and kicked Shmuel's leg with all her might. He howled in pain and grabbed his leg. Everyone stared at the seven-year-old girl, shocked by her terrible act. But before someone could reach out to catch the little rebel, she took off running.

"Are you all right?" Ahuva asked.

"Yes...yes..." Shmuel mumbled, shocked by the piercing pain.

"I'll rip her leg off when we get home," Sarah promised.

"No, it's my fault. I should have told her myself," Hassan said quietly.

"Well, we'd better get going. We'll catch her before she gets lost again," David said.

The family parted from Rivka, Shmuel, and Hassan and left on the journey back to Tholet. They caught up with Hamama at home, milking Yamima and crying.

In Tholet, the days passed slowly and drearily. Hamama had turned eight years old, and Kadya was six. Sa'adia left to live with Garfi, the blacksmith, and Sarah walked around aimlessly, embittered by the dearth of wedding proposals. David was away from the house more and more often because of many long, distant journeys, and Ahuva grew paler, thinner, and less able to conduct the housework. She constantly complained of intense headaches, and even though she tried to appear healthy in front of her daughters, she couldn't fool her family.

Hamama tried to help as much as she could. She and Kadya took on Hassan's old tasks, in addition to their own: washing the laundry and hanging it to dry, fixing jugs with dried mud, bringing water from the well, taking care of Yamima and the chickens, helping Ahuva in the garden and in the kitchen, and sewing up holes in old clothes. Hamama and Kadya spent most of their time together, and so became nearly inseparable. But still Hamama found plenty of time to mourn Hassan's absence. She taught Kadya all the games she had learned from him and retold all the stories he told her, and when these ran out, she simply made up new ones. Kadya looked up at her the same way she looked at Hassan, and although it made Hamama proud it also reminded her of how much she missed him.

One day, David came home bearing a surprise. On a recent journey, he went to El Be'aden to check on his family. And when he told Rivka about Ahuva's condition, she and her husband decided to come to Tholet for Shabbat with their little daughter, Shoshana.

Hamama didn't run to hug her sister, and she avoided Shmuel. But Rivka wasn't bothered—from the moment she had arrived, she hadn't left Ahuva's side for even one moment. The women played with the baby, and Hamama set the Shabbat table and went outside. She sat by the door and looked up at the night sky, overcome by a great sadness.

David, Sa'adia, and Shmuel walked up the path toward the house, humming a Shabbat melody.

"*Shabbat shalom*, Hamama," David said.

"*Shabbat shalom*, Father," Hamama answered and kissed his hand.

David entered the house, and Sa'adia mussed Hamama's hair with atypical friendliness. Before she managed to wonder about his strange behavior, Shmuel sat down next to her. Hamama fidgeted uncomfortably, taken aback even more by the men's strange behavior—even slightly worried.

"*Shabbat shalom*," he said to her.

"*Shabbat shalom*," she replied quietly.

"My leg hurt for a whole week after your kick."

"I'm sorry."

"That's all right. I know I deserved it. I took away your boyfriend."

Hamama immediately stood up and shook with anger. "He's not my boyfriend!"

Shmuel protected his legs and smiled. "Are you going to kick me again?"

"No."

Shmuel stood. "Anyway, I just wanted to tell you that he's getting along very well at the workshop, and that he's very talented."

"I don't know why you think I care," Hamama said. "We need to go inside. Father is waiting for Kiddush."

Hamama went inside without waiting for Shmuel, her heart beating rapidly. *Hassan isn't my boyfriend. He's also not a brother.* And then, *Why didn't he come? Why did he leave me alone when everything is so sad all the time?*

Baby Shoshana was in a good mood and made everyone laugh. Even Hamama couldn't resist the baby's charms, and she played with her a little bit.

"I knew you'd break," Rivka said with a smile.

"She's cute," Hamama said.

"Ah!" Ahuva was struck by another one of her headaches, and Rivka went to take care of her.

"Mother, come to the bedroom. I'll massage your head with oil," she suggested.

Sarah and Rivka helped Ahuva stand, and then they headed to the bedroom. A few minutes later Sarah came out.

"Mother said you can sleep here today," she told Hamama. "It's warmer."

Sarah, Hamama, and Kadya cleared the food and dishes, and David spread out the mats.

"I like sleeping by the ovens," Kadya said cheerfully.

Hamama said nothing.

When David and Shmuel went outside, and it appeared all her siblings were asleep, Hamama snuck upstairs to the bedroom. She hid inside one of the closets and sat, grasping her legs, under cover of darkness. Weak sighs came from the mat, every sigh a knife stabbing her little heart.

"I can't breathe, ya Rivka," Hamama heard her mother's voice.

"Here." Rivka tried to lift Ahuva's head a bit, but the heaving didn't stop.

"Water," she barely managed to say.

Hamama's eyes quickly acclimated to the darkness, and she saw Rivka trying to give Ahuva water, but her mother couldn't swallow. The water spilled out the sides of her mouth, and her face and chest got drenched. Rivka wiped her face and gown gently, but Ahuva kept on heaving. Hamama shut her eyes tightly. *God! Please help Mother stop heaving!*

And then there was silence. *She is breathing again.* Hamama felt relief. Rivka left the room, and Hamama thought of sneaking back downstairs, but then Rivka, Shmuel, and David entered.

"I think she's gone," Rivka said in a broken voice.

David went to his wife who lay quietly on the mat. Hamama didn't understand immediately, but then her father started to weep.

Hamama screamed. "Mother! Mother! Mother!"

She jumped out from the closet and lay on top of mother's body. Her screams woke the others, and they ran upstairs and cried together.

David sat down on the floor and held his wailing children.

Because it was Shabbat, the family did not leave the matriarch's body. The corpse somehow didn't rot—a miracle, said David— but as soon as Shabbat ended, the Jews of Hassabyein prepared to accompany the woman to her eternal resting-place. They all marched together, the Arabs of Tholet holding up the rear, paying their last respects.

Hamama walked along, but she could not comprehend how her feet possibly moved, one after the other. It was confounding. Her feet burned with anger at the ground that intended to take her mother from her, and so she raised her gaze. As soon as she could, she took off and climbed one of the trees to watch from afar. No one saw her leave or noticed her absence.

She had cried throughout the Shabbat, and now her throat was sore, and her eyes burned. She saw her siblings tear their clothes and knew she was supposed to do the same. She followed the ritual and tore her own as a symbol for the rupture in her life. And when her mother's body was lowered to the ground something exploded inside her. She couldn't cry anymore, but also, she couldn't stand the pain, and so she ran back home.

The shiva passed in a daze. Hamama watched Rivka sit with Shoshana who played with Kadya's hair. Sarah sat on the ground and ignored everyone around her. The men sat together to study, dedicating their learning to the memory of Ahuva. Relatives from Hassabyein worked tirelessly to feed the many people who came by—

every day at least a minyan of men. Their children came, too, but this time there was nothing joyous about the many Jewish kids playing outside. Hamama walked out onto the porch to watch them and wallowed in her sorrow. As she sat, she heard two women talking.

"Poor man. A widow with such little children."

"And he still has to marry them off."

"I tell you, the ways of God are mysterious. Such a righteous man, and this is his reward?"

"Don't worry, he'll find a match soon, and she'll take care of the kids."

"Maybe they'll make a deal instead of the dowry? He'll take a woman, and in exchange, give the daughter?"

"That's a good idea. Then he won't have to worry that there's no money."

"Do you know a family with a boy and a girl who need a match?"

Hamama was outraged by the gossipers' conversation. She stormed in from the porch and bumped into Sarah, who was heading out. In her rage, she failed to notice that her sister was in tears. Hamama lay down on her mat. Many thoughts flooded her mind. How dare they talk about a match already, when the *shiva* wasn't even over yet? The thought of a new mother, a stepmother, filled her with dread. Not only did Sarah and Sa'adia pick on her, but she would also have to put up with a new woman? *And Father is hardly ever home!* She rushed to find Kadya.

"Kadya! Listen! They're going to find Father a new woman."

"Already?" Kadya's voice rose in alarm.

"Not right away, but soon. We have to run away."

"What?"

"Run away, Kadya! We'll wait until Rivka and Shmuel leave; we'll keep our distance and follow them. We'll run away to El Be'aden, Kadya."

"And what about Father?" Kadya asked, and Hamama was overcome by shame. Once again, she was thinking only of herself, while her younger sister was the one acting responsibly.

The two sisters sat quietly for a few minutes. Hamama was disappointed at the inadequacy of her plan, and although she was itching to run away, she was once again forced to struggle with the tight boundaries of her home. Kadya must have sensed her sister's inner conflict.

"Hamama, you go," Kadya said. "I'll stay with Father. That way I can also tell him that you went after Rivka and Shmuel, and he won't worry about you."

"But what about you?"

"I'm here. Maybe if he really does get married, I'll join you."

Hamama hugged Kadya and then started to pack. Kadya helped her bundle together an extra set of clothes and some food for the journey, and the two hid the bundle in the vegetable garden.

When the *shiva* ended, Rivka, Shmuel, and the baby said their goodbyes and headed out. About half an hour later, when everybody was preoccupied, Hamama headed up to the first floor. Kadya was waiting for her, bundle in hand. Hamama gave Yamima a little kiss on her cheek and headed out on the trail, holding on to Kadya's hand.

"Good luck," Kadya said.

"Thanks! I'll be waiting for you in El Be'aden," Hamama said.

The sisters parted with smiles, and Hamama was filled with excitement. Little did they know that this would be the last time they were to see each other.

Hamama began her journey without looking back. The excitement of the journey ahead filled her with strength, and within a quarter of an hour, she saw the profiles of Rivka and her family. She slowed her pace, knowing that if they discovered her while they were still so close to Tholet, she would be forced to go home. She stopped when they stopped and walked when they walked. As darkness fell, she saw them set up camp in one of the caves on the mountainside. Hamama could sleep in a different cave, but she was afraid of missing their departure in the morning. She decided they were far enough from home that she could join them.

"Hamama? What are you doing here?" Rivka screamed.

"I'm coming with you," Hamama said decisively.

"No, you're not! How could you run away like this? Father must be going crazy worrying."

"He's not worried. Kadya knows, and she'll tell him."

"Shmuel, we have to take her back home." She turned to her husband, but he smiled at Hamama and answered, "I don't think so. I've already missed a lot of work."

"But Shmuel—" Rivka protested.

"They won't worry about her. You heard. She'll stay with us, and later, your Father will come on one of his journeys and take her back."

Rivka calmed down, but still frowned at her impetuous little sister. Hamama, on the other hand, felt a renewed fondness for Shmuel. They lay down to sleep, and in the morning, continued on their journey, eventually reaching El Be'aden.

The village of El Be'aden wasn't all that different from Hassabyein. Many Jews lived there. People came up to Shmuel and Rivka on their way home and expressed their sorrow over Ahuva's passing. The villages were far apart, but the news traveled fast, which surprised Hamama.

Then she remembered Hassan. *How will I act around him?* She hadn't thought of him until that very moment.

As they arrived at Rivka and Shmuel's home, Hassan came out to greet them, concern and sorrow on his face.

"May she rest in peace. I'm so sorry," he told Rivka.

"Thanks, ya Hassan, I know you're also mourning," Rivka answered and patted him on the shoulder.

Suddenly, he saw Hamama, and a look of surprise filled his face.

"She ran away from home. Followed us," Shmuel explained.

Hassan smiled, but quickly wiped his smile away at the sight of Hamama's scowl. He turned to her gently. "I'm sorry, Hamama. About everything."

Hamama ignored him and walked into the house.

The family walked in through a heavy wooden door. Hamama glanced around with curiosity. She faced a large courtyard. To her side, she noted a vegetable garden that closely resembled her mother's. Here, too, were a chicken coop and two goats. Shmuel's workshop was on the other side of the courtyard, filled with a variety of strange tools she had never seen before.

Hassan helped Shmuel carry their packs from the journey. Rivka showed Hamama around the house as Shoshana slept in her arms.

"Shmuel and Hassan work here all day. It's different from Mother and Father's house. Shmuel is here all the time."

"That must be nice."

"Yes, we eat lunch together every day."

"Rivka, I'm sorry I ran away like that, but I promise I'll behave," Hamama said, her eyes fixated on the ground.

"I know. And if you'd like, you can stay. I'll need more help soon," Rivka said with smile. Hamama looked at her in surprise:

"You're pregnant?"

"Yes."

Hamama stared suspiciously at her sister's belly.

"Well, there's still some time. Come, I'll show you our house and your room."

Rivka and Hamama crossed the courtyard toward the stairs that led to the kitchen, the *diwan*—the large guest room—and the bathroom. Hamama glanced around in awe of the large, spacious house.

"I'm staying here," she said.

"Come see your room."

"My room? Alone?"

"For now, when Shoshana is older, she'll sleep here with you."

On the top floor, there were three bedrooms and a porch.

"One for us, one for Hassan, and one for you."

With Rivka and Shmuel, Hamama no longer had to watch herself or be careful not to annoy them all the time, and no longer had to worry about endless pinching and kicking. She didn't have to fight for food or attention, and she enjoyed helping with whatever she could. Shmuel sent her father a letter with a merchant to tell him that his daughter was at his house, safe. Her father sent back a letter and told them that he had found a match and would try to come visit sometime in the future.

"Father needs help at home, Hamama," Rivka said when she saw the pain in Hamama's eyes. "Otherwise, how will he go to work?"

"I know...it's all just happening so fast."

"Her name is Ahuva. Just like Mother," Rivka said quietly. Hamama tried to comfort Rivka, but her sister shook it off quickly and went back to the task of separating the beans from the dirt. Hamama crushed garlic, vegetables, and peppers for the *s'hug*, as tears flowed down her cheeks.

"Are you crying?" Rivka asked.

"It's the peppers," Hamama said defensively.

The two burst out laughing.

Hamama quickly adjusted to her new home, and all her worries about how to behave around Hassan turned out to have been unnecessary. She almost never saw him. When he was in the workshop with Shmuel, she stayed away from there. Sometimes, he would even eat his meals while working, since he was in a hurry to go launder the clothes of the town's wealthy Arabs.

In the evenings, he would go back to the workshop to finish his work, and later go back out, his head wrapped in a *kafiya*, a traditional Middle Eastern square scarf, like the Arabs, to smuggle Jews to Sheikh Ott'man. From there, those Jews would continue to Aden, which was occupied by the British; from there they could board a ship to the Land of Israel. Sometimes, Hassan would disappear for three days to a week, and then Shmuel would start worrying, but Hassan would always come back and talk about his journey with a sparkle in his eyes and excitement in his voice.

"He's been doing this for a year already," Rivka said.

"I'm not surprised," Hamama said, not noticing that a smile had crept onto her face.

She admired him for his bravery. It was well known that if he were to get caught, he would be severely punished, and if they were to discover that he did this work on a regular basis, he would probably be sentenced to death. And the danger didn't come only from the soldiers—the desolate desert was populated by murderers and robbers. Hamama worried whenever he left on such a journey but refused to show it. She came to terms in her heart with the fact that their relationship would never go back to the way it was because they were no longer friends, no longer siblings, if they ever had been. She didn't talk to him, and he didn't persist but left her to her own affairs.

But Hamama wasn't lonely. She found a new friend. Miriam was a chubby girl with a wide smile and deep dimples.

One morning, the girls headed out together to pump water from the well. The main well in El Be'aden was famous. It was called "The Well of Rabbi Shalom Shabazi." It was built like a bell: its opening was narrow, but its body widened as it deepened. The water was clean and never dried out. To maintain the well's cleanliness and to make the long line more efficient, a Jewish man sat at the bottom of the well; he would receive the buckets, fill them, and send them up. Arabs and Jews from all over flocked to the well.

Hamama and Miriam didn't like to go to this well because of the long line, but the small well that was closer was often dry. On a day when the two had to wait in line, Miriam took the opportunity to tell Hamama the tale of the well.

"This well is special because Rabbi Shalom Shabazi put a plank in it, and blessed it so it would always have water," Miriam explained.

Another girl waiting in line intervened. "Do you know the story of the Arab who took the plank out?"

"No."

"There was this Arab, who didn't know about Rabbi Shalom Shabazi's blessing. He was gathering wood, found this plank, and took it from the well. When he tried to burn it, it didn't burn. The Arab was surprised and tossed the plank aside. In the meantime, the well dried up. Everybody went to the father of Yehuda Ya'akov, who was a great rabbi at the time, and they told him, 'Rabbi, Shabazi's well dried up. What should we do?' He immediately knew what had happened and went to that Arab's home. He told him, 'Give back the wooden plank, as it is blessed.'

"The Arab refused, and wanted to extort money and possessions out of the Jews in exchange for the plank. Yehuda Ya'akov's father held his own, and miraculously, the man froze on the spot. He stood in place, unable to move. Yehuda Ya'akov's father took the plank and went back to the well, followed by all the townspeople. A spirit of Rabbi Shalom Shabazi came and blew the plank out of Ya'akov's father's hands far away, somewhere no one would ever find it; everybody witnessed the miracle. The well immediately filled with water, and all the people rejoiced."

"But what happened to the Arab?" Miriam asked.

"His son came to Yehuda Ya'akov's father and begged, slaughtered a sheep in his honor, and brought presents—but the father didn't want to hear any of it. He told him, 'I came to him with good intentions and he refused.' The Arab's son stood there and cried. Finally, the rabbi assented, and cancelled the curse."

At dinner, Hamama told everyone the story she had heard at the well.

"You see? El Be'aden is a special place," Rivka said with pride.

"The Land of Israel is more special," intervened Hassan. "How many miracles happened there? How many righteous people live there?"

Shmuel burst out laughing. "You'll get there, too, Hassan Salem, be patient. But first, find a wife."

Several months passed. Rivka gave birth to twins, Efraim and Menashe. The births were difficult and the recovery long. Hamama made herself as helpful as she could. After Rivka recovered, Hamama took care of the rambunctious babies, and guarded them from their envious sister. Shoshana would try to sabotage the pair of intruders at every opportunity, sometimes pinching and sometimes pushing, but the two would only laugh out loud, unmoved by her failed attempts. Miriam would join her whenever she could, and the two became friends in heart and spirit

Hamama was happy in El Be'aden but often thought of her village and the family she'd left behind. The guilt of leaving her younger sister became unbearable when terrible news arrived: Kadya went out to collect wood and was killed by some monstrous beast. She and Rivka cried for hours, but as soon as the tears dried up, Hamama buried her pain deep down. She didn't like to talk about Kadya but dreamed of her at night, missing her. Now she really had no more reason to return, and Tholet became a distant memory. Whenever she saw Kadya's little face in her thoughts, the image of Ahuva immediately appeared, smiling and hugging her. This image was, to her, a mix of grief, longing, and consolation.

Miriam, in her wisdom, knew she had to distract Hamama. The two friends always found new adventures, veering off from the daily chores to an unknown world. One of these adventures, in fact, nearly cost them their lives.

El Be'aden stood between the desert and the forest. The shepherds took the sheep to eat in the forest where good weeds grew, but for the past two weeks they had steered clear of the area because of rumors of a *tahash*—a leopard. No one saw it themselves, but the shepherds found three corpses of sheep. The villagers, Arabs and Jews together, went out, armed with weapons, but couldn't find anything.

The rumors were like a twist of the blade in Hamama's open wound, a wound still sore from Kadya's passing, and her fear of the leopard grew. She refused to leave the house, and neither Rivka nor Shmuel succeeded in lifting her spirits. Hassan didn't even try. Hamama wasn't angry with him— she knew that he shared her grief. She was always surprised by his ability to hold it all inside—tough, serious, melancholy. She tried with all her might to be like him, but just couldn't get over that damned leopard.

"You know how to get rid of fears?" Miriam asked her one day.

"How?"

"You go to where the fear is."

"Are you crazy?"

"Well...we have to gather wood today, and the forest has the most."

"You've completely lost it."

"I'm going there. You're sending me alone?"

Miriam got up without waiting for an answer and started marching toward the forest. Hamama froze. She didn't want to leave the house and certainly didn't intend to go into the forest, but she also didn't want her best friend to go alone. What if something happened to her, and Hamama wasn't there to help?

So, she ran after her friend. When Miriam saw her, she started running, too, so that Hamama couldn't stop her before they reached the forest. Finally, Miriam stopped, breathing heavily, surrounded by the first trees. Hamama arrived after her, also breathing heavily, pale and frightened.

"Let's go back, Miriam."

"Here. We made it."

"Miriam..."

"Come on, Hamama, we won't go deeper. But look, on the ground, lots of dry sticks."

Miriam started gathering sticks, and Hamama stared at her with fear.

"Are you planning to go home empty-handed? You're here already," Miriam said.

"Quiet!" Hamama said.

Miriam quieted down, perplexed by Hamama's sternness.

"And there it is," Miriam whispered as warm urine flowed down her legs.

Hamama watched the leopard sleeping under one of the bushes. His stomach was swollen, and it looked as if he'd recently eaten and fallen asleep. They might make it out alive. Hamama turned to her frightened friend.

"We have to get out of here. Quietly." Hamama kept her voice low and reached her hand out to Miriam.

"I don't think I can move," Miriam said. "Also, I wet myself."

"You don't have much choice. You want to be his next meal?'

"You think he likes girls in urine sauce?"

"Oh my God, Miriam! We're about to die and you're still joking around?"

"Well…at least, you'll remember me as funny."

"Enough nonsense. Take my hand already."

Miriam held on to Hamama's outstretched hand, and the two girls slowly walked backwards, careful not to step on any twigs. Their eyes almost popped out of their sockets, examining every hurdle on the ground, as any missed detail could cause an unexpected sound.

A crow called out. Miriam's sweaty hand slipped from Hamama's, and she struggled to contain the instinct to drop the sticks and start running. Hamama held her breath, expecting the *tahash* to leap at them. But the beast remained still. The two marched quietly out of the forest. When they felt they were far enough away, they took off running toward the village, dropping all the sticks they had gathered. When they arrived at the village, they told the first man they saw where they saw the *tahash*. He organized a group, which included Shmuel and Hassan, and they went out to hunt the leopard. Rivka and Miriam's mother took care of the frightened girls.

"What were you two thinking to go to the forest like that?" Rivka yelled.

"Miriam wanted to cure my fear and ended up with one herself," Hamama responded.

The girls burst out laughing, but Hamama's body wouldn't stop shaking, and Miriam's turned yellow. When the men returned with the leopard's corpse, the girls were crowned the village heroes. But the two were already on their way to the village *machva* expert. The expert made Miriam drink her own urine to cure her jaundice, and afterwards, they sat down on the bench and held hands through the pain of the *machva*.

Hamama awoke in her room. Hassan was there, looking at her with concern. He hugged her tightly, and then left the room. Hamama could have sworn she saw tears in his eyes.

2008

"The night that Miriam and I got the *machva* together was worth more than any kids' blood oath," Grandmother says. "From then on, you couldn't find us apart for even a moment. We came to Israel together and settled in Pardes Hanna together. But then, when they finally built the houses here, she got the lot in the neighborhood up the hill, and I got the one here. Back then it didn't bother us, but now we're both old and can hardly walk. Can't visit each other. It's good that there's a telephone."

A week later, Grandpa didn't feel well, and Grandma contracted what he had, and because of my pregnancy, they forbade me from visiting.

"What a pair," my mom tells me over the phone. "He infects her, and by the time she's better, he gets infected again. The transition between seasons is really dangerous. Are you taking care of yourself?"

After I promise her that I'm taking care of myself, staying away from air conditioners and drinking lots of water, she says, "You know? It does them really good that you visit every week."

I want to tell her that it does me good, too, but I'm not used to talking about my feelings with her, so I don't say anything.

You could say that for many years, I practically lived with Grandpa and Grandma, and then for many years, I only came by for Shabbat meals.

At least I did that. Every Shabbat, we would eat *jachnun*, a Yemenite pastry, and tomato puree at Grandma's, then sit around for a few hours talking and snacking on sunflower seeds together.

Now, I only come for one Shabbat each month.

It was really important to me that Grandpa live to the end of this pregnancy, that he meet my daughter. But what kind of man will she know? Not really my Grandpa. Not what I grew up with.

I go over the folder on my computer where I keep the videos of them telling their stories, and here—here he's laughing, and here he's smiling that rambunctious smile of his, and here he's telling me about the work at Shmuel's workshop. He's reaching for the memory of it.

"It doesn't matter. It was a long time ago," he says.

CHAPTER 3

After the incident with the leopard, Hassan no longer kept his distance from Hamama. He didn't plan on letting her push him away anymore, and he didn't care whether she liked it or not. He had lost little Kadya. They all did. But losing Hamama was not an option. As long as he was around, he kept an eye out for her—he refused to let her and Miriam gather wood alone, or even go to the well by themselves. Hamama feigned some objection and pretended to be deeply offended, but secretly she like to see Hassan caring for her so plainly

One day as they waited for Miriam by a stone fence, Hassan picked up one of the bricks.

"Look, this brick's hollow. It'll be our hiding spot. Whenever I launder rich people's clothes, they give me good things, which I'll then leave here for you."

Hamama smiled.

Over the next few weeks, Hamama found various surprises under the brick: raisins and almonds, sweet dates, and *lokum* —the gel confections known as Turkish delight.

"Are you still angry with me?" Hassan asked one day as they waited for Miriam.

"No," Hamama answered, as a stone lifted from her heart, "but can I still tease you?"

"Did you wait a long time for me?" Miriam had arrived, interrupting their moment.

"Yes," Hamama said and contorted her face, pretending to have suffered the whole time spent with Hassan.

Hassan started to walk, and the girls followed.

"You really don't have to accompany us," Hamama said.

Hassan didn't answer.

"And anyway, you walk fast, and we're slow, so why should you come?" Miriam added.

Hassan didn't answer her, either.

"Shmuel needs help at the workshop," Hamama said. "There's high demand for jewelry in anticipation of the upcoming holidays."

"He's not listening," Miriam said.

"He doesn't talk much, either," Hamama said.

"Why not?" Miriam asked.

"How should I know?" Hamama asked, then she quoted from *Pirkei Avot,* "He who speaks often with a woman commits his soul."

"But he spoke with you. I saw, earlier."

"I'm like his sister. Or at least I was, before he left us and came here."

Hamama and Miriam continued walking and teasing their escort, but he didn't react to anything, and it seemed he wasn't listening to them at all.

"I have an idea. Maybe he's ashamed of you?" Hamama asked.

"Of me? Why?" Miriam was surprised.

"I know he's looking for a wife. Maybe he's thinking of you?" Hamama laughed.

Hassan tripped, and the girls giggled.

"But I'm already engaged to Ben Tzion," Miriam said.

Hamama stopped short, then saw Miriam and Hassan keep going and ran to catch up. "Really? You're already engaged?" Hamama was absolutely shocked. She thought she knew Miriam well, but this was the first time she had heard of her engagement.

"We've been engaged since we were two. The moment we were born our families promised us to one another."

Hamama stared at her friend in disbelief. She couldn't comprehend how Miriam, who was so adventurous and carefree all the time, could be somebody's wife.

"When will you get married?" Hamama asked.

"Actually, soon..."

"Well, I don't ever want to get married!" Hamama said with contempt.

56

She thought of her mother left behind when she was sick, of Rivka always busy with the kids; on top of that, she didn't think there was anybody she'd want to live with for the rest of her life.

"You won't have a choice, Hamama. We're already twelve," Miriam said with a certain know-how that annoyed Hamama.

"Why can't I go out to work or travel to the Land of Israel like Hassan?" Hamama asked with a rising anger. "Why do I have to stay home all the time and raise annoying kids?"

Hassan stopped walking, and the girls nearly bumped into him.

"You can work," he said. "And you can go to the Land of Israel. But you have to get married first. Who knows, maybe our families will even emigrate to Israel together?"

"Or maybe you'll just go alone and leave me behind—again."

"I won't leave you behind anymore. Ever. I promise," Hassan said.

Hamama was still upset—Hassan could see this. She felt like everyone was moving on with their lives while she was left behind, stuck in the mud. She was angry at Miriam for getting married, she was angry at herself and the life that was forced upon her, and most of all she was angry at Hassan.

She knew he had a good heart, and that he didn't think he was lying to her, but what will happen to them when he gets married? How could they possibly stay close? She tried to gather herself, to fight back her tears. And then, although they were on a public road and Miriam was standing right beside him, Hassan took Hamama's hand without a moment's hesitation, and looked into her eyes.

"I promise," he repeated.

Miriam fidgeted awkwardly. Hassan noticed and started to walk again. The girls hurried after him, but neither said another word.

Hassan did, in fact, try to find a wife. He believed he could fulfill the mitzvah of *yishuv ha'aretz*—settling the land of Israel—only after fulfilling the mitzvah of getting married. In his monumental Halachic work Maimonides describes the four reasons for which a person is permitted leave the land of Israel, and one of them is to find a wife. So, in Hassan's mind there was no sense in undertaking the journey to Israel, only to leave again. In addition, he wanted to make *aliya* as a complete man, which required finding a woman and getting married.

But whenever he met with a family, they would reject his offer as soon as they learned of his smuggling. The Jews who favored immigration to Israel had already organized themselves into groups, and those who weren't as keen didn't want to be involved with such a dangerous crime against the authorities.

They were also worried about the bride's fate. Smuggling Jews out of Yemen, as Hassan did, was punishable by death, and then what would happen to the smuggler's wife? Who would support her? Hassan grew restless. He swore he wouldn't immigrate to Israel before getting married, and every additional journey on which he embarked, endangered him once more. He yearned to stay on the other side of the border, never to return.

Miriam's wedding took place a few months later. The village of El Be'aden was filled with joy and festivity—and entire two weeks' feasting, dancing, and ritual. Hamama sat with Miriam and watched as women dotted and drew on her skin. Miriam was excited.

"I think I prefer your regular skin," Hamama said.

Miriam started to laugh, but one of the women silenced her.

"Don't move! And you—" the woman turned to Hamama, "make yourself useful and fetch some water for the bride."

Hamama left the room, but not before she twisted her face behind the woman, which caused Miriam to burst into laughter.

A parade of women entered the room singing, some drumming along rhythmically. Hamama gave Miriam the water and tried to get away from all the happy aunts.

"Aren't you happy for Miriam?" Rivka asked Hamama when she returned home.

"I'm happy."

"So why the sour face?"

"We always liked pumping water and gathering wood together, and now that won't happen anymore."

Rivka smiled. "Ah! It'll happen. She'll just live by Ben Tzion's family and not at her house."

"But she'll have to bear children."

"Not yet, Hamama. Also, Ben Tzion is too young. By the time she'll bear children, you'll be married, too."

Hamama forced a smile and walked out. She felt she was suffocating. It wasn't really the trips to the well or the forest that she was going to miss, but rather her one true friend.

The preparations continued. Miriam was immersed in the river, accompanied by an audience of women. Ben Tzion underwent the haircut ceremony; Miriam was dressed in the traditional bridal clothes, and on Thursday evening, the wedding ceremony took place. Miriam insisted that Hamama stand beside her despite the latter's apparent chagrin, and indeed, Hamama couldn't help but be overtaken by the excitement of the ceremony. For a moment, she thought about commenting on the heavy miter, adorned with gold and jewels, that Miriam was forced to carry on her head, but when she saw the sparkle in her friend's eyes, she decided to stay silent.

Ben Tzion and his entourage arrived in song and dance, and Hamama decided that she couldn't help but like the skinny boy who appeared before them. His festive attire only made him look skinnier. He saw Miriam and smiled broadly, which immediately caused Miriam to choke up. This amused Hamama, and so she was surprised to find that her eyes had also welled up with tears.

The wedding celebrations continued throughout the night and all of the following Shabbat. Hamama tried to visit Miriam as much as possible, but her friend was trapped amongst many women she didn't know and had to host dozens of guests and visitors.

Rivka misunderstood Hamama's frustration with her friend's wedding and spoke with Shmuel.

"I think it's time to find Hamama a match," she told her husband.

"Did she say something?"

"She seems to oppose the idea, but she already reached marriageable age. And it's not safe for her to stay unbetrothed."

"I'll send David a letter to get his permission."

At dinner one night, part of the family was missing. Hassan was away on a smuggling run and wasn't supposed to return for another few days. Rivka turned to Hamama.

"How's Miriam?" Rivka asked.

"Happy," Hamama answered through a mouthful of food.

"Good. When I married Shmuel, I wasn't happy at all at first, but with time I got to know him better." Rivka smiled at her husband.

Hamama barely swallowed her food, growing suspicious of direction of the conversation.

"Hamama, you've reached the age where we need to find you a husband, and…" Rivka began.

"I don't want to get married," Hamama interrupted.

"You don't have a choice," Rivka said with a stern tone. "Shmuel already sent a letter to Father."

Hamama grunted in anger. Everyone was scheming behind her back. Rivka continued to bring Hamama to her side.

"Hamama, you know what happened to Rachel. It's very dangerous to leave you without a match."

Hamama didn't respond. The thought of a stranger, another person, ruling over her life, did not appeal to her at all.

"Look, Hamama, we're not your parents," Shmuel intervened. "You're allowed to refuse. We won't force you to marry someone you don't want."

Hamama looked up at Shmuel. He really was a good man.

"Fine," she agreed, "as long as I'm allowed to refuse if I don't want the man."

Rivka sighed in relief.

But Hamama exercised her veto power liberally. That one had a limp, and another one was old, that one was dumb and another one was just too ugly. The propositions continued to come to their home, but none struck Hamama's fancy. The villagers thought she was picky, but she didn't see herself as such. She would just look closely at the match that was offered to her and asked herself: *Do I want to live my whole life with this man?* The answer was always, "No."

One day, she heard Rivka and Shmuel talking about her.

"The Tan'ami family offered a match," Shmuel announced.

"Oy," Rivka grunted, "what did they see in her?"

Hamama wasn't offended. She understood the problem. The Tan'ami family was one of the most respected Jewish families in town. Their son was a learned professional. If she refused, her name would be besmirched, and the whole village would look down on Rivka and Shmuel.

"I already heard some women in the souk teasing us and talking about how we treat the girl like gold, and are trying to make money off her, and so on," Rivka complained.

"We really do treat her like gold." Shmuel smiled at his wife.

"That's the problem. We haven't pressured her. She'll always refuse."

"But you know that we won't achieve anything by force," Shmuel said. Hamama knew he had a gentle soul, a manner resembling her father's. "Maybe she's just not ready yet."

"We already put her name out there. She has to be ready." Rivka sighed again.

Hamama lay on the mat and tried to convince herself to agree to the match. But she understood that all the good qualities that were pointed out to her, about his talents and his family, were also his deficiencies. If she were to marry him, she would never immigrate to the Land of Israel. He wouldn't agree, and his ties to the authorities would endanger his whole family. And so, she found herself growing angrier and angrier with Hassan. If only she had never met him. If only he hadn't enticed her with his stories of the Holy Land.

Hamama found herself stuck. Although she didn't want to disappoint or hurt Rivka and Shmuel, she couldn't bring herself to bury her dreams. She tried to find a solution, a way out. *A way out. She could run away again!*

The first time she ran away from home, she ended up here, with her loving sister and her husband. And with Hassan. Who knows where a second getaway might lead? And, of course, by leaving, she could avoid marrying a Tan'ami without embarrassing Rivka and Shmuel. She couldn't run to Tholet, because there her father would set her up with the first eligible man he met, but she could go to Aden, and from there—to the Land of Israel!

Hamama knew that Hassan would never agree to help her. He himself wasn't planning to leave until he was married. But if she followed him, right up to the border with Aden, he wouldn't have to know.

Hamama got up and started packing a bundle of clothes and food for the journey. She had to find a temporary place to hide, close to the village, from where she could follow Hassan and find out his plans to go on another journey. She left the house quietly, with no regrets or worries. She exited the village with excitement in her heart, moving between the shadows of houses to avoid being seen.

Hamama left El Be'aden, the forest to her left and the desert to her right. She chose the desert, and after two hours of walking arrived at a deserted ruin. Hamama entered the old house, which apparently served as a public restroom for passersby. The smell was nauseating, but she gathered her courage and climbed up to the attic, where she found a small hiding spot far from the flies. She fell asleep.

Hamama slept deeply, and she only woke up in the late morning to the sounds of woeful calls. She recognized Rivka's voice and jumped up with fright. She hit her head, and the sharp pain reminded her of last night's events. And only then did the idea of running away seem stupid and selfish. Her bleary eyes welled up with tears at the sound of her sister's sorrow.

That's a terrible way to wake up. And a terrible way to behave. She felt ashamed.

Hamama imagined Rivka tearing out her hair in grief, and Shoshana and the twins crying with no consolation. She now wholeheartedly regretted her decision to run away; alas, she was also too embarrassed to return. She continued to hear voices calling her name.

"Hamama! Hamama!" She recognized Shmuel's voice.

Somehow, she hadn't thought this would happen. She didn't think enough. She crawled deeper into her hiding spot in the attic, trying to meld into the wall without uttering a sound.

"Hamama!" Shmuel called.

Shmuel, Hassan, and two more men entered the ruin.

"She was here," Hassan said as he pointed at the small footprints on the floor.

Hamama's heart skipped a beat.

"You don't see any more prints next to her? With her?" Shmuel asked, worried.

"No. She's alone," Hassan said. He tried to follow the footprints, but the two men followed him and covered the tracks.

"What are you doing!? Now I can't follow the tracks." Hassan grunted angrily and left to find another lead outside the ruin.

Hamama had never seen Hassan angry. Shmuel stayed behind, staring at the walls around him. After everyone left, he held his head and exhaled quietly.

Is he crying? Hamama was alarmed. She was beyond embarrassed. Her anger at herself was unbearable, and she hoped that they would leave soon so that she could stay there and die. Shmuel followed Hassan, and Hamama watched as the delegation continued on its way.

Hamama sat in the stinky ruin for two days, subsisting on her small provisions. She didn't care if she ran out. She didn't care about anything. She sank into a deep dreariness, silent and sorrowful. She was alone, but if she had felt any comforting presence, she would have chased it away. She didn't deserve any consolation. She didn't deserve anything. She was just a stubborn, spoiled little girl who did whatever she felt like doing. Sarah and Sa'adia were right all along. They saw her bad nature. She only thought about herself, her own future, her own dreams. She shamed her dead mother and her loving father, as well as Rivka and Shmuel who had cared for her and treated her like gold.

Hamama couldn't escape the difficult, accusing thoughts, nor did she want to. Every once in a while, she fell into a disturbed, dream-filled sleep. In all of them, she saw Rivka screaming and crying, filled with pain. She would wake up drenched in sweat.

The flies had arrived and were feeding off her sweat. She didn't even try to get rid of them.

Another two days passed, and the pangs of hunger started to bother Hamama. Even though she accepted them lovingly as the punishment she deserved, she climbed down from the attic to stretch her legs in one of the ruin's rooms. She lay across from the open window, staring at the sun with mild hallucinations. She didn't notice when someone entered the room. It was an Arab shepherd from the village, stopping in to use the latrine. The shepherd saw Hamama's outstretched arm in one of the rooms and approached her. He immediately recognized the dirt-covered girl and began yelling and cursing.

"Is that you, Hamama? *Il'an abuk!* A curse on your father! Do you know everyone's looking for you?"

Hamama didn't bother to answer. In light of the new presence, she felt a sudden relief and passed out. The Arab shepherd woke her up and gave her water. He then instructed her to come with him, and when she refused, he picked her up like a sack of yams and carried her straight to the village to Rivka and Shmuel's house.

Rivka was so excited to see Hamama alive that she forgot to get angry. She hugged and kissed her little sister and cried and laughed. But when she calmed down and realized what Hamama had done, she slapped her across the cheek.

"I'm sorry, Rivka. I'm sorry!" Hamama cried.

"That's all right," Rivka said. "The important thing is that you're healthy. That's it. I'm done trying to find you a match. You can become an old spinster and raise my kids, for all I care. So long as you're fine."

Hamama laughed and cried, and Rivka joined her. Shmuel and Hassan stood in the corner with their arms crossed, drawing a blank as to what they were witnessing.

"Where were you?" Hassan's voice was harsh.

"In the ruin you went to," Hamama said, partly in fear and partly with pride because she managed to hide from him.

But Hassan just nodded and left the room.

The great fear he felt when Hamama disappeared, the great fear for her life—that was the strongest emotion he had felt since his mother's passing. He was happy she had returned, but he had difficulty calming down. The incident with the tiger had also stirred deep emotions in him. He attributed them to the years he had spent growing up with her, the period of their childhood that now seemed so far away. Hassan leaned on the wall, breathing in the fresh air. He remembered how she came to hang the laundry with him in Tholet, and how they played the game with the alb seeds. He remembered her eyes, watching him with awe and amazement, and her smile, teasing him, making him laugh. He realized how safe and strong he always felt beside her and how joyous his life became when she moved in with them. When she was angry with him for leaving Tholet he watched her from afar, waiting for a chance to get close to her again, to earn her trust, her forgiveness. He cared for her. He wanted to do good by her, and that made him become better. Escorting her and Miriam to the well - those walks together every morning - it wasn't only to keep her safe but it also kept him centered.

She was his favorite person, and he could have lost her. Again, tears welled up in his eyes. He hurried to the workshop, but the anger disrupted his delicate work, and he sat down, helpless.

Rivka took Hamama to the washing room and cleaned all the dirt, the dry sweat, and the stink that clung to her. Miriam also came by and watched the sisters.

"You're completely crazy, Hamama," Miriam said. "Now no one will ever want to marry you."

"That's all right. I'll take care of everybody's kids," Hamama said without any remorse.

Two weeks passed with the usual routine. Hamama, who was worried that Hassan might still be angry with her, was relieved when she found out that he was again leaving her little gifts under the hollow rock. She and Miriam continued to help with the household chores, and Hamama heard all about Miriam's strict mother-in-law.

"I'm telling you, I'll be the first to join you in immigrating to Israel."

"She's that bad?" Hamama asked.

"If she stands over my shoulder one more time while I'm cooking, I'll step on her on purpose."

"And you wanted me to get married."

"Yes! Ben Tzion is so charming. I love being married! I want a huge family! Just...without his mother."

Hamama laughed. She liked the fact that Miriam came over to cook with her, and to get away from her controlling mother-in-law. Shoshana shadowed them both and tried to figure out how to do the daily chores. Now that Menashe and Efraim had started going to the *mori alial,* the school for toddlers, Shoshana was left without an object for her badgering.

Hamama was happy with the routine. But then one evening, Hassan announced he had met a girl, and he planned to become engaged.

"Congratulations," Shmuel said.

"How did you find her?" Rivka asked.

"It was during the last journey I led," Hassan explained. "Menachem Gamdani's group. We stopped at her village, next to Taez, and her family, Gamlieli, hid us in the pen so the neighbors wouldn't inform on us."

"And she served you food and drinks, and you saw her beautiful eyes?" Hamama teased. Hassan ignored her quip.

"No," he answered. "I didn't even see her. I spoke with her brother, and he told me about her. Said no one wanted her, so I offered myself, and we agreed that I would visit them next week."

"And what else do you know about the family?" Shmuel asked.

"That they have the fear of heaven in them and that the girl is educated."

"And you didn't see her at all?" Hamama insisted.

"Not everyone needs to inspect so carefully as you," Rivka scolded.

"I actually agree with Hamama," Hassan said. He gave Hamama a smile. "After all, the woman is the one who will carry the burden of the family while the husband comes and goes. It's only reasonable for her to be very careful about whom she decides to devote her life."

Everyone was silenced by his words, and Hamama's heart leapt with joy at Hassan's encouragement.

In the absence of a father, it was Shmuel's responsibility to find Hassan a match. Although he trusted the boy's wisdom and good heart, he wanted him to act properly and work with a matchmaker.

"Who will you go with?" he asked.

"Pinhas Aharon."

"That's good." Shmuel nodded his approval.

Later, before she headed to bed, Hamama went to Hassan and took his hand.

"Good luck tomorrow," she said with a wide smile.

His heart widened with joy at her smile, but at the same time a pang of sorrow cut through him. Getting married would undoubtedly change their relationship once again. It seemed as though they had only just started becoming friends again.

"Thanks, Hamama," Hassan said and forced a smile. "Good night."

The following day, Hassan went to the girl's village with Pinhas Aharon, a well-known matchmaker. The girl's family welcomed him respectfully, and he entered the diwan like a king.

"*T'fadlu.*" The head of the Gamlieli household led them to colorful mats and embroidered pillows.

Hassan looked around the living room and was impressed by the wealth surrounding him, but he then remembered that Pinhas Aharon had told him that families often borrowed such possessions from their neighbors in order to make an impression. Hassan didn't care.

Gamlieli's son, whom Hassan had met in the pen, sat down next to him, and pointed at a girl of about eleven who sat in the corner.

"That's my sister, Leah."

"I'm Hassan."

"I know," Leah answered shyly as she lowered her head.

Hassan quieted and let Pinhas Aharon handle the negotiations. He started praising Hassan, his character and achievements. The whole time Hassan looked at the girl who was bound to be his wife, and he was overcome with excitement.

"His hands are in everything," Pinhas Aharon began. "Already at a young age, he learned various handicrafts, and there isn't much he can't do. The residents of El Be'aden, both Arab and Jew, will confirm that he has done many repairs and renovations to their homes. And further, he even washes *talitot* and takes any available jobs in order to support himself and his family." Pinhas Aharon paused for a breath before continuing with his praise of Hassan. "He also acquired the skills of gold craftsmanship from his relative. Finally, let me tell you about his bravery and faith in God. He is an emissary of good deeds and leads groups of Jews to the Holy Land."

"Regarding this mission," interrupted the father of the girl, "will he stop this dangerous occupation after the wedding?"

"Yes," Hassan answered. "I will give the bride one year to stay at her family's side, and then we'll immigrate to the Land of Israel."

Pinhas Aharon pinched Hassan discreetly, but the lad's words had already cast their impression on the family. The girl burst into tears and left the room. Her mother followed her, and her father stood up.

"This wasn't discussed," the father said with a frown on his face.

"You're a Jew," Hassan said. "How can you desire to continue living here as the days of redemption come upon us and the Jewish people return to their homeland?" He ignored another one of Pinhas's pinches. *I can't handle any more rejections. How many trials does God want to put me through? Am I bound to walk up to the entrance of the land without going in?*

The winds calmed in the colorful room. The brother whispered something into the father's ear, and the latter sat down again:

"You seem like a good lad, and all the praise has touched our hearts, but we don't want to part with our daughter," explained the father.

"Then don't marry her off," Hassan answered. He himself was surprised by the audacity of his words. *I sound like Hamama*, and the thought of her encouraged him.

"What did you say?" the father asked as if he hadn't understood.

"I meant that when your daughter becomes a woman, her will and her husband's will be what counts," Hassan said. "You won't be able to decide where she'll live after the wedding."

"We'd like to discuss this a bit before deciding," the brother said as he led his father to another room.

"You can't be allowed to open your mouth," Pinhas Aharon said with a sharp tone. "You can't. Next time I'll go without you to the girl's house."

"But they have to understand that they're giving away their daughter. They can't maintain their control over her after that. Not over her and not over me."

"Hassan, you're an orphan, I'm sorry. And that's why you don't understand the family's need to stay close to their daughter."

"Then they should immigrate with us to the Land of Israel," Hassan insisted.

The Gamlieli men, the father and the brother, entered the room and sat down:

"We like you," the father said. "We'll agree to a match with some conditions. The dowry we'd like is five hundred riyals."

Hassan stood up in anger.

"Just say that you don't want to marry the girl off," Hassan shouted.

Pinhas Aharon stood by Hassan. They parted from the two and left the house with great agitation. Hassan walked briskly, and Pinhas Aharon remained silent for a few minutes.

"It's true the usual dowry is about one hundred riyals," Pinhas Aharon began. "The family's request was too high, but I know you're keen on getting married, so I don't understand your stubbornness."

Hassan didn't respond. After half an hour of walking, Pinhas Aharon tried again.

"But you have the money," he said.

"And what will the money help? First, they don't want to give the girl up, and then they try to sell her to the highest bidder? I don't understand them and don't want to be a part of it." Hassan became angrier with each word he spoke.

"All in due time, Hassan. All in due time." Even though Pinhas Aharon was trying to encourage him, his words were like salt to his wounds.

"The time is due," Hassan yelled.

The two walked together for a long hour. Hassan battled his feelings. The ground burned beneath his feet, as if urging him to hurry and run from it. Every step stung with pain. Every step filled him with disappointment. He was not stepping on the Yemenite ground; the ground was trampling him.

"Hassan, I know you're upset," Pinhas Aharon said, "and I sympathize, but let me tell you a story that happened in the lands of Ashkenaz."

Hassan remained silent, which Pinhas Aharon must have taken as sign to continue so he began telling a story.

"In the lands of Ashkenaz, there was this one rabbi, Rabbi Yekalesh. One night, he dreamt a dream, and in that dream, someone told him to travel to the city of Prague and that there, by the king's courtyard, under the bridge, there was a buried treasure. Rabbi Yekalesh woke up and dismissed his dream with a smile. But the dream came back three more nights. Every night someone told him the same thing. He decided and acted. Rabbi Yekalesh went on a journey to Prague. He underwent many hardships on the journey, but finally made it to the king's courtyard, next to the bridge. But what? Many soldiers stood guard, and he couldn't get to the bridge. He walked around restlessly for several days. He ran out of food and money. One day an officer saw him and asked, 'I've seen you here many days already. What's your business?' So, Rabbi Yekalesh told him about his dream. The officer laughed and said, 'And why would you listen to such dreams? I also had a recurring dream for a few nights now, where in a town far away there's a treasure hidden in the oven of some Rabbi Yekalesh. Does that mean I should go out and search for this man?' Rabbi Yekalesh heard this, returned home, dug in his oven, and found the treasure."

Pinhas Aharon finished his story and looked at Hassan, who burst out laughing.

"Hamama is my treasure?"

He stopped laughing and wondered: He cared for Hamama deeply and she was, undoubtedly, his favorite person. She was also like a sister to him, but then again, she was also much more than that. Great joy filled his heart as he realized the truth of his feelings for her. He was amazed at how this idea had escaped him until this very moment. In all his efforts to find a wife he never thought to look inside, to search for love, and now suddenly he was overwhelmed by the good fortune of finding this treasure—his treasure. "How come you never said anything before?" Hassan asked.

"Well, I actually did say something to Shmuel. I told him: 'it is not proper for Hassan to go out and look for girls when his unmarried cousin is sitting at home.' He had the same idea but still instructed me to follow you wishes."

"So, Shmuel thought about it, too?"

Pinhas Aharon laughed,
"Everyone thought about it."
"Hamama too?" Hassan was alarmed.
"Well, no. She's as blind as you."

The two continued on their journey, and when the rooftops of El Be'aden peeked out from under the horizon, Hassan's heart leapt with joy: Hamama.

Shmuel and Rivka were happy to hear about Pinhas Aharon's idea. They, too, had thought of it earlier, but Rivka said she hadn't dared to make the suggestion.

"I love you both," Rivka told Hassan. "I have imagined a joint future, but both of you have seemed oblivious to the idea. I began to doubt it could work."

"I'll go ask for her hand from David," Hassan said.

"And what'll we tell her?" Rivka asked.

"Nothing. Don't tell her anything." Hassan smiled.

"Great idea." Shmuel laughed.

"Why don't you just bring Father back with you, and we'll hold the engagement here?" Rivka suggested with a wide smile on her face.

"Great idea." Shmuel kept on laughing. "We'll make sure Hamama doesn't know anything."

The following day Hassan accompanied Hamama to the well.

"I'm going to visit your father. Should I pass something along?"

"Regards," she answered.

Hassan left on the journey excitedly, and Hamama returned home with the jug of water just like every other day, not suspecting a thing.

The next day Hamama noticed that Rivka was fussing about her excitedly. Hamama couldn't comprehend Rivka's strange behavior, so she preferred to go outside.

"Maybe you shouldn't go outside," Rivka said.

"And who will gather wood? Menashe or Efraim?" Hamama answered as her suspicions grew about her sister's behavior.

Rivka paused. "Well, perhaps you're right," Rivka said. "Go and gather some wood. Maybe we'll have some guests today."

Hamama shrugged. She left to gather wood with Miriam, then returned home to clean the house and prepared the *nargilot* in the *diwan*. She went out to the workshop:

"Shmuel?"

"Yes, Hamama?" Shmuel raised his eyes from the workbench.

"Something weird is going on with Rivka."

"Yeah?"

"I think she's not feeling well."

"Ah…"

"Shmuel? Who's coming to visit today?"

"What? To visit? Eh…Customers from another village…hmm, coming to check out the merchandise." He held in a chuckle.

Hamama shook her head. Whatever was going on with Rivka, Shmuel must have it, too. She preferred to deal with the rest of the chores than with those two and their strange mood. She left to help Miriam with her chores, and when she finally returned toward evening, she was so exhausted that she had to pinch herself to stay awake.

"Hamama? What are you doing?" Rivka asked.

"I'm tired…"

"Why don't you go to sleep?"

"Sleep?" Hamama was surprised. "We still have to prepare dinner and *j'ala* for the guests, and who will serve them?"

"Go. Take a nap. It's for the best. Shoshana will help me."

Hamama was suspicious of her sister's motive, but she succumbed to her exhaustion, went upstairs, and was soon fast asleep.

In the middle of the night, Hamama was stirred from her slumber by the sounds of singing and music. She dressed slowly and tiredly, and with her eyes still half shut, she headed toward the noise. To her surprise, she saw that the yard was full of people, among them her brother, all singing joyfully. Hamama recognized her friend Miriam and tried to get her attention.

"Psst!"

Miriam heard her friend and hurried over to her with a wide smile.

"What's going on here, Miriam?" Hamama asked.

"What? You don't know?" Miriam was surprised. "They betrothed you."

Hamama was alarmed. Now she was wide-awake.

"What? To whom?"

"To Hassan Salem."

Hassan. That makes sense.

She smiled at Miriam and went back to bed.

Hamama saw again in Hassan a friend, a brother. She loved him very much and felt comfortable in his company. She loved teasing him at every opportunity and enjoyed playing with him and laughing together. But still, the situation had changed. Something stood in the air when he entered the room. She could no longer ignore how handsome he was, the build of his body and his green-gray eyes filled with life. These thoughts caused her embarrassment, and she couldn't help but blush whenever she ran into him. The fact that they lived under the same roof didn't help.

"Hamama, could you bring the men their breakfast?" Rivka urged her on.

"I don't feel well," Hamama said and ran upstairs.

Shmuel and Hassan exchanged amused glances.

"That's not nice. We can't live like this," Rivka reprimanded them.

Later Hassan accompanied Hamama and Miriam to the well. Hamama made sure to keep her gaze glued to her feet and to refrain from uttering a word.

"Is everything okay? Hamama?" Miriam asked.

"What? Yes," Hamama whispered.

Miriam smiled as Hamama started to blush, but the latter was so overcome by embarrassment that she tripped, fell and broke her jug.

"Oy! Hamama!" Miriam kneeled down next to her friend.

"Oy! Rivka will be so mad at me," Hamama said with regret.

Hamama looked around shamefully and noticed that Hassan had disappeared. She hoped he hadn't seen her mishap.

"You're acting very strange," Miriam said as she helped Hamama get up.

Hamama gathered the pieces of the broken jug when Hassan suddenly reappeared, this time with a new jug filled with water. He placed the jug at her feet and left without saying a word. Miriam watched him leave and burst out laughing.

"You two are so cute!"

She left Hamama with the new jug and went to fill her own.

When Hamama returned home, Hassan was gone. She sighed with relief and continued her chores. The next morning when Hamama went to the kitchen, Hassan was again not around.

"He's eating in the workshop," Rivka said. She sounded angry.

"What?" Hamama said.

"And Shmuel is with him, so he won't be alone," Rivka continued, "all because you're being a little girl."

Hassan stopped accompanying Hamama and Miriam to the well, but Hamama kept on finding little surprises under the hollow stone. It didn't matter what she found—Hassan's presence, his thinking of her, filled Hamama's heart with such joy, she felt she would explode.

"What did he leave for you this time?" Miriam asked, appearing behind her.

"Raisins," Hamama said and shared the treasure with her friend.

"So that's it? They trust us to go alone? Now, when we're not single anymore?" Miriam laughed.

Hamama didn't answer. Suddenly, she noticed Hassan's back amongst those walking to the well. He didn't walk with them, but rather went to launder the *talitot,* the fringed garments worn by the very religious Jews. Hamama stared at Hassan's back, at the part that wasn't covered with the *talitot.* For a moment, she thought that she hated those shawls. What's their business with Hassan's back? The thought warmed her stomach, and she blushed and lowered her gaze.

"Hamama! Here's your Hassan," Miriam cried when she noticed the lad.

Hamama was now embarrassed not only by her body's strange reactions to Hassan's presence but also by her friend's announcement, so that when her eyes met Hassan's her feet once again grew confused and she tripped and broke her jug.

"Not again!" Miriam said.

The next morning, Rivka handed Hamama a new jug.

"This jug is from Hassan. And he said he'll stop walking by the well, because he doesn't want to waste all your money on new jugs."

Hamama grabbed the jug and left the house to the sound of Rivka's laughter.

Hamama's embarrassment didn't stand in the way of her great excitement. So, when Hassan left on one of his journeys, she couldn't be comforted.

"When he was here, you tried to avoid him at all costs, and now—when he's gone—you're looking for him?" Rivka said when they sat down together to sort beans. "You look miserable."

"I…forget it, you don't understand," Hamama said hopelessly.

"Oh, I understand." Rivka smiled and hugged her.

These were the days just before Rosh Hashanah, and there was much work to be done in anticipation of the holidays. There was also high demand for jewelry and gifts, so that when Hassan returned, he couldn't be found. He worked at the workshop until late at night, and in the morning, he left very early to launder prayer shawls and dresses close to the well. Miriam noticed Hamama's yearning, mistakenly believed that a chance meeting between the two would bring joy to her friend. Miriam agreed to go to the well with her the following morning, after having found out that Hassan would be there.

Hamama waited by the meeting spot, but Miriam was nowhere to be seen. Hamama was surprised Miriam had chosen such an early time to meet and was growing suspicious that her friend had overslept. It was still dark out, moments before dawn. Hamama yawned loudly and decided to go to the well alone, and later, she would yell at Miriam. With every step the sky brightened, and when she finally arrived at the well, the sun rose, and Hassan's figure emerged, atop one of the hills, hanging laundry on one of the dry *hilfa* bushes. Hamama felt weakness in her feet.

"Ah! I see my girlfriend is coming to bring me some more water." Hassan called out, a wide smile across his face when he saw Hamama standing by the well.

Hamama blushed with shame, so when she bent down to grab the rope and pull the bucket, she tried to hide her head between the well's rocks. She subsequently tripped and fell into the cold water. Hassan, who at that moment had bent down to pick up some more laundry, didn't see what had happened, and so he kept on working.

The cold water hit Hamama's body with shock, and the weakness in her feet turned to freezing paralysis. She was alarmed and grasped for the outcroppings in the stones on the well's walls, but the walls were too smooth, and she slipped back into the water. The water was silent and cold. She shook off the intense cold, trying to move her legs and hands to stay above water. She managed to raise her head out of the water and took a deep breath, but again failed to grab onto anything, so the weight of her wet clothes pulled her back down. As she struggled, she prayed not for her own life, but that Hassan would not notice she had fallen into the well.

But Hassan did notice that Hamama had disappeared, leaving her jug beside the well. At first, he was amused at the thought that she had run off, but suddenly he understood what had transpired, and he ran to the well.

"Hamama!" he cried out.

He looked down to discover that his fears had been right. The girl struggled to stay above water.

"Catch the bucket! Hold on to the rope, and I'll pull you up!" he yelled and tossed the bucket toward her.

Hamama was so embarrassed, she barely managed to hold on to the rope, as Hassan pulled and rolled up the rope until Hamama's head popped out of the well's entrance. Hassan grabbed her hand quickly and pulled her out of the well.

Before she could utter a word, Hassan slapped her across the cheek.

"You're about to die, and you're too embarrassed to call for help!" he yelled.

Hamama, shocked and hurt by Hassan, burst out crying and ran off.

When she arrived home, Rivka was alarmed to see her little sister drenched and crying ceaselessly.

"What happened, Hamama? What happened?" she asked and wrapped her up in several blankets.

Hamama couldn't stop shaking and crying, and only a few minutes later said, "Hassan slapped me."

Rivka hugged her sister.

"Just wait until he comes home. Wait and see what I'll do to him! Who does he think he is? That if you're his, he can behave like this?" Rivka paced around the room like a lion in a cage.

An hour later, Hassan entered the house and looked at Hamama, sitting down and covered in many blankets, her eyes red from tears.

"Hamama—I…" Hassan tried to apologize.

"What do you think you're doing?" Rivka interrupted. "Who gave you permission to touch her?"

"Rivka, she fell into the well, and she fell because of her shame. She almost drowned, and out of shame, she didn't want me to pull her out!"

Rivka looked again at Hamama, then back to Hassan:

"In that case, you should have slapped her twice," she said.

Hamama looked at her, surprised, and Rivka couldn't contain herself and burst out laughing. Hassan, too, started laughing, and Hamama, who finally realized how stupidly she had acted, joined in. The laughter released her tension, calmed her, and cleared the air of bad feelings. Hassan sat down next to Hamama:

"I'm sorry I slapped you," he said quietly. "I was scared."

Hamama looked at his green-gray eyes, and her heart was flooded with warmth and love. She didn't know what to say, but she knew he understood.

Hamama counted the days to the holiday of Sukkot, the Fest of Tabernacles, at which time her family would arrive from Tholet, and the wedding celebrations would begin. Shmuel and Rivka's house filled with guests, and an enormous sukkah was built in the yard. Hamama looked at Shmuel and Hassan tightening the sheets around the sukkah and at Efraim and Menashe prancing around them and trying to help. Hassan raised his head and smiled at Hamama. She smiled back. Hassan had never been so happy. *But now we can't see each other for a whole week. How will I manage that?* He knew Hamama admired him for his strength and courage, but she didn't know that he drew those things from her, from her innocence and her smile, her spunk and sincerity.

"Uncle Hassan!" little Menashe interrupted his thoughts. "You're going to lift me up to lay the *sekhakh*, right?" The little boy was so excited to cover the sukkah.

"Of course," Hassan answered with a smile. He glanced back up at the terrace, but Hamama no longer stood there. She had probably gone inside to help Rivka.

The following morning, he ambushed her on the way to the well.

"Hassan! What are you doing here?" Hamama smiled at him.

"I came to say goodbye. See you at the wedding," he said, and after a moment reached out and took her hand.

Warm waves of fondness swept over the two. Neither wanted the moment to end, but other girls approached on the path, and Hassan let Hamama's hand drop as he hurried off. Hamama's whole body burned with joy, and she smiled when she discovered that he had deposited a fragrant jasmine flower in her hand.

Hamama paced around the house excitedly. She insisted on helping Rivka with all the preparations, even though her sister objected, saying that in her state she caused more harm than help. But Hamama didn't mind her sister's teasing. She and Miriam stood in the kitchen, prepared various treats, went out to gather sheets and blankets from the neighbors for all the guests, washed the laundry, and hung it to dry. Hamama was ever grateful to Rivka and Shmuel for taking her in, for caring for Hassan, and now for marrying them. So, when Shmuel gave her a gold necklace he prepared himself, she immediately burst out crying:

"It's too much, Shmuel!"

"It's not. The whole time you worked here and helped out, it's the least we can do."

Hamama hugged him.

"Ah, a hug from the girl who kicked my shin." Shmuel laughed.

Hamama smiled at him.

"Hamama! Father's coming! And Sarah and her husband, too!" Rivka yelled from the yard.

Hamama left Shmuel, placing the gold necklace in her pocket. David spread his arms out as she approached him.

"*Mabruk, ya Hamama.* Here, this is Ahuva," David said to his daughter, who was already fully engulfed in his arms.

Hamama looked at her stepmother. She was short and very pretty: her round cheeks seemed to smile at all times. Her dark skin radiated. Nothing about her resembled her late mother. Nothing except for her name.

"Mazal *tov*," Ahuva said, and the two embraced.

"Thank you!" Hamama said, then turned to Sarah.

Sarah stood by her husband, a very gaunt man. Hamama approached her for a hug.

"Thank you for coming," Hamama said.

"Well…you didn't come to my wedding, at least I'll be nicer," Sarah teased. Hamama knew her sister well enough not to be offended.

"And Sa'adia?" Hamama asked.

"His wife is about to give birth. He couldn't leave her this time," David explained.

Hamama saw Sa'adia the morning after the engagement. He told her about the woman he had chosen. She was divorced, and older than him, but she made him happy. When he had visited Hamama, her belly was already large, but this time he didn't want to leave her.

Hamama led her small family to the house. Assigning rooms was easy because it was Sukkot. The women slept in the house, and the men slept in the Sukkah. Hamama spread out her mat between Sarah and Rivka and was happy that the sisters would sleep together, like past times, but her plans were disrupted by the celebrations that started that night. The men slaughtered a sheep, sang, and danced in the yard. The women sang and danced for Hamama in the house.

Hamama sat amongst the cheerful ladies, but in her heart wished to be far away from the others; alas, this time she could not escape. She was at the center of attention.

"I know exactly how you feel," her friend Miriam whispered.

"What?" Hamama asked as she kissed the hand of one of the old aunts.

"You want to go out and find Hassan." Miriam laughed.

"Will you help me?" Hamama begged.

"No." Miriam laughed again.

"You're evil."

"You're dumb."

"You're really evil."

"You really think Hassan would be happy to see you run off and disobey the *halacha*, the Jewish law? And what will you do when you see him? Break a jug?"

Hamama didn't know how to answer her friend, so she pinched her and turned to face the rest of the guests. She decided to take this opportunity to get to know her stepmother better. Ahuva was very friendly and smiled happily when Hamama turned to speak to her.

"Rivka told me you work as a midwife?"

"Yes, I do."

"It's probably helpful to have some additional income, but aren't there very few Jewish babies in Tholet?"

Ahuva smiled with kindness.

"I go to Hassabyein, if they call me. Also, the Arab women in Tholet often use me."

"She's really good," Sarah said. "Quite in demand."

"And Kadya? Tell me about Kadya," Hamama said quietly.

Ahuva's face fell.

"Kadya was such a good girl. As soon as I came, she was happy for me, and helped me with everything. She was like my own daughter. I called her my girl." Ahuva grew silent.

Hamama took Ahuva's hand, and they comforted each other. Later, when Ahuva left the room, solace came from an unexpected place. Sarah, who saw the sorrow written on Hamama's face, sat down next to her.

"You know, Ahuva is infertile, which is why nobody except father wanted to marry her."

Hamama twisted her face in disapproval, but her sister continued.

"You see, she really did take Kadya to be her own daughter, and they both made each other very happy."

Hamama was touched by Sarah's attempt to cheer her up. Even though her sister could use Hamama's decision to desert Tholet against her, this time she chose to be kind.

The celebrations—singing and dancing—continued throughout the holiday. In the course of three days Hamama's body was covered with dots of *k'tat*, a gentle color that was used to decorate the bride's body. At dawn of the fourth day Hamama went down to dip in the river, accompanied by friends and the women in her family. She was not alone. As each of her companions entered with her, the water took on the holiness of communal bonding, and it elevated her to new heights. She felt stronger and braver, yet very feminine. She grew more conscious of her body, and when she returned from the river, wrapped in her clothes, she felt she was no longer a girl.

That night was the groom's *henna* night. During a big feast one of the men kneaded the *henna* dough and spread it on Hassan's hands and legs while the others danced and threw riyals before him. The green-brown mud circles on his palms, which later would leave brown-red marks, were the ransom paid to keep the demons away from the bride and groom but seeing them just reminded Hassan of the stories told about him when he was born and about his late parents. He suddenly missed them terribly and felt alone in the happy crowd. Only the thought of Hamama provided him with comfort.

The wedding ceremony passed as if in a dream. While standing next to each other for the first time in five days, both Hamama's and Hassan's hearts filled with joy. The rabbi read the ketubah, the Jewish marriage contract, and finished with sheva brachot, the seven blessings.

"Baruch Ata HaShem Elokainu Melech HaOlam, Asher Barah Sasson VeSimcha, Chatan VeKalah, Gila Rina, Ditza VeChedva, Ahava

VeAchava, VeShalom VeRe'ut. MeHera HaShem Elokeinu Yishama BeArei Yehudah U'Vchutzot Yerushalayim, Kol Sasson V'eKol Simcha, Kol Chatan V'eKol Kalah, Kol Mitzhalot Chatanim MeChupatam, U'Nearim Mimishte Neginatam. Baruch Ata HaShem MeSame'ach Chatan Im Hakalah."

"You are blessed, Lord our God, the sovereign of the world, who created joy and celebration, bridegroom and bride, rejoicing, jubilation, pleasure and delight, love and brotherhood, peace and friendship. May there soon be heard, Lord our God, in the cities of Judea and in the streets of Jerusalem, the sound of joy and the sound of celebration, the voice of a bridegroom and the voice of a bride, the happy shouting of bridegrooms from their weddings and of young men from their feasts of song. You are blessed, Lord, who makes the bridegroom and the bride rejoice together."

At the end of the wedding ceremony, Hassan left with the men to pray the evening prayers, and the women walked back to the house. Afterwards, came the feast. The guests sang and told stories all night long. Hamama wasn't asked to help, but even if she had, she wouldn't have been able to move because of the heavy bride's outfit. Her white dress was sewn especially for her, embroidered with red and orange, but the jewelry and miter belonged to the bride dresser.

"How could you stand it?" Hamama asked her friend Miriam, as she sat, sweating, burdened by the heavy jewelry.

"It gives you something to concentrate on. To be stable. Not to fall."

"I asked the dresser to give you more jewelry than any other bride," Rivka said.

"Why?" Hamama asked.

"So, you won't be able to run off suddenly." Rivka laughed.

The other women burst out laughing, and Hamama twisted her face. All the women in El Be'aden knew her past, but it didn't bother her in the least. She just wanted this night to conclude so she and Hassan could be together.

Hassan and Hamama lived in Rivka and Shmuel's house, the house that was occupied by all the wedding guests. So, Miriam and Ben-Tzion lent their house to the newlywed couple.

"I left you raisins and nuts in the room," Miriam told her.

"I want to be there already."

"Yes, but remember that my evil mother-in-law still lives there. She didn't volunteer to leave. But she knows she's not allowed to disturb you."

"It'll be fine," Hamama said, but as she was comforting Miriam about her mother-in-law, she herself started to worry. What was going to happen? What would they do there? Was she ready? Rivka already explained to her that it was too early for them to have kids, that they themselves were still kids, and that she shouldn't worry. But what if nobody told Hassan the same thing? *It'll be fine—I can handle Hassan.*

The celebrations continued throughout the night, and the following morning the men and women led Hassan and Hamama in a procession to Miriam and Ben Tzion's house. Rivka and Sarah were already waiting for them. They welcomed them, then quickly left. Hassan and Hamama were alone.

"Finally," Hamama sighed.

"Makes sense that you suffer at these kinds of events." Hassan laughed.

They entered Miriam and Ben Tzion's room, searching for the evil mother-in-law, but she was nowhere to be found.

"Maybe she decided to leave the house for a few hours," Hamama said.

They sat on the mat, staring into each other's eyes. Suddenly, Hassan grasped Hamama's hand and held it. Hamama's whole body was flooded with heat, only this time she noticed that Hassan was also blushing.

"*Mazal tov*, Hamama," he said.

"*Mazal tov*, Hassan," she smiled.

She could drown in his beautiful eyes, and she found herself leaning on him. He wrapped his arm lovingly around her, and they both fell into a deep sleep, exhausted from the long celebrations.

"Hassan? Hamama?" Rivka's voice resounded outside the house.

Hamama awoke slowly, her gaze following Hassan, who got up to answer the door.

"Good morning, Rivka." Hassan blessed his sister-in-law.

"Morning? I brought your lunch. Lahoh and meat soup."

"Thanks," Hassan said and took the food inside.

"Did she leave?" Hamama asked.

"Yes. Are you hungry?"

"For meat soup? No. But I'll have the *lahoh*," Hamama said as she got up, trying to straighten out the creases in her white dress. Yesterday, she had hardly eaten anything, and she still wasn't hungry, but she loved the spongy pancake-like bread.

"I didn't tell you yesterday, but you look very beautiful," Hassan said, smiling at his wife.

Hamama was embarrassed. "You don't have to say things like that to me. It's too weird," she said.

Hassan placed the food aside and went to Hamama and took her hands:

"But I want to. Because you're my wife."

"That also sounds weird." They sat down to eat and then rested a bit, enjoying each other's company. They both wanted this moment to last for a long while, but a knock at the door disturbed their peace.

"Time to honor the guests," Rivka called.

"Already?" Hamama complained. "What does she do? Sleep outside our door?"

"Perhaps she doesn't trust me?"

Hamama didn't say anything. The couple walked out, accompanied by Rivka and a group of women, and headed back to Rivka and Shmuel's house, where they were greeted by the many guests and family members who had travelled from afar. The men sat together and learned Torah while the women chatted about the wedding.

Hamama was twelve when she got married, and Hassan was fourteen.

Rivka watched the happy couple, and Hamama knew her older sister thought about the day Hassan and her would leave her house and go to the Land of Israel.

"I don't want you to leave," Rivka told them.

"Come with us," Hassan said.

"I don't want to leave you, Rivka," Hamama said as she held her sister's hand.

"I don't know if we're ready," Shmuel said as he looked at his saddened wife.

"We'll wait until you're ready," Hassan decided.

Hamama didn't believe that she could love him any more than she already did. She knew how much he yearned to immigrate to the Land of Israel. Everyone knew, and still his loyalty and love kept him back. It was a difficult time for Jews who stole the border. There were many robbers on the roads and soldier checkpoints near the border with Aden. The gradual disappearance of Jewish families from Yemen made it harder for those who stayed behind to leave without notice.

But even though they didn't plan to immigrate quite yet, Hassan wasn't deterred from helping others cross. He insisted on continuing to perform this mitzvah, a fact that cost Hamama many hours of lost sleep. She didn't say anything, but every journey on which he embarked scared her senseless. When she wasn't busy with various chores, she would sit and wait by the well next to the dry *hilfa* bushes, where Hassan hung the laundry when he was home.

"This isn't healthy," Miriam said one day.

"He's a day late. He should've been home by now," Hamama said, wringing her fingers.

"He's been late before, Hamama. Sometimes more than two days."

"I know!" Hamama was angry. Miriam sat down next to her and took her hand:

"Maybe you shouldn't wait for Rivka and Shmuel anymore," she said, "Next time he goes, go with him."

"I don't want to leave everyone."

"You won't leave everyone. Ben Tzion and I will come with you," Miriam said, smiling.

"Really?" Hamama asked, and the first smile of the week crept onto her face.

"Yes. We talked about it. I really want to leave his mother behind." Miriam laughed.

Hamama and Miriam embraced. They headed down from the hill, and each went to her respective home.

But Hassan still hadn't returned.

Rivka followed her sister, who was growing paler and paler from fear. Two days later, Shmuel returned home, also pale.

"I heard a rumor that Hassan got sick on the way," he said.

"And? Where is he? What does he have?" Hamama demanded.

"I don't know."

"Where is he?" she kept asking, this time addressing only herself.

As they spoke, there was a knock on the door. Shmuel opened it and spoke with someone. He closed the door and looked confused.

"That was little Gamdani. He said he heard a rumor that Hassan has died."

Hamama immediately grew weak and fell to the floor. Rivka hurried over to her.

"Don't believe the rumors! These are just rumors! You know Hassan!" Rivka tried to encourage Hamama. But Hamama collapsed into herself and refused to talk or listen to others.

Another week came and went. Shmuel left the workshop and went out with a group of trackers to try and find Hassan. Hamama didn't eat or drink anything.

"You have to take care of yourself!" Rivka scolded her. "What if Shmuel comes back with him? You'll have to take care of him!"

Hamama listened to her sister and tried to eat some of her lunch. Dining felt so out of place, and the food remained stuck in her throat, where her tears also stood. She couldn't. Just couldn't. Hamama quickly ran to the bathroom and vomited.

Rivka and Miriam took turns watching over Hamama.

"I'm afraid she'll go look for him or something," Rivka said, caressing Hamama's hair.

"She won't. She can't get very far like this."

The next morning Shmuel returned without any news from the journey. A month had passed since Hassan had gone missing, and Rivka and Shmuel organized a shiva with broken hearts for they too truly loved Hassan.

"She's only a girl," Hamama heard Rivka mumbling through her tears. Shmuel hugged his wife tightly, but Hamama could not comprehend the sorrow that surrounded her.

Hamama refused to take part in the shiva. She didn't believe in her beloved's death. She couldn't watch the mourners sitting on the floor and crying over her husband. It didn't make any sense to her. Every day, she left the house and wandered in the village with Miriam following her. Hamama knew her friend was watching over her, but she didn't care. She didn't speak with anyone. She didn't have the strength to utter a word. She sat down by the stone fence and hugged the empty hollow rock. The villagers who walked by, both Arabs and Jews, looked at her with pity She knew why: only twelve and already a widow. Hamama fell asleep by the stone fence, and Miriam called Shmuel to help take her home. That's what she did throughout the shiva. She would walk to the stone fence and fall asleep there, and Shmuel would come and carry her back home. Rivka insisted on feeding her like a baby, so she prepared diluted porridges, so she wouldn't throw them up, but they didn't always find their way to her stomach. Hamama felt sorry for her older sister. She knew that they must be blaming themselves for not leaving with Hassan right after the wedding. But she wasn't angry with them. How could she be angry? She also wanted to wait for them.

Two more weeks passed. Hamama sat in the kitchen preparing to make the *kubaneh*, the traditional yeast bread, when she suddenly heard children's screams outside.

"Hassan Salem is alive! Hassan Salem is alive!"

Hamama and Rivka ran outside. Shoshana, the twins, and the neighbors congregated outside the house and the children chattered in excitement.

"This isn't a game!" Rivka scolded.

Hamama approached cautiously and then saw him. A man she didn't recognize helped him walk. Hamama ran, parting the sea of small children, out through the gate, to the village path, to Hassan. Tears of joy and sadness crossed paths as they ran down her cheeks at the sight of Hassan: sick, gaunt, and walking at a snail's pace—but alive. Hassan smiled at her with happiness mixed with exhaustion. Hamama replaced the man who helped Hassan walk. He wrapped his arm around her shoulders and leaned on her, looking at her with his green-gray eyes.

"Hamama..." Hassan groaned.

"Shh... You're home now. We're together," Hamama said, tears still flowing down her cheeks.

They came home. Rivka and Shmuel helped Hamama lay Hassan down in his room, which was now his and Hamama's room. He immediately fell asleep. Hamama sat with him a few more minutes and stared at him, just to make sure he was actually there. Then she went out to the kitchen, where Rivka and Shmuel waited.

"I need to eat," she said.

Hassan fell into a troubled sleep, and his body burned up with a fever. Hamama stayed by his side and took care of him. He mumbled words she couldn't understand, sometimes with anger, sometimes with panic. Hamama felt helpless in the face of his illness but thrilled to have him back with her. Shmuel sent letters to Tholet to refute the news of Hassan's passing, and Rivka diligently kept the couple fed.

Then Hassan's fever let up. He awoke and found Hamama sleeping at his side, her arm wrapped around him. He looked at her sleeping, calm but pale, and kissed her on the forehead.

The next morning, he managed to stand up and the couple went downstairs to the kitchen to eat breakfast with Rivka, Shmuel, and the kids.

"So? Shmuel asked. "What happened?"

When Hassan was awake only intermittently, Hamama hadn't bothered him with questions. She simply enjoyed watching him as he looked at her.

"I managed to get the group across, but on the way back, I was caught by soldiers who stopped me for questioning. They wanted me to confess to smuggling Jews."

Hassan stopped for a moment to take a sip of his coffee. "This is good."

"Why don't you let him drink his coffee in peace? He'll tell the story after," Hamama said.

"That's all right," Hassan said. "I didn't stand a chance in their jail. They planned to torture me until I died."

He stopped. He looked at Hamama and wished he had moderated the story a bit.

"But there was one soldier, who usually worked at the border, and this was the man I would bribe to look the other way when I brought the groups across. He didn't turn me in from fear of being arrested himself, and maybe because of this fear, he wanted to help me. A good guy. He could have killed me just as well, but instead helped me escape. He said that now he doesn't owe me anything and that I shouldn't come to the border anymore; otherwise, he'll arrest me."

Hassan quieted down, letting his words sink in. He ate slowly, and only a little, from the pieces of bread Hamama had cut for him.

"So, don't smuggle Jews anymore," Shmuel said.

"No," Hassan said, "just our group."

Shmuel and Rivka looked at one another and nodded with silent agreement. Hassan knew it meant that this time they wouldn't take any more chances by waiting.

"Get well, and we'll head out," Shmuel said.

2008

Grandma stops. A nurse wheels Grandpa out to the porch. They fired the previous one because of his drinking problem. Now, she brags, she got a teacher. Rami. His Nepalese name is Raundi, but he forgives her the little details.

"Did you hear that? Get well, and we'll head out," Grandma repeats her last words.

Grandpa waves her off. He barely talks these days. He sits on the wheelchair, a black, round pillow under him, his legs covered with a thick sheet instead of pants and wears a short undershirt because of the heat.

"I need to go," I apologize, and part from them with a kiss.

On the train to Tel Aviv I try to enjoy the view, as I always like to do, but the image of Grandpa in the thick sheet is deeply engrained in my mind. I'm furious that it's come to this. I'm furious about my complete inability to do anything. I'm furious about the tinge of relief I felt as I left their house.

Get well, and we'll head out? To where? And in any case, he can't get well anymore. I find myself trapped in a cycle of fury and sadness and close my eyes. That way I won't see him. I picture him young, strong, like in the photos. I wish I really knew him like that. Smuggling his family from Yemen to Aden.

CHAPTER 4

Throughout the history of Yemenite Jews, there was constant contact between them and the settlers in the land of Israel. Letters, books, news and halachic innovations crossed the desert, especially when both Palestine and Yemen were under the rule of the Ottoman empire. Yemenite Jews who wanted to make *aliyah,* to immigrate to Israel, had to do so illegally, since leaving Yemen was forbidden. The economic dependence of the Muslims and Jews was so entangled that the Muslims felt they could not afford to lose "their Jews".

When Hassan and Hamama were about to embark their journey, the British Mandate of Palestine was a geopolitical entity under British administration, and the few immigration certificates they gave were mostly reserved for German Jews who needed to escape the Nazi regime. Like many Yemenite Jews before him, when Hassan decided to make *aliyah* he did not think of the laws of men but rather the laws of God, and so started to plan his departure.

The rumor sprouted wings, and a little bird whispered to the Jews of El Be'aden that Hassan was planning to smuggle out his last group. More than eight families asked to join the journey, not including Miriam and Ben-Tzion, Rivka, Shmuel, and the kids. Hassan didn't want to turn down these brave Jews who had come to such a critical decision, not to mention that the disappearance of some of the village's Jewish families would make it much harder for the others to escape later. But he couldn't take that many people with him.

"I can lead a group. I'll stay one day behind you," offered Yefet, Shmuel's brother. He was a cloth merchant and knew the roads well.

"That could be a good idea," Hassan said.

"We'll join Yefet," Shmuel said. "That way the other people will see that he's trustworthy and will agree to join him."

"Are you sure?" Hassan asked.

"Yes. The important thing is that we'll meet in Aden."

Hassan wasn't too happy with Shmuel's decision. He understood Shmuel was trying to do good by his brother. He was kindhearted like that. Hassan, however, had a hard time trusting his loved ones to someone else. But all he could do now was teach Yefet what he knew, to prepare him for this dangerous mission. And so, they sat down and sketched the path from El Be'aden to Aden and agreed on places to stop.

"The shortest way to the border is to go down southeast, but that's exactly where the robbers and soldiers are waiting." Hassan pointed on the sketched map with his finger. "I usually head south through the mountains, and sometimes we find shelter by the families in the adjoining villages. Remember, Yefet, that it's always better to travel through the mountains than the forests because there you have better visibility." Hassan finished and looked at Yefet.

"Maybe we can get permission from the Imam?" Yefet asked. "I heard that a few families asked for a permit and crossed the border easily."

"I wouldn't recommend that," Hassan said. "These permits are very rare. It's much more likely that you'll be flagged, and then it'll be even harder for you to leave."

While the men planned, Hamama, Rivka, and Shoshana packed their housewares and clothes.

"Hassan said to take as little as possible, but mostly items of some value, which we might need on the journey," Hamama said as she packed the gold necklace Shmuel had given her as a wedding present.

The house buzzed with excitement. Yefet's group left that night. Hassan insisted that Yefet lead so that he could follow him to make sure he stayed on course. At their time of departure, Hamama and Rivka hugged quickly, as if they weren't really parting, and the group headed out.

That night Hamama didn't sleep very well.

In the morning, she wandered around with Miriam to say farewell to the village and the memorable corners of their childhood.

"Do you think I can take this stone with me?" Hamama asked and pointed at the hollow rock under which Hassan used to leave surprises for her.

"I think you're taking the real thing with you. That's better." Miriam laughed.

"Maybe you're right," Hamama said. "I packed enough rocks."

"Rocks?" Miriam was surprised.

"I had to take one of my millstones with me. Who knows what they have there, in the Land of Israel?"

"I don't know, but I'm sure they have rocks."

Hamama shrugged. The girls pumped water together, this time to fill the leather pouches they would carry with them on the journey.

The day passed with dreadful slowness. Hamama couldn't wait to head out on the journey. Hassan saw her impatience and tried to soothe her nerves.

"You're so excited that you're not noticing something very important," he said.

"What?" Hamama snapped.

"We have the whole house to ourselves." Hassan smiled.

But his comment only caused her to notice the empty house more. The excitement was extinguished, replaced by mild melancholy.

"I didn't mean that," Hassan said when he noticed her sad face, and he sat down by her, his shoulder flush against hers.

"It's strange to suddenly leave everything," Hamama said.

"For me, too."

Hassan lifted his finger and turned Hamama's chin toward him. He passed his hand over her cheek, and Hamama felt her body quiver. Hassan hesitated for a moment, then asked quietly, "Are you going already in the ways of women?"

"No. Not yet," Hamama said. She was thirteen and had not yet gotten her period. She knew what to expect, as she had seen her sisters, but while they started early and got their periods at eleven, she was late.

"We have time," Hassan said as he hugged Hamama, neither one of them knowing that many months would pass before they would once again have a quiet moment to themselves.

About two hours after sundown, Hassan's group headed out. The Jewish travelers dressed as Arabs, which was considered an offense to the Shariah laws and was thus very risky. But then again, so was leaving Yemen without a permit. Hassan had his usual *kafiya* wrapped around his head. Hamama smiled at the sight of her brave husband, and her heart filled with pride. Hassan led out front, followed by two men. The three were followed by the women and children, with Ben Tzion and the other men taking up the rear guard. Occasionally, the group stopped to hide. Hassan would run forward to survey the area, and after a while, he would return, and the group would continue to march. Two days passed like this on the journey from El Be'aden to Aden. On the third day, Hassan had a worried look on his face.

"What's going on, ya Hassan?" Hamama asked.

"Nothing," he said, averting his gaze.

But that night he ordered the group to stay in one of the caves in the mountains, and he went to a nearby village to find food. Hamama watched him leave and knew something was off. A few hours later, Hassan returned with fresh food and disturbing news.

"I lost Yefet's group."

"What?" Hamama was stunned.

"Yesterday, I noticed we were walking on untouched ground, which means they hadn't passed here before us. So, I thought maybe he took a different route. But we agreed to leave a sign at a meeting spot in the village, and that wasn't there, either."

"What are you saying? Did something happen to them?" asked Zacharia, one of the men in the group.

"Not necessarily," Hassan answered.

"What does that mean, 'not necessarily?'" Hamama, with tears in her eyes, demanded.

"It means that maybe Yefet decided to go a different way and ignored the route we agreed on," Hassan said. "Maybe because of soldiers or robbers. Maybe they had to stop for someone. It could mean many things, and not necessarily bad ones."

"So, what should we do?" Miriam asked.

"What do you mean?" Zacharia said. "We must continue the journey to Aden."

"But what about them?" Hamama asked. "We're not going to look for them?"

"Zacharia is right," Hassan said. "We don't know why they went off course, but they're still going to the same place where we're going. I think we'll continue and hopefully meet them in Aden."

Even Hamama knew they couldn't start looking for Yefet throughout all of Yemen, and they could only hope that the other group was fine, and they'd all end up in the same place as planned. But still, day after day, her little heart ached with anxiety.

"What's that?" Ben Tzion asked one evening, pointing at a strange vehicle while hiding behind some rocks with his group.

"That's an automobile," Hassan said.

"What's an automobile?" Zacharia asked.

"It's used instead of a camel or horse, made of metal, and drinks flammable fluid," Hassan explained. Automobiles were rare at that time in Yemen, and in the villages, people grew up without knowing that such beasts existed.

"Do you think we could get closer to see?" Zacharia asked.

"No. No doubt only bad news will come out of such a meeting. But when we get to Aden, you'll see many automobiles and large ships that sail the sea."

"I want to see ships." Miriam clapped her hands and looked at Hamama, but her friend returned an unenthused look. Miriam squeezed Hamama's hand, and Hamama knew she was trying to take her mind off the missing family members.

After a journey of eight days, the group reached the border. Again, hidden from view, the men surveyed the border crossing between Yemen and Aden. Many soldiers patrolled along the border.

"That's definitely not good," said Kapach, another man in the group.

"We have no choice," Hassan said. "We'll have to pass like ordinary citizens."

They returned to the rest of the group, and Hassan laid out his plan.

"This isn't the first time this has happened. There's no reason to worry. But you'll have to be brave and have faith in God."

The group sat in silence.

"I'm your leader," Hassan said. "The Kapach and Gamadi families came to visit relatives. The Ben Tzion and Sharabi families, as well as Hamama—you came for the women, who are on a health retreat. In any case, everybody came for a limited time, and you plan to return to Yemen."

"That's dangerous," Zacharia said.

"Yes. That's why you'll have to be strong and fearless. We'll walk toward them and stop a few meters from the crossing, in order to get 'refreshed.' The women will prepare coffee, and we'll sit and eat. We'll appear calm, as if we have all the time in the world. And if we're lucky, maybe the soldiers will partake of our meal, and we'll befriend them."

The group gathered its courage and carried out Hassan's plan. As expected, a few soldiers sat down with them, drank some of the fresh coffee and chatted. Afterwards, the group members gathered their belongings and began to cross the border. While crossing, Hamama noticed that Hassan grew pale. One of the soldiers recognized him and stopped the group.

"You!" the soldier pointed at Hassan, "come with me."

Hassan was taken outside the crossing station. The rest of the group stood in place, waiting. Hamama's heart pounded. She felt Miriam squeezing her hand forcefully. Hamama didn't know if that was out of fear, or if Miriam was trying to encourage her, but the squeeze hurt her and left a bruise. Hamama glanced at the group members and pretended to be surprised rather than terrified. She gathered courage from their reaction and kept her fear at bay as much as she could.

The soldier led Hassan to a side corner and pushed him to the wall.

"What are you doing here, Jew?" the soldier whispered with fury.

"This is the last time. Really. I have money, just let us pass in peace," Hassan whispered back.

The soldier glanced around, trying to see if his friends suspected him, but they merely smiled back. They were used to scaring the passersby in order to extract some bribes. Even if people were innocent, they feared the Yemenite soldiers and tended to pay generously.

"No. I warned you."

"But still, you have to believe me," Hassan said. "Believe me that after today, you'll never see me again."

"Why should I believe you?"

"My wife is here."

For a moment, Hassan thought he caught a glimpse of a smile on the soldier's face. After all, considering the time the two had known each other, they might have been good friends, not to mention that this soldier had saved Hassan's life.

"Congratulations," the soldier said.

"Now you believe me?"

"Not yet. Let me see her."

The soldier dragged Hassan by his arm, smiling at his chuckling friends. They stood in front of the group, and Hassan pointed at Hamama. It looked as if he had hurt her with the wave of his hand, since she immediately froze and grew as pale as the dead.

"Take this," Hassan said as he surreptitiously snuck the money into the soldier's pocket. He was quite adept at bribing the soldiers, but he looked forward to the day he would no longer require this skill.

The soldier returned the money as quickly as he had received it and whispered, "You'll need it more." He pushed Hassan into the group and opened the gate to their freedom.

The group hurried to pass, almost tripping over each other.

"Slowly," Hassan said, and the confidence in his voice calmed the group. As they walked further from the border, Hamama caught up to Hassan.

"What happened there?" she asked.

"That was the soldier who had saved me that time. He was angry that I had returned. But I promised that this was the last time."

"But why did he look at me?"

"I told him you were my wife and that we were leaving and not planning to return."

"I could've been anyone. How could he have known I was really your wife?"

"He knew," Hassan said, and smiled one of his warm smiles at her.

After leaving Yemen's borders, the group was free to march during the day without worry. Fear of the soldiers turned to excitement and an exhilarating sense of freedom. Despite the anxiety about their relatives in the other group, Hassan and Hamama couldn't help but enjoy the moment. As they entered the city of Aden, a whole new world opened to them.

Aden was a large, booming port city. Connecting Yemen with Somalia and Ethiopia, Europe and India, it was a city of major commercial and strategic importance. Because of its centrality and vitality, it served as a meeting place of merchants, scholars, and politicians.

Under the British administration, it was also the intermediate station for Jews leaving Yemen and immigrating to the land of Israel.

Men and women walked around in modern attire, and the colorful souks were overflowing with goods. The tall, crowded houses were similar to those in the villages, except that there was hardly any room to pass between them, and their heights reached above six stories. Beyond the houses, they could still see Yemen's mountains, and on the other side, the port and sea. The streets were paved, and those strange automobiles described by Hassan passed by frequently. Carriages with horses carried merchandise, and the sounds of sellers from the souk filled the air, one promising a bargain and the second raising his voice to market fresh fish. Spicy aromas rose from the spice stand and a huge bag of freshly ground turmeric reminded Hamama of her father. The vibrant colors and varied smells aroused the group members who up until then had marched together, but now were being pulled in different directions.

"Let's get to Ma'uda's house, so you'll know where we'll sleep," Hassan directed. "After that each person can take off on his own." Hassan was eager to get lost in the big city.

Ma'uda's house was adjacent to the souk and easy to find. It stood behind the jewelry stand that glimmered in the sun. On the way, the group members passed between the necklaces and pearls of the market, blinded at every turn. When they reached the end of the souk, they met a short, bearded man standing across from them with outstretched arms.

"Welcome! I'm happy to see that you've succeeded in your journey." Their host, Ma'uda, blessed them.

"Everybody, this is Rabbi Ma'uda," Hassan said as he made the introductions. "He's hosting us in his rooms."

The men hurried to shake Ma'uda's hand, and he pointed the way inside, hanging back with Hassan.

"So, you're Hassan, he whose name precedes him?" Ma'uda asked and patted the lad's back.

"I didn't know my name preceded me," Hassan said. There was only one thing on his mind. "Was there word of another group of Jews?"

"Your second group? I read in the letter that there's another one, but I haven't seen or heard anything," Ma'uda said.

Hamama and Hassan exchanged glances but didn't say anything. The group members settled in their rooms and unpacked their few belongings, anxious to go out and relieve some of the stress they had endured during the journey.

Hassan and Hamama wandered through the souk. The scents and commotion had a powerful effect. Hamama was taken in by the abundance around Aden, and it instilled in her a sense of calmness. She so yearned to leave her worries, to be fully present in this moment, with Hassan buying fruit and leading her hand in hand across the sea.

"My mother would sit at the sea for hours," Hassan said. "Sometimes I would sit with her. She was so sad. I was happy to leave the sea behind after she passed away. But this smell, the salt, makes me miss her."

Hamama squeezed his hand.

"I wish she could've met you," Hassan said, and he didn't let go of her hand for a long hour.

On the way home, Hamama and Hassan saw Zacharia and Kapach closely examining an automobile. Hassan laughed.

"Well? Are you impressed?" he asked.

"Listen, it's a nice idea, but how will it go up the rocks? The mountains?" Zacharia questioned.

Zacharia and Kapach joined Hassan and Hamama on their way back to Ma'uda's house. Zacharia's and Kapach's booming laughter overwhelmed Hassan's and Hamama's silence. They crossed in front of the jewelry stand and arrived at the house, where they noticed Ma'uda's glistening smile:

"I got you all a spot on a boat that leaves Saturday night," he said with pride.

"Oh…" Hassan said.

"Oh? That's your reaction?" Ma'uda sounded surprised.

"He doesn't know how to express joy, Rabbi. A serious guy." Zacharia laughed at first but then grew silent when he looked at Hamama.

"I'm sorry, Rabbi," Hassan said. "This is great news, and I'll be happy to tell my people, but Hamama and I will stay here a bit longer, until the second group arrives."

"Do you have relatives in the group?" Ma'uda asked.

"Yes. Two people who raised me and her."

"I understand. God willing they'll arrive in peace. We'll pray for them."

On Saturday night, the rest of the group boarded the boat with tears in their eyes. They were headed to the Land of Israel, but Hassan and Hamama—as well as Miriam and Ben Tzion, who insisted on staying with them—were left behind.

The four lived in Aden for half a year. Ma'uda needed his rooms to host other groups of travelers, so the two couples rented a room at the house of a Jew named Tiram. Hamama and Miriam found housekeeping work, and Hassan and Ben Tzion became porters. Their employer grew especially fond of Hassan and was quite forgiving when he occasionally disappeared for a few days. During that half year, Hassan would steal the border back to Yemen, and would pay people out of his salary to look for Yefet and his group. Hamama knew about this dangerous activity but didn't try to stop him.

One day, Hassan returned from his travels with a letter in hand. When he entered their room, he kneeled by Hamama. She grew frightened.

"It's Shmuel," Hassan said. "The rumor passed along in this letter says he died. They don't know anything about Rivka and the kids."

The two sat together, stunned by grief. Miriam approached them and tore a bit of their clothes as was the ritual.

"He was like a father to you both," she said.

Miriam and Ben Tzion helped organize the shiva, but Hamama remained outside. Hassan sat down next to her.

"This can't be," she said.

Hassan didn't say a thing. She repeated her words, this time with laughter and delight in her voice. "This can't be!"

"Are you all right?" Hassan asked, worried about his wife's state of mind.

"Yes. On Passover, the Passover when you left us, I dreamt a dream. In my dream, Shmuel and Rivka joined us on the journey to Israel, only Mother and Kadya didn't, and they died. But Rivka and Shmuel have to immigrate. That's how it happened in the dream. They're alive."

"What are you talking about, Hamama?"

"Something must've happened to his hair," Hamama said, partly to Hassan and partly to herself.

As Hassan began questioning his wife's sanity, she took off out the door, shouting "Shmuel! Shmuel!"

Miriam and Ben Tzion came out of the house to see what the fuss was.

"She's gone crazy," Hassan said. Then he looked ahead and saw what Hamama had seen.

"Shmuel!" he cried.

Shmuel was marching toward them. He was thin, pale, and almost bald. Hamama embraced him warmly, and he sighed with exhaustion.

"Ma'uda said you live here now," he said weakly.

"What happened, Shmuel? Where's Rivka?" Hamama asked.

"She's fine," he promised. "I'll tell you everything."

But when Shmuel finally reached their room, Hassan took over and wouldn't let Hamama near him with her questions. He served Shmuel food and offered his mat. Shmuel was tired from the journey and immediately fell asleep. Hamama sat by him the whole time and heard him mumbling his twins' names.

The next morning, they all sat together for breakfast, but besides drinking coffee, no one touched a thing. Everyone expected Shmuel to start talking, but when he didn't, Hassan urged them all to eat before heading out for another day of work. And so, breakfast passed in utter silence. Shmuel sat with them but didn't touch the food.

He knew they were waiting for him to speak, but a strange and powerful force pushed his words back into his throat, as if threatening him that if he spoke, he would confirm the truth of the events.

But still, Hamama's stares and everyone's worries had an effect. And gradually, Shmuel found it in him to begin his story.

"We'll start at the beginning," he said and sighed. "Yefet led us along the route Hassan sketched, and at one of the villages, he stopped. He had heard that the governor of Ra'ida was passing out passage permits. He convinced us that this would be safer than stealing the border."

Hassan fumed in silence. Shmuel raised his arms and shrugged, as if to say, "what could I do?" then continued.

"We headed to Ra'ida, where we found out that the rumor was false, and was in fact a trap. The governor of Ra'ida imprisoned us and charged us with an attempt to leave Yemen without permits. We stayed in Ra'ida, but luck turned against us, and Shoshana caused a fire in one of the fields. She was working for some women while we were imprisoned. She hadn't learned how to cook well yet, and lost control of the fire. In an effort to not burn down the entire house, she somehow managed to move it outside, but the fire spread and burned someone's field… This could have been a funny story, except that we didn't have the money to compensate the owners for the destroyed property. We were now in even greater debt and could no longer bribe our way out of it."

Shmuel paused for a moment.

"And then, a plague spread across the city," he said eventually, tears welling up in his eyes. "It took mother and Efraim and Menashe."

"Oh!" A cry escaped Hamama's lips, and she fell to her knees.

"Blessed are You, the Lord our God, King of the universe, the true Judge," Ben Tzion said with a heavy heart.

"We tried to pass messages to you through messengers, but, because of the plague, nobody could get out, and then the message was mixed up, and you heard that I died."

Shmuel stopped, giving them time to digest his story.

"We only received that message today," Hassan said.

Hamama tried not to think about the boisterous twins she knew and loved since the day they were born. She tried to hold on to the fact that if he said they died, then Rivka and Shoshana did not.

"Because of the plague, the governor released most of the prisoners, so they could help clear the bodies and take jobs to help manage the city anew. When he heard that I was a goldsmith, he insisted on keeping me around to work for him because his goldsmith had died in the plague. And the plague didn't just pass over our family. All of us, except Shoshana, were infected. When I had to bury the twins and Mother, I asked for permission to inform my family in Aden. The governor agreed and gave me a permit, but I was forced to leave Rivka and Shoshana with him to ensure that I returned. They're working as housekeepers for the governor's wife."

Shmuel finished his story, and everyone remained silent.

"What were the signs of the illness?" Hassan asked, his mind already searching for a way to save Rivka and Shoshana.

"They couldn't eat, whatever came in, came back out. Gauntness, hair falling out. Why do you ask?" Shmuel wondered, trying to banish the horrifying images he recollected.

"I need to know how it looked, I want to be able to describe this illness."

Shmuel stared at him in alarm.

"You're not going back," Hassan explained. "I'll go instead of you and tell them you died."

"And what about Rivka and Shoshana?" Shmuel asked with a frown on his face.

"Have faith in God. I'll bring them back soon," Hassan said.

Hassan didn't waste a minute. He took Shmuel's passage permit and dagger and went out to the souk with Ben Tzion, to gather donations from Aden's Jews to help with the release of Shmuel's family. After collecting enough money, he prepared to depart.

"I want to contribute something, too," Hamama said.

"But you don't have anything," Hassan answered while bundling his gear.

Hamama took out the necklace Shmuel had given her as a wedding gift.

"You don't have to."

"First, go to the governor's wife and make sure she likes you," Hamama advised. "Visit Rivka and Shoshana.

Hassan took the necklace and stuffed it into his shirt pocket.

"I'll return with them, and we'll all go to the Land of Israel together," he said.

"I know," she answered.

A moment before he left, she stood up on her tiptoes and kissed him on the lips. Hassan held her tightly then released her and left.

Hassan's journey was long, but his determination to bring Rivka and Shoshana back was so strong that he almost didn't make any stops on the way. He crossed the border with Shmuel's permit without worry, since lone travelers had no problem entering Yemen. He did hope he would be able to manage to obtain return permits, to avoid endangering Rivka and Shoshana after all they'd been through.

As he entered Ra'ida, he saw the ruins left by the plague. Whole houses were burnt down out of fear of contamination. At the city gate, he was greeted by weepers who warned passersby not to enter the city.

"What brings a lad into the city of death?" one mourner screamed out as the others wept with sorrow.

Hassan ignored the sobbing women and continued walking. His heart pounded in his chest when he saw the horror. Gaunt men carried bodies down the street, and others wandered around searching for a loved one, or for food. Hassan was overcome with sorrow over their plight, a sight of such suffering that it became indelibly etched in his memory. He tried to toughen his heart as he marched toward the governor's house. It was easy to recognize the house since it was the tallest and most splendid of all, and dozens of people were knocking at the door begging for help. A stench permeated the air, and Hassan restrained himself from vomiting. He made his way through the skinny, bald people lying on the floor and turned to one of the guards:

"I have to speak with the governor's wife," he announced.

"Who are you?"

"Hassan Salem. A Jew bearing tragic news for her maids."

"Maybe you should leave your tragic news outside the house?"

"If only I could."

The guard entered momentarily, and when he returned, he led Hassan inside into the central courtyard of the governor's house. The governor's wife was watching her young children playing in the courtyard while Rivka and Shoshana swept the ground. Was that Rivka? Hassan's heart sank when he saw how emaciated they had become. Rivka's hair had all fallen out. They stopped when they recognized Hassan but waited for their employer's permission to speak with him. The governor's children felt the air shift and also stopped playing for a moment then quickly resumed their game.

"Blessed are you, woman of valor," Hassan greeted the governor's wife.

"What words do you have for me?" she asked, curiously examining the handsome lad standing before her.

"I have news for your maids, but I would first like to thank you for guarding over them and taking care of them during such a difficult time." Hassan removed Hamama's heavy necklace from his shirt pocket.

"It's beautiful," she said as she gathered the necklace in her hands, inspecting it with excitement.

"It was made by the pitiful goldsmith who came to our home to tell us his fate and the fate of his family, and who then took his last breath in my arms."

Rivka heard this and fell to her knees. The governor's wife quickly helped her back up, and Hassan pleaded with her. "Tomorrow, I will ask your husband to release the two to mourn their husband and father in Aden, where he is buried. Please, help me convince him to let them go."

The governor's wife nodded, and, together with Shoshana, led Rivka inside. Hassan left the courtyard.

The next morning Hassan came to see the governor. He was a strong and well-built man, with an irate face.

"My condolences for the many losses endured by Ra'ida," Hassan began.

"I understand you want the woman and girl," the governor said without wasting any time.

"And not as an act of kindness, despite the governor's benevolence. I also came to pay for the damage they caused," Hassan said and handed the governor the money he had gathered. The governor took the bag and handed it to one of the soldiers, who began counting the money. Afterwards, the soldier whispered into the governor's ear.

"And yet, this isn't enough," the governor said to Hassan. "If it were up to me, I would release the prisoners. But because the debt isn't to me but to one of my subjects, who puts his faith in my just judgment, I cannot accept only a part of the value of the field that burned."

"Well, you seek justice, and for that you cannot be faulted," Hassan said, "but still, I understand there's another prisoner here, by the name of Yefet?"

"Yes. He was a merchant, and now works at the smithy, repairing some damages of the plague."

"If he stays here to work, to repay the full amount, would you agree to release the widow and the orphan?"

The governor thought for a moment and then agreed.

"Thank you, your honor. I'll go speak with him immediately."

Hassan left and turned to find Yefet. When he found him, Yefet was overjoyed at the sight of the lad, and his eyes immediately welled up.

"Oh, Hassan! It's all my fault. If only I had listened to you."

"Listen, you have the chance to make up for it."

"I will do anything. The death of my mom and nephews is weighing heavily on my soul. May they rest in peace. May I be at peace!"

Hassan felt sorry for him. He felt guilty about using him. But when he explained his plan and the governor's request, Yefet almost cried with relief.

"I'll stay here and pay off the debt. Thank you for finding a way for me to atone for my sins!"

That day the two weren't allowed in anymore, but the next day the governor was available early in the morning. In light of Yefet's promise to stay in Ra'ida until the debt was repaid, the governor pardoned Rivka and Shoshana, and even helped them obtain passage permits, so the two, who had already lost half of their family, could mourn the loss of another third.

As the mother and daughter left the governor's house, Rivka fell into Hassan's arms with tears of agony.

"He's not dead. Shmuel's not dead." Hassan whispered in her ear.

Rivka took a step back from Hassan and looked into his eyes, scared and confused.

"Hassan?"

"I lied. To get you out. Now let's get out of here before this governor changes his mind."

Hassan lifted Shoshana onto his shoulders and marched out parting without any regret from the ruined city.

After walking for an hour, the three met a man with two donkeys who was waiting for Hassan.

"*Shukran*," Hassan said and paid the man, who then immediately left the place.

"You shouldn't have," Rivka said as she mounted the donkey.

"You've gone through enough," Hassan said.

"And with the money for the donkeys you couldn't have released Yefet as well?" she asked.

"We raised as much as we could, but it wouldn't have been enough. He still would've had to stay." Hassan helped Shoshana take her seat on the donkey.

The three rode the donkeys until the Yemen-Aden border, where they crossed with the governor's passage permits. Rivka kept quiet throughout the entire journey, while Hassan tried to amuse little

Shoshana. When they reached Aden, Shmuel and Hamama ran toward them, and the cacophony of cries and laughter that ensued caused the passersby to look at them with curiosity, but not with surprise. Death, family reunions, and joy mixed with endless sorrow were very familiar to the people of Yemen from days past.

A ship was preparing to leave for the Land of Israel on Saturday night. The reunited group sat to dine together in silence. Shoshana sat on Shmuel's lap and refused to leave him, and Shmuel held Rivka's hand tightly and wouldn't let go. Hamama looked at them with sorrow. When she first saw Rivka, she nearly went mad with pain. Her sister, who was once chubby, was now skin and bones and bald. Now she understood that they were not ready for the journey ahead.

"We'll wait for you," Hamama said quietly.

Shmuel glanced at Hassan. "No. You've waited enough. More than enough."

"We have patience," Hassan said.

"No. We'll stay here. We'll mourn a full year for our relatives who were buried without a gravestone in Yemen's soil. You'll immigrate, prepare the ground, and we'll follow you."

The group continued to eat in silence. When the women cleared the dishes and the men sat outside with Shoshana, Rivka took Hamama's hand.

"Don't let him wait any longer. We'll come. I promise."

"I know you'll come. I dreamt all this many years ago," Hamama said and embraced her sister.

"And what about the blood? Did it already come?" Rivka asked Hamama after Shabbat was over, and Hamama had finished packing.

"No, but I'm nervous about it."

"It's all right, I'll tell you about it."

"Can I join?" Miriam asked.

"Good idea," Rivka smiled.

"You're still young. When the blood comes, you'll turn from girls to women, and after the period of purity, the men will be able to come to you."

She paused.

"It's important to remember—only if you're willing. And if you're scared, it's better that you wait. They'll wait for you. After all, respect for the partner's feelings is the basis of a successful marriage."

Rivka kept it short:

"The coming of blood tells you that your body is ready to have children, and in order to have children you must be intimate with your husbands. His manhood would lead him to you, and you will lead it to the opening where the babies will come, with God's help."

Hamama had so many questions, but the topic was so private, so suppressed, that she decided to wait until the moment of truth to discover everything. She wasn't worried in the least, since her partner was Hassan. Strong, loving Hassan, who always protected her from all evil.

Hamama and Hassan, Miriam and Ben Tzion gathered their bundles and headed toward the harbor. Shmuel, Rivka, and Shoshana escorted the four to the boat and parted from them with sadness diluted by excitement.

"It's finally happening, ya Hassan." Shmuel embraced Hassan.

"We'll wait for you," Hassan answered.

Rivka and Hamama didn't say a thing, just hugged and cried. Hamama detached herself from Rivka's embrace with great difficulty, and Miriam supported her on the walk onto the boat. Many people were crowded together, excited to leave. Hamama looked back, but Shmuel and Rivka had already left. She assumed they didn't want to prolong the parting.

Hassan led them after a group of people into the cells. But the sight of all the crowds and the stench of dust and sweat chased the four back onto the deck.

"We'll stay on the deck outside," Hassan said. "It might be cold, but at least we'll be able to breathe."

They walked back up onto the deck and found a place to sit, together with their small bundles. More families joined them, and after they secured their place, Hassan let Hamama and Miriam walk around and explore.

"But stay together and don't split up. And if something happens— scream," he instructed.

"You're cute," Hamama said in an attempt to irritate him.

"This ship is new to him too, so he's worried," Miriam said.

"He was worried also on our daily walk to the well…"

The two wandered along the deck and examined the boat from end to end. When they reached the stern, they grasped the cold metal poles and gazed over at the port. Suddenly, a loud horn blasted through the air, and a man on the pier released the anchor, and two men brought it up on the deck.

"We're moving," Miriam exclaimed with excitement in her voice.

"We're leaving Yemen!" Hamama cried.

The two burst out in gleeful screams. Their exhilaration rubbed off on the other passengers, who joined them in the calls of excitement as the boat pulled away from the pier.

The boat left the beach, but they still sailed parallel to it. As they sailed in Yemenite waters, north toward the Suez Canal, the passengers' excitement abated. An unfounded fear of being arrested by the soldiers still ate away at their hearts.

While the passengers dealt with their worries and excitement, the workers on the boat were happy. They were dark-skinned people, with round and plump faces. Their smiles were wide and their eyes shone with glee.

"Such happy people," Ben Tzion said.

"It's happiness out of drunkenness," Hassan said with disdain. Later, Hassan made sure Hamama and Miriam didn't walk around after dark and that they'd sleep by the men's feet. Hamama laughed at his fears but knew that they were not unfounded. The deck hands had stared at her more than once.

One evening, some of the Jewish men joined the sailors' celebrations.

"What are you doing?" Hassan shouted at them. "They'll get you drunk and will then go to your wives!"

"And who are you to speak such vile words?" one of the men jeered at him.

"Have you ever been on a boat?" another man inquired.

"Well, no. This is my first time," Hassan answered.

"Then how do you know that this is what they'll do?" the second man confronted him, taunting Hassan.

"He's just a pervert whose wife is still too young!" laughed the first man, who was already quite drunk.

Hassan was ready to pounce on him, but Ben Tzion stopped him:

"He's drunk and stupid. Let's not risk our place on the boat because of honor games," he whispered in Hassan's ear.

Hassan stepped back slowly, swallowing his pride like a bitter pill.

Not two hours later, a woman's screams could be heard from the other side of the deck. Hassan and Ben Tzion jumped up and ran toward them. Hamama and Miriam exchanged glances and immediately took off after them. When they reached the other side of the deck, they found a ring of people surrounding a crying girl. Hamama and Miriam were the only women in the circle, and they made their way through the men to hold and cheer up the girl.

"He came to rape me!" the girl yelled. "He came on to me! And I screamed, and he ran away!"

The captain, a tall, broad-shouldered man with a deep and frightening voice, asked, "Who was it?"

Silence fell on the deck. Even the crying girl barely managed to answer him.

"One of the deck hands! I don't know who…"

"Where's your man?" the captain asked.

"Here," said an elderly Jew dragging a drunk man behind him. The drunken man was alarmed by all the people surrounding his wife. Hassan looked at the two men who had fought with him earlier, and they lowered their gaze.

"I want you to tell me who this villain is!" the captain said angrily. It wasn't clear to whom his anger was directed, and so everyone was taken aback. He ordered all the deck hands to stand in line on the deck. Hamama and Miriam helped the frightened girl stand up.

"Who did this? I won't tolerate this kind of behavior on my boat!" the captain yelled.

The girl, shaking from fright, looked helplessly over all the men.

"I can't recognize him! It was dark, and his face was dark, and I don't recognize him!" she wailed and started crying.

"In that case, I'll punish all the deck hands," the captain threatened. "Who tried to perpetrate this crime?"

There was silence on the deck. Only the girl's yelps could be heard.

"I thought so. I forbid any more drinking for the rest of the journey. Don't let me catch any one of you drunk!" the captain yelled.

The crowd dispersed, and the deck hands returned to their posts. Hamama and Miriam supported the girl.

"Will you come sleep with us tonight?" Miriam asked.

"Yes," the poor girl said weakly as she left her drunken husband with his friends.

The women lay down together by Hassan and Ben Tzion's feet and fell asleep. She woke up crying numerous times, but Hamama and Miriam hugged her and calmed her down until she fell back asleep. When morning came, they all got up and found the drunken husband, sober and full of regret. He was down on his knees, begging for the girl's forgiveness.

"It's my fault! Will you forgive me? I'll never leave you and will protect you always. You're my treasure!"

The girl looked at him dolefully but accepted his apology and left with him. Why did she forgive him? Because of his clear remorse, or because there was nowhere else to go on this boat, sailing to a new land? Hamama could not be sure which it was.

2008

Grandpa and Grandma immigrated to the Land of Israel in 1942. After eight days at sea, they finally reached the Suez Canal, where they were greeted by guides from the Jewish Agency. There, after disembarking from the boat, a moment after they kissed the ground of the Land of Israel, they underwent their first DDT disinfection and received numerous shots. From this uncomfortable experience, Grandma mostly remembers the first time they got an orange and margarine.

"The *Mahazris* didn't know what to do with the margarine. You know, it didn't taste very good. What did they do? They spread it all over their hair and face." Grandma laughs, as do I.

"I really loved the oranges, so every time they distributed food, I would exchange the bread and margarine for an orange," she tells me.

Grandma smiles as she recollects these moments, and I enjoy watching her smile. A large bowl of oranges sits atop the table on the patio. I suddenly remembered that whenever oranges were in season, that bowl was always in the same place. Filled with oranges.

I remember Grandma sitting on a plastic lawn chair on the grass in the yard, a patch bordered by a live fence of khat bushes to the north, loquat, and pecan trees to the south, palm trees and Grandpa's room to the east, and, to the west, more loquat trees and large white planters that were once used for spices and herbs and now held the leftover food for the cats. Grandpa sits on an old pique blanket spread over the grass, a wooden stand for holy books in front of him, and we, the girls, sit around him and eat sweet orange slices from his hands.

"I think he woke up," Rami says, and Grandma goes inside. I also awaken from the memory. I leave the patio and look at the yard that is no longer there.

Grandma comes out again and hands me a white bag with oranges.

"Here, I made you a bag! It's good for the pregnancy," she says.

I thank her and take off before they bring Grandpa out to the patio. Grandma doesn't judge me. I know.

CHAPTER 5

Hamama, Miriam, Hassan, and Ben Tzion, together with a few other families, were tossed from side to side in green-gray trucks. A large canvas covered the truck, preventing the air from circulating. They were all oozing sweat on the drive from the beaches of the Suez Canal to the Land of Israel.

"Maybe we should fold up part of the canvas?" one of the men asked the truck driver.

"I'm driving fast, and the sand will get in your eyes. Is that what you want?"

Even before they had a chance to decide, Ben Tzion, who managed to suppress his seasickness on the boat, couldn't handle the suffocating crowdedness and the bumpiness of the road and vomited all over the truck's floor.

"Oh, great. That'll help the smell," one of the women said.

"Yes. Maybe now we won't have to smell you," Miriam retorted in defense of her sick husband.

"It's not just me, it's everyone," the woman replied. "It's the smell of the sulfur, from the spraying."

"It really is hard to get the smell out," Hamama said, but she was quickly silenced by Miriam's angry glance.

The driver stopped the truck in frustration, and the passengers jumped out.

"Maybe we'll make this our lunch stop," the driver suggested, and without waiting for an answer left the group to sit under the only tree in the area, where he lit a cigarette. The passengers prepared the food, and Hamama helped Hassan wash the truck floor.

"It's a desert," she said to him.

"Yes," he said.

"Where are we going?" she asked.

"I don't know," he answered.

After that first break, they continued on their way. They drove for three days, feeling like animals on their way to slaughter, and the occasional attempts to lift the mood with songs and jokes didn't help. Every once in a while, when they stopped, they saw small towns or groups of black tents, but toward the end they saw the sea.

"If we see the sea, we're not going to Jerusalem," Hassan said.

He was right. The immigrants from Yemen were led not to Jerusalem, but to the transit camp Atlit. At the camp, the immigrants would receive some guidance and would be sorted out to different towns.

Hamama noticed a large boulder standing near the camp's entrance. Its presence there bothered her. A man in short khakis exited the camp and hopped onto the boulder. *Ah, this is what the boulder is for.* Hamama calmed herself, as if the rest of the view wasn't disturbing enough: a tall barbed wire fence, a guard tower with an armed guard, and enormous wooden sheds that waited on the other side of the entrance.

"Welcome to Atlit," their guide said. "This is a transit camp meant to help you acclimate to the country. After a short period of acclimation, we'll assign you to various towns throughout the Land of Israel."

As the guide spoke and introduced the camp, Hamama tried to turn Hassan's attention to the guard tower, but he insisted on paying attention.

"After these words of introduction, I'd like to ask you to split into two groups—one of men and one of women," the guide said.

The sounds of dissatisfied mumbling emerged from the group of immigrants.

"What do you mean 'split into two groups?'" one of the men asked.

"This is just a transit camp. We don't have a house for every family, so we separate the men from the women and house them in separate sheds. After all, we wouldn't want to have any indecency here."

"We were together on the boat the whole time, and no one ever said 'indecency' to us," Ben Tzion said.

"Here in the camp, there are rules," the guide said. "If you don't obey the rules, your assignments will only get delayed. It would be a waste of everybody's time. As you'll see, there are very many immigrants here and a long line."

Hamama held onto Hassan's hand as the crowd started separating into men and women.

"Miriam will take care of you." Hassan smiled at his wife. "And soon we'll see each other again."

Hassan joined the group of men, and they followed the guide inside. Hamama looked at him walking away from her and immediately felt pangs of longing. A moment later, two female guides wearing short pants came to the group. The Yemenite women were stunned at the sight of such immodesty.

"The important thing is that there shouldn't be any indecency here," Miriam dead-panned, and Hamama laughed out loud.

"Welcome!" one of the guides, who had red hair and freckles on her cheeks, announced. "Join this line, please."

Miriam and Hamama hurried to be first in line out of their group, but in front of them stood a long line of other groups, at the head of which sat two women wearing white gowns.

"When he said, 'long line' he meant a long line," Hamama said.

"This is worse than the line at Shabazi's well," Miriam said.

Hamama noticed that the women at the front of the line were getting some kind of treatment and sprayed.

"Not another spraying!" she cried.

"There are shots and spraying and then showers. That's what I heard," the woman standing ahead of Hamama said, with an accent Hamama didn't recognize. The woman's Hebrew sounded very different from Hamama's, but they could still converse.

"But they already did that to us," Hamama insisted.

"That's how it is," the woman explained. "It's important. It's for your health. I was a nurse in Romania."

"What's a nurse?" Miriam asked.

"You know, like the women there, giving shots."

"I really don't understand how those shots work," Miriam said. "And it's uncomfortable. They just prick you like that."

The woman from Romania looked at her with surprise.

"It's like a needle for sewing, only hollow inside," she explained. "That's how it gets the medicine into the body."

"In Yemen, we used to heal all the illnesses with a white-hot metal rod," Miriam said and showed her the scar she had received from the machva.

The Romanian was taken aback and went silent.

"You should have explained it to her like she explained to us," Hamama said. "Told her about the medicine we make from plants. Now she'll think we're like animals."

"And what do you think the guides here think of her?" Miriam asked. "Look how they're staring at all of us."

The line progressed slowly, and when they arrived at the table in front, Miriam and Hamama tried to explain that they had already undergone the DDT spraying in Suez.

"Yes, but we really can't know for sure," one of the nurses said. "There's no time. What's the name?"

"Hamama."

"What's 'Hamama?'"

"A dove."

"So why isn't your name *Yonah*, the Hebrew word for dove?"

"If you want, you can call me Yonah. Not sure I'll answer you though."

"How old are you?"

Hamama looked at Miriam questioningly.

"Fourteen?" Miriam whispered.

"Fourteen," Hamama said.

"Married?" the nurse asked.

"Yes."

The nurse said something to her friend in a language Hamama and Miriam didn't understand. The first nurse tilted her head, and the second one laughed.

"She's so arrogant. Look at them and say something to me," Miriam said in Yemenite.

"Here, I'm looking and talking with you," Hamama said in Yemenite.

"Good, now we'll also do an evil laugh. *Yalla*," Miriam said, and the two friends burst out laughing.

The nurse became annoyed and moved Hamama on to the other woman and started interrogating Miriam with the questions.

"I'm giving you a few shots now to prevent illnesses," the second nurse explained.

Hamama extended her hand. The nurse noticed the prick wound on Hamama's arm.

"Did you recently get a shot?" she asked.

"Yes, when we arrived at Suez."

"Do you know what you got?"

"No."

"Hold on a second," the nurse said and gave directions to another woman. "Go ask Reuven what they got, so they don't get it twice!"

She turned back to Hamama.

"Did all the other women in your group also get the shot? Ugh, what a mess!"

She sent Hamama to get another DDT spraying. An hour later, the nurse received her answer. Nobody knew what shots the women had already been given.

"We can't take a chance," the nurse said to Hamama apologetically, as she pierced her with the needle again.

Half a day passed from the immigrants' arrival until the end of the registration and vaccination procedures. The guides handed out fruit and encouraged them to keep going. Next, they arrived at the showers. Ruti, the red-haired guide, led Hamama, Miriam, and about ten other women to one of the sheds. A different guide, whom the girls later found out was known as Soapy, took them to the next room. Soapy stood in the center of the shower room and demonstrated, as she had done for many others before them.

"This is a faucet," she began. "You open it like this and water comes out, then you close it, and there's no water."

Hamama was surprised by this new method and immediately liked it. Soapy smiled at the women's surprised looks.

"It wasn't like this in Yemen, eh?" she said.

"Finally, something to be happy about in the Land of Israel," Hamama said to Miriam.

"And this is soap." Soapy showed them a white, rectangular block. "You rub it on your body, and it removes the dirt and bad smells."

"Sounds good," Miriam said. "We can finally get rid of that sulfur stink."

"Good," Soapy said. "Now let's go back to the previous room, where you'll undress. Ruti will gather your clothes, and I'll help you shower this first time. Then you'll know how to do it alone."

The women went back to the first room and started to undress slowly and hesitantly.

"We're all women here," Ruti encouraged them.

We're all women, thought Hamama, but she had never stood completely naked in front of another person aside from her mother and sister. When she dipped in the mikveh on the eve of her wedding, her body was covered with *k'tat*, and she didn't feel naked like she did in that shower. She looked at the older women and felt shame for them.

"Come on. There are other groups waiting," Ruti said as she started to gather the women's clothes.

Hamama undressed completely and handed her clothes to Ruti. She stood embarrassed for a moment and then looked at Miriam.

"You have large breasts!" Hamama said, surprised.

"And you're flat as a boy!" Miriam laughed.

"Girls, I'm opening the faucets," Soapy warned.

A stream of cold water attacked the women from the ceiling. Hamama didn't hesitate and immediately tried to run from it. Soapy caught her, put her back in her place and handed her soap.

"Here, smell this. It's nice," she said.

Hamama smelled the soap. It really was nice. Soapy showed her how to rub her body with it. Miriam copied her. A moment later, Hamama got used to the cold water, and she started to enjoy the shower, washing all the dirt from her body, all the negativity. *Maybe they're right, maybe this is how we should start a new life. With a shower.* But when the shower ended, she could still smell the spray.

Soapy handed them towels.

"Fresh from the laundry," she said with a smile.

"Where are our clothes?" one of the women asked.

While she was still talking, the redheaded Ruti entered with a pile of khaki clothes.

"Where are our clothes?" another woman repeated the question.

"We sent them to be burnt," Ruti explained. "We can't be sure if they're contaminated or not. It's better this way."

"What's 'better this way?' Do you have any idea how much the cloth for my dress cost?" another woman yelled.

"And who gave you permission to burn our clothes?" Miriam cried.

"Calm down," Ruti said. "Here, we brought you new clothes. Clothes of the Land of Israel."

She handed each woman a bundle. When Hamama realized what she was holding, she started yelling, too.

"Shorts? I'm not wearing this. Shame! *Tfu!*" She spit on the ground.

The other women joined the fray and chased Ruti out, throwing the shorts at them. After she left, Soapy groaned:

"Now she won't return anymore."

The women looked at her and then at themselves: a group of half-naked women, wrapped in towels, yelling and fussing. They realized the ludicrousness of the situation and burst out laughing.

"I'll go get you something else," Soapy said and left. A few minutes later, she returned with skirts, but unfortunately those were too short.

"Really, we can't wear these," Hamama said.

"You were so eager to burn our clothes," Miriam added, "and now we'll go out, and you'll accuse us 'indecency.'"

"I have an idea," Soapy said and left again. This time she came back with long pants.

"Wear this and over it—the skirts."

"I guess this is the best we'll be able to find here," Miriam said.

"I'm a seamstress by trade," one of the women said. "I used to help my husband in the workshop. I'll sew something more fitting for us."

The women wore the new khaki clothes and examined one another.

"You had a long day," Soapy said. "I'll show you to your shed, so you can go to sleep. Tomorrow you'll get your work plan."

Nobody had the strength to ask her what work and when they'd be assigned to the various towns. Hamama, Miriam, and the rest of the women walked to a large wooden shed, exhausted and defeated. Each one had a strange-looking bed that stood off the ground, but this didn't bother Hamama. She lay down and immediately welcomed the lethargy that overcame her body. She slowly relaxed every muscle, shutting her eyes and picturing Hassan's face. Beautiful, smart Hassan. *I wonder how his day went.* She promptly fell asleep.

In the morning, Hamama awoke to the sound of yelling. Two women were arguing by the end of the shed.

"What a way to wake up," she groaned.

Miriam was already up and talking to another woman, and she smiled at her slowly rising friend.

"Hamama, this is Shimona. She's also from Yemen."

"Nice to meet you," Hamama said, rubbing the rheum from her eyes. Shimona was older than Miriam and Hamama, and more experienced, since she had immigrated a few weeks earlier.

"Weeks?" Hamama was surprised, "How long do we have to be here until we get our assignments?"

"Three months," Shimona answered.

"What?" Hamama was shocked.

"And during this whole time, there's just one hour each day to go to the fence to talk to the men," Shimona added.

"One hour?" Hamama became angry. At this point, she was no longer happy about having woken up and buried her face in the bed once more. From there, she heard Shimona explain more about the shed.

"Those are the Moroccan ladies, over there. You should beware of them because they have big mouths." Shimona pointed to the edge of the shed. "And in the middle, you see the Polish and Romanian women. You'd think they'd be friends, since they're all Ashkenazi, but they hate one another. Not like they hate us, but enough."

Hamama didn't like to hear what Shimona was saying. Her words had wickedness in them. *We're all Jews. We're all in the same shed, with the same rules.* She tried to imagine Hassan's calming face again, but to no avail. The thought of seeing him for only an hour a day upset her. It's good that Rivka and Shmuel stayed back. They wouldn't have survived this, not after all they had been through.

Despite the early hour, the sound of women's chatter grew, and Hamama felt as if she was trapped inside a beehive, only without the taste of honey. She was happy when Shimona returned to her bed, and Miriam was no longer occupied.

"Did you see the size of this shed?" Miriam asked.

Hamama raised her head and looked at the many rows of beds along the walls. Many women sat amongst small bundles that contained whole worlds. Some of them hung clothes or sheets between the beds to allow for some privacy, but they could always see, hear, or smell through them.

"I have to get out of here," Hamama said as she stood up.

"*Yalla*," Miriam said, and the two friends left the shed, only to run into a new guide they hadn't seen before.

"Where to?" she demanded to know.

"Don't know," the two answered.

118

"Get back inside. I'm reading the work schedule," the guide ordered and followed them back inside. She was tall and older. Her white hair was tied back, where it erupted like a fountain on her the nape of her neck. She was called the commander, both behind her back and to her face, not because her position was above the others' but because her loud, demanding voice, and her sternness transformed her requests into orders and her words to a constitution that couldn't be overstepped.

"Good morning and welcome, new girls," she opened. "At six o'clock, breakfast. Then we'll split into four groups: laundry, cleaning the shed, cleaning the bathroom and showers, and kitchen and lunch preparation. At one o'clock, lunch. Then a round of showers and visits with the family. Women who have children in the children's house will take showers last. At seven o'clock, dinner. At nine o'clock, lights out. Questions?"

Miriam raised her hand hesitantly.

"Yes?" the commander asked.

"What's o'clock?" Miriam asked.

The commander, without any surprise or ridicule, pointed at a large, round clock hanging over her head.

"It's time to learn to read a clock, girly. Shimona?" she turned to the experienced woman. "Make sure you teach them."

The guide started reading out women's names and splitting them into the groups she mentioned earlier, while Shimona tried to explain to Hamama and Miriam how to read a clock.

"Don't worry, you're probably with me in the laundry today," Shimona assured them.

"We'll probably find normal clothes there," Miriam said.

Hamama stared at her surroundings. She had room for just one thought: her schedule contained only one hour with Hassan. She missed her old schedule in El Be'aden where she and Hassan walked to the well, or to gather wood.

"Hamama!" Miriam cried, "Do you understand how the clock works?"

"I didn't pay attention," Hamama said quietly and followed the other two to the dining hall.

All day she waited to see him, contemplating the many things she wanted to share with him. But when she finally saw him, Hassan stood before her without the usual spark in his eyes. The delight that always radiated from him when he spoke of the Land of Israel had disappeared. He didn't know what to tell her. He was confused and hurt. In all his dreams of living in the land of Israel with Jews from all over the world, he could never have imagined that he and his family would be treated like cattle.

Hamama's heart broke at the sight of his disappointment. She abandoned everything she had wanted to tell him and only tried to encourage him:

"Do you smell the sea?" she asked.

"Yes. How do they treat you over there?"

"They're respectful."

"That's good."

Hamama reached out and touched his hand through the fence. She couldn't believe that this is what they had come to. His eyes were cast downward, as if he didn't want Hamama to read the sorrow that had welled up in them, but she already knew. She cast her eyes down at the deceptive earth about which they had dreamt, and suddenly she noticed a large rock.

"Hassan?"

"Yes?"

"Do you see this rock?"

"Yes."

"Look under it every once in a while. I'll leave you some surprises."

Hassan smiled at her. For the remainder of the hour, they sat across from one another. When they parted, Hassan smiled at her encouragingly.

"I love you, Hassan," she told him for the first time.

"I love you."

They never had to say it before, but now, with no other means of conveying their love, they were forced to use words. That night, Hamama left a flower made out of an orange peel under the rock. She didn't have any almonds or raisins to give, and in any case, food wasn't in short supply now, but she kept looking for ways to cheer Hassan up. One day, an old Ashkenazi lady saw her and handed her a book.

"Here. This is for your husband," she said.

"Thank you!" Hamama said, ashamed that she couldn't read what the book was about.

Life at the Atlit camp was different from anything Hamama had ever experienced. She was used to getting orders at home, and following them, but she knew that here the orders didn't come out of love and so she didn't tend to obey them. In fact, she often tried to get out of any and all work, especially cleaning the bathrooms. Whenever she was sent to clean the bathrooms, she complained of stomach aches and refused to get out of bed. This trick worked the first three times, but as soon as the commander recognized the pattern of Hamama's illnesses, she pulled her by the ear and angrily pushed her over to the bathrooms.

But that pain hurt less than her separation from Hassan, especially since she knew he wasn't happy.

Hamama wasn't the only one who suffered from the separation between men and women at the camp, and many women tried to get around the camp's rules.

One night, Hamama awoke to the sound of yelling.

"A man! There's a man here!" one of the women screamed.

The shed's lights were turned on, and the women awoke to find one woman's husband lying under her bed. The counselors came in.

"What's going on?" one of the tough ones asked.

"She's hiding her husband here!" one lady informed the counselors

The counselors led the embarrassed man out, but his wife didn't think it was funny and attacked the informer.

"Hey! Stop her!" the informer yelled.

Other women got involved and separated them.

"I'll show you!" threatened the woman.

"I'm not scared of you."

"Really?" the woman made a fist and pretended to attack again, and the informer was taken aback, to the laughter of the others.

"One more month," Hamama mumbled.

And that month eventually passed. The men and women sat together at the camp's wide yard, waiting for their assignments. They spread across the ground like a grey and brown patchwork quilt, their possessions in hand, ready to leave. The sparks in their eyes that had dimmed during their stay at the transit camp were reignited with the promise of a new home, as stories of different cities and settlements passed from ear to ear.

"We have to get to Tel Aviv," Ben Tzion said.

"Why Tel Aviv?" Miriam asked.

"I heard from the other men that it's the best town. There's work, the sea, a souk."

"I'm going wherever Hassan and Hamama are going," Miriam said and grasped Hamama's hand.

Hamama noticed Ben Tzion tense response.

"Shalom and Yona Vazif—Pardes Hanna" the counselor read from the list.

So that's what they decided to call us, thought Hamama.

"Miriam and—what's this? Ben Tzion? Is that a last name or a first name?" asked the counselor.

"Last name," Ben Tzion answered.

"And what's the first name?"

"I don't have one," Ben Tzion answered, to the sound of laughter.

The counselor shook his head in exhaustion:

"Miriam and Ben Tzion—Pardes Hanna."

"Great!" Miriam cried and hugged Hamama.

"But I want Tel Aviv," Ben Tzion cried.

"I don't want Tel Aviv," Miriam whispered to him.

Ben Tzion was embarrassed by the attention he drew, and his face grew red with shame. He tightened his fists.

"You're my wife, and you'll come with me!"

"What!?" Miriam was astonished.

"I always follow you when you go after Hamama, but now you need to follow me."

"What happened? You came to a new land and turned into a man?" Miriam asked angrily.

"I'm going to Tel Aviv, and you'll follow me if you want me," Ben Tzion said angrily and got up. Miriam remained in her seat, embarrassed by the others' gazing eyes.

"Do you want to go after him?" Hamama whispered.

"I want him to come after me," Miriam answered.

"Fine then. So, come with us, and he'll regret this," Hamama said.

"Why are you so sure?" Miriam asked.

"Who wouldn't want to be with you, ya Miriam? He'll go to Tel Aviv, he'll miss you and come crawling back."

Miriam, Hamama, and Hassan got up with the rest of the immigrants and headed over to the trucks that would lead them to their new residences. They were happy to get out of the camp, and the excitement once again filled their hearts. They didn't know anything about the uncomfortable surprise awaiting them in Pardes Hanna.

2008

"Zecharya ben Ezra"
By Yaakov Orland
Translation from Hebrew: Ronen Gradwohl

I am Zecharya ben Ezra
And my bread is the bread of affliction
And I live in the ma'abara
By Netanya, by that direction

In winter, oh, the cold's relentless
In summer, I suffocate
But I don't demand, no more, no less
I'll take what's on my plate
Here all the rich and destitute
Find deficiency or fault
Only one, that Yemenite
Is happy with his lot

Oh to hope and oh to pray
That remember me He may
If that'll happen when He will bring
The Messiah, the Lord King
It's all worthwhile, if good, if bad
So Zecharya ben Ezra said

Of a renewed heart was I the other day
To Nes Tziona it took me
Then to Sde Boker, on the way
Ben Gurion I went to see

I told him listen mister
Don't you be distraught
As long as there's a Heavenly Master
Zecharya's in your flock

Then his heart was silent with exaltation
And perplexed grew his tongue
Oh Zecharya blessed be this nation
That has you as its son

Blessed are the nation and its people
If they're so strong and they're so fertile
And so my march was not for naught
My steps with purposefulness were fraught
It's all worthwhile oh Lord
That's his speech, Ben Gurion's words

Grandpa and Grandma were like that. Innocent and hardworking, not quick to complain. I admire them for everything they accomplished in their lives and built with their own hands, but I can't help but wonder if their lives could've been a bit easier. Of course, I can't talk to them of exploitation or discrimination. They taught us that there is no such thing. People build their own futures for themselves. I wonder what they'd say if I told them about what I've learned, that the immigration from Yemen was encouraged because of the idea that the Yemenite Jews would replace the Arab workers as cheap laborers. They probably wouldn't believe it. Well, maybe today they would believe it.

I watch an old video in which Grandpa speaks with Etti, his first grandchild, who had left for the United States many years earlier.

"Grandpa, tell Etti how much you miss her," my sister's voice is heard in the background.

Grandpa is sitting atop his very high bed in the old room. Above are bookshelves covered in dust, and across him a reading desk. On top of the desk, I spot the white, powdery mint candies that I always loved.

"I miss you," he says.

Etti left many years ago, and because she lived illegally in the United States, she couldn't come back to visit. If she were to return to Israel, it would be permanently.

"Tell her to come back," my sister says.

"Why should she come back?" Grandpa asks. "What does she have here? There's no work. She should stay there, where there is."

I stop the film. Atlit and the pains of Aliyah, the pains of labor leading to Israel's birth, have all been overcome. But now that Grandpa is older, he can only watch as his expanding family struggles in vain to secure their livelihood in the place he has chosen to live. He tries to hide his disappointment, but I could feel it lurking beneath his half smile.

CHAPTER 6

The road came to a sudden end on a bare hill that was destined to become a basketball court. Hamama, Miriam, and Hassan got off the bus in amazement with the rest of the settlers. The guide—a Yemenite lad wearing khakis and a round, brimless hat—came up to them with a smile.

"My name is Moshe Mahatzri," the lad said. "I'm your guide for the settlement of Pardes Hanna. You can come to me with any problem. Welcome!"

"Where are the houses?" one of the men asked.

"Here." Moshe pointed at a pile of black tarps. "Every family will take a tent. It's temporary, of course," he insisted, noticing the looks of horror. "Until they build your permanent homes."

Hassan took a tent for himself and Hamama and an additional one for Miriam. The men helped each other build the tents while the women prepared lunch.

"Don't worry, he'll come back to you," Hamama comforted her sad friend.

"If he doesn't come back soon, I'll crack and go to him," Miriam said.

"It's not like you to talk like this. You're stronger than him."

"That's right," Miriam said, but Hamama could hear the doubt in her voice.

When the tents were ready, the women went inside to arrange the interiors. Finally, Hamama could open her bundles and organize their few possessions to create a homey feeling. When Hassan came in, he smiled at the sight of the stone grinders Hamama had dragged all the way from Yemen.

"Finally, a home," he said.

"Our own home!" Hamama laughed.

When the tents were set up, everyone gathered at Moshe's call, this time more excited and generally happier. Everyone had found his or her corner in the Land of Israel.

"Now we'll head down to the employment office. Don't worry; we won't talk about work tonight. It's just our largest building, and tonight, we light the first candle of Hanukkah. Come on!" Moshe started marching down the hill, at the same time happily chatting with one of the immigrants. Miriam marched next to Hamama, and they both chuckled.

"Even his walk is jovial." Miriam tried to imitate his flapping gait.

Hamama laughed. Something about the guide's confident stride, the way his limbs floated across the ground, comforted her.

The Hanukkah party at the employment office was a great success. The warm welcome that the immigrants received consoled Hamama a bit over the many discomforts they had undergone s since entering the country. Their own housewarming—temporary houses, but still houses—was also celebrated with delight. Moshe and two female guides walked around and handed out *levivot* and *sufganiot*—potato pancakes and jelly donuts. Hamama felt the warmth, the joy, and the comfort fill her heart. Tonight, she could even sleep in the same room as Hassan after so much time apart. She saw him glance at her from the other side of the room and knew that he was thinking exactly the same thing.

"Good morning to the Yemenite pioneers!" Moshe announced outside the tents early the next morning.

The jovial guide passed around bread, eggs, and sour cream to all the people in the tents. The men stepped aside for the morning prayer while the women prepared breakfast. They then reconvened for a joyous meal, filled with hope and ready for anything.

"Ladies and gentlemen, let us march to the orchards," Moshe said. "There's much to do and little time."

"I told you that you could work in the Holy Land," Hassan said to Hamama, before walking ahead to allow the two friends to be together.

He worried about Miriam and thought of going to Tel Aviv to speak to her husband, but he knew that she wouldn't want him to do that. Ben Tzion had to understand on his own. He looked at the two young women and thought back to their joint trips to the well in El Be'aden. Miriam was a good friend to both of them for a long time now. He hoped Ben Tzion would come to his senses. Usually, it was his job to calm Hassan's burning temper. He did it on the ship from Aden and a number of times in Atlit. He prayed his friend would have a change of heart.

Hamama and Miriam marched in silence, trying to become accustomed to their new shoes. When they arrived at the orchard, the men worked to renew and maintain the pits around the citrus trees while the women picked oranges, clementines, and lemons.

"That's one heck of an orange!" Miriam cried as she pointed to a large fruit.

Moshe suddenly popped out from behind some trees.

"That's a grapefruit," he explained. He peeled the fruit and gave her and Hamama a taste. "But don't get used to this. It's not our orchard."

"So, whose is it?" Hamama asked.

"PICA, the Palestine Jewish Colonization Organization."

"Who?"

"A private company of Baron Rothschild's. They buy land in Israel and build settlements. Pardes Hanna is just one of the towns he built. Hanna is his cousin."

"When will we meet him?" Miriam asked.

"That'll be difficult. He passed away eight years ago," Moshe said and left to help two men with their pits.

Hamama climbed onto the tree quickly, and Miriam opened the bag she held.

"Catch?" Hamama asked as she started tossing the fruits into the bag.

"Careful, Hamama! You don't want them to explode!"

"So, catch them!" Hamama said and started tossing the fruits faster than Miriam was able to catch.

"Very funny!" Miriam cried. "Maybe I'll climb up, and you'll catch them below?"

Hamama slowed down, and Miriam filled two bags. They went over to the next tree, and then the one after that. When evening fell, Hamama returned to the tent with scratches and cuts on her hands and feet—and with a wide smile across her face.

Ben Tzion's Tel Aviv was indeed the big metropolis he had imagined, but the Yemenite immigrants were led to a rather a noisy and crowded neighborhood by the name of HaTikvah. Ben Tzion recognized many of the Yemenite families who had settled there, and an old couple from El Be'aden even invited him for coffee.

"Where is Miriam?" Asked the woman. "That girl could light a dark cave with her smile! Is she okay?

"She's so funny!" added the old man. "Her laugh always reminded me of the flutter of songbirds."

Ben Tzion felt shame wash over him.

"She is waiting for me in Pardes Hanna. I just came to visit a cousin."

The old woman was delighted.

"Oh, which cousin?"

Ben Tzion was not accustomed to lying, especially not to elderly people. His mouth was dry and his ears rang. With nothing to answer them he got up and, with a quick thank you, hurried away.

One rainy afternoon, Ben Tzion arrived in Pardes Hanna. He wandered around for a few hours until he met an Ashkenazi man riding a horse, who pointed him toward the tents on the hill. No one waited outside to welcome him, and he stood there drenched in rain in front of the black cloths. A strong wind blew and threatened to uproot the tents. Many men came rushing out of the tents to strengthen their temporary housing. Among them, Ben Tzion recognized Hassan. Then Miriam came out of the neighboring tent. She hurried to tighten the pegs in the rain and didn't see her wet husband standing and watching her. Ben Tzion hurried to help her. They didn't exchange a word about the argument, and when they finished tightening the tent, they went inside as if they had never parted.

Hamama and Hassan enjoyed their new daily routine. Working with their hands and living independently in their own "house" was wrapped up deeply with the dream of living in the Land of Israel. And life in Pardes Hanna was in many ways reminiscent of life in El Be'aden. The veteran residents, the Ashkenazim, reminded them of the Muslim residents in the village, since they had larger, "real" houses. Pardes Hanna also had soldiers, not Yemenite but British. The 1917 Balfour Declaration, which had been incorporated into the terms of the British mandate, stated that a national home for the Jewish people would be established in Palestine and permitted Jewish immigration up to a limit that would be determined by the power of the Mandate. After this declaration Britain was presented with the problem of mediating between the resident Arabs and the increasing numbers of Jews, forced to keep a look out for both parties.

Moshe, the guide, warned the women more than once about the British soldiers. His insinuations led the women to imagine all sorts of horrendous things about them, and they always walked around in pairs and carefully avoided eye contact with these "lonely lads who are far from their homes."

The work in the orchard included digging, pruning, and picking, which filled the Yemenite immigrants' days. There was no longer a need to gather wood since there was always some around, and they didn't have to pump water from the well. At the edge of the hill of tents, there stood a shed that served as a shower, and inside and outside of it, there were faucets. The water came from the pipes feeding off infrastructure built long ago. Hamama and Miriam grew accustomed to the showers and enjoyed washing themselves after a long day of work.

Everything was refreshing—except cooking. Their payment for labor was always food, but it was always the same: bread, eggs, and *lakerda*, a pickled bonito fish. Hamama was annoyed:

"I can't stand this fish anymore," she complained and handed the *lakerda* to Hassan.

"Well, you married the son of a fish merchant!" She chuckled, and he continued, feigning disapproval, "Like the children of Israel leaving Egypt, you've already forgotten the poverty you left behind?"

"We may have been poor, but at least the fish was fried and the food tasty!"

"I can't argue with that," smiled Hassan.

"Maybe we should say something?" Miriam suggested.

Although she was rebellious and stubborn, Hamama never dreamed to turning to someone older, let alone a man, with complaints. When she expressed her displeasure, she did so within a close circle of friends and family, to those she considered her equals. But in the new country, with the new rules and joint work in the orchard, she felt empowered. Perhaps she could, after all, stand up and speak her mind.

"Maybe I'll really say something," Hamama said. She didn't wait for the end of the meal but got up and went out to look for Moshe.

"I've got to see this," Miriam said and got up after her. Hassan and Ben Tzion quickly followed.

"What's this?" Hamama asked as she handed Moshe the food they had received.

"It's food. What do you want, Hamama?" Moshe asked.

"I want money. If we're working, we need to get paid," Hamama said.

"We're teaching you how to work," replied Moshe.

Hamama grew angrier, her fists clenching tightly. Moshe was taken aback.

"You're teaching me how to work? I'll teach you how to work!"

"Hamama—" Moshe tried to calm her.

"Don't call me 'Hamama!' I want you to get us a fair wage, in money, and I'll decide what I want to eat with my money."

The other immigrants erupted in cheers and claps. Hamama looked back and saw that Hassan was among them, smiling and clapping, too. She felt herself blush, but immediately returned to her enraged demeanor, looking at Moshe expectantly.

"I'll look into it with my superiors," he answered. He almost smiled at the furious girl, but the group of immigrants that crowded around them was much more serious.

"Look into it, look into it," Hamama said. "Until then, we won't return to work." Moshe waited for Hamama to leave, but the girl kept standing in front of him with clenched fists and a furious expression. Moshe walked back slowly and left the tents. Hamama returned to her friends.

"There you go," she said.

They laughed and returned to eat the fruits of their labor. They were on strike for a whole week, a week they used to improve their "homes" and synagogue, but at the end of it their request was granted. Hamama was happy that she had managed to influence Moshe and help everyone, but forced to consider it, she really didn't know what to do with the money. She went to the grocery store, owned by Yosef Toledano, a chubby and cheerful Sephardic Jew. Toledano examined the girl who had entered his store, looking at the variety of goods and slowly choosing.

"I want this," she said in a near whisper and placed all her money on the counter.

"Let's see how much you have," Toledano said. He counted some of the coins. "I only need these." He pushed the remaining ones back toward her. "And this is your change."

"Thank you," she said quietly and left the store. That day she cooked Hassan and herself a rich, flavorful lunch.

Hamama loved to go to the store and surround herself with all the goods. She grew accustomed to the coins and learned how to pay with them. Toledano always treated her kindly. One day he surprised her.

"Do you like *Samneh*?" he asked.

"Of course!" she said.

"I'll make you a good price. I know that you Yemenis don't like the margarine here, but what can you do? Butter is expensive." He handed her a glass jar.

"Oh! I'll make something delicious with this, and bring you some," she promised, and returned home happily. standing by the shed they used as a synagogue. When she saw Hassan and other Jews standing across from them, with Moshe nearby, she grew alarmed and started running, but by the time she arrived, the soldiers had already left.

"What happened?" she asked Hassan.

"There was another fight at the synagogue." Hassan sighed.

"What now?"

"They decided to say the prayers in the *Shami* version. One clown got up and switched to the *Baladi* version in the middle. He was beaten up."

"You can't fight in the synagogue," Hamama reprimanded him.

"What can I do? This can't go on. They think all the Yemenis are the same, but these are two very different versions."

Hamama nodded and went inside the tent. Hassan stayed outside to talk to the other men. Miriam joined Hamama inside.

"Such children," Miriam said.

"True, but they're right. Everyone wants to adhere to the path of his ancestors. Honestly, can't understand a word of the *Baladi* version. They should make two minyans."

"Right, but then they'll fight over which minyan goes first. You know, that's how it is with Jews."

"At least Moshe is trying to bridge between them," Hamama said.

"Moshe? Ha!" Miriam snorted. "That Mahatzri is on their side. When the clothes packages come, who do you think he calls first?"

"Really? So why didn't you say anything?"

"I'm saying it to you now. Go to him. He's scared of you." Miriam laughed.

"But we don't use old clothes anyway," Hamama said. "Yona sews them for us."

"But still, just out of principle, you should yell at him."

"All right," Hamama agreed.

That evening Hamama spoke with Moshe. She didn't even have to yell. He apologized immediately, promising that from this day forth he would call everyone as soon as the packages arrived.

The relative equality between men and women at the orchard was new to the Yemenite immigrants, and they didn't object to it. Together they tended the land and the trees, as if they were one big family operating a family business. But when the Jewish Federation guides tried to organize co-ed history and Hebrew lessons, there was a great uproar. Learning history or Hebrew was similar in their view to studying Torah, a daily mitzvah only for the men. Eventually, they reached a compromise: one weekly class for women and two for men. That's why Hamama and Miriam were surprised when Hassan and Ben Tzion announced that they were heading out to a class at the employment office, after having learned twice already that week.

"Why are they going to another class, and we're not?" Miriam asked after they left.

"What are they going to learn?" Hamama wondered.

The two sat outside the tent, caring for each other after a day of work at the orchard.

"I have an idea," Miriam said as she pulled a thorn from her friend's hand. "Let's follow them."

"Great idea," Hamama said and sucked the blood from her finger.

The two friends followed their husbands from afar. But when they descended the hill toward the Labor Office, they suddenly heard shooting from the amphitheater that was on the way to the office. They jumped into the bushes and hid.

"Look!" Hamama said. "Hassan and Ben Tzion aren't frightened at all! They're just walking as usual!"

"You're right. And I also hear the sound of horses. Do you see any?"

It was dark. The girls approached the source of the loud noise and climbed to the top of the hill, from which they could gaze into the old building.

What they encountered was a new kind of magic: through the windows, a huge, bright picture appeared before their eyes. A movie was playing, in which men with brimmed hats rode on horses and waved guns around. Hamama held onto Miriam's arm tightly.

"This is some kind of act of demons." She breathed heavily.

"What is it?"

"I don't know, but I'm staying here," Hamama said. "It's more interesting than the men's class at the employment office."

Hamama and Miriam sat in silence, watching a movie for the first time in their lives, entranced by the new discovery. They were spellbound by the large, impressive figures moving on the screen and were moved by the love story. Even though they sat on twigs and thorns on the little hill, the two didn't feel the time pass; it was as if they had entered a new world. When the hero rode off into the sunset, leaving his love behind, Miriam wiped a tear away. Hamama pinched her hand.

"Ouch!" Miriam yelled.

"Shhh! Look!" Hamama pointed.

As the movie came to an end, the lights in the amphitheater were turned on, and an entire audience of British soldiers came into view, stretching and getting up on their feet.

"God help us!" Miriam called out in surprise.

"Look! We have guests!" cried one of the soldiers who had heard Miriam.

"They saw us! Run!" Hamama yelled.

The two girls started running up the little hill toward the tents. Five soldiers ran after them, laughing. Hamama and Miriam ran faster, scared to look back.

"Wait for us!" one of the soldiers called. His call was to no avail as the girls, who didn't understand any English, translated his words into death threats. They ran quickly, huffing and puffing, until they reached the tents, where they hid. They didn't even notice that they were holding hands throughout their escape. The soldiers didn't enter the tent area, and the two girls breathed with relief.

"What a scare!" Miriam said.

"In Yemen, we had leopards and here, the British…" Hamama tried to catch her breath.

"We can't tell Ben Tzion and Hassan about this." Miriam wiped the sweat from her forehead.

"I think I peed my pants," Hamama said and examined her undergarments.

"That's not pee. It's blood," Miriam observed.

The girls looked at one another.

"Congratulations, Hamama. It's about time. Hassan will be happy." Miriam laughed, even though she was still frightened by the events of the evening.

Hamama smiled momentarily but still hadn't internalized the meaning of what had happened. Her feet still shook from the fast running, and her temples were beating like drums. She looked at the bloodstain again and at Miriam's smiling eyes.

"Oh! I have to wash everything now." Hamama sighed loudly, but her heart, only now released from fear, leaped with excitement. She was finally a woman.

Hamama remembered the instructions she received from Rivka. After she told Hassan that she was going in the ways of women, Hassan left to sleep outside the tent. They continued walking to work together, but Hamama didn't directly hand him anything. Instead, she would place an object on the ground, and he would pick it up. She felt butterflies in her stomach and noticed that Hassan was also a bit nervous. Her sister's words echoed in her mind. "He'll wait if she's not ready." But still, she was fifteen and a ripe woman. Up to now, they had only slept together and hugged. Now, after counting seven clean days, they would be expected to consummate their marriage for the first time. Her apprehension was mixed with great excitement, but she had no doubt that she was ready. When the time came, Miriam accompanied Hamama to the women's *mikvah*.

"Are you excited?" she asked.

"Yes."

"It's strange," Miriam said. "Now, when I know what you're going to do tonight, I think I'll take Ben Tzion for a midnight stroll as far as we can from your tent."

"Great idea," Hamama replied, somewhat embarrassed. Privacy wasn't the tents' strong suit.

Miriam and the *balanit*, the woman in charge of the *mikvah*, waited for Hamama as she undressed. Hamama had already showered in the shed and only had to wash the dust from the road from her feet. She had to make sure that there wasn't anything on her body that could separate her from the pure *mikvah* water. Hamama passed her hand over her thin body. *Soon Hassan will be the one to pass his hand here.* Embarrassed by the thought, Hamama shook her head and called the *balanit*.

When she came, the *balanit* led her to the chilly mikvah room and Hamama—who had hoped to cool her enthusiasm—was surprised to discover that the water was warm.

"Kosher," the *balanit* announced.

Hamama immersed herself in the water again, spreading out all her limbs and coming back up for air.

"Kosher," she heard a muffled sound.

Hamama immersed herself a third time and stayed underwater for a bit. She remembered the immersion in the river on the night of her wedding. The singing voices of her female relatives rang in her ears as she ascended from the water once more.

"Kosher."

With a strange feeling of the past merging with the present, Hamama wrapped herself in a towel. She felt something shift within her. Or perhaps nothing had changed at all.

Hassan was waiting for her at the tent. She made sure to close the tarp tightly behind her and turned to look at him. The tent was dark, but she felt his body shiver. She came close to him, if only to soothe his shivering. The couple were overcome with a deep serenity and a feeling of wholeness.

In the spring of 1944, Hamama became pregnant. Hassan was very excited, and even though she was only at the onset of her pregnancy, he insisted that she stop working in the orchard. Work that involved pruning shears and tree climbing did seem inappropriate, and so Hamama gave in to his worries, even though she disliked sitting around aimlessly. This was the first pregnancy amongst the immigrants from Yemen, and everybody took part in the excitement and anticipation. The construction of the large synagogue in Pardes Hanna was sped up so that the place would be ready before the birth. Hamama was afraid that she would give birth to a girl, and all the hopes of inaugurating the synagogue with a *brith* would turn to disappointment.

In addition to the fear of disappointing the whole community, Hamama was angered when Hassan shared with her the prophecies foretold by the Arab women in his late parents' village.

"When my father died at the same time as I was born, they said I ate him." Laughed Hassan, "And as revenge my son will eat me!"

"Why are you telling me this?" Hamama was outraged.

"I thought it was kind of funny."

"It's not funny!"

Hassan was so serious that his sense of humor could be more than a little off-putting.

"Hamama!" he insisted. "There are no demons in the Land of Israel."

"Hassan! I have enough worries even without thinking that you'll die on me, God forbid!"

"*B'khyat*, Hamama, it's just a story."

"Well, you found a very opportune time to tell it," she said. "Listen, I can't sit at home and wait anymore. I have to go out and work."

"But what about the baby?"

"What about him?"

"You have to take care of him. You can't work with shears. I can't take care of the baby."

"Well, at least I'm not the only one who worries." Hamama snorted.

"Fine," Hassan conceded. "I'll speak with Moshe. We'll see if there's some safer work for you."

And Hamama jumped on Hassan with hugs and kisses. Hassan burst out laughing: "If only everyone was as eager to work as you!"

Not all the women from the tents worked in the orchard. Some of them worked in the homes of the veteran residents. Moshe added Hamama to the group of women who wanted to work in such housekeeping. She stood with a bulging belly between other women who were too old to work in the orchard or refused to work alongside men. After twenty minutes, a group of Ashkenazi women came to examine the workforce. One of them, a tall blonde, stood in front of Hamama.

"I want this one," she told Moshe.

Moshe came over to Hamama.

"Do you want to watch over her children?" he asked.

"Just watch over the children? No housekeeping?"

"Yes."

"Fine."

Hamama followed the tall blonde to her house, wondering how hair could possibly be so yellow. The Ashkenazi woman tried to slow her gait, so the girl wasn't walking behind her. Hamama bumped into the woman's leg and nearly tripped. The woman quickly caught hold of Hamama.

"Let's just walk together," she suggested.

"Fine," Hamama answered.

They marched together in silence. But when they arrived at the large house, Hamama couldn't help but show her admiration for the fertile vegetable garden. The woman smiled and pointed at all her hard work.

"I have lettuce, beets, kohlrabi, and radishes," she said. "Also, cabbage, cauliflower, and green onions."

"Your garden is beautiful!" *I hope one day I can have a garden this lovely.*

"Thank you. I love growing the food myself."

The Ashkenazi woman had yet to introduce herself, and when Hamama looked at her, the woman extended her hand.

"My name is Rosa," she said. "What's your name?"

"Hamama."

"What month are you, Hamama?"

"I don't know."

Rosa raised her eyebrows but only pointed to the garden. "If you want vegetables, you're welcome to take some home."

"Thank you."

"Come, I'll show you the house."

The house consisted of two stories, and beside it was an enormous covered patio. Rosa led her into the house. Two cute blonde children, a boy and a girl, ran toward them.

"This is Hamama, and she'll watch over you," Rosa told the children. "Hamama, my children's names are Tzyviah and Aryeh."

Rosa left the children with Hamama, and they immediately dragged her throughout the house and showed her their rooms, their toys, and finally—the animals they raised behind the house. They had rabbits, a turtle, and four geese.

The large house, the vegetable garden, and the livestock reminded Hamama of the villages in Yemen, only here the houses were whitewashed. As were the people.

She loved to come watch over the children, and the children loved her. She taught them the games Hassan had taught her when they were children. She was reminded of Kadya, and Menashe and Efraim.

"Hamama, why are you crying?" Tzyviah asked.

"I'm crying?" Hamama asked as she wiped her tears. "It must be from the pregnancy."

"What do you have? A boy or a girl?" Aryeh asked.

"I don't know," Hamama answered.

"I hope it's girl!" Tzyviah said.

"I hope it's a boy!" Aryeh said, and the two children started fighting and roughhousing to the tune of Hamama's laughter.

One day Rosa asked Hamama to watch over the children on Shabbat.

"A lot of guests are coming over," she explained.

"I understand. But could I bring them to our tent for the Shabbat meal?" Hamama asked.

"I think they'd really like that," Rosa said.

On Shabbat, when Hassan went to the synagogue, Hamama marched over to Rosa's house. She thought about how much the kids would be excited to see the tent and how the Shabbat meal would be filled with children's giggles. She missed Shoshana. *She must be so big now.*

Hamama approached Rosa's house, and her heart skipped a beat. Rosa was picking leaves of lettuce from the ground—on Shabbat, a day of rest from work as decreed by God. Hamama was taken aback. She didn't know what to think or do. She followed Rosa quietly. Rosa washed the lettuce and placed it aside to dry, and then she headed out to the livestock. Hamama continued to follow her with her gaze, hiding behind the bushes. Rosa headed straight for the rabbit cage, humming some song to herself, and with the perfect calmness of a woman adept at her work pulled a chubby rabbit out of the cage, placed it on a flat wooden plank, and raised a butcher's knife. Hamama's heart pounded, and she yearned to shut her eyes, but the treasonous pair refused to heed her desire. With eyes wide-open, Hamama saw Rosa butcher the rabbit and carry it to the kitchen. Hamama's knees shook, and she began to feel sick. The rabbit's head was left lying on the grass, and the other rabbits were fidgeting uncomfortably at the sight of the blood. Hamama couldn't stand the sight any longer and vomited into the bushes. She then immediately took off running. To kill a rabbit—a non-kosher food? On Shabbat?

Hamama came to the tent hill just as the men returned from the synagogue. When she recognized Moshe, she ran to him and beat him with all her might:

"Why did you send me to work at an Arab's house?" she screamed. "How dare you?"

"Hamama, what are you talking about?" Moshe was taken aback but managed to avoid her fists.

"She picked lettuce! On Shabbat! And then slaughtered a rabbit!"

Moshe started laughing, and Hamama began beating him again.

"Why are you laughing?" she demanded.

"She's not an Arab. She's a Jew, only secular."

"What's secular? A Jew is a Jew!" Hamama asserted and stormed off.

On Sunday, Moshe told Hamama that he had scolded Rosa.

"I told her you Yemenis are old-fashioned and keep the Shabbat and keep kosher," he said. "She promised to be more sensitive. I hope you'll give her another chance."

Rosa came to the tents.

"I'm sorry, Hamama," she told her. "I should have done those things before you came."

Hamama didn't look at her.

"I'd like you to continue working for me," Rosa said.

Hamama thought about Tzyviah and Aryeh. She would miss them a lot. "I can't work for you," Hamama whispered then stood up and left.

The Jews of Yemen were religiously observant, ignorant of the existence of Jews who lived secular lives. When one stream of Yemenite Jewry wished to combine secular studies—geography and mathematics—together with religious studies, this led to a huge dispute over education and created a rift between the two sides that exists to this day.

When the new immigrants arrived in the secular Jewish land, they were surprised to find many Jews who were not at all observant. They fought for control over their children's education and a modest dress code for men and women, but the veteran residents viewed the conservative Yemenite culture with contempt and tried to "help" the immigrants adapt to the socialist Zionist vision.

World War II raged, but the news hadn't reached the tent hill.

Hamama started temporarily working at Toledano's market. Even though he spent many hours and days writing letters to his family in Spain, letters that probably never made it to their destinations, Toledano tried not to worry the pregnant girl. Hamama wondered how long it could possibly take to write letters, but she didn't complain too much. She was fond of the chubby man who liked to joke with her and teach her his business. He wouldn't allow her to carry heavy crates. He placed them on a tall bench when they were unpacking, so she wouldn't have to bend down.

"The young lady Vazif," he said jokingly, "you can organize the cucumbers here, and the carrots, over there, just like the sign says."

"The sign?"

"Hmm...I understand," the storekeeper rubbed his forehead. "Can you read, Hamama?"

"No," she said, and lowered her eyes.

"Well, I suppose we'll have to do something about that."

Hamama didn't like going to the *Ulpan*, where the immigrants were taught Hebrew. She was quite proficient at math but found reading and writing very difficult. During his free time, Toledano taught her as much as he could, so that at least she learned the names of vegetables and fruits, but most of the time he left Hamama alone and went out on business.

One day, Hamama planned to organize a few of the shelves, but her foot got caught on a loose floorboard, and she tripped. *I'm so clumsy! I hope nothing happened to the baby.*

She sat down on the floor, examining her growing belly and waiting for the baby to let her know he was fine. The well-mannered fetus immediately kicked, and Hamama sighed in relief. She looked at the floorboard *Maybe I'll ask Hassan to fix it. It's too dangerous.* She tried to move the board back into place, but when she pulled on it, she was surprised to find a handle. Hamama yanked it, and a square of the floor opened up and unveiled an entrance to a hidden room. Hamama immediately closed the door and got up to see that no one was around. Her curiosity overcame her desire to respect her employer's privacy, so after checking that nobody was approaching the store, she hurried down into the hidden room. It was rather small, and when her eyes grew acclimated to the dark, she saw guns, pistols, and a number of boxes standing one on top of another.

"Hamama?" a voice called from the store.

Frightened, Hamama hurried back upstairs to find Toledano standing in front of her.

"I didn't see anything," she promised.

"You really didn't see anything. Because if you had seen something—every Jew in Pardes Hanna is in danger," he scolded her.

"Why do you have all this?" Hamama demanded to know.

Toledano shut the door but didn't answer.

That entire day she noticed he avoided her.

She tried to find a way to ease the tension. The next day, she showed up with an old rug in hand. Without a word, she spread it in the center of the store so that it covered the loose floorboard. Toledano saw but said nothing.

It was only long afterward that Hamama learned about his efforts to organize to fight the British. He probably had wanted to tell her that the British might now be fighting the Nazis, but they were refusing to allow Jews to emigrate from Nazi Germany; he probably wanted to say that the solution to the Jewish problem was a Jewish country. But he didn't tell her those things, and she didn't ask. It was only much later that she realized he was protecting her.

"Do you notice that the men are disappearing at night more and more often?" Hamama asked her friend one evening.

"They have more classes," Miriam answered.

"Why them and not us?" Hamama wondered.

"That's how it is, I guess." Miriam went back to sewing in silence.

Hamama looked at her quiet friend and felt like something was going on around her, something she wasn't a part of, especially after what she saw at the store. Miriam's silence only heightened her curiosity. The circle of silence now also included her good friend, and she was left alone. Alone with her large belly.

Hassan returned late that night. Hamama, who had planned on yelling at him, was defeated by the fatigue of the ninth month and had fallen asleep. He came in and looked at her lovingly, tired and worried. Difficult days lay ahead of them, and here she was lying on the floor in a little tent, completely unprotected. The fear and anxiety had begun to eat away at him, and he couldn't fall asleep. Again.

Hamama's suspicions disrupted her sleep. She tried to get Miriam to open up, but her friend continued to avoid her. Hamama was convinced that Hassan was involved in something terrible. Now that he was done smuggling Jews out of Yemen, living and working in the land of his dreams, what other dangers was he chasing? He couldn't be stealing or doing anything like that! And Miriam and everyone else seemed to cover for him, keeping secrets from her.

Hamama looked at her bulging belly and felt gigantic and unwanted. It was then that the idea that he might be cheating on her with another woman struck roots in her mind. But she couldn't understand why Miriam wouldn't tell her. Because of the baby? Because she didn't want to upset her? She also couldn't imagine Hassan doing such a thing. It was unthinkable. But on the other hand, why else would he be so distant? With no other explanation to grasp on to, her worries grew and grew. Everyone walked on eggshells around her, and she was on the verge of bursting.

One evening, when Hassan claimed he was going to a class, an evening in which Hamama had confirmed with Moshe that there was no class, she decided to follow him.

"I'm going to bed early tonight," she told Miriam and left for her tent, certain that Miriam didn't suspect a thing. Instead of going to her tent, Hamama snuck out and followed Hassan across Pardes Hanna. His gait was suspicious, and he repeatedly glanced behind him. A few moments later, Ben Tzion seemed to appear out of nowhere, and joined him. Well, he certainly wasn't cheating on her.

The two continued marching, but Hamama felt a sudden weakness and couldn't follow them anymore. She felt a contraction in her stomach and stood still for a moment, but she was afraid she would lose track of the two in the dark. A moment later, she started walking again and was glad to find that the two had finished their journey in one of the abandoned sheds in the orchard. She sat down on the ground, exhausted, and stretched her legs.

After a few minutes, a man came outside to guard the door and noticed the pregnant woman stretching her legs by the shed. He quickly went back inside.

"What are you doing here, Hamama?" Hassan called out.

"I followed you," she answered lethargically.

"Why?"

"I wanted to make sure you weren't cheating on me."

Hassan suppressed a smile and chastised his wife.

"You don't trust me?"

"You've disappeared a few nights already, and you don't tell me where you're going!" Hamama argued.

Hassan looked back at the shed and sighed. "I joined the ETZEL."

"What?" Hamama was shocked.

She heard all about the Zionist underground military organization. In contrast with the Haganah, which worked under the British role in efforts to protect the Jews from Arab uprisings, the ETZEL plotted against the British soldiers and was considered illegal. It would've been better had he cheated on her with another woman.

"And now that you have found our meeting place, we'll have to find a new one," he said.

"Hassan! You can't join the ETZEL! We're about to have a baby!" Hamama's eyes filled with tears.

"I know. That's why I'm doing it. Because our child needs to live in a safe place." Hassan helped his wife stand. "Now come home. You shouldn't walk so far in your state."

Hassan held her hand, and the two walked back home in silence. When he lay her down in their bed and covered her gently, he whispered in her ear.

"I told you I'd never leave you again."

Hamama said nothing, but her miserable eyes convinced Hassan to lie down beside her and miss that night's meeting.

The ETZEL, also known as the Irgun, was not the only Zionist paramilitary organization that operated in the British Mandate of Palestine. The Haganah, which later became the core of the Israel Defense Forces, was one of the first such organizations. It originated in order to defend the Jewish settlement, and then joined forces with the British army during World War I and World War II. Their alliance with the British made them one of the enemies of the ETZEL and of their more radical and violent cousin, the LEHI.

As the threat of war with Germany increased during the 1930s, Britain believed the support of the Arabs to be more important than the establishment of a Jewish homeland, and so in spite of The Balfour Declaration, the British Mandate shifted to a pro-Arab stance. They thus limited Jewish immigration, triggering a Jewish insurgency.

Hassan recognized Hamama's ambivalence toward the British soldiers—they reminded her of the governor's police in Yemen, keeping the peace inside and outside the neighborhoods. But he knew better. As long as the soldiers remained, there would be no Jewish state. So, the only way to truly make Palestine a Jewish state was to fight for it.

The next day Hamama worked at the store. Toledano was busy organizing some new merchandise, and Hamama took care of a number of women who came in to shop.

"Hamama, you look like you're about to explode any minute!" Gamdani's wife told her.

"Yes," Yona said. "I sewed her this dress, but that's it. From now on, I just want to tighten your figure." Yona laughed.

Hamama smiled at the two. She knew them already from Atlit, and they had been living in the same tents for two and a half years.

"Did you hear about the ETZEL's actions against the British?" Gamdani's wife asked.

"Yes!" Yona's voice raised in excitement. "The explosion at the headquarters of the secret police in Jerusalem?"

Hamama moved uncomfortably. The women either didn't notice or interpreted her teetering as a symptom of the pregnancy.

"Maybe you should sit down for a bit?" Yona suggested.

But before Hamama could refuse, Toledano burst in, panic-stricken.

"They're here!" he screamed. "And they're drunk!"

The other women were afraid, but Hamama, whose large belly gave her some confidence, took control:

"Quickly, girls! Go out the back door to the orchard. From there, you can run home. We'll delay them."

Toledano rushed the women to the back, and then came back to help Hamama drag the table over the rug.

"Where are all the women?" one of the officers yelled as he stumbled into the store.

Hamama stood behind the counter, afraid. Up until now she had managed to avoid these men, and now she was standing across from them without any protection, a cache of illegal weapons hidden under her feet. Four additional soldiers marched in. Toledano quickly offered for them to sit around the table, and he brought in more chairs from the back. The five sat down, following their prey with their eyes. With trembling legs, Hamama brought a pitcher of wine and a loaf of bread to the table. One of the soldiers grabbed her from behind.

"Come here," he snarled.

His drunkenness deceived him into thinking that he had found the prey he was seeking, but when he pulled her toward him, he noticed her large belly, and immediately let her go and apologized. Toledano hurriedly served them another loaf of bread and some cheese. The soldiers attacked the food voraciously, and Hamama, who up until now had imagined the British as devilish men with horns, realized that the lads before her were about her brother Sa'adia's age. One of them occasionally stole a glance at her; his eyes didn't project evil but sadness. *Maybe he has a wife and baby at home.* She looked at Toledano, who stood with a pale face by the soldiers, waiting for orders. *If only we could all live in peace.* Hamama felt her feet burning over the weapons that might harm these lads. They wanted to abuse women, so she tried to harden her heart toward them, but to no avail. The soldiers partook of another bottle of wine and left the store. Toledano and Hamama breathed a sigh of relief.

When Hamama told Hassan what had happened, his eyes burned with anger, and he forbade her to go back to work in the grocery store. Hamama's furious reply was so intense that she was struck by severe contractions that lasted a whole day. Hassan was at work, and Hamama wandered aimlessly around the tent. The strong pains she felt were a few minutes apart, which she interpreted as anger, but as the contractions became more frequent and closer together, she understood that she was actually in labor. She wandered around the tents to find someone, and luckily, one woman who had stayed back that day saw her and ran off to call a midwife. When the midwife arrived, she ordered the messenger to spread clean sheets in Hamama's tent and to boil some water, while at the same time she turned to examine Hamama:

"It's time, Hamama," she said with a smile. "The synagogue is ready."

In that moment, Hamama forgot about the ETZEL and the British, and she forgot about the tents and her anger with Hassan. She just wanted to see him, the fruit of her womb. In her mind, she called him Rachamim—mercy. *God, have mercy, mercy for your people, for Israel.*

And then he was there, a beautiful, honey colored baby. The midwife cleaned him a bit and handed him to Hamama gently. Hamama looked at her son and was overwhelmed by great pleasure. But then the midwife took him back.

"Now the placenta," she instructed.

Hamama stared longingly at her son who rested in the midwife's arms. He started crying and screaming, and finally, when she was ready, she took him to her bosom. She refused to let go.

"Hassan! Hamama gave birth to a boy!" The news spread quickly throughout the orchard. It took Hassan a few moments to digest the news. His heart raced with excitement. He dropped his tools and took off running toward the tents, accompanied by his friends' cheers of joy. The way to the tents felt so much longer than usual.

Finally, he entered the tent and found his exhausted wife hugging their small, screaming son.

"He keeps on crying," she said with a smile.

Hassan stood, paralyzed.

"Take him. Come on, don't be scared," Hamama encouraged him.

Hassan fearfully approached the baby and picked him up. The baby calmed down momentarily, as if entering a familiar place, but a few seconds later, he started crying again. Hassan glanced quizzically at Hamama, but when he saw that she had already fallen asleep, he crept quietly out of the tent with the baby and introduced him to Pardes Hanna.

Rachamim was the first baby privileged to have his *brith* in the great synagogue. Many of the town's residents took part in the joyous occasion. The young parents, tired and bleary-eyed, were proud of their small son and his strong, loud cries. The rest of the residents' enthusiasm was a bit less—they were proud, but the need for more insulating stone walls between the tents intensified.

As part of the Socialist Zionism and because of the unsafe environment in the immigrations' tents, all infants and babies were instructed to stay at a "Children's House" during the day. The nannies and nurses in charge of the children came from the more established parts of Pardes Hanna and weren't very fond of their new neighbors.

Rachamim was the first baby, but there was no shortage of small, dirty, browned-skinned, barefoot children who ran around the house, caused trouble and made a mess.

A month after the birth, Hamama returned to work in housekeeping, and every once in a while, she would come back to breastfeed Rachamim at the Children's House and enjoy his company.

One day, when Rachamim was two-and-a-half months old, Hamama came to feed her little son.

"He's sleeping," the nanny told her.

"How can he be sleeping when he hasn't eaten yet?" Hamama asked.

"Sleeping. What can we do? You don't wake a sleeping baby."

Hamama left for the tent and returned an hour later.

"Still sleeping?" She was surprised.

"Yes," the nanny answered.

Hamama, who was familiar with her son's hungry and loud nature, was shocked. She pushed the nanny aside, went into the room and found Rachamim lying there motionless, his stomach swollen.

"He's not breathing!" she yelled. She grabbed the boy and ran to the medical clinic. The doctor saw her immediately and returned the boy's breath.

"You still need to go to the hospital," he told Hamama and organized a ride for her.

Hamama took the ride with her child, examining every one of his limbs and trying to get a smile out of him somehow, or at least some other normal reaction that would calm her. The twists and turns of the drive and the enormity of her fear caused her to feel queasy, but with great effort she managed to hold herself together. At the hospital in Afula, they took Rachamim to be examined, and Hamama was left alone. Only then did she have a second to breathe, and then she remembered Hassan:

He will worry so much!

"Hassan! They arrested Toledano!" Ben Tzion hurried over to his friend in the orchard.

Hassan dropped his tools and ran with a few of the men to watch from afar as soldiers took weapons out of the hidden room in the grocery store.

"They're looking for Hamama," Miriam said as she walked over to them. "They know that a pregnant woman worked with him, and they want to interrogate her."

Hassan's heart stopped. He ran to the tent immediately, and when he couldn't find Hamama, he ran to the house where she worked. They too turned him away empty-handed. The young man was held by a great terror. Up to now he hadn't fully understood why his joining the ETZEL caused Hamama so much angst. He was so sure in his righteousness—so sure that he had closed his heart to her fears.

But now he understood. Rachamim! *She must be with our son.* He ran to the Children's House.

"The boy was choking, and she rushed him to the clinic," the nanny reported sheepishly.

Hassan ran all the way to the clinic in the center of the settlement.

"The doctor sent them to the hospital in Afula," the nurse explained.

"Afula?" Hassan wondered.

"They had to make sure the boy hadn't suffered any damage."

As he left the clinic, Hassan didn't know what worried him more. Hamama and Rachamim were on their own, in another city; Rachamim was sick; and Hamama was wanted by the British police.

"Hassan!" Miriam was running toward him. "They told them she died in childbirth."

"What?" Hassan stirred from his thoughts.

"Everybody in the tents is in agreement, and they told the soldiers that Hamama died during childbirth."

"I see.," He let his face fall, to fit the reaction the soldiers expected from him.

"They want you to go with them to the interrogation," Moshe told Hassan when he arrived at the tent hill.

"I have to go back home," Hamama said.

"What do you mean? You have to stay here to breastfeed," the nurse told her.

"But my husband -"

"I'm sure the doctor in Pardes Hanna will tell him what happened, and where you are."

"But then he'll worry."

"Okay, and who will feed your baby?"

Hamama grew silent. Of course, the nurse was right. Hassan was a big boy who could take care of himself, but Rachamim was just a little baby. He needed her.

"You can sleep with us in the nurses' shed," the nurse offered.

"Thank you," Hamama said softly.

The days at the hospital passed slowly. Hamama, who wasn't accustomed to not working, helped the nurses with cleaning and cooking. The nurses liked her—and liked to belittle her. They would call her, "Pardes Hanna, come here," or "Pardes Hanna, your baby wants you." Her attempts at teaching them her name were to no avail. When the head nurse saw that the girl was often helping out, she called her to her office.

"Would you like to work here until your baby gets better?" she asked.

Hamama shrugged in agreement. She didn't believe that they would actually pay her, so she only sometimes helped out, sorting lentils in the kitchen or preparing potatoes. But most of the time, she would wander off, sit on the grass and think about Hassan.

Anger overcame her at times. *Why doesn't he come visit me? Surely, he must know where I am. How could he leave me alone?*

Hamama lived in the hospital for two months, and she never heard a word from him. She got to know all the nurses and their amusing personalities. They taught her Hebrew expressions she didn't plan on telling even Miriam. Her main comfort was Rachamim, who was growing and getting fatter, under full supervision, with all the nurses taking care of him and following his development.

When it was finally time to leave, the head nurse called her over and handed her a large sum of money.

"This is your salary for your work with us."

Hamama was shocked by the amount of money, and in her heart, she regretted not having worked more. The nurses accompanied her and Rachamim to the car that would take her back home.

"Goodbye and see you later, Pardes Hanna!" they called to her with a smile. "Take care of Rachamim, Pardes Hanna!"

Hamama waved goodbye, holding onto her large baby and excited to see Hassan again. Regardless, she went over all the curses and the angry speech she planned to hit him with for not coming to visit her.

After an exhausting week of interrogations by British soldiers, Hassan was released. They were convinced that he was a simple husband, unaware of events around him, and his sad story about the wife who died at childbirth convinced them not to arrest him and send him with Toledano and the other ETZEL people to the detainment camp in Eritrea, Africa. The two months following his release were difficult to bear for him. Hassan suspected that he was still under surveillance and so he couldn't contact Hamama or try to find her. He had to continue his life as usual, and he even gave up the secret ETZEL meetings. Every once in a while, Ben Tzion would come to update him on news and class materials, and Miriam tried to obtain information about Hamama through the clinic. Unfortunately, the clinic didn't have telephone lines yet, and Hassan had to settle for his faith in God and endless patience. A month after his release, the surveillance was lifted, but Hassan didn't want to endanger Hamama, so he continued as usual, until the day he returned from work and found her sitting in the tent with a large baby who was supposedly his young son.

"Hamama!" Hassan cried out in surprise and hugged his wife and child.

"You're lucky. Miriam already told me why you didn't come looking for me and your son. She saved you from an hour of curses." Hamama eyes welled up with tears.

"You're still welcome to curse," Hassan said as he examined Rachamim with the same curiosity with which Hamama had examined him. "I'm so sorry I couldn't come visit you or write. They kept an eye on me. I'm sorry about Toledano. I know he was your friend."

Hamama noticed cuts and bruises on Hassan's face and hands, and her heart skipped a beat.

"What happened to you?" she asked, afraid to hear his answer.

The child stretched his arm to his father's nose and gurgled joyfully. Hassan hesitated for a moment, taking refuge in his son's touch. He didn't want her to know how he was interrogated, abused and hurt. Her innocence and pureness of heart were what he loved about her the most, what he was feeding off of, what he needed in order to keep his own strength. In the end he just smiled apologetically.

"I had a small accident in the orchard."

"Well, I hope now that we're back, you'll be able to concentrate better at work."

Hassan smiled at his wife's scolding. At last, after the longest weeks of his life, he once again felt at peace.

"It's good that you're home," he said.

The little family was happily reunited within the black tarps, as life outside continued to beat down.

For the next few weeks, Hamama refused to send Rachamim to the children's home. The nannies would claim that the tents were dangerous, but of course Rachamim had almost died while in their care.

But the tents really were unsafe. Fires broke out every once in a while. Not all the women liked cooking in the same kitchen and so fights broke out. They tried cooking in the tents, but the tarps caught fire and quickly destroyed the temporary house and everything inside it. Hamama also cooked in the tent, but Hassan, who was smart with these things, dug a deep pit and filled it with charcoals, which he then covered with a metal sheet. That way the oven would heat the tent during the cold nights and was safe for cooking, without the danger of a spreading fire. But as summer returned, the immigrants were to face yet another threat.

One night, Hamama awoke to the sound of loud panting, which came from the tool chest.

"Hassan! Wake up!" she whispered in his ear.

Hassan opened his eyes and heard the panting, too.

"Take Rachamim and go outside!" he whispered.

Hamama gathered the sleeping baby to her bosom and left the tent. Hassan, stick in hand, marched quietly toward the tool chest. He lifted the lid fearfully and discovered a large female snake, whose swollen belly indicated she was pregnant. Hassan immediately closed the chest and left the tent. Quietly, all the men woke up and gathered around. Moshe the guide, who, unfortunately, had already witnessed such occurrences on numerous occasions, organized them to action.

"She's bound to wake up and bite, so we won't touch the tool chest. We'll move the tent and belongings aside, and then set the tool chest on fire."

The men quickly dismantled Hassan and Hamama's house and moved all their belongings aside. Hamama stood shaking from fear and disgust, with Miriam's arm wrapped around her. The sound of loud breathing emerged from the chest, and the snake peeked angrily out of the tool chest. The men were already prepared with sticks. They stabbed the snake's body quickly and tossed her into the burning fire. She moved around the flames violently for a moment, and then her body exploded, and blood sprayed all over, bystanders included.

"Hold Rachamim!" Hamama choked.

Miriam hurried to take the baby from Hamama's arms as the mother turned back and vomited.

The events of that night tested more than Hamama's stomach, but also the tent dwellers' patience. The next morning the immigrants went on strike from work and turned every tent on the hill inside out, in search of more snakes. Toward the evening, they gathered and decided to go out to Jerusalem to protest, across from the Jewish Agency's offices. As the consoler Moshe was the main target for their anger, but he still tried to calm their spirits and help them organize their demonstration.

"We've been living in these tents for three years." Damari said. "They promised us that these were temporary dwellings!"

"These houses are unsafe for our families, and especially now, when nearly all of the women are pregnant," added Ben Tzion, to whom Miriam had recently revealed that she was pregnant.

"I understand you," Moshe said, "and am ready to help with the protest, but you have to understand that the British don't like such commotion, and so it has to be done wisely." Then he laid out his plan.

"We won't all take the same bus, since that's suspicious. We'll start a round early in the morning, and throughout a whole day, we'll get six men onto each bus to Jerusalem. Also, these men won't sit together like they're organized, but rather separately, as if each is going for their own business. In Jerusalem, you'll split up and set a time to meet in front of the Agency building, and then you'll start the protest."

The men listened to him and took buses to Jerusalem, six men at a time, to protest across from the Jewish Agency's headquarters. Hassan looked at the large building resembling a castle where the leaders of the Jewish people sat. He was overcome by a deep respect, and yet, he was determined to obtain for his family those things that the leaders didn't view as important or hadn't found the time to do. The immigrants started chanting slogans toward those in the building, and a few minutes later, a Yemenite man came out to them.

"Someone who speaks Hebrew well can come with me and make your argument," he said.

The men chose Moshe and Hassan, and they entered the Agency building. Hassan never imagined that the castle would turn out to be a simple office building. He didn't meet Ben Gurion, the head of the Jewish Agency and later the first prime minister of the state of Israel, but he and Moshe were led to one of the rooms, where a mustached man named Noah Shapiro awaited them. Moshe made their case and told the story of the snake. Hassan thought he saw a brief smile creep onto Shapiro's face as the story came to its shocking end.

"So, you have a son?" Shapiro suddenly asked Hassan.

"Yes," Hassan answered.

"And there are many families with children." Shapiro repeated.

"There are some who immigrated with kids and others with babies on the way," Hassan said.

"I'll send a committee to check it out," Shapiro said. "We'll do this formally. I hope we'll be able to help you soon."

Hassan and Moshe were led outside. The men expressed satisfaction at the man's answer, but Moshe, who was more experienced, stayed quiet. But despite the guide's lack of faith in the speed of the institutions, a group from the Jewish Agency did show up at the tent hill less than a week later, and they decided that indeed there was an urgent need for real houses. As World War II came to an end, the immigrants from Yemen received funds to build a neighborhood they named Rambam, the Yemenite neighborhood.

2008

Blessed are the nation and its people
If they're so strong and they're so fertile
And so my march was not for naught
My steps with purpose they were fraught
It's all worthwhile oh Lord
That's his speech, Ben Gurion's words

(From "Zecharya ben Ezra" by Yaakov Orland)

Today I'm supposed to meet them. Mom already told them that my husband accepted a position in Chicago, in the United States. I think we all know that this step is necessary for his career. Especially if we want to come back to Israel, and if he wants an academic position here. But I never thought I'd be the one to leave. All these years in youth movements and Zionist education, and even with the growing awareness of the latter's misdeeds, to leave Israel? To leave them? There's not much time left, I know. I don't believe that Grandpa will be waiting for me when I come back.

Grandma greets me happily and touches my large belly.

"You're so ugly," she compliments me.

"I know you say that against the evil eye, but it still hurts," I say with a smile.

She returns an amused smile. Grandpa sits behind the house, and we join him and bask in the sun. This time I am not consumed by his ill appearance, but rather encouraged by Grandma's youthful quips.

"At least, we'll get to see your little girl," Grandma says.

"Yes. She needs to get out already. I'm hot," I answer, trying to make her laugh and succeeding.

CHAPTER 7

The move into houses marked the beginning of a new period in the lives of Hamama and Hassan. The modest houses consisted of one room per family, with one bathroom and a shower shared by every four rooms. The bathroom, a small shed with a hole in the ground, and the showers were small and narrow, but the security of being surrounded by stone walls made the lives of the Yemenite immigrants much happier.

"Yefet, Malka is calling for you!" Hamama yelled at her new neighbor Yefet Tiram one morning as they both hurried to the bathroom.

"Oy," Yefet sighed and hurried back to his house, limping slightly.

Hamama quickly entered the bathroom and locked the door behind her, laughing. Yefet came back furious:

"Hamama! Next time you do that I swear I'm going to crap in front of your house!"

But Yefet forgot his anger when he experienced Hamama's cooking that evening, together with all the residents of the neighborhood. The Yemenite immigrants celebrated together in one of the yards nearly every night.

"I can't believe the lottery put you in an apartment on the other end of the neighborhood," Hamama complained to Miriam.

"Well, you'll have some space away from me." Miriam laughed and left to serve the *j'ala*. Hamama followed her with her gaze, sighing in jubilant relief at the sight of the small community that had flourished here in her yard. The eucalyptus trees between the houses added a soothing green touch, and she dreamed of a vegetable garden in front of her house. The many neighbors sat on mats and chairs, smoked a *nargilah* together, and chatted happily. The women, after passing out the *j'ala* to the men, sat together with the fancier plates and laughed out loud. Hamama loved the mixture of toasted corn seeds with the peeled sunflower seeds. She worked all afternoon to toast a large amount together and now filled her hand with the salty delicacy and stared at her new life with contentment.

Then a truck of ETZEL soldiers arrived at the yard. A few young men hopped off and passed some flyers around. Hamama glanced at Hassan, who was chatting with one of the fighters. *He looks so determined, fearless.* His fearlessness caused Hamama's fear to double. But she didn't say anything to him about her worries. They had a silent agreement: she knew what was important to him, and he knew what was important to her, and they both respected that. There was no point in dissuading Hassan from involvement in the ETZEL, and Hamama didn't want to argue with her loyal husband.

One evening a group from Shfayim came and joined the immigrants in their feast.

"They have come from an ETZEL fighting course," Hassan pointed out proudly.

Hamama remained silent and served the merry group. A few days later, soldiers from the Haganah arrived. At that time, the Haganah cooperated with the British.

"Who is Shalom Vazif?" one of the Haganah soldiers asked.

"I am," Hassan said as he approached them.

"Did you have out-of-town guests this week?"

"No," Hassan lied.

"Just so you know, if something happens, like a bombing, it'll be your responsibility," the soldier threatened.

"If you say so," Hassan answered fearlessly.

Hamama overheard and became angry.

"He's not responsible, and I'm not responsible for anything that's going to happen! What are you a soldier for? Go guard! Don't go looking for people to blame before anything even happens."

Hamama's eyes burnt with such fury that the Haganah fighter took a step back and returned to his car. Hassan laughed.

"Hamama, you could've been a great soldier," he told his wife.

Hamama didn't laugh at all, and instead spilled her fury right onto Hassan.

"What are you thinking?" she yelled. "That you're this great hero? You're willing to risk yourself and your family so easily?"

"But Hamama—"

"Don't 'but' me! You have a little boy. You promised you wouldn't leave me anymore."

Her glaring anger and pain wiped the smile from his face. He struggled to find the words to explain himself, and just stood before her in silence. In no mood to wait for him to regain his speech, she turned her back to him and stormed off.

Hassan knew that Hamama's worries weren't unfounded. The British and their allies were quite skilled at scaring the rebels. He knew that she often thought about Toledano, who was imprisoned in Eritrea. She also could have ended up there. Hassan didn't tell Hamama, but he had nightmares of her imprisoned, far from him. How could he continue to live when she faced such a danger? When at any moment, she could arbitrarily be arrested and taken from him?

Hamama noticed that Hassan was troubled. She left him alone, sorry to have saddened him. She felt mad at herself for not simply letting him be himself, but it seemed to her, Hassan was looking for adventures, for danger, and it made her blood boil. What's not to like in their new neighborhood? In their little community, in the work at the orchard? Hamama preferred not to think about the war, and when it snuck up and into their agendas, she quickly distracted herself. She especially hated the animosity between the Haganah and the ETZEL. Their mutual lack of understanding reminded her of the difference between the *Shami* and *Baladi* versions of Yemenite prayers. The fact that they would still argue in the synagogue became a kind of bad joke to her. But the fact that Jews were reporting other Jews to the British, arresting them, or flogging them was incomprehensible to her. What was the point of a Jewish country if they couldn't live together? She didn't share these thoughts with Hassan. With the little amount of time they had together, she preferred to snuggle in his arms rather than to fight with him.

Miriam, instead, became the target of Hamama's frustration.

"I don't understand these men. Always looking for trouble," Hamama said as she picked thorns out of her friend's cracked hands. Rachamim and Yair, Miriam's son, were roughhousing between their legs.

"What are you talking about?" Miriam asked.

"Playing soldiers," Hamama answered.

"It's not a game, Hamama!" Miriam suddenly grew angry. "It's a very important struggle!"

"Why are you upset?"

"I'm upset because you're mocking people who are willing to sacrifice their lives so that you'll be able to live in peace. In a Jewish country."

"You're exaggerating! Life under British rule isn't so terrible." But Hamama knew it wasn't true.

Miriam stood up, her face flushed. The tension both scared and amused Hamama.

"So apparently you didn't really like your previous employer, eh? I'm sure he's enjoying lovely cakes over there, in his prison in Eritrea. And you played with the nurses in Afula while Hassan was under interrogation. You didn't see how he came home. If you would've seen his swollen face, maybe you wouldn't talk like that."

It was as if a bomb had exploded between the two.

Sadness flooded Miriam's face. "I'm sorry, but it's true," she said. "I just don't understand why you find any of it amusing. Come, Yair, we're going home." She grabbed her son.

Hamama stared at her in silence. Rachamim stuck to her feet, trying to find comfort within the anger that filled the room. A moment before Miriam left, she turned to Hamama with measured anger.

"And it's not just a man's game. I'm also in the ETZEL. You can understand why I didn't tell you sooner." Then she left.

Hamama sat after her friend's departure, confused and enraged. *Miriam was in the ETZEL?* The two had grown more distant when Miriam returned to work in the orchard after the birth of her son, while Hamama worked in housekeeping because she was pregnant again. But how long had she kept this secret from her? And above all these thoughts floated an image of Hassan's face, beaten and humiliated, an image she tried to distance from her mind's eye. When she returned after two months, he said he had a small accident in the orchard. He had a few scratches, and Hamama teased him that he should concentrate at work. *How bad was the injury? What had they done to him?*

When Hassan returned home, Hamama hugged him with eagerness but also with great sorrow.

"Hamama, what happened?" he asked.

"Ah…I fought with Miriam," Hamama said. She didn't want to bother him, she only wanted to be comforted.

"I'm sure you'll work it out. You two are inseparable."

Hassan could see that his words failed to relieve Hamama's pain. He liked having her apart from everything that was happening—an island of preserved serenity. But shielding her shouldn't come at the cost of her best friend. Softly, he spoke:

"Tomorrow the ETZEL has a meeting. You could join me, just to hear them out. Miriam will be there."

The next morning Hamama joined the ETZEL meeting. She found her friend in the crowd, walked over, and quietly stood next to her. Miriam smiled.

"We have good news," announced Eliahu, the head of the organization in Pardes Hanna. "Our brothers from the Haganah movement decided to join us in the struggle against the British. From now on, we won't be the ETZEL, but rather the Jewish Resistance Movement."

His news was received with calls of joy. All were held by great excitement, including Hamama.

After the end of World War II, when the horrors of the Holocaust became known and Jewish immigrants from all around the world sought refuge in Palestine, the British maintained their pro-Arab stance and did not allow enough Jews to immigrate. This policy brought the Haganah, ETZEL, and LEHI together against the British, and led them to form the Jewish Resistance Movement.

Ten months of unity, eleven major actions, and nine months of Hamama's pregnancy came to a violent end. The Jewish Resistance Movement successfully released 200 illegal immigrants, most of them Holocaust survivors, from the British detention camp. In addition, in what came to be called "The Night of the Trains" and "The Night of the Bridges," members of the movement bombed major British supply routes all over the country and attacked British police stations. Working in unity was inspiring and filled the Jews of Palestine with hope and a sense of how it would feel to be led by their own future government. But after the bombing at the King David Hotel, the Haganah members distanced themselves from the action, and the Jewish Resistance Movement was dismantled.

This last action was a disaster that cost ninety-one lives. Civilians—British, Arab, and Jewish—were killed, and, in order to placate the British, Haganah members informed on ETZEL and LEHI activists. In Pardes Hanna several ETZEL members from the neighborhood were turned in to McNab, the British commanding officer in charge of the military base in Hadera. When they were finally released, their faces swollen and their bones broken, a great cry erupted from the little neighborhood. That night, at the ETZEL meeting, the activists decided to assassinate that violent British commander.

"There's no doubt that this was a scare tactic, a warning to us not to continue our actions," Eliahu said.

Hamama, in an advanced stage of pregnancy, looked at him fearfully. On the one hand, she hoped that he would heed the warning, but on the other hand, her whole body burned with the desire for revenge.

"But we won't be silent," he continued. "If there's no justice or compassion in the British system, we can take justice into our own hands. McNab is cruel and dangerous, and he deserves to be sent off to the next world. After the meeting, all the fighters will stay, and we'll plan the action."

A young couple from the group of fighters suddenly stood up.

"We'll do it," Asher and Ayala offered. The two had recently completed their training in Shfayim and had a good friend amongst those who returned injured. Hamama looked at the couple in astonishment. They weren't much younger than she was, but their gentle features betrayed a life lived in comfort and without much hardship. The boy was tall and skinny as a twig and the girl looked like a fresh flower that just blossomed. She hoped Eliahu would refuse their offer.

"No," Eliahu said. "We need a larger crew to complete the action. The Hadera base is very scrupulously guarded, and McNab is always surrounded by other soldiers. This isn't an action for two."

"But then more people will be endangered, and we still have so much to do!" Asher insisted.

Eliahu refused, but the two refused to listen.

The next day, Asher and Ayala boarded a bus to Hadera, with a pistol hidden under Ayala's shirt. When they saw the commander head toward one of the coffee shops, they followed him and sat at a table in the same coffee shop, pretending to be a happy couple with no worries weighing down their hearts. They shared a moment of joy, peace, and love, a moment before it was all about to end. Asher and Ayala glanced at one another, holding hands. Asher's hands trembled, and Ayala calmed him with her glance. The cruel commander noticed the young couple in love and smiled. The girl reminded him of his daughter in Liverpool. He missed her dearly and was angry and frustrated at being stuck in this warring country. How he longed to return home. Asher and Ayala rose from their seats. The commander averted his gaze out of politeness, and in this critical moment, Asher pulled the pistol out from under Ayala's shirt and shot him dead. The surrounding soldiers immediately returned fire and killed the couple on the spot.

The funeral was well-attended, and many came to accompany the couple to their eternal peace. Hamama and Malka Tiram, both in the ninth month of their respective pregnancies, decided amongst themselves to name their babies after the couple. Hamama gave birth to a boy and called him Asher, and Malka gave birth to a girl she named Ayala.

Asher's birth wasn't easy. He was a skinny, unlucky baby who, at the young age of six months, caught a fever that refused to leave him. It was as if the tumultuous atmosphere in the country affected his restless, combative character.

In the future, many would blame his troubles on a childhood accident, but Hamama always insisted that it all started the day he was born.

"I don't know what else to do," Hamama said helplessly to the good doctor. She was ever grateful to him for saving Rachamim's life, and now Asher's life was also in danger.

"To tell you the truth, I don't either. I'm sorry that I have to send you away from here again, but I recommend the Hadassah hospital in Tel Aviv. Asher will be in good hands there. They have better equipment."

The doctor equipped her with all the paperwork, and after she informed Hassan that Miriam would take care of Rachamim, she left for Tel Aviv with her sick son.

Asher didn't make the journey easy, but his loud cries and wild arm movements comforted her. If he cried so loudly and strongly—that must be a sign of health. But when he finally fell asleep, she breathed in relief and looked at the sea that accompanied her along the way. In Tel Aviv, she asked the passersby how to get to a bus station to the hospital, and hurried there for her son's sake, without paying any attention to the lively metropolis she had found herself in.

When she arrived at the hospital, the child was taken from her, and Hamama waited on the bench outside the room. She watched everyone hustle by. The nurses looked busy and serious, and the many sick patients depressed Hamama.

A few hours later, one of the nurses came to Hamama:

"Are you Yona? Asher Vazif's mom?"

"Yes."

"Come with me."

Hamama walked briskly, trying to match the nurse's quick pace. They came to a room, and Hamama stood across a glass wall. On the other side of the wall, beds with babies were organized in an orderly fashion.

"Here he is," the nurse pointed toward Asher.

"Can I hold him?"

"No."

"Breastfeed him?"

"We'll take care of feeding him. You can visit him three times a day."

"Like this? Through a glass wall?"

"Yes, I'm sorry," the nurse said. But she hardly sounded sympathetic.

Hamama stood staring at her ill baby lying on the other side of the wall, unable to get to him. A few minutes later, she went outside for some fresh air. She didn't ask what he had, and no one told her anything. She only knew that he had to stay there, and she couldn't touch him. Her mind raged, and she took off wandering around the city, which was also raging. The cacophony, the mess, the people.

She boarded a bus back to Pardes Hanna.

Hassan saw Hamama's tormented face, and after confirming that the boy was being taken care of, he didn't say another word. His silence didn't help her, and her suffering heart wanted this man, who was immersed in work and fighting, to take his weapon and break the glass wall that separated her from her son. She found some comfort in Rachamim, who grew fast and talked without end. Miriam's sons, Yair and Yoav, would also come by to play, and Hamama could not help but vent to her friend.

"How can I?" Hamama raged at her friend's suggestion she go back. "I can't go there! I need to take three buses just to stand behind a glass wall. Without touching? Without feeding? My heart is broken! I want so badly to be with him, but not like that.

"Hamama—"

"How? Ya Miriam? Tell me, how?"

Her friend stayed silent, and Hamama dragged on with her daily work routine, bearing a grudge against her husband and keeping away from him until he rescued her from her situation.

But salvation came to her from elsewhere. Hamama did some housekeeping work for a nice elderly Ashkenazi lady named Hedva, who also happened to be one of the first settlers with a telephone in her own house. Hedva couldn't help but notice Hamama's grief.

"So? Come here," she said after she heard Hamama's story. "We can call the hospital from my telephone, so you can hear how your little one is doing!"

Hedva called the Hadassah hospital, and asked to speak with the children's division.

"This is the employer of Yona Vazif, Asher Vazif's mother. She wants to know how he's doing." Her voice commanded attention.

Hamama approached the earpiece and heard a woman reporting on her son.

"Asher? He's doing much better, but he needs to stay here a while longer."

"All right, we'll keep calling for updates," Hedva said, partly to the nurse and partly to Hamama.

Hamama was overcome with joy and impulsively hugged her older employer. From then on, she received updates about the child over the phone.

One day the nurse told her, "You should be ashamed for not coming to visit your child. I'll give him a stick when you come, so he can hit you."

"I…I have another child at home and work…" Hamama mumbled.

She didn't know how to react to the criticism handed to her by a total stranger. The voice on the other end of the phone was both playful and threatening, rendering Hamama speechless and tearful. Hedva, who was listening the whole time, grabbed the receiver.

"Mind your own business. We only asked you about the child's wellbeing."

"I'm sorry," the nurse said. "I understand. Don't worry about him. We're taking good care of him here, and he's quite rambunctious."

After the call ended, Hedva looked at Hamama, who was shaking from shame and grief.

"What does she know? Probably not even married." Hedva tried to cheer the girl up.

Hamama thanked her, and that day, left for home earlier than usual.

Hassan was also upset, missing his son terribly, but even more than that he was distraught by his inability to comfort his grieving wife. This time, a surprise under a rock wouldn't suffice. Frustrated, he devoted all his time and energy to fighting the British. He learned as a child to translate agony into missions.

After Asher was hospitalized, Hassan participated in an attack on the train in Hadera. A month later, he helped bomb the British Air Force base in Ein Shemer. Every action was preceded by weeks of organizing and planning, and Hassan, who worked in the orchard all day and fought all night, came home exhausted and thus managed to escape his wife's accusatory stares. After successful attacks on the officer's club and food storage unit in Hadera, the ETZEL activists celebrated their victory together. But Hassan, sitting across from his rejoicing friends, was overcome by such painful loneliness that he left everything and nearly ran to his home.

He entered the room quietly, longing for some comfort, and found Hamama embracing Rachamim, crying in her sleep. His throat burned, but his eyes were unwilling to express his grief. There was no place for him in the little room. There was no place for his pain. Hassan went outside and slept under the stars.

One day, as Hassan cleaned the pits around the orange trees, tired from another night of sleeping outside, he heard the work manager calling his name. There were many reasons one might be summoned, but he preferred to imagine it was Hamama who asked for him, that Hamama wanted to tell him that Asher was back, together with her own love and forgiveness for her husband. He knew it was not his fault the child was sick. He knew she wasn't really mad at him. But he did promise her a land of milk and honey, and he did promise to make her happy.

It wasn't Hamama waiting for him at the work manager's hut, but it was the next best thing.

"My goodness, Hassan! You look like a grown man!"

And you look like an old one, thought Hassan when he saw Sa'adia standing in front of him. Sa'adia's face was scorched by the passing years and its untold sorrows. The two men embraced for a long moment. Sa'adia and Hassan had never been close friends, even though they lived together as brothers for a period of time. But now, in this new land, each found a bit of comfort for his troubled heart in the other's arms.

"Come! Let's get you to your sister!"

Hassan obtained permission from his work manager and walked with Sa'adia in silence toward the small neighborhood. He had many questions but sensed that Sa'adia was in no hurry to talk. Hassan wasn't blind to the many wrinkles and graying hair on the young man walking next to him. He also noticed the absences of Sa'adia's wife and children. He wanted to bring Hamama joy by reuniting her with her brother but was afraid of the bad news borne by this gift.

Hamama's wide smile and the sudden bliss that spread across her face at the sight of her brother finally tore down the dam blocking Hassan's tears, and his tired eyes welled up uncontrollably. He didn't want anybody to see him in such a moment of weakness, so he made an excuse and disappeared behind the house.

"Sa'adia!" Hamama called out happily.

"Hamama!" Her brother returned the merry call and lifted his sister in the air.

"How did you find us? When did you get here? Where are Rivka and Shmuel?"

"Slow down, Hamama. Won't you offer me something to drink first?" Sa'adia laughed.

Rachamim snuggled up to his mother's legs, and Sa'adia picked him up.

"I can't believe you have a child. You're still a baby yourself."

"And another one at the hospital..." Hamama said with sadness, but then stopped when she realized that Sa'adia was standing across from her alone, without his family.

Sa'adia did not speak at first, and when he did his words were barely audible. "Mine passed away in Yemen. The wife and children."

"I'm so sorry," Hamama said.

Sa'adia's tragedy put her own struggles in perspective. She never even got to know his family, and now they were all gone! She hugged her brother and they both wept. It seemed like there weren't enough tears in the world to wash away all their sorrows, but her wise older brother was more adept at quickly shifting from the dead to the living.

"Well? What's this little one's name?" Sa'adia asked.

"Rachamim."

"Sounds about right." Sa'adia smiled and pinched the poor child's cheek. When he let go, the boy was happy to escape from his uncle back to his mother. Hassan came in and invited Sa'adia to sit down.

"I'll go make some coffee," Hamama said to her husband.

Hassan noticed the softness with which she said those words and her loving glance calmed him. He heard Sa'adia's news and saw the two crying and wondered how two broken hearts can mend each other, and why his own wasn't enough for his wife. Then he thought about how he ran outside to cry alone while the two of them wept together. He didn't know if he would ever be able to do that.

The small house felt so warm, so comfortable. *It's good to be in a home*, Sa'adia thought, painfully remembering his house in Aden, wondering how to tell these two what he had suffered.

Hamama handed him a cup of fresh coffee. "What about Rivka and Shmuel?" she asked.

"They're stuck in Aden. Also, Sarah and her husband, and Father and Ahuva, are in the Hashed camp. The gates were shut, and I was one of the last ones to get out."

"What do you mean 'the gates were shut?'" Hassan asked.

"What's the Hashed camp?" Hamama asked.

"There's been a blockade of the Suez Canal because of the war. And now the British are preventing people from crossing."

"And the family?"

"Rivka and Shmuel are fine in Aden. They have work and an apartment. But by the time the others arrived, there was no more room or food, so they opened a camp outside of Aden, the Hashed refugee camp, and that's where they live. The British, those bastards, aren't letting people immigrate any longer."

"And what about livelihood? And food?"

"Donations. Don't ask more questions, Hamama."

"But Father! Father's there!"

"I know. That's why I'm here. I came to fight them, the British bastards, so that we'll be able to establish a Jewish country here."

"You sound like Hassan." Hamama said.

Hamama and Hassan invited Sa'adia to live with them, and Hassan found his brother-in-law work in the orchard the following day. Sa'adia was happy about his new place and was friendly with everyone, avoiding all questions about Yemen. But three nights later, the neighbors lost their patience and gathered in Hamama and Hassan's yard. They all wanted to hear about their relatives who were left behind. Sa'adia was slow to answer, but after filling up on wine, he was more forthcoming, and with great sadness, he started describing the fate of Yemenite Jews these past few years. Hamama was sorry she had listened to him because she couldn't sleep at all that night.

"You're here," her brother had told the group. "You arrived. You made it. Like you, many thousands more Jews tried and succeeded in stealing the border to Aden. Only those British bastards aren't handing out any more permits, aren't letting anyone leave Aden. All these years, more and more Jews are leaving Yemen, coming to Aden, and waiting for salvation. The streets are filled with refugees; families are sleeping under the stars. All the money they brought with them, after selling their possessions to immigrate to the Land of Israel, was spent on food, on a roof. The Jewish community in Aden gave food and donations, and it still wasn't enough. People are turning into skeletons, and children are dying. I'm talking about thousands. Filling the streets, feces and urine and vomit. It didn't take much until the plagues started."

Sa'adia quieted down momentarily, and then sighed. When he saw their watery eyes reflecting their painful concern for the relatives back in Yemen, he continued.

"Then the emissaries from the Joint and the Jewish Agency came and opened the Hashed camp—which they actually called Redemption Camp—outside of Aden. They organized the refugees in little sheds and tents and provided medical aid for the sick and food and clothes for the needy. As much as they helped, more Jews kept on coming. Even the Imam came out with a statement for the Jews, urging them to return home and promising that they would get their possessions back. And some of those who had suffered so much did lose their spirit and returned to Yemen. The rest are waiting."

The pioneers of the Rambam neighborhood sat in shock and dismay. Each and every one of them had some family there. The fear for their relatives and the worry about their wellbeing was part of their daily bread, and as Sa'adia talked, loud sighs were heard all around, and those who stayed silent—their hearts broke silently. They all felt the grief and responsibility for their brothers. Sa'adia spoke again:

"I lost my wife and child in Aden. How many more need to die before they open the gates? I came to fight them. The British. To save our families!"

A number of men supported the slightly swaying man with tears in his eyes.

"We're already working on it, ya Sa'adia," Damari said.

The next day Hassan took Sa'adia to an ETZEL meeting. Sa'adia immersed himself in actions against the British leadership, which was seen as responsible for the condition of Yemenite Jews. And looking at her brother, Hamama, found herself fully on the side of the struggle against the British. If not actively, she now at least gave her full support to Hassan and Sa'adia. And Miriam.

"We received a letter, Hamama," Hassan announced one evening. Hamama hurried toward him.

"A letter from the hospital," he said. He opened the letter and read quietly.

"Well?" Hamama asked impatiently.

"He's back to full health. We can come take him!" Hassan smiled.

Hamama jumped for joy and hugged the man she loved to be angry at all the time. Sa'adia clapped happily. And Rachamim, even though he didn't understand a thing, quickly joined and partook in the sudden outburst of excitement. His brother was returning home.

The next morning, Hamama boarded a bus and left for the hospital, then hopped on another bus, then another. When she finally arrived at the children's division, a nurse led her to one of the rooms.

"Here he is," the nurse said.

Hamama looked at all the children in the room and failed to recognize her son amongst them.

"Well? Won't you pick him up?" the nurse asked and looked at Hamama.

Hamama broke down in tears:

"I don't know which one is my son."

"That's all right," the nurse said kindly. "Three months is a long time in a baby's life. Here, this is him, the rowdiest one of the bunch."

The nurse lifted Asher and handed him to Hamama. Hamama looked at the chubby, light-skinned boy who stared back at her curiously. A moment later, she hugged him tightly and started crying again.

"All right, that's enough, that's enough. You don't want to scare the boy," the nurse said and handed her a tissue.

Hamama packed the few belongings the baby had received from the hospital and left for home. Her heart was filled with joy, and she couldn't wait to show the boy to Hassan. She held him tightly when he napped during the ride, alternating her gaze between the sea and his peaceful face. Hassan and Rachamim waited impatiently for their return, but when Hamama handed the boy to Hassan, he immediately said, "That's not our baby."

Hamama didn't hesitate for a second. "That's what they gave us so that's what we got."

The two were suspicious of the boy's light skin, but when they noticed that he grew darker and more tanned the longer he spent time outside, they realized that the paleness was a result only of his hospitalization where he had been always indoors.

But soon, the community would face renewed threats. After the ETZEL's attack on the military base near Hadera and the taking over of its food pantry, the British soldiers began rummaging through Jewish homes in search of clues. They came up with very little, so they randomly arrested men to be interrogated. One of them was Sa'adia.

"Give us names!"

"I'm Sa'adia. That's my name."

"Give us the names of your friends!" the British officer snapped back.

"I don't have any friends. I'm a new immigrant," Sa'adia answered with an innocent expression.

The officer left, and the commander came in. Sa'adia recognized him from the photos in the ETZEL meetings as one of their main targets. The commander was sent to the military base in Hadera after McNab was murdered, and only waited for an excuse to take his revenge on the fighters.

A shudder spread through Sa'adia's bones at the sight of the commander's grim smile.

"Do you recognize me?" the commander asked as he pulled closer.

"I'm a new immigrant from Yemen," Sa'adia answered.

"I heard they have those in the ETZEL, too."

"I'm a new immigrant."

"And I'm an old one. And a tired one. Give me names, or we'll have to do this the hard way."

"I'm a new immigrant," Sa'adia answered a moment before his lip was torn open, his cheek turned a dark red, and his eye was swollen shut.

"And now?"

"I'm a new immigrant," he mumbled and spit a tooth out of his bleeding mouth.

Sa'adia's body was thrown on the ground, freezing water was thrown in his face, and his ribs were broken.

When Hamama received her beaten brother back to her care, she banished for good the image of the young and sad British soldier from Toledano's store who had garnered her sympathy. The British were now the enemy.

Hamama examined her brother's wounds while the doctor removed the meager bandages the British police had wrapped around him.

"You have to take him to the hospital, Hamama," the doctor said. "He has a few broken ribs, and we need to see if there's any internal bleeding."

"He's spitting up blood," Hamama said as she passed a sympathetic arm across his forehead. It hadn't been too long ago that he had teased her and stolen yams, and now he was lying there half dead, blood covering his clothes and body.

"I can take him," said the nurse who had accompanied the doctor. She saw Hamama's small children and patted her shoulders.

Hamama looked at the short nurse with a Moroccan accent who was so generous and smiled. "What's your name?" she asked.

"Penina," she answered.

"Thank you, Penina."

"It's my pleasure."

Hamama let the doctor and nurse take her brother to the car, where she said good-bye. He had just arrived, the rest of her family was far away, and now he was being taken away from her again? And who knew if he would ever return?

Hassan tried to be around more often. He may not have been able to cry with Hamama or talk about how he felt, but he could do other things. So, he planted a vegetable garden around the house, and bought her two goats. Hamama was pregnant again, and the new work in the garden made her feel stronger, yet more relaxed. She taught Rachamim to care for the garden, and both struggled to prevent Asher from getting trampled by the goats. She managed to distract herself from the bloody battles surrounding her as she immersed herself in the yard she and Hassan had fashioned after a Yemenite village.

Hamama kept calling to check on Sa'adia from her employer's phone and was surprised to hear that Penina, the nurse, was still taking care of him. She and Penina started talking often and getting to know one another, and so she was delighted to learn that the two decided to get married. A month after he was admitted to the hospital, Sa'adia came back whole, healthy, and ready to start a new life.

After a small but happy wedding ceremony, Sa'adia moved in with Penina to a newly built room behind the Noam School, a high school yeshiva that had just been completed.

The school was so close to Hamama's house that she heard the students' prayers every morning. She enjoyed the Ashkenazi style of prayer, and occasionally, when she walked over to Penina's, she would linger by the school, picking some flowers and listening with enjoyment to boys singing together in harmony and infusing her surroundings with holiness.

Penina also loved to visit Hamama, who had welcomed her to the family and the neighborhood with love despite, her Moroccan origins.

The growing family of pioneers comforted Hamama over her distress about the missing part of the family still stuck in Yemen.

On the twenty-ninth of November 1947, the United Nations approved a plan to separate the British Mandate of Palestine into two states, one Jewish and one Arab. As part of this plan, Jerusalem would be under international control. The United Nations Partition Plan for Palestine, or United Nations General Assembly Resolution 181, was not successful in creating two states—the Arab world strongly rejected it and fighting between Jews and Arabs began almost immediately after the resolution's passage. Nonetheless, it was a jubilant moment for Palestine's Jews.

Or at least for most of them.

Hamama and Penina were sitting in the yard together, separating leaves of coriander from their stems and discussing the differences between *s'hug* and *harissa*, a Maghrebi hot chili pepper paste, when Miriam ran, panting, into Hamama's yard.

"Hamama! Hamama!" Miriam cried. "The British are leaving!"

"Now?" Hamama said in amazement.

"No. In half a year. But that's it, they decided. They're leaving."

"How do you know?" Penina asked.

"From the radio at my Ashkenazi woman's house," Miriam panted.

"And you just ran off like that in the middle of work?" Hamama laughed.

"How can you be so indifferent? Aren't you glad?"

"I'm glad," sighed Hamama. "But I'll believe it when I see it."

Miriam returned to work, disappointed by the lack of enthusiasm and slightly fearing her employer's reaction upon her return. Hamama and Penina were left behind, going back to their small talk, but each thinking about their husbands and the actions in which they were going to participate.

"It's a girl!" the midwife called out.

Hamama breathed a sigh of relief. She had wanted a girl. She already had two boys, and she thought maybe were easier to raise. The dark, hairy baby shrieked, and Asher and Rachamim burst into the room to see their baby sister.

"Get out!" the midwife yelled as she covered Hamama.

The midwife pushed the two out, and they both ran to their father, who was just returning from the orchard. Asher, who had only recently learned to walk, fell a few times, but quickly caught up to his brother with scratched, dusty knees.

"It's a girl!" Rachamim cried.

"Ga." Asher attempted to mimic his brother's words.

Hassan happily tossed Asher in the air and hugged Rachamim. The three returned to the house, this time waiting for the midwife's permission before entering.

The appearance of little Kokhava in the family changed Hassan. Up until then, he took pleasure in his young boys after work and on Shabbat, and their playfulness amused him and lifted his spirits. But the little baby girl who liked to be comforted in his arms awoke something inside of him. He felt more vulnerable than ever, as if his thick skin had eroded, and he could feel her and everything around him more purely. As the ETZEL's activities nearly ceased following the British announcement of withdrawal, the father and daughter grew closer. Hassan built Kokhava a crib, along with several new wooden toys for her brothers. While Hamama had appreciated Hassan's work in the yard and his efforts to be more present in her life, seeing him assemble and design again brought tears to her eyes. It hadn't been so long ago that he had made various toys for her when they had run barefoot on Yemenite soil.

Thinking of her distant childhood and the family that is no longer with her, Hamama couldn't help but feel melancholy and nostalgic. Even during the most joyous moments, she never forgot Rivka and Shmuel and everything they had done for her. She wondered how Shoshana looked now, and if they were well. She longed for her sister's warm embrace. She thought about their parting moments in Aden, their too-brief goodbye, and how they tried to hold themselves together to avoid falling apart. And then she remembered how tightly they held each other the day the Arab returned her home safely, after her foolish attempt at running away from El Be'aden. She was a stupid selfish child, but her sister loved her unconditionally.

Nearly every night, Hamama, Hassan, and the children dined with Sa'adia and Penina. Hamama's and Sa'adia's eyes would meet, and each saw his own worries reflected in the other's gaze.

The British base in Pardes Hanna, Base 80, was never approached by the ETZEL because of its proximity to the town. The soldiers on the base knew the residents and met them in the grocery stores, in the orchards, and in the synagogues whenever some conflict arose in the neighborhoods. The ETZEL leaders also avoided any action because they were worried about acts of revenge on the settlers. But after the United Nations Partition Plan for Palestine, the different Jewish leaders felt the urgency to prepare and arm themselves. Soon the Jews of Palestine would be left alone with the Arab forces in a battle for the land. The need to gear up grew more pressing, and so even dangerous actions like attacking Base 80 became an option. The ETZEL still refused to use the group of Yemenite immigrants from Pardes Hanna, and so the latter heard the tale of the attack only much later.

The story they heard was that fifty ETZEL fighters prepared for the action at Base 80. Every one of them a hero, every one without flaw, all wearing the uniform of the British army. At their head, stood the ETZEL commander, Menachem Begin. Begin was the most wanted ETZEL fighter—his pictures were spread out on every British command table—and still the British failed to recognize the man who stood before them. The fake soldiers split up, some going to the supply storage units and others planting bombs throughout the base. Begin himself entered the office of the base's commander to update him on various issues, and then he shoved a note in his pocket that read, "The man with whom you just spoke is Menachem Begin." Begin left, and the commander ran after him with fright. But then the sounds of explosions all over the base ripped through the silence. All the ETZEL fighters boarded trucks carrying weapons and ammunition and escaped from the base, leaving chaos behind them. The remaining British soldiers were so afraid, they boarded the trucks that were left and fled the burning base.

The Yemenite residents cheered excitedly as they heard this story. It was long after they survived the anticipated act of revenge.

"Hassan? What are you doing?" Hamama asked in fright as Hassan burst into the house and started throwing clothes around.

"We have to destroy evidence," he mumbled.

Hamama led the children outside, carrying the baby. Hassan ran out with a British uniform, a pistol, and ammunition. Hamama followed him running off in the distance. Together with some other men,

Hassan buried all the equipment near the Noam School. He then ran back to Hamama, holding on to their immigration certificates and their children's birth certificates. He glanced at her briefly, standing in fright, holding his children.

"We'll get through this, and it'll all be over," he said.

"Hassan! You're scaring me."

"The British will come, and they're going to flip everything over. You're all coming with me to the amphitheater."

Hamama, Hassan, and their children started marching with the rest of the neighbors and their families to the safe old building. The boys and rabbis from the Noam school marched with them, helping families carry their young children. People flowed into the building and waited to proceed underground. Rachamim hugged Asher, and suddenly Hamama grew anxious about what she would feed Kokhava. Throughout the evacuation she hadn't thought about food at all, but now, seeing all these people—all these children—she wondered how long they would be kept away from their homes.

"Residents of Pardes Hanna, we've come to the moment of truth," Eliahu announced on the amphitheater stage. "They're coming for us, and they're angry. Be brave. If they ask you to show identification, show it to them from afar and don't give it to them. They're bound to confiscate it, and then arrest you."

"But they can't do that! It's illegal!" Ben Tzion interrupted.

"Right now, they're not thinking about the law. They're thinking of revenge. The fighters and I will try to draw fire in a different direction, and you'll wait here and be brave!"

"Long live the ETZEL!" called the men, Hassan amongst them.

Eliahu and his men left the amphitheater, and Hamama drew close to Hassan in fear. As long as Kokhava was asleep, she didn't have to worry, she tried to comfort herself. *It'll be over quickly*, she thought. But she did not know what would happen.

It started off with a silent, nerve-wracking wait. And then the shooting started.

"The fighters are drawing fire in a different direction," somebody said.

The residents remained quiet. The boys from the yeshiva read Psalms. And then a burning stench permeated the air. The men quickly climbed the walls of the building to peek outside.

"Hassan! Your house is on fire!" one of the men said.

Hamama's heart sank. She hoped that they had released the goats. *How could I not release the goats?*

Kokhava woke up and started crying. She was hungry. Asher tried to make her laugh, and Rachamim tried to sing to her, but to no avail. Her cries infected the other babies and a depressing choir threatened the residents' sanity almost as much as the burning of their houses.

"I'll go get them food from the village center," Hassan said, eager to run off.

"You're not going anywhere!" Hamama cried.

"It's in the other direction!" Hassan insisted, and before Hamama could object, he took off running.

A few minutes later, Hassan returned with some bananas that he handed out to the kids, but Kokhava was too young to eat the fruit and kept on screaming loudly. Hassan looked at his little daughter, and her cries scathed his heart. He took advantage of a moment in which Hamama helped Asher eat, and once again ran outside, this time toward the houses.

He hopped between the trees and bushes, up toward the old tent hill. From there he continued on, always on the lookout. The sounds of guns were further away, and he didn't encounter a soul. When he arrived in his neighborhood, he saw that the smoke came from the Noam School rather than the houses. In his yard, the two goats were crying in fear.

Hassan petted them a bit, snuck onto his knees and climbed in through the window. The smell of burning tickled his nostrils as he stood helpless in the corner of the little kitchen.

I made it here. Now what? He chose a pot that he knew was dairy and mixed a bit of corn flour with milk on the fire, constantly checking to see if someone was approaching. When he finished, he wrapped the pot in some towels that he found and hopped outside again, finding his way back to the amphitheater. Hamama was waiting for him, in utter shock.

"*Ya majnun!* You're crazy! The girl should die, not you!" she yelled at him in anger.

Hassan sat down next to the baby and started feeding her calmly, waiting for Hamama to stop yelling. When she calmed down, helpless in the face of a father's love for his daughter, he looked at her lovingly:

"Our house didn't burn, and the goats are fine."

Hamama refused to talk to him that whole long, exhausting day, until Eliahu showed up. All the residents of Pardes Hanna, as well as the rabbis and their students from Noam School, stood in silence and looked at the tired leader whose arms were covered with bandages. Sweat, blood, and dirt didn't cover the smile on his face when he announced that they could all return home. Hamama sighed with relief and squeezed Hassan's hand.

A month later, on May 14, 1948, Ben Gurion announced the establishment of a Jewish state in the Land of Israel. The yeshiva students broke out in song and danced together with the residents and their children. The men slaughtered three sheep and the celebrations could be heard from afar. The war intensified as Syria, Lebanon, Jordan, Egypt and Saudi Arabia joined the Palestinian forces against Israel, but the small Jewish country fought with all its might and won.

In Yemen, news of the establishment of a Jewish state in the land of Israel was met with mixed feelings. While Yemenite Jews were overcome by joy and saw this event as the beginning of the *geula*, the anticipated salvation, they also grew more fearful for their personal safety. The 1947 UN Partition Plan led to pogroms against the Jews of Aden and of Sheikh Othman, and the fear of additional hostilities further compelled the Jews to leave. Driven by the civil war that broke out after the assassination of Imam Yahya and the blood libel of which the Jews of Sana'a were accused, along with the severe drought, the lack of personal and economic security, and the promise of a state of their own, many Jews throughout Yemen sold their property and left for Israel.

They marched on foot for days. The journey was arduous, and they were frequently robbed by bandits and forced to bribe anyone who promised safe passage to the gate from which they could leave for Israel.

They arrived at Hashed camp, drained and exhausted, where they joined tens of thousands of other Jews waiting for an airlift organized by the state of Israel and the Joint (The American Jewish Joint Distribution Committee). Their situation was dire; terrible overcrowding, a blazing sun, and water shortages rendered the refugees weak and lethargic. The camp, which was built to accommodate 1,000 residents, at times housed over 12,000. The medical team that came from Israel treated eye diseases and tried to help the refugees, but there were also those who exploited the immigrants and treated them with cruelty.

The new state of Israel, which planned to absorb the Jews of Yemen at a moderate and gradual pace after dealing with their contagious diseases, was forced to change its approach when it heard of the distress of the masses of immigrants filling the refugee camp. The famous "Operation on the Wings of Eagles," the impressive airlift of 50,000 Yemenite in one year, became a rescue mission. And although praise of the operation reached mythological proportions in the public consciousness, the suffering of the immigrants and the hundreds of casualties were eventually forgotten.

2008

"Well, Grandma, since I'm already filming you, maybe it's a good idea for you to give me a recipe now."

We laugh. Whenever I call from Tel Aviv and ask her through the phone to tell me how to make something, such as steamed vegetables, jachnun, kubaneh, she explains what I need and demonstrates with her hands:

"A little bit of this and a little bit of that, to your taste."

"Grandma, I can't see you over the phone!"

Now, while I'm filming them in Pardes Hanna, my baby crawls toward Grandpa and chews his shoes. He smiles at her and makes funny noises. She leans back and smiles. Here she is, only a few months old, and already she manages to connect with him, something I haven't succeeded at lately. Grandma interrupts my thoughts.

"Fine. What do you want to know?"

"Your jachnun!"

"Well…that you have to come and make with me sometime."

"Sure. And who will watch over my little one?"

"Your mom, who else?"

"Eh…at least give me the recipe in the meantime, and later I'll come and make it with you."

"If I tell you, you won't come."

"I'll come!"

Of course, I didn't come. The first time I made the jachnun, I was already in New York, and it wasn't baked enough. My Swiss in-laws were very polite and ate the warm, unbaked dough, despite my protests to throw away my failed experiment.

Grandma stretches, makes sure that Grandpa and the baby are getting along, and I turn on the camera.

Grandma's jachnun

1 kg Osem flour (that's the blue and white one)

1 tsp baking powder

A little bit of salt, and little bit of sugar. ("Grandma! How much is 'a little bit?'" "Your mom measured it for you: a little bit of salt = 1 TBSP, a little bit of sugar = 5 TBSP")

3 cups water

250 grams soft margarine (don't heat it up!)

Make dough out of all the ingredients—except for the margarine. Leave it on the side.

Knead thoroughly. The dough has to be not too soft and not too thick. Leave it to rest half an hour, and twice during the half hour pass an oiled hand around it.

After half an hour, divide the dough into ten balls and leave them for another half an hour.

Prepare an oiled work platform with a bowl of the soft margarine on the side.

Take a ball of dough and stretch it really well, in the shape of a square or rectangle, on the oiled platform. Generously spread margarine on it. Fold the square in half, so that it becomes an elongated rectangle. Stretch and roll, stretch and roll, like you would fold tights (or a sleeping bag, for you).

Do this with all the balls and put the jachnuns in a baking dish with a baking sheet. Bake half an hour on high heat. ("Grandma! How many degrees?" "Let's say 200 Celsius or 350 degrees Fahrenheit.") After that, you have to organize the jachnuns in an oiled pot. Like this, one next to the other. Cover it with a paper towel, and then aluminum foil. Now put it on the hotplate on Friday, and let it stay there until the following morning. Every once in a while, check it, but don't wait until noon the next day, otherwise it'll dry out.

CHAPTER 8

As the War of Independence came to a close, the country, and especially the immigrants' camps, were filled with chaos. Hamama didn't sense much of it in her little home in Pardes Hanna, until the start of austerity.

When she came to the new grocery store one morning, she was surprised to see a large sign on one of the doors. She still hadn't gotten used to the grocer's Romanian accent and wondered if the writing on the sign was in Romanian or Hebrew.

"What's this?" she asked him.

"That's it," the grocer said. "They've all gone crazy. I have to hand out food according to what it says there. And with no money. You have to bring coupons."

Hamama didn't understand. The grocer, chubby with a red face, came out from behind the counter excitedly and pointed at the sign.

"Here: Milk powder. Egg powder. Margarine. It tells me here how much I can give each person, and the rest with coupons."

"What coupons?" Hamama asked.

"There's a meeting tonight. They'll probably hand out the coupons. Every coupon will give you meat, or coffee.

Hamama looked at the grocer in disbelief.

"But let's ignore it for now. I still have some merchandise here from before they brought the boxes with all their powders. Come, buy. Today's the last day. After this, it's all coupons."

Hamama bought all the legumes she could afford. *Tough days are upon us.* She left the store and hurried to Miriam to update her.

"Yes. Ben Tzion already told me about the meeting." Miriam sighed.

"Quickly, go buy while there's still something to buy," Hamama said.

"He's still selling?" Miriam was surprised.

"Apparently."

Miriam quickly jumped up from her seat, grabbed her wallet, and ran to the store. A few minutes later, she was back.

"I was too late. There were so many women there, rummaging through the store! The only thing I managed to grab was a bag of flour."

"Oh no!" Hamama said.

"And the poor grocer looked so depressed. He was just staring at his empty shelves, talking to himself. Something about the store being reduced to a mere government office."

All the food stores changed. The opening hours were adjusted to fit the times the merchandise arrived, and long lines crept from the stores' doors all the way down the town's main road. The grocer, the greengrocer, and the butcher sold their merchandise only according to the government's instructions, depending on the size of the family. Hamama quickly learned how to handle the coupons, and the decreased availability of food stressed her, but not terribly so. After all, she had grown up in poverty.

She would prepare green-yellow lentil soup, rich and thick, whose smell would whet her children's appetites; and a small bowl of it could leave even Hassan content. She would also add corn flour to various dishes to thicken them, so that they would fill her family. Hassan often praised her for this, and although she didn't think it was something out of the ordinary, she loved the way he smiled at her, pleased and proud.

In addition to the stores that operated under the guidelines of the government, there was also a black market. In Pardes Hanna, most prominent was the Arab egg merchant who would come with his cart and who would practically be attacked by all the women. Hamama wasn't used to all the physical jostling amongst women and would usually leave with only three or four eggs. She was always amazed that despite the battling, the women managed to never break a single egg.

Hamama found another source of food with one of her employers, who was called "the soldiers' mother." She would always leave her a quince and some raisins meant for the children. This woman was older, and every morning an army jeep would pick her up and take her to cook for the Jewish soldiers, who were now stationed at the rebuilt formerly British Base 80. Everything the soldiers left behind, and that couldn't be kept for the next day, she would collect and bring to those in need in the town. Hamama was ashamed to take anything from her until one morning the lady stayed behind to speak to Hamama as her jeep honked for her.

"Look, I'm late because of you," she chastised Hamama. "Why don't you take the food I prepare for you?" she asked Hamama. "You have children. Give to them! I eat with the soldiers and also get coupons. It is too much for me alone. What am I going to do with all the food?"

From that day on, Hamama was no longer ashamed and would take the various foods that her employer left her, but she made a habit of leaving her door open and handed out food to hungry passersby. Her days were busy with housekeeping at Hedva's and the soldiers' mother's, and every afternoon, she worked for three hours with a large crew at a geriatric center.

Hassan also switched jobs and started to work at a plywood factory in Kibbutz Mishmarot, adjacent to Pardes Hanna. In the beginning, he would leave on foot early each morning. The journey to the factory took over an hour, and Hassan led an early prayer and learned his daily Torah portion at the synagogue. There were many men who left for work early, and the family breakfast turned into a quick coffee for the parents, while the kids still slept. Hamama packed meals for Hassan, as the kibbutz—most of whose residents had emigrated from Russia and did not keep kosher. Two of the factory's founders were actually grandchildren of a great rabbi, and Hassan couldn't understand what had happened to the tradition that was always his guiding principle. In time, he grew to know the people with whom he worked side by side. Their stories of fighting in the Jewish Brigade in the British army, helping the Ma'afilim—the illegal Jewish immigrants—and the secret weapons industry led by the Haganah found their way into Hassan's heart, and his appreciation for them grew, even though he continued to maintain a tough demeanor toward them. As a veteran ETZEL fighter, he reminded them of the Haganah's atrocities, and he also criticized them for not being religiously observant. The arguments during work didn't detract from their fondness of him and his appreciation of them. Although his salary as an "outside worker" was lower than theirs, he enjoyed coming to work and building furniture and roofs for sheds with his own hands. He finally felt like he was building the Land of Israel.

"What are you doing?" Hamama asked him one afternoon when she saw him gather wooden planks behind the house, while Rachamim and Asher fussed around him.

"Building a shed."

"What do you need a shed for?"

"My workshop."

Hamama smiled. After years of acclimation and survival, of struggles and births, Hassan would finally find his craft. And indeed, Hassan didn't waste any time. Every day after work he came home, built the workshop and acquired tools. Then he started assembling and building ovens and furniture to enrich his house. Together with some workers from the Kibbutz, he found various parts and built himself a bicycle, which shortened the time it took him to get to work.

Rachamim and Asher would run after the bicycle, but one Friday, Hassan locked himself in the workshop for many hours, and wouldn't let them in. The two left to bother their little sister until they heard his call, and then they ran to the shed.

Hassan appeared on his bicycle and connected to its rear was a wagon with a screen in which the two could sit.

"Do you need anything from town?" Hassan called from outside, and without waiting for an answer, he took off, his sons accompanying him with shrieks of excitement from the wagon in the rear.

In light of the food shortages, Hassan started to expand the vegetable garden, and slowly turned the backyard into a blossoming garden. He bought seeds and fruit trees and planted pecan trees and persimmons, and soon, peaches and pomegranates, then mango and guava, sweetsop and various citrus trees. Rachamim and Asher helped their father as much as they could, and after several years of work, Hassan and Hamama's house turned into the healthy, Yemenite version of the candy house *Hansel and Gretel*. All the neighborhood kids liked hanging out in the backyard, filling their bellies with fresh fruit.

Hassan never chased them off. He imagined that they were human scarecrows that would scare the birds away with the noise they made. Or maybe it was just that the skinny children indeed resembled scarecrows. Certainly, the noise they made practically scared him away from the house.

Hamama enjoyed her flourishing garden most of all. She loved the smell of freshly picked fruits and the rich flavors the herbs added to her cooking. She treasured the idea that her mother would have been delighted by this colorful haven. But most of all she felt this garden was their own piece of land in Israel, a genuine way to put roots down.

"Rivka and Shmuel have arrived along with Sarah and her husband!" Hassan shouted as he waved a postcard with a few words on it in front of Hamama's eyes.

The immigration of Yemenite Jewry, which came to be called Operation on Wings of Eagles—officially Operation Magic Carpet— was in full swing, and Hamama was in suspense waiting to hear news of her family. Every week a different person from the neighborhood would happily report that his family finally had arrived, and Hamama could no longer sleep and eat because of the suspense and frustration. When Hassan waved the postcard in front of her with a huge smile on his face, her heart nearly exploded from joy.

"Finally! What about that? Did they write something?" She grabbed the postcard, examining it with love despite her inability to decipher the writing.

"Only that they're in Atlit. They'll come visit after the assignments next week. Everybody is feeling fine."

"Mother! Asher took all my sticks!" Rachamim pulled at her dress.

"And there aren't enough sticks in the yard?" But Hamama was distracted. The upcoming family reunion excited her, but many questions filled her head. At night, when Hassan was already in deep sleep, she still lay with eyes open and a wide smile.

Hamama looked at the view through the windows of the bus. She had learned to despise the sands on the road to Tel Aviv. They reminded her of her baby boy and the large glass wall. She instead shifted her gaze toward her family. Hassan studied Torah, and Kokhava lay sleeping in his arms. Every five minutes she looked back, to make sure Rachamim and Asher were behaving nicely. Asher was almost two years younger, but somehow managed to drag his older brother down a bad path. The family had already received two complaints about the noise the two brothers made.

But this did not bother Hamama today. Today, they were traveling to Tel Aviv to spend Shabbat with Rivka and Shmuel.

Their first meeting had been filled with great excitement and confusion, part of the arrival in a new land. Hamama tried to find out from her sisters everything they had undergone, but they were too busy being astounded by her children. The need to summarize several years in three hours was unbearable, and as they left, Hamama felt something was missing.

But on this visit, they'd be able to spend the whole Shabbat together, and would be able to enjoy each other's company without being rushed. Through the housing lottery, Sarah and her family were sent to the town of Rosh Ha'ayin. Hamama had never heard of it until their assignment. Rivka and Shmuel were sent to Kfar Shalem, an immigrant neighborhood on the outskirts of Tel Aviv.

"Hamama! Hassan! Welcome!" Rivka hurried toward them.

The boys fussed around Hamama's legs. They weren't yet accustomed to their short, gaunt aunt.

"Rivka! I still need to get used to seeing you here! I'm so happy!"

Hamama hugged her older sister until she saw a gorgeous young girl run towards them.

"Hamama!"

Hamama ran to the girl. "Shoshana!"

"I can't believe how big you got. I want to hear all about your adventures in Aden!"

Shoshana giggled and turned to gather Kokhava, who had just woken up, to her bosom, and led the boys to play with her younger brothers. Rivka had given birth to three boys in Aden, all of them strong and resilient, a living memorial to the two poor twins who were left behind.

"She is very good with small children. Like you were," said Rivka.

"I still am!" laughed Hamama.

Shmuel came out to them and gathered their belongings. Hamama had already noticed during their previous meeting that despite his young age, Shmuel's hair had grayed, and wrinkles of worry had appeared on his face. Her heart contracted with grief, but she smiled at him lovingly.

Hassan and Shmuel embraced warmly.

"I'm still not used to seeing you as such a man." Shmuel squeezed Hassan's shoulder.

"Time passes," Hassan replied, embarrassed. Next to Shmuel he still felt like a child.

Sarah also came outside, with her large belly.

"Sarah?" Hamama was surprised to see her sister. "You still haven't given birth? When you were at our place a couple of weeks ago, it already looked like the end. Where are your husband and children?"

"I left them in Rosh Ha'ayin. I told them, 'I'd like a bit of quiet before the next baby.'"

The group went inside.

"Thank God, this is a lovely home," Sarah said to Hamama. "Where we live, everybody's still in tents. If I had known it was this nice here, I would have visited sooner!"

"We also lived in tents for three years, until they built us houses," Hamama explained.

"Well, Rivka here already has a house, so I guess you have to know where to go, eh?" Sarah sharply replied.

Rivka twisted her face angrily behind Sarah's back. When the latter went to the bathroom, she turned to Hamama:

"She's driving me crazy with her evil eye. I already put garlic all over the house and hung a *hamsa*[1] in the yard."

Hamama laughed at the sight of her worried sister and followed her to the kitchen.

"Don't get me wrong," Rivka said. "I love this house, but I'm scared to death because there are evil spirits here from the war."

"Come on, Rivka, there are no evil spirits in Israel."

"Say what you want, but when we moved here, there were still tools and pictures from the previous family who lived here. Sarah is crying about the tents, but sometimes I feel like I'd prefer to start over and not inherit an Arab family's house."

"What do you mean 'an Arab family's house?'"

---

[1]The *hamsa*, the five fingers of the hand, is believed by some, predominantly Jews, Christians, and Muslims, to provide defense against the evil eye.

"The houses in this neighborhood have been here for a long time. During the war, Arab families ran away out of fear, since the Jews won, and now we live here."

Hamama was stunned. She hadn't known that Jews were living in Arabs' old homes. She hesitated. "O.K...but still, you don't want to live in the tents."

Hamama told her sister about the female snake that visited them in Hassan's tool chest, laughing at her sister's horror. Finally, the two began to prepare the kubaneh for Shabbat.

Hamama found the family meal pleasant, and it reminded her of days long gone. The sounds of children's laughter mixed in with the adults' conversation, and they enjoyed the traditional meal that Rivka had prepared with her own trusty hands. Hamama smiled at the sight of Shoshana, who ruled over all the little ones, and wondered when the girl she'd helped raise grow so mature.

After they put the kids down to sleep, they all sat around the table and enjoyed the *j'ala*. Sarah swayed uncomfortably from side to side because of her large belly, and Rivka helped her out with a few pillows.

"Well, Hassan, now—when you're already in Israel—what stories do you tell on Friday night?" Shmuel asked with a smile.

"Me?" Hassan asked. "I tell the kids about the childhood in Yemen."

"He likes telling them about ghosts and evil spirits. After he told them about the *makhva*, Rachamim didn't sleep all night." Hamama laughed.

"It's a shame Penina and Sa'adia couldn't make it," Sarah said.

"Yes. Sa'adia wasn't feeling well," Hamama answered, thinking Sarah wanted to join forces with her old companion, but alas, Sa'adia was much different now.

"How are Miriam and Ben Tzion?" Rivka asked.

"They're fine, thank God. Two boys. Yair And Yoav."

"Send her my regards," Rivka said.

Hassan opened a Torah book and started learning the weekly portion with Shmuel, while the women kept on chatting.

Late at night, when the stars outside were the only source of light in the house, Hamama woke up to some noise. She thought maybe one of the children had to go to the bathroom and had forgotten his way around the unfamiliar house, but when she opened her eyes, she saw a figure moving around the house, holding a benzene flashlight.

For a moment, she thought that an Arab evil spirit was wandering about. But then, the short, skinny figure resembled her Rivka. *Why is my sister walking around with fire on Shabbat?* She quickly got up, put on her gown, and followed.

"Hamama! You scared me!" Rivka jumped back.

"You're the one who scared me! What are you doing with a flashlight on Shabbat?"

"It's Sarah. Come."

Hamama hurried after Rivka to the kitchen and saw her sister sitting on the floor, her face covered with sweat, holding her stomach in pain.

"I don't know what to do!" Rivka said with alarm.

Hamama understood her sister, who had taken care of their mother when she was on her deathbed. She was brave and wise, but after losing her two boys and mother-in-law in Ra'ida, she was overwhelmed by fear that something terrible might happen. Hamama took charge.

"Go get me scissors, string, and a needle," Hamama ordered Rivka. She helped a shivering Sarah lie down and looked into her eyes:

"Don't hold him in. If the baby wants to come out—let him."

"Do you know what you're doing?" Sarah asked fearfully.

"Yes."

"You won't take advantage and take revenge on me?"

Hamama laughed at her sister's fears. The two were never particularly close and fought for most of their childhood. Hamama remembered how mad and hurt she was by her sister's teasing and mean tricks, by how Sarah and Sa'adia excluded her from their games. But never in her life had she sought revenge. Even the thought of it alone seemed ridiculous.

"That's you. Not me. Luckily, the situation is reversed here."

Sarah smiled weakly, as if proud of her sister's retort, and lay down on the ground, breathing heavily. Hamama spread out the clean towels that Rivka had brought earlier, and Sarah could barely lift her behind so that Hamama could get the towels under her.

"I can't anymore. I have to get him out," Sarah mumbled. She breathed deeply a few times, started to push, and a baby's head, covered with white vernix, started to emerge.

"Here's the head!" Hamama announced as she wiped her hands from washing. She hadn't even finished preparing, and the baby was almost out! Rivka appeared from behind her holding scissors and a bag of sewing supplies.

"Hamama!" Rivka screamed.

The baby's head was blue.

"Why isn't he crying?" Sarah panicked.

"Just push him out," Hamama said as she quickly worked to untangle the umbilical cord that was wrapped around the baby's neck.

Hamama lifted the baby to help it breathe and saw that it was a girl. After the air entered the baby's small lungs, she started to scream loudly. Sarah sighed with relief, and Rivka stood frozen with the fear that held her.

"Everything is all right, big sister," Sarah said to Rivka as she worked to push out the placenta.

"What will you name her?" Hamama asked her while wiping and wrapping the tiny creature who had just come into the world.

"Yamima."

"After Mother's cow?" Hamama said with surprise.

"She doesn't have to know that," Sarah said, a slight grin on her lips.

"She should at least know I saved her life," Hamama said and handed the baby to Sarah.

"I'll think about it," Sarah said and gently hugged little Yamima.

Sarah wasn't very fond of their late mother's cow, but Hamama guessed it was something to hold on to, a memory of their mother and her favorite cow. Sarah's choice warmed her heart, and through such little acts, her tough sister's kindness and thoughtfulness was revealed.

Hamama noticed that Rivka had disappeared. The placenta, blood, and excrement covered the kitchen floor, and Hamama sighed and dragged Rivka from the other room to wash and clean Sarah. Hamama gathered the placenta into a bag and buried it in the ground behind the house. She then scrubbed the kitchen floor clean.

She worked for about an hour, and then washed herself with cold water. When the work was complete, the three sisters lay together in Sarah's bed, while the new mother tried to breastfeed little Yamima. As the sun started to rise, the three fell asleep, exhausted.

In the morning, the magical unity of the three sisters was shattered by Sarah's grumbling, followed by the neighborhood rabbi's ruling that Sarah had to go to the hospital. Hassan and Shmuel invited the rabbi to tell the stubborn woman himself because no one wanted to argue with her. The rabbi refused to give into her demands.

"I don't have to go to the hospital," Sarah said.

"You have to call for an ambulance so that the mother and baby will go to the hospital," the rabbi insisted.

"But I already gave birth," Sarah said.

"And still, your health takes precedent over Shabbat laws." The rabbi looked at Rivka and Hamama. "But it's not good for her to go alone, so we should send someone with her."

"I can't leave the house. I have all these people to take care of," Rivka said. She looked at her younger sister.

"No, no, no. I don't travel on Shabbat," Hamama said.

"You delivered the baby?" the rabbi asked.

"Yes," Hamama answered.

"The Midrash Rabba tells us the he who starts the job must complete it," The rabbi said. "What did you do with the placenta?"

"I buried it in the yard."

"That's a problem. They need the placenta."

"I'm not going to dig up now," Hamama said. "And anyway, it's all destroyed!"

"Here's what you'll do: Go with her to the hospital and tell them that you're a relative, but you don't know anything. Only that she gave birth, and you brought her there."

"I don't want to travel on Shabbat," Hamama objected angrily, as she noticed the twinkle of a smile on Sarah's face.

"I'm the rabbi, and I'm telling you to go."

"Because of you, I'm violating the Shabbat," Hamama grumbled at her sister as they both sat swaying back and forth in the back of the ambulance.

"I didn't ask you to come," Sarah said and returned her attention to Yamima.

Hamama looked at the five-grush coin Shmuel had given her so she could return home. She felt her entire body tense. She didn't understand why they had to rush new mothers to the hospital if everyone was fine. At the hospital, they delayed her with questions she thought were unnecessary.

Sarah was admitted, and Hamama received all her sister's dirty clothes. Hamama looked at her sister lying in bed. Sarah didn't even toss a quick glance back at her. *She didn't even say thank you*, Hamama fumed as she left the hospital. She didn't know what upset her more, violating the Shabbat or violating the Shabbat for someone who did not appreciate or even acknowledge her help. She threw Sarah's clothes into the trash and started walking from the Hadassah hospital back to Kfar Shalem.

She thought that the experience she and Sarah had undergone the night before would change the nature of their relationship, but it looked as if Sarah wasn't interested. *If so, I'm not interested, either!* Hamama tried to convince herself, but still her heart ached with disappointment, and she felt like that little girl who so yearned for her sister's love.

The squelching heat of Tel Aviv tired her out, but still she tried to comfort herself. *I don't have to make such a big deal out of this walk; it's much shorter than the distance from Tholet to Grandma's house. And this time there's no jug of lassis on my head, and I'm even wearing shoes!* But then thought of Sarah alone in the hospital: a new immigrant, without any family by her side, in a strange city, and just after giving birth. And Hamama hardened her heart. She would have to deal. She kept on marching, the anger and frustration feeding her legs.

Again, she wondered how she could be so good and patient to strangers but completely impatient and filled with anger toward her sister, her own flesh and blood. And again, she tried with all her might to halt the desire to go back running to the hospital.

She was deep in thought when she arrived in the HaTikvah neighborhood. People she knew from El Be'aden sat on a porch and waved to her.

"Hamama Vazif!" One of the women called out. "Our village hero!"

"Oh, nice to see a friendly face." Hamama sighed, her whole body drenched in sweat.

She went inside while the woman told her children the story of how Miriam and Hamama found the leopard in the woods. Hamama smiled as the happier memories soothed her torn heart. She accepted a drink.

"Will you stay with us until the end of Shabbat?"

"Unfortunately, I can't. They're waiting for me at my sister's house in Kfar Shalem."

"Well, you made it this far, it's not much farther now."

Hamama thanked them and continued on her way. Just as she arrived at the house, Hassan and Shmuel came out to greet her.

"Why didn't you take a taxi?" Shmuel asked, a frown on his face.

"I already violated the Shabbat once. Why should I violate it again? Here are your five grush."

Hamama handed him the coin, went inside, and sprawled out on her bed.

After Shabbat, the family members discussed who should go to Rosh Ha'ayin to tell Sarah's husband about the birth. Hamama, who figured they would make her the victim again, threatened Hassan.

"Don't you dare send me."

"But Hamama, I have to work tomorrow, and so does Shmuel."

"Rivka can go."

"Rivka doesn't know the way, she's new," Hassan insisted. "She's been through a lot…"

Hamama grumbled in discontent and reluctantly boarded the bus to Rosh Ha'ayin. But in her heart, she thought maybe this drive could make up for the fact that she had left Sarah alone in the hospital.

When she arrived in Rosh Ha'ayin, Hamama was greeted by enormous black tarps. She guessed that at least fifty families lived in each tent. The lucky ones lived in the old booths that had belonged to the British army. Memories from Atlit that Hamama wished to forget flooded her. She entered one of the tents to track down Sarah's husband. Inside the tent was a cacophony of colors. Only the ceiling was left black. White and colorful sheets hung everywhere, creating little cubicles of intimacy. Each family tried to create some separation between itself and the others, but loud noises of argument and children's cries filled the suffocating air. Suddenly, Hamama's little tent in Pardes Hanna, snake and all, looked like the Garden of Eden.

Hamama maneuvered around the sheets, peeking in bashfully.

"What are you looking at?" one of the immigrants snapped at her.

Hamama hurried on and noticed two women holding on to an embroidered shirt.

"That's mine!" one of them yelled.

"It's mine! You stole it from me!"

Hamama kept on marching and suddenly heard a scream. She turned around and saw a man rush toward the two women and tear the shirt in half.

"Here. Will you shut up now?" he said angrily. The two women jumped on him with their fists.

"Thinks he's King Solomon," said an old man who sat on his bed. Hamama smiled politely at the wrinkled man:

"Tell me, do you maybe know where..."

"Hamama!" Sarah's husband called out.

"Here you are!" Hamama sighed with relief. She had already forgotten the old, wrinkled man and all the others. "Sarah gave birth! A girl!"

"Thank God. I knew she wanted to get away from here to give birth in peace, but she left me worried."

"Everything's all right. She even gave her a name already— Yamima."

"Thank God, thank God. Where is she now?"

"At the Hadassah hospital in Tel Aviv."

"Thanks, Hamama. I'll take the kids and head over there now. In a few minutes. Will you come with us?"

"No, I have to get back home," Hamama said. She wanted to get out of there. She suddenly felt a strong yearning for her little house in Pardes Hanna, a strong desire to be next to Hassan and hug her children. The suffocating tent caused her to shudder and for good reason. This temporary housing situation was terrible. The arguments between the immigrants only increased, and life there became unbearable.

Three months after Yamima's birth, Sarah got into a fight with one of the villains there. The man, blinded by fury, wanted to stab her with a knife, but instead hit her husband, who had rushed to protect his wife. Sarah's husband died from his wounds that night, leaving Sarah a widow, and more bitter than ever.

After the hot summer, came the great freeze of 1950. Hamama sewed a lining into Hassan's coat and watched him ride his bicycle against the wind. The children tried to rebel against the many layers surrounding their bodies, and Hamama couldn't help but laugh when she saw them moving around like stuffed dolls. She purchased a wool scarf and didn't feel the need for any additional layers. She was pregnant once again, and the heat waves she often felt protected her from the winds and the cold. Inside the house, the family sat close together to warm up. Hamama tried unsuccessfully to remember if it was just as cold in the tents. *Maybe the oven in the ground in the center of the tent warmed us*, she thought, or maybe that winter was particularly cold.

One morning, Hamama wanted to go out to the communal bathroom in the yard but couldn't open the door.

"Hassan! Hassan! Wake up!"

"What happened, Hamama?"

"I can't open the door."

Hassan rose and washed his hands in a bowl of water he had prepared the day before, while Hamama jumped around uncomfortably because of her rebellious bladder.

"Come on, Hassan. I have to go."

Hassan looked at his wife and smiled. He went to the door while rolling up his sleeves. He wondered when Hamama had become so weak.

"Here!" he announced as he pulled the door. But the door refused to open.

"What's this?" he moaned and turned away from Hamama's grin.

"Let's try together," Hamama suggested, and the two pulled the door with all their might.

The door barely opened, and something white and cold spilled into the house.

"What's this? Milk?" Hamama asked.

Hassan picked up some of the snow that had come into their house and shuddered at the unexpected coldness.

"Ice, I think."

He glanced outside, and in the light of the dawn, noticed that the ice was about a meter high, and blocked the entrance to the house.

"I think you'll have to pee in the sink."

Hamama went to the kitchen, and after she finished peeing in a very uncomfortable position, she opened the faucet to wash the urine, but no water flowed out.

"Hassan!"

"Use the water from my handwashing," he told her from the entrance. In the meantime, Rachamim woke up.

"What happened, Mother?"

"Go, look outside."

Hamama washed the sink with Hassan's handwashing water while Hassan and Rachamim gathered ice in one of the bowls. Then Hassan melted the ice over a kerosene burner.

"The water froze from the cold. Also, in the pipes. Now we'll have to heat it to make coffee and cook."

Asher and Kokhava woke up and joined the strange activities. They then happily helped their parents shovel the snow from the entrance, so they could go outside.

"I don't think we'll be able to go to work today," Hassan said.

"What do you mean? We have to," Hamama insisted.

They both went outside to look at the white view. The sight was amazing. As the sun rose, the whole world sparkled and blinded them. They no longer cared about the cold. The children ran past them and jumped into the snow, playing and going wild. Hassan lifted Hamama into the air, together with her large belly, and gently placed her on the thick snow to the sound of the children's roaring laughter.

"Are you crazy?!" Hamama yelled, but she smiled, and immediately threw some of the cold material underneath her at him.

This throw was the opening shot of a snow fight between them all, except for Kokhava who sat with great seriousness on her little bum and shoved handfuls of snow into her mouth. Asher, who felt personally offended by Kokhava's calmness, gathered a fistful of the cold white stuff and shoved it between his sister's back and her shirt. Kokhava immediately burst out screaming, and Hamama hurried to pick her up and bring her inside. This act led to the end of the wild play, and Hassan instructed his sons to head inside and prepare for the morning prayer.

After the pregnant mother's wakeup call and the early morning adventure, the Vazif family headed back inside. The rest of the neighborhood preferred to wait until a more comfortable time to slowly rise to the strange morning. Adults and children managed to pave their way outside, some through their doors and others through the windows, and stood dumbfounded by the beauty that greeted them. It was a normal weekday that turned into a holiday, and many got to know and love the white snow, which visited them that year and then never returned.

The great freeze harmed the crops in the orchards and also in the vegetable gardens at the residents' homes. Hamama worried about the two goats, and when she felt it was about to get particularly cold, she brought them indoors to Hassan's dismay and the children's delight. Luckily for Hassan, since he changed the source of his livelihood from work in the orchard to the wood factory in the Mishmarot Kibbutz, he didn't face any loss of work. And when spring arrived, he worked extra hours to save the young fruit trees and the other vegetation in the garden. Hamama felt as if she hadn't seen him a whole month when he came to her with a letter, a smile spread across his face.

"From Father?" she asked with excitement.

"Yes," Hassan answered. Hamama jumped for joy and embraced him.

"Slowly, slowly, you're no longer skinny and small," Hassan said jovially as he caressed her large belly.

"I'll go to them. I don't want them to be stuck in Atlit any more than they have to be," Hamama said. After asking Hedva for a few days off, she headed north toward Atlit. She hadn't been back since she had left the place eight years before. *Eight years!* she thought with amazement. *Had so much time really passed?* Back then she was still a young girl; she hadn't even consummated her love for Hassan, and now the fourth child was on the way. The memory of the fence that had separated her from Hassan suddenly reminded her of how much she loved him. Their daily routine was always full and exhausting, but Hassan never stopped leaving her little surprises every once in a while: fragrant jasmine flowers, an orange, or a new piece of furniture he had built. They had been through so much. She looked at the sand dunes and the blue sea through the windows of the bus, and a shiver passed down her spine. She was no longer angry, no longer disappointed. Now everything was all right. And Father was there.

"I came for David and Ahuva Shar'abi. From Tholet," Hamama said to one of the Agency guides. The guide, who was younger than Hamama, led her through the interim camp. Hamama looked around, seeing but not absorbing. She walked through the place she had lived for three months, but now everything was different. There were many large tents throughout the camp, as the wooden sheds no longer sufficed. A group of women walked together behind one of the guides, and for a moment, Hamama thought she saw Soapy leading them, but changed her mind after taking another glance. The salty smell of the sea penetrated her nostrils and sent a shiver down her spine once more. She looked at the old guard tower, but it was unmanned.

"Here's the secretary. You'll have to explain to them that you want your parents to live with you, and believe me, they'll happily let them out of here. This place is overcrowded, and if you ask me, people will just live here for a few years until they find a place for them."

Hamama thanked the guide and faced the secretary.

"Are you sure?" a woman with short hair asked her, after listening to Hamama's request.

"Yes. He's my Father."

"But you have a one-room apartment."

"And here there are tents."

"You're right about that."

The woman signed a few papers and then suddenly looked behind Hamama, then returned her gaze to her.

"Here, Itzik already brought them. They're here, behind you," she said. Her expression softened as she observed the family reunion.

"Father!" Hamama yelled and ran to hug David. He was old and gaunt now, and his back was crooked from his life's burdens. Hamama buried her face in his chest and refused to look at him. *For just another moment*, she told herself. Be strong. Don't show him how terrible he looks.

"Hamama…Hamama…Where's my girl?" David asked affectionately as he took a step back to look at Hamama with her protruding belly.

"I haven't seen you since your wedding," he said with tears in his eyes. "How many years have passed since then? Ten years? More?"

"Too many years," Hamama said.

"You're a beautiful woman now, no longer the skinny little girl who trudged after me every morning," David said.

The encounter with her father suddenly reminded Hamama how much she missed her mother. Hamama could no longer control her emotions and burst out in tears. David hugged her warmly and then stepped aside, and Ahuva hugged her. Hamama kissed her stepmother, on whom the hardships of the journey were also clearly visible. Now Hamama felt even happier that her stepmother was there and had been with her father all these years after all his children had left him behind. She had endured the long, hard journey with him, from Yemen to Aden and from the Hashed Camp to Israel.

After the three calmed down a bit, Hamama walked David and Ahuva to the secretary and the two signed an exit form. Hamama then led them to the tents, waited as they gathered their few possessions, and walked with them to the bus station. By then, she had regained her strength and told them all about her life in Atlit, the tents, and the house that awaited them in Pardes Hanna. David and Ahuva asked about the children, and Hamama enjoyed telling them everything.

David and Ahuva immediately fit into the family life and found work to occupy themselves. Ahuva cooked meals in the Noam School, where she was considered a mother by the students there. David took care of the goats and chickens in the yard. Because Hamama was so busy, she only found time to milk the goats, but when David arrived, he started making various cheeses out of the milk, always spicing them differently, adding chives and garlic or nigella seeds.

Hamama was happy to see that even though her father looked old and feeble, he was still healthy and strong. And thanks to his healthy habits, he kept all his teeth until the day he died. The help Hassan received from David in the yard gave him time for his other activities. The first thing he did, in light of the new congestion in the house, was to erect a hut between two eucalyptus trees. Together with David, he then built a porch.

But David loved Rachamim best. He liked to sit with his grandson, to teach him various crafts and to tell him stories. Rachamim enjoyed cuddling up with the grandfather, who had suddenly joined their lives and who provided a new calmness to his raging soul. He was just a little kid when he became the older, responsible brother. And not only that, but the rambunctious Asher and spoiled Kokhava commanded all his parents' attention, and he always had to help out. Only with Grandpa David could he finally be a kid again, getting lost in far and ancient lands. He loved to hear Grandpa's stories of little barefooted Hamama.

"Mother, did a big monkey really chase you through the neighborhood?" he asked her one day.

"Mother, how many times did you run away from home?" he asked another day.

"Mother…how much trouble you caused—and you keep chastising Asher for acting out?" Rachamim kept on teasing his mother, until she had enough.

"What happened, Rachamim? Don't you have friends your own age, that you keep hanging around the old man?"

But Rachamim quickly replied. "The parents have eaten sour grapes, and the children's teeth are set on edge."

"What?"

"You ran away from your father, left him. Now I have to stay with him."

David, who sat watching from the corner of his eye this whole time, burst out with such laughter that he could hardly breathe. Hamama pretended to be angry, but in her heart, she was grateful for the connection these two had forged.

Ahuva also easily integrated into her stepdaughter's household. She helped around the house, but her favorite activity was going to the movie theatre. The magical world that had so fascinated Hamama and Miriam became the old lady's new addiction, and even though the two could enter by paying only rarely—with the help of the usher's protectionism—she didn't wait for the loyal friend's shift and spent most of her money on tickets, ready to sit and watch the same characters and the same story over and over again. One afternoon, Hamama returned from work, tired and exhausted.

"You remember that we're going out for a movie tonight?" Ahuva asked.

"Did you ask Miriam if she wanted to join?"

"She can't."

"All right, but I still have to do the laundry and organize the kids."

"I'll help with the kids," Ahuva said, and hurried to feed and bathe the three, while Hamama, with her protruding belly, bent down on her knees to scrub a basket full of sweatpants. The difficult laundry work exhausted Hamama even more, and she started to feel cramps in her belly. She ignored them, washed the laundry, and hung it on a rope while dreaming of a young Hassan hanging laundry in distant El Be'aden.

The warm memories distanced the pain, and she quickly finished her work.

"I'm going to shower," she said to Ahuva as she tossed a glance at her bathed children, lying together on the mattress in the room.

Hassan, who was sitting and studying Torah on the porch, smiled at his diligent wife and her strange hobbies. He never understood the fascination with those movies, and after joining her a couple times in the amphitheater, staring at the same huge screen, he lost interest. In the first movie, which was a Western, he could understand why people might get excited by the action, but the movie about Moses and the Ten Commandments was simply…inaccurate.

After laying out his critique, Hamama pardoned him from this burden as long as she could go to the movies whenever she wished, while he watched over the kids.

Hamama entered the little shower Hassan had built about two months before. It was in a very small room, but still preferable to the shared showers. Many of the residents in the neighborhood used their money to expand their houses, and a year later, the public showers were dismantled.

The water that splashed onto her exhausted body woke her slightly, but the cramps suddenly intensified, and she realized these weren't cramps from hard work, but contractions from labor. And tonight, there was an Indian film. *I really love those Indian films.* Disappointment filled her as she dried herself.

"Auntie, no movie tonight," she announced as she left the shower.

"What happened?"

"Contractions."

Hassan jumped up. From the moment Sarah had given birth on Shabbat, and the rabbi had insisted on sending her to the hospital, Hassan had decided that Hamama's next birth would also be in this protected place.

"Hamama! This time you're giving birth in the hospital!" he announced.

"Tell that to the baby," Hamama said. "He's already coming."

Ahuva quickly moved the sleepy kids to the porch and prepared the bedroom for the birth.

"You're going to the hospital!" Hassan insisted.

"Leave me alone, ya Hassan, I don't have the energy for a hospital. Ahuva's here, and she's a professional midwife. What more could you want?"

"I'm not asking. I'm telling. This time you're giving birth in a hospital."

"Fine, said Hamama. She looked at his startled face. "Well? You better go get a taxi!"

Hassan ran all the way to Neve Asher, to the taxi station. It took him about half an hour. Following the last contraction, Hamama paced around the room swaying from side to side, trying to convince the baby to stay inside until Hassan returned. Suddenly, she felt a warm liquid between her legs. Ahuva looked at her, and she knew there was no choice. She couldn't wait any longer. Hamama lay on the improvised platform that Ahuva had prepared, and while her stepmother was busy washing her hands, the head started to come out.

"At least wait for me, if not for Hassan," Ahuva commented with a smile. She had told Hamama once that she always liked the easy births because she had seen so much pain and grief in her life, and she liked to wish pregnant ladies a birth as easy as a chicken laying an egg. Without tears, without complications, without the deaths of babies or mothers.

"It's a boy," she announced as she lifted the screaming newborn. She cut the umbilical cord and placed the baby on Hamama's bosom.

"Hassan will be angry..." Hamama said, tired but happy.

Hassan was indeed angry and tried to insist that Hamama and the baby drive to the hospital. But when he saw how exhausted Hamama was, he went outside, defeated, paid the taxi driver for the drive home, and returned to hold his newborn son.

"He's got light skin. Like you," Hamama said with exhaustion.

"Next time—hospital."

"Why is that so important to you?"

"Because there you'll truly be able to rest. Just you and the baby. Without all the kids around."

Hamama's heart warmed at Hassan's words, and she was sad that because of the post-birth restrictions they couldn't embrace each other. Hassan felt her sorrow and sat beside her, holding the boy who had fallen asleep on his chest while Ahuva cleaned the room.

"I'll sleep with the kids on the porch today...so you'll have a bit of room," Hassan said.

After Ezra, the baby who was born during that year of austerity, Hamama gave birth to one more boy and one more girl. They were both born in the hospital.

2009

Today, the weather is pleasant, and I'm sitting with Grandpa and Grandma outside, behind the house. We're leaving in a few months. I left my daughter with my husband and came. Finally, he's returned. Operation "Cast Lead" is over, and I thank God that despite his advanced degrees, the army decided that they want to use my husband as a truck driver. It's hard to send loved ones to war.

We're sitting on a cement platform that was once a triangular, grassy area; on one of its corners stood a hollow tree covered with mushrooms. When I was a girl, this was my favorite spot. I would sit here reading books or cleaning lettuce. Here Grandma would prepare the *s'hug* using the special stones she had brought from Yemen, long before she bought a food processor and switched to a more convenient method. Here there was a short path that led to the room behind the house, the room Grandpa had built with Kokhava when she was twelve. Behind the path, there were loquat and pomegranate trees, and many herbs and spices. On the other side of the grassy corner were the mango and papaya trees, and a few *Khat* bushes.

"Do you remember the hollow tree that stood here?" Grandma asks, reading my mind.

"That was Aharon's tree," Grandpa says quietly. I know he means Aharon Nahari, my uncle whom I'd never met.

"Now it's all cement," he adds.

Grandma doesn't like her sick husband's despairing tone and chastises him immediately:

"And what's this? Look, Ezra made you a whole line of *Khat* bushes! And Asher planted flowers!"

I look over to the edge of the cement platform to a white faucet under which wild basil has started to grow.

"And the basil, Grandpa!"

He smiles with difficulty. "But this is nothing compared to what there used to be—and you know it."

I remember well. I was born at the time of the pecans and loquats, when all the other trees were but a distant legend. But I remember Grandpa in his blue work robe, sometimes the gray robe, walking around the yard with a ladder and fixing the watering system. I liked following him and learning about what he was doing. When he stopped for a moment and gave me a taste of the fruit of his land.

CHAPTER 9

Hamama's and Hassan's lives were exhausting but happy. Their small house was packed, and their yard filled with fruit trees. The kids were always running around, and although from the outside the young parents looked angry or were constantly chiding, their hearts were filled with pride.

Hamama liked to sit with her family in the yard every Shabbat, the kids frolicking around her. Little Simcha and Shira, who were born a year apart, sat on the ground, waiting patiently for the pieces of fruit Grandpa David handed out. Kokhava tried to forcefully comb Ezra's hair because she believed with all her heart that ever since he was born, he was a live doll that she had received as a gift. The small boy had green eyes and blond hair, and all the passersby stared at him in disbelief.

Shira also had golden hair; many people assumed at first she was adopted. Only David and Hassan saw Nadra in the two of them.

One Shabbat, the adults were sitting around, happily listening to Rachamim and Asher running around the fruit trees behind the house.

"Hey, Rachamim, look at this beautiful persimmon!" Asher said, without knowing that others were listening in.

"It really is a beautiful persimmon. But don't even think about it! You can't pick fruit on Shabbat!" Rachamim warned him.

"I won't pick it, I swear, but look—I'll close my eyes, and you'll bring me closer to it, so that I'll be able to eat it straight from the tree," Asher suggested.

Hamama, Ahuva, and David burst out in laughter and looked at Hassan, who was shaking his head:

"Well, Hamama, call your little rebel so he won't cause the boy to sin," he said.

"Asher!" Hamama yelled. "What are you two doing there?"

"We're just playing," he answered. "We'll be right there, Mother!"

Asher's wild nature often drove her crazy. Back then, they would slaughter the meat in the yard. Hassan would call the butcher, *Mori* Aharon, to come, and Asher would watch intently as he hung the goat or sheep on one of the trees and slaughtered the animal. *Mori* Aharon would then clean the meat so that Hamama could cook it.

One day, Asher called Rachamim to the room, and held up the sharp butcher's knife.

"Do you know what this is?"

"It's for slaughtering," Rachamim answered.

"Yes, but do you know how to slaughter?"

"No"

"I know."

"How do you know? You have to learn it."

"And I learned it! Here! Come here, and I'll show you how it's done."

Asher motioned to Rachamim to lie down, and then he exposed his big brother's neck. For a moment, he rested the knife on his throat, and with great luck and God's Providence, he did this with the blunt edge of the knife. Rachamim started to scream. Hamama ran in.

"Asher! What are you doing? *Il'an abuk!*"

Asher was taken aback. He tossed the knife aside and tried to run from the room, but Hamama caught him by the ear. She dragged him toward Rachamim with her free hand carefully checked his neck. Only after verifying that everything was in place and the boy healthy and whole did she grab his ear as well and pull.

"What do you think you're doing? What kind of a game is this?" she yelled angrily. But in truth she was as frightened as she'd ever been.

"I just wanted to show Rachamim how to slaughter the goats," Asher said to defend himself.

"What are you trying to do? Slaughter your brother?" Her voice trembled with rage and terror.

Hamama dragged the two by their ears into the yard and tossed them toward Hassan, who was sitting down and studying.

"Next time you need an animal slaughtered, go to the *mori* and slaughter it there. I don't want the kids to see it in our yard ever again."

Even though Asher was the wilder of the two, Rachamim was the first to land in serious trouble. One day shortly before the holiday of Shavuot, when all were busy with preparations, Rachamim went out to wander around the neighborhood with two friends. They stopped by Ma'atuf's grove.

"Let's go in," one of the friends suggested.

"I don't think that's a good idea," Rachamim said.

"Fine, you don't have to. But stay outside and stand guard," his friend answered, and the other two entered the grove to steal some fruit.

Unfortunately for them, Ma'atuf decided to walk around his grove, to unite with the Creator before the holiday. Suddenly, he noticed the mischievous boys gathering the fruit of his land.

"Thieves!" he yelled.

The two friends quickly ran out of the grove, shoving Rachamim out of their way. The surprised and frightened boy froze, and only after noticing Ma'atuf furiously running at him, did the strength return to his feet, and he took off.

Rachamim entered the house huffing and puffing, his frightened eyes looking around to see if anybody could see his pounding heart. Since a man's home is his refuge, Rachamim sat down in the corner and hoped to blend into the walls.

A few minutes passed, and there was a knock at the door. Kokhava opened it and in marched Ma'atuf, yanking Rachamim back into the spotlight.

Hassan sat mending his children's clothes. "Your son is a thief!" Ma'atuf shouted at him.

Hassan carefully placed the sewing tools aside, and quietly looked into Ma'atuf's eyes. Ma'atuf was taken aback.

Rachamim crept into the room. "There he is," Ma'atuf said. "Tell your father the truth! Tell him you were with your friends today in my grove."

"It's true that I was there, but I didn't steal. They made me their lookout," Rachamim said defensively.

"I'll report you to the police! That's what I'll do," Ma'atuf threatened.

Rachamim looked at his father's very pale face, and the pain of having shamed his father burned him so deeply that he jumped up and ran from the house. Hassan didn't follow him out and didn't say a word. Ma'atuf, who remained standing across from him, started to fidget uncomfortably.

"Hassan, we've known each other for a long time—"

"Go to the police," Hassan interrupted his neighbor. "I won't be angry with you."

"I don't really want to call the police. It's just—I said it to educate the boy."

When Hassan heard the word "educate" his pale face whitened even more. Ma'atuf's words stung him even more than his child's actions. While Rachamim made poor choices and acted foolishly, Ma'atuf suggested it was Hassan's responsibility, that he was not an effective father. Had Hassan ever been so humiliated?

Ma'atuf saw his expression, and so left him. There was nothing more to say.

All the members of the household sank into deep silence at the sight of Hassan's unnatural stillness. Hamama pulled Asher and David toward her.

"Go find Rachamim, make sure he doesn't do anything stupid," she whispered to them.

Asher left and, together with all his friends, ran around the neighborhood looking for the lost brother. David marched slowly, wondering where his favorite grandson had disappeared. All the while, the time passed, and the police didn't come, nor would they come. Hassan sat in silence and Hamama, increasingly worried, started to whimper. Hassan heard this and said angrily, "You're crying about your thief of a son? It'd be better if he doesn't return home."

"How can you say something like that!" Hamama answered, also with anger. "He's your son. Even if he made a mistake, he's still your son."

Shira started to cry, and Hamama lifted the toddler and tried to calm her. Kokhava took charge of the kitchen duties, and Hassan didn't budge from his spot. He continued to mend the children's clothes, without betraying any signs of worry when Asher returned to announce that he couldn't find his brother.

David continued to march up the hill toward the Noam School. He loved Hassan deeply, but he knew his stubborn and difficult nature. The children always looked up to him in admiration, especially Rachamim, of course. David worried about Rachamim and his gentle soul.

Suddenly, he heard whimpering by the water pools. He lifted his head and was frightened at the sight of Rachamim sitting at the edge of a pool with a height of fifteen meters.

"*Ya* Rachamim! Come down!" David called.

Rachamim looked at his beloved grandfather. He wiped away the tears and blew his nose into his sleeve.

"I'm not coming down."

"What is there for you to do up there, *Ya eini?*" David asked.

"I'm going to jump."

"Jump?!"

"Father is mad at me."

"It'll pass."

"I made him ashamed."

"He'll live."

"And me? How will I live? Even if I return home, he'll probably beat me until I die."

David hurried home and told Hamama. She immediately ran to the pools.

"Come down, ya *ibni*! Father won't touch you."

"That's not true."

Hamama hurried home and berated Hassan, "Look, your son is ready to jump."

"So, let him jump."

Hamama grabbed the clothes out of Hassan's hands and tossed them to the ground.

"So why are you mending his clothes if you want him to jump?" Hamama demanded. "And who made you such a tough judge that even the Lord Himself is more forgiving than you? The boy is all grief, he understands that he shamed you, he understands the moral lesson. Now go tell him to come home!"

"You tell him."

"Hassan!"

"Tell him that I won't beat him. He can come back." Hassan picked up the clothes Hamama had tossed to the ground and continued with his mending.

Hamama ran back to the pools and saw David trying to get through to the boy.

"He promised he won't touch you," she said breathlessly. "Now come down. It's a holiday tonight."

Rachamim came down from the cement pools into his mother's arms, and they walked home together.

But the moment Hassan saw his eldest son's face, he forgot his promise, grabbed his belt, and started hitting the boy's feet.

"My son won't be a thief!" he yelled.

Rachamim started to cry, and Hamama tried unsuccessfully to hold Hassan's hand back. Finally, she stepped in between her husband and the boy, which was when his belt struck her.

Hassan was shocked by the intensity of his fury and his wife's anger that was about to burst, but Hamama quietly and sternly spoke.

"If you touch any of our children like that ever again—holiday or no holiday—I'm taking them and leaving you."

The intensity of their fury and the first public fight between the two turned the atmosphere in the house unbearable to all its residents. The children and Grandpa David ran off to the synagogue, followed by Ahuva to Penina, after the discomfort brought on by Hamama's words. Hamama was left on the porch, looking out at Hassan, who sat outside refusing to go to the minyan.

They sat like this for an hour, in silence. As the holiday evening prayer was usually short, Hamama wondered why the family hadn't returned. They probably had gone to Sa'adia and Penina's.

"So?" she asked after a long hour. Hassan didn't answer, instead continued to wring his hands.

"We need to finish the prayer and pick up the kids," she said. "Everybody's probably at Penina's now."

"I can't pray while I feel this way."

"What happened? You need to keep hitting your children some more?" Hamama immediately regretted her words. Hassan's expression was fallen and serious. It appeared as though not only Rachamim had learned his lesson that evening.

"Don't tease me, Hamama. I don't want my son to turn into a criminal."

"Then *talk* to him. Why do you go straight to violence?"

Hassan came in to wash his face and started the evening prayer of the Shavuot holiday. Hamama set the holiday table, wondering if the kids had already eaten something at Penina's. She was embarrassed that her father and Ahuva had witnessed the whole scene. Hassan finished his prayer and marched with Hamama on the path next to the Noam School. The two enjoyed a gentle breeze that made the evening heat more bearable. Hamama noticed some lizards running away from them into the bushes around the school, and she smiled. She looked over at Hassan, who was walking erect with a soft expression. *We need to walk like this more often. Together. In the evening.*

Shadows pranced across the earth outside Sa'adia and Penina's house, a testament to the ruckus inside. When the couple entered the brother's house, all immediately grew quiet and looked at them with anticipation. Hassan smiled calmly and blessed everyone, looking, beyond the others, directly into Rachamim's eyes.

"*Hag sameach.*"

"*Hag sameach!*" everyone answered in unison.

"Will you join us for dinner?" Penina offered.

"My table is already filled with many good things, and you didn't plan to host," Hamama said.

"And still, it's a holiday, and it'd be great for us all to be together," David said.

"If so, at least wait so we can go back and bring some of our food here," Hassan suggested. "Rachamim, will you come help me?"

Rachamim, head still hanging low, joined his father on the short journey home. Hamama noticed that the boy's head slowly ascended as the two walked further and were swallowed by the darkness.

Like every couple, Hamama and Hassan had various disagreements. For example, they often argued over the children's education—an argument in which Hamama always had the upper hand, since most of the burden in this area fell on her. But with the other arguments, Hassan could be stubborn. There was anger and frustration, but always also mutual respect. Hamama hoped that the incident with Rachamim and the embarrassing conflict in front of everyone was a one-time occurrence, but of course it was not.

Hassan was a Renaissance man; he always had been. In addition to the furniture he built and the vegetable garden and blossoming orchard he helped nurture, Hassan liked to prepare various medicinal herbs in accordance with the writings of Maimonides, the medieval physician-philosopher. He even started to make wine and arak.

In the beginning, only close family and friends enjoyed the liquor, but after people heard about the quality of the Vazif-made alcohol, they asked to purchase some from him. Hassan committed to provide a few bottles to the Nahari brothers, to whom many of the men turned for entertainment, purveyors of hookah, card games, and gambling. These were considered a source of release for the Yemenite workers. Hassan, who avoided the place, was convinced to come celebrate the deal they had made, and, afraid of offending them, drank a bit too much. His head spun and those surrounding him no longer looked friendly. When the Nahari brothers got up to manage the gambling, Hassan jumped at the opportunity and left for the fresh air outside.

It was winter, and a cold wind sent a quiver down his spine. The rain started to pour over his body, but neither the wind nor the rain stirred him from his drunken stupor. This was the first time being truly drunk, and he enjoyed the feeling of freedom and power. When he came to the little house, he walked in with a loud ruckus, and Hamama immediately jumped.

"Why are you waking the whole house?" she hissed.

Hassan ignored her and almost knocked over one of the chairs. Surprised, Hamama caught it in time. Her surprise quickly turned to disgust and disappointment.

"Are you drunk? Stop prancing around like a bewildered rooster whose feathers were plucked! It's disgusting!"

Hassan was stung by Hamama's disrespectful words and felt a strong urge to shut her up. He raised his hand and slapped her across the cheek.

Hamama stepped back, surprised by Hassan's reaction. The only time he had struck her on purpose had been back by the well. There had been love and concern there but now he was standing before her drunk and arrogant, ready to hurt her without any reason. Her pain took over, and she felt the need to hurt him where he was most vulnerable.

Hamama looked straight into her husband's eyes.

"Where did you learn to treat women like that? From your mother's clients?!"

Hassan, shocked by Hamama's words, immediately shook off his stupor.

"Get out," he ordered.

"Hassan…"

"Get out."

"What are you going to do? What about the children?"

"Get out."

"But Hassan—it's cold…"

Hassan repeated his command slowly and viciously:

"Get out!"

He grabbed Hamama's wrist and tossed her out of the house. Hamama, wearing only her nightgown, was immediately struck by the cold. She tried to get back in, but Hassan had locked the door.

She was too ashamed to yell and wake all the residents of the house, so she stood rubbing her body to get warm. *Like a dog, he threw me out, threw it all out.* Tears streamed down her cheeks, and the cold moisture sent a shiver through her body.

She started to worry. *What if one of the kids wakes up in the middle of the night and looks for me? What will Father and Ahuva think of us? I stepped over the line. I shouldn't have cursed his mother. Maybe he lost control because he was drunk, but I hurt him on purpose.*

Freezing, Hamama went into the pen to lie down between the two goats, where she warmed up a bit. *But still, he shouldn't have hit me! Or thrown me out of the house in the middle of the night! In the cold!* She vacillated between grief and anger, disappointment over her broken relationship and a calculated analysis of the night's incident and distribution of blame. She passed the hours with these intrusive thoughts, until she finally fell into a frenzied sleep.

She awoke at dawn, meeting the kind gaze of the goats. Suddenly, she saw the house door open, and Hassan stepped outside, his face filled with worry as he looked all around. *Here, now he understands what he did.* She continued to hide in the pen, and after he walked to the back of the house, she hurried inside. She quickly put on a robe and breathed with relief, enjoying the warmth that spread through her body. The door opened, and she pretended to be busy preparing breakfast. Hassan entered the kitchen and stared at her, the straw in her hair and dirt on her feet. His heart sank, but he didn't forget the way she spoke about his dead mother.

"Who told you to come in?" he managed to mask his sorrow with a gruff voice.

Hamama took a deep breath before turning around and staring straight into his eyes, where she saw concern and love. But still, she had to say it.

"Shut up, or I'll break this *finjan* on your head." She held the coffeepot up to her husband's face. "What did you think to yourself? That you're drunk so you can be a big macho hero and can throw me out? Like a dog? I don't want to hear another word from you."

Hassan was encouraged to see that Hamama's spirit wasn't broken, although he was sure that her heart was. Otherwise, how could she have said what she did about his mother? He made his lunch and left for work.

And so, the days passed. Hamama continued the housework as usual but didn't exchange a single word with Hassan. Hassan wanted to work things out but had no idea how to approach Hamama. After a few weeks, he figured he might never find a good way and so just asked bluntly:

"How long will you be angry?"

"Until you behave like a human being. I'll never forget that you threw me out of the house."

Hassan was silent. Two days later, he returned to Hamama:

"I promise not to drink ever again."

Hamama realized that this was the closest to an apology she would ever get, partly because she was also a bit guilty and hadn't apologized, either. She accepted the offer but wondered at what point their relationship would return to normal.

Hassan indeed made sure not to drink beyond the Kiddush and Havdalah, and every time he had to check the arak and wine product, he would call Hamama to taste and see if it was ready. Despite this arrangement, the two were still filled with guilt. After all, Hamama didn't need her husband to swear off alcohol.

Maybe it was the arguments, or the crowded conditions during the hot summer days, but after six years of living in Hamama and Hassan's house, David and Ahuva moved to a small one-room apartment on the outskirts of town. Hamama was saddened by the parting but tried to encourage her kids.

"It just means you have another house in the neighborhood to go to and play!" she said with a smile.

217

"But we already have a porch, and when Father sleeps in the tree, we have enough room," Rachamim told his beloved grandfather.

"Rachamim, you're a big boy," David answered. "Soon you and Asher will want your own rooms. And this is too much. But your mother is right, *Ya eini.* Come to us, we're not far at all."

The children helped the elderly couple move. They carried their few possessions on their backs, and some they stuffed into the basket on Hassan's bicycle. Hamama, who stayed behind, glanced painfully at her emptying house, but knew that her father was right.

Like always, Miriam knew when to come by to cheer her good friend up, and when she came, the two went out to the yard to visit the pregnant goat.

The goats gave birth to many kids. The males went to the slaughter, and the females stayed in the yard. Hamama had a nasty habit for every birth of a first kid. She would purposefully disfigure him a tiny bit, so that she wouldn't have to dedicate him to a *kohen*, a descendant of the Holy Temple priests. Although there was no Holy Temple, the God-fearing Yemenite Jews didn't feel completely at ease using what should have been the *kohen*'s property.

"So, you came to make sure she won't give birth without you around, eh?" Miriam teased.

"Laugh all you want, Miriam. And what will I do with an eldest goat? There's no Holy Temple. Why should I give him to the *kohen*? And which *kohen* will take him?"

"You're stingy. That's what you are. Your scissors, did you already bring them?" Miriam continued to tease.

"And what about your goat? Did she already give birth? Let's see what you'll do." Hamama was annoyed by the teasing.

And indeed, when Miriam's goat was about to give birth, Hamama stood there and watched. Miriam refused to disfigure the goat and dedicated it to a *kohen*. The goat grew and became wild. Miriam couldn't slaughter him, and there was no *kohen* willing to take him off her hands. He would ram into the other goats and threaten to break the yard's fence.

Hamama teased her friend for her righteousness, but Miriam kept insisting she had done the right thing. In the end, she found a solution—she donated the goat to a school's petting zoo.

"You won," Hamama said.

"And now, will you finally stop disfiguring them?"
"Well, no."

As the new year came, Hassan spent more time with Rachamim in preparation for his upcoming Bar Mitzvah. One day, they both sat in the hut atop the eucalyptus tree, and Hassan taught Rachamim how to read his Torah portion in the Yemenite style. Kokhava forced Ezra and Shira to play school at the small table Hassan had built for her. She was the teacher and they had to do as she said.

Simcha, in contrast, insisted on spending his time with Hamama in the kitchen. He enjoyed following every move she made. He took note of the amount of each ingredient and observed intently as her hands caressed then pressed the dough. She let him take part in her baking.

Asher went outside to play with Shimon Ma'atuf and their friends near the Noam School.

The Noam School consisted of a large area filled with many attractions for young children: the large basketball field, the empty dormitories that they could enter through the windows, the enormous synagogue with treasures to be found under the seats, and, most interestingly, the new construction area.

The elder Omsi, who stood guard at the entrance, didn't mind these young ones too much and was happy to see them around the older, more serious boys who studied Torah. Maybe he should have been more attentive that day. Pangs of regret would accompany him for the rest of his life. He didn't notice that the boys were heading toward the construction area.

Usually, they played far away from there, but without Omsi noticing, the boys snuck over to the forbidden area. Asher and his friends skipped between the long pipes, eventually encountering an enormous pit. This pit served the workers as a place to store their tools. Although narrow, it was very deep, going down about five meters deep.

It was the evening of Rosh Hashanah, and the construction zone had been abandoned. The Romanian workers, who rented a room in the neighborhood, were preparing for the major holiday.

The elder Omsi heard the cries of excitement, which he knew couldn't be good. He hurried over to the jovial group as fast as his tired feet could carry him.

The children had been daring one another to jump over the pit.

"Hey! That's not a game over there!" he yelled.

The guard's yelling created a frenzy with the boys, and Asher, who claimed he could jump over the pit, approached the edge and stared at the sharp tools that stared back at him from the bottom of the pit. And his little heart beat nervously, and he found himself unable to make the jump.

"What are you doing?" Omsi roared.

And at the sound of the old man's yell, Shimon Ma'atuf impatiently pushed Asher into the pit. Asher fell straight down and onto the sharp tools, hit his head hard, and lost consciousness.

Omsi forgot his age and ran toward the pit. The children stood in shock as they watched blood gush from their friend's head. As he approached the scene, Omsi realized he couldn't get down into the pit to help Asher.

"Parchi, Gamdni," he yelled, "run quickly to the Romanians and tell them to bring the rope!" He stared at Asher in shock.

All but Shimon, frozen in place, ran off. Omsi screamed at the motionless and silent Shimon.

"This is a game, you think? That's how you want to kill your friend?" Omsi roared at him. "Run and get Hassan!"

But Shimon Ma'atuf didn't move.

"Coward," the old man mumbled. He truly wanted to blame the boy, but deep down he knew that he, the guard, was the sole guilty party.

With the children leading the way, the workers came running. With great skill, they quickly lowered one of their crew down into the pit. The worker held the unconscious boy, and the other workers pulled the them up.

Although the Vazif residence was next door to the Noam school, the family didn't hear a thing until a tumultuous procession approached them. Kokhava was the first to see the boy and the blood.

"Asher!" she screamed.

Hassan immediately jumped down from the tree, and Hamama ran out from the house. Omsi and two workers came to the front door, holding the unconscious Asher on their arms. The rag they had tied to his head was completely drenched by his blood.

Hamama took Asher into her arms, her face white as a sheet.

"They played there, by the pit," Omsi said, "and Shimon Ma'atuf pushed him. But I'm guilty, I should have stood guard, and I didn't."

But Hamama wasn't listening to him. She looked at her sleeping son and searched for something to hold on to.

"Where's Hassan?"

"Ran to get the taxi," Omsi answered.

The Romanians left the shocked family. Rachamim looked over at the group of kids and clenched his fists in rage. The group quickly dispersed, while the family members sat in a protective circle around the injured brother until Hassan arrived with the taxi.

"Get Grandma Ahuva to stay with you, all right?" Hamama directed Rachamim, a moment before she got into the taxi with Hassan and Asher. Rachamim, whose Bar Mitzvah was only two months away, took the responsibility, as always.

At the hospital, the parents sat across from the doctors who were trying unsuccessfully to control the bleeding. They were then taken out to wait in the hall.

"Do you want to wash your hands?" Hassan asked.

Hamama noticed that her hands were drenched with Asher's blood, as was her dress. A shiver shot down her spine, and she started to cry. Hassan tried to calm her, but the two were lost in the sterile space.

"He'll live," the surgeon announced a few hours later, "but he'll suffer from a mental disability."

The doctor explained his prognosis, but Hamama only yearned to meet her son and see his smile. She sent Hassan back home to be with the kids during the holiday, while she sat with the unconscious boy, waiting for him to wake up and return to himself.

When Asher finally opened his eyes, his face quickly contorted in pain. Hamama hurried to place a hand on him. He smiled at her, and her injured heart healed immediately.

Rachamim was the first to discover the change in his brother. They had always been close, and so he noticed that Asher was no longer as jovial as he used to be and lost his temper easily.

At school, the boy's life was even worse. Shimon Ma'atuf, who for many nights dreamt over and over about the moment of the push, was overcome with such shame and guilt that he thought he could no longer contain it. But then he found a way to channel the burden into fury, and the pain into a desire to inflict pain. From the moment Asher returned to school, Shimon and some of the other children bonded together to tease Asher, curious to test the changed boy's reaction.

"Stupid and dumb! Sucking his thumb! Looking for Mum! To her baby she'll come!" they teased, hinting at Asher's difficulties at school. Asher stood, pale with fury, and almost attacked one of them. Rachamim and Kokhava quickly grabbed his hands.

"Get out of here before I let him break your teeth!" Rachamim yelled to the offenders.

"Is that a threat, cry baby?" Shimon teased. "Come on, guys, let's go, so he won't start crying and go jump off the edge of some pool again."

Rachamim swallowed his saliva and held onto Asher tightly, but Kokhava left her brother and pummeled Shimon with relentless punches. The lad was caught completely by surprise, and before he realized what was going on, Kokhava had already stepped back and spit on him.

Asher and Rachamim burst out laughing, and the laughter infected the other kids.

"So, you let a girl beat you?" Asher laughed.

Ma'atuf shook the dirt off his clothes and walked away angrily. Asher and Rachamim hugged their sister and returned to class.

Asher's siblings tried to protect him as much as they could, but sometimes they too were the objects of his uncontrolled rage. One time, when the kids were in the yard with Hassan, Ezra angered Asher, who held a hoe in his hand. Asher lifted the hoe and hit his younger brother on the back. Ezra immediately burst into tears and Hassan— who saw everything but hadn't managed to prevent it—was himself overcome with such anger that he started beating Asher with his belt.

"Are you trying to kill your brother?" Hassan yelled.

Hamama hurried out to protect her disabled son.

"Stop, ya Hassan!" she called. "Don't you understand that this won't help him?"

Hassan stopped his beating, and Asher ran to the edge of the yard. Hassan and Hamama brought the whining Ezra into the house and iced his red back.

"You shouldn't have angered him, *ya* Ezra," she mumbled, partly to Ezra and partly to herself. Later, she took Asher aside for a talk:

"Look, *ya ibni,* you're strong. You can kill a human being. And then what will you do?"

"What can I do, Mother? When I'm angry, I can't control myself."

"Run away, *ya ibni.* You'll have to run away."

The mother's advice helped Asher avoid further conflicts, but she discovered that the price was steep. Nearly every day, she heard from the teachers that the boy had run away from school.

"They're laughing at me. I don't want to hit them, so I run away," he explained.

Hamama thought about this. "But you can't just skip school, you still need to learn…"

"I'll try, Mother," the boy promised, and he kept his promise.

Asher needed an enormous amount of self-control, as Shimon Ma'atuf never stopped teasing him and making his life difficult. Asher wasn't one to complain about his former friend, but his silence and attempts at ignoring and running away only encouraged Shimon to continue. Rachamim, Kokhava, and even Ezra—who had forgiven Asher about his back—hung around Asher during recess to watch over him, but during class, Asher was bound to fall victim to Shimon's pranks. One day, when the teacher had his back toward the class, Shimon threw fruit from the Margosa tree, which the kids called "gulguls," at Asher's head.

Asher closed his eyes and took a deep breath, picturing his mother's face. Another gulgul hit his head. *Father*, he thought, *Father's belt*. Another gulgul. *Rachamim and Kokhava*, he thought, *instead of playing with their friends, are watching over me every recess.*

"Asher!" the teacher roared, which pulled Asher out of his deep concentration.

"What, teacher?"

"Get out! How dare you throw things at me?"

Asher noticed the bag of gulguls on his desk, and Shimon's face covered with a wide smile.

"It's not me!" he said angrily.

"So who?" the teacher asked.

Asher was silent. It would be so easy to blame Shimon. But he wasn't a snitch. And in any case, that evil kid had already placed all the fruits on his desk, so how would he ever prove his innocence?

"Get out of here," the teacher said again and opened the door.

Asher rose. Helpless, the shame and anger boiled inside his small body, the rage of atrocious injustice burned in his bones, and the disappointment over his great efforts that amounted to nothing churned in his mind. He felt a sharp pain in his head. Teary-eyed, he left the classroom.

Once outside, Asher gathered stones and threw them at the school windows, shattering them. The teachers' and students' yells encouraged him, and he ignored his siblings running toward him. No one could stop the weeping boy from shattering the windows. By the time the police arrived, he was sitting on the ground, exhausted. Alone. Holding a piece of broken glass and threatening all those who attempted to approach him.

"Someone made him angry," Hamama said to the police officer in the station. "I'm telling you. It's not his fault! He is a good kid with a bad luck. Listen, I'm not just saying that—he has documents from the doctor saying that you can't make him angry."

"Bring all the documents, and everything will be all right," the officer promised as he handed the quiet boy over to his mother.

Hassan glanced over the report from the officer, noting the date and time when the boy was supposed to stand before a judge. He understood that it wasn't really his boy's fault, but nonetheless he didn't know how to protect him. He looked at Hamama, who hugged Asher and led him outside.

"God help us," he mumbled and followed them out of the station.

Hassan, Hamama, and all the kids, bathed and dressed neatly, sat across from the judge with expectant eyes. Rachamim held Asher's hand, partly to comfort Asher and partly to comfort himself.

"Asher Vazif. Here in court you must tell the whole truth. Tell me, why did you break the windows at school?"

Asher stood uncomfortably and lowered his gaze.

"I was mad at the teacher," he said.

"Why were you mad at the teacher?"

"He accused me of something I hadn't done. And I was trying really hard."

"I understand your medical condition. Do the kids at school also understand it?"

"Yes."

"And still they tease you," the judge said in a very quiet voice. He looked at the tense family facing him. "I understand that you're a supportive and loving family, but the boy's environment isn't good for him. We already talked about his missing school, and the teasing by his peers, both in and after school in the neighborhood.

He looked down that the paperwork in front of him. "A psychologist who tested the boy found enormous potential that is repressed because of the constant need to deal with the environmental hardships we mentioned. I must recommend moving him to a new home, a foster family away from here, where he could start over, and reach his potential."

The judge grew quiet and waited for the family's reaction. Asher was still standing, but his legs shook. Hassan grew pale, and Kokhava started to cry. Hamama stood. In her mind's eye, she remembered Asher's tears, his running away from school, his sadness. She took Asher's hand.

"I won't object," she said. "He should go where he'll be happy."

Asher left to live with a foster family in Jerusalem. The couple that took him under their wings were a pediatrician and a psychologist who were unable to bear children. Their house was home to a few other children sent there by the court, who all quickly bonded with Asher.

At first, Asher was sad about parting from his family and home, and he kept thinking about his brothers and sisters, his parents and the orchard in the back, but with time he discovered that he was loved in the new place as well. And without Shimon and the others teasing him, he managed to concentrate at school and to succeed. Occasionally, he received permission to go home, and when he returned his family was always overjoyed to see him. But during one visit, he found his mother crying.

"Mother! What happened?"

"You still call me Mother? And I gave you to someone else."

"And because of that I have two mothers who love me," he comforted her with a hug.

Hamama wasn't the only one who felt guilty about sending Asher away. Rachamim also developed a deep wound. The thought that he hadn't been able to look out for his brother, that he failed to protect him, ate at him from the inside. That wound widened, refused to heal, and created a deep emptiness in the elder brother's heart.

Hassan, who was adept at hiding his feelings, never said a word about the rip in the family. Instead, he busied himself building and constructing. He spent more time with the children, and, together with Kokhava, built an additional room behind the house, next to his workshop. When it was completed, he allowed Simcha to bring a dog into the house, and although the black animal was scary and dangerous, Hassan respected the boy's choice.

Everyone in the neighborhood feared the large dog, and Simcha, who until then had been a largely unnoticed boy, enjoyed strolling around the neighborhood and collecting others' stares of admiration. Simcha and Yechiel, Miriam and Ben Tzion's third and youngest son, forged a strong bond, and thus, another generation was added to Hamama and Miriam's unbreakable friendship.

The two young friends walked this monstrous dog around the neighborhood every weekend. One Saturday afternoon, they noticed Shimon sitting on one of the fences. Simcha knew Shimon Ma'atuf only as the boy who terrorized his brother, who caused his departure. Anger filled him, and he loosened his grip on the leash.

No one knows how the dog read his owner wishes like that—some said it was all planned and practiced and some criticized the dog as a dangerous beast. But the fact is that the dog attacked Shimon viciously. He bit a piece off his behind.

His parents came and demanded the animal be put down.

"A bull is put down after three infractions, and this is the dog's first, so why should I put him down?" Hassan asked.

"You're happy about what happened," answered Ma'atuf's father.

"Don't rejoice at your enemy's fall," Hassan quoted Proverbs with the greatest indignation he could muster.

Ma'atuf the father huffed angrily and left. Hassan turned to his smiling children.

"Now the dog has done wrong. And I don't want another incident like this."

They all nodded obediently and hurried to write to Asher about the incident. Shira, the youngest sister, licked the stamp, and the following day rode in the basket of Hassan's bicycle and slipped the letter into the mailbox in town.

2009

Nine hours of interviews on video tape. I'm sitting in Chicago, transcribing Grandma's stories. Every once in a while, the camera pans over to Grandpa. Tired. Quiet. I feel as if I don't have enough of him in the story.

I should have taped this interview before he grew ill—when he still spoke, told stories, laughed. What was he thinking in this moment? What did he feel?

I was always so in awe of my grandfather, Hassan, the smart and strong man. The man who smuggled Jews from Yemen to Aden. The man who protected women on the boat. The man who survived Atlit and built Pardes Hanna.

In all my admiration, I couldn't see—I didn't want to see—my grandfather growing old, sick, suffering from pain, asking to die. I couldn't see the large diapers that poked out of the blanket that covered his feet. I couldn't stand his dependence on others. I was ashamed for him.

I was jealous of my sister and my cousin. They could sit with him and make him laugh. But when I sat with him, alone, the silence permeated the air. And I knew that in my gaze, he could see his great past.

I'm nostalgic. We left Israel only a few months ago. The girl is almost a year old, and there's another one on the way. When we parted, Grandma cried. I tried to make her laugh a bit. I promised to come visit in the summer.

Grandpa didn't say a word. My daughter climbed on him and managed to extract a tired smile.

"I love you, Grandpa," I said. Me, the one who doesn't talk about feelings. I knew that I was seeing him for the last time.

CHAPTER 10

"You're killing me," David said angrily. "Why did you send him there all of a sudden?"

Hamama tried to ignore her aging father, who had walked all the way from his house just to yell at her.

"Why did you have to give him away?"

"I didn't give. They took," Hamama said irritably. *He's talking as if I'm not worried at all!* Her fury mounted.

"What do you mean 'took?' How did they know to come?"

Hamama tried to be patient with her aging father. Since Ahuva, Hassan, and Hamama took care of all the bureaucracy involved with his *Aliya*, opening and handling his bank account, his house registration and taxes, David was quite unaware of how thing worked outside his small, comfortable radius.

"When kids are born, they write it down. And when they turn eighteen, they come and take them to the army," she explained.

"You shouldn't have let them write it down when he was born," the old man insisted, and sat down. He thought of Rachamim, tall and smiling in a green uniform and beret.

She maintained a tough and apathetic front with her father, but in her heart, she worried about the boy. She had last seen him a month earlier, but they hadn't heard from him since. She was relieved when Miriam came by for a visit that afternoon and distracted her from her own angst.

"How about taking a trip tomorrow?" Miriam suggested.

Hamama smiled. Her friend always knew how to cheer her up. The next day, she packed cakes and other treats for Rachamim, and the two friends boarded a bus heading south toward the Nitzanim base. Again, the sands blew on the way. *Sands and sands. Sands and sea. The sea. Nadra and the sea, Hassan Shalom and the sea, Hassan and me by the sea in Aden.*

"What're you thinking about?" Miriam asked.

"About the past."

"Just yesterday we ran away from the tiger. And now?"

"Now it is their lives. We're just their caregivers," Hamama said sadly.

"Not true. Now it's their life, and they...they're our lives," Miriam said with a victorious smile.

"You're right. But still, I think I'll spend Shabbat with Rivka."

"That's a good idea. That way you can let her spoil you a bit."

The two chatted until the driver told them they had arrived.

"This is the place," he said.

Hamama looked out. "But there's nothing here," Hamama said.

"True. You get off here, keep heading in that direction, cross the railroad tracks and continue straight. Then you'll see a road, which will lead you to the base. But if you see a fence, don't cross it. It could be a mine field."

"Ah, thanks for the warning," Miriam said, only slightly amused.

The two got off in the middle of nowhere and started marching. The sea breeze stung their eyes, and the taste of salt on her tongue sent a shiver down Hamama's spine. Atlit.

"It's scary," Miriam said as the two prepared to cross the tracks. "I hope we don't get stuck here when a train comes." They looked in both directions to see if a monstrous engine would appear from nowhere.

"That doesn't make sense," Hamama said. "Even if it were to come, we'd have enough time to cross. Come on." Hamama pulled Miriam across the tracks. They continued along the trail to the base, walking in the heat of the day. In front of them, they saw a soldier carrying an enormous backpack. As they approached, the dusty soldier greeted them.

"Is this the way to the base?" Miriam asked.

"Who do you come for?"

"Rachamim Vazif. You know him?"

"Of course, I know him, but it's not good that you came here, ma'am."

Hamama was overcome by a slight nausea at the sound of the word ma'am. "Why is that?" she asked.

"They've been out in the field, away from the base, for a month already," the soldier continued.

An Army jeep stopped by the three. The dusty soldier dropped his backpack and saluted.

"What's going on here?" the officer asked.

"They came to visit Rachamim Vazif, sir," the soldier answered.

"But he's in the field," the officer said.

"That we already heard," Hamama said.

"I'll tell him you dropped by," the officer said. "He's supposed to have a vacation in a couple of weeks. I'll make sure he comes home for a visit."

"Could you give this to him?" Hamama asked as she handed him the cakes. "And if he doesn't come soon, the other soldiers can eat it."

"Thank you very much," the officer said and continued on his way.

"So, do you know where we can find the bus station back to Tel Aviv?" Miriam asked the soldier.

"Come with me," he answered with a smile and drove them off.

The consolation for Rachamim's enlistment came with Asher's return home. When he turned seventeen, the foster period came to a close, and he began to study at the professional school in Kfar Ha'Roe, where he prepared various tools at the workshop.

"This is great work," the instructor complimented him one day. Asher looked at the hammer he had just made and was filled with pride. He aspired to be like his father.

"You know what? Take it home with you. It's yours. Show your parents."

Asher was glad, although he didn't need tools in order to instill pride in his parents. Their great love, partly driven by guilt, left him little room to breathe. Hamama cooked his favorite dishes, and Hassan taught him Jewish laws, since the boy grew up with a secular foster family. Asher returned home happily and jovially, but at the entrance into town, he was greeted by Shimon Ma'atuf, together with Nahari's eldest son and other hooligans.

"Lookie, lookie who came home," Ma'atuf teased.

"The retard," Nahari the eldest said. "That's what I heard. He looks normal, no?"

"Please let me through," Asher said.

History tends to repeat itself, and Omsi the elder, who was now even older and no longer a guard at the school, sat on his porch, watching.

"Leave the boy alone," he warned them with a shaky voice.

Shimon noticed the old man. He quivered momentarily, recalling that terrible day, and his hatred of Asher intensified.

"Well, Nahari, show this cripple what a man you are," he said as he pushed his friend forward.

Asher looked at the circle of lads closing in on him. He was neither afraid nor angry. It seemed like the regular order of things. At some level, he even anticipated this. Being away under the care of his adoptive parents helped him better control his urges.

And growing up with other forsaken children taught him the art of fighting. Nahari the eldest, whose body was amazingly built and his arms wide, walked toward him with a threatening look on his face. With catlike grace, Asher moved his hand down to his bag and tightly grasped the hammer. His hand was moist with perspiration, and he prayed he wouldn't have to face this test.

"Nahari, stop," Asher warned.

"Why? What's a skinny kid like you gonna do?" Nahari laughed and threw a punch.

Asher quickly moved aside and pulled out the hammer. Nahari never hesitated before pulling out a knife. The circle of boys grew excited. Omsi barely managed to wobble over to the edge of the porch.

"I'm calling the police," he threatened.

But no one listened. Onlookers from the neighborhood ran toward the circle to try and stop the fight, but it all happened too quickly. Nahari jumped Asher with the knife, and Asher responded by smashing the hammer on Nahari's head. With one blow, Nahari the eldest fell to the ground, unconscious. Asher dropped the hammer with regret and stood motionless until the police officers managed to carve their way through the spectators and arrest him.

"He just returned home!" Hamama said with disbelief to the police officer at her door. Suddenly, she noticed a strange procession with Omsi the elder at its head.

"We witnessed the whole thing," the old man announced. "It was self-defense. We came to testify."

And indeed, Omsi and the other people from the neighborhood testified in defense of Asher, and the case was closed.

Except it wasn't the end of the story. The following morning, they called from the school to warn Asher not to come, since the injured boy's family were waiting for him at the entrance to town, waiting to take revenge.

"And what will we do now? He won't leave the house!" Hamama protested to Hassan that evening, after Asher spent the entire day with her.

"Come with me," Hassan said to his son. The two went outside and marched down the path toward the Nahari home.

"Behold, the fire and the wood, but where is the lamb for the burnt offering?" Asher quoted from Genesis jokingly, but in his heart, he was tense and nervous.

"God will show us the lamb for the burnt offering, my son," Hassan answered sternly.

The Nahari home consisted of two rooms. One was the gambling den to which Hassan provided liquor. The second room, which was no smaller than the first, formed the family living quarters. Hassan knocked on the door, and Asher felt as if he was pounding on his heart. The head of the household opened the door with surprise.

"Hassan Salem?"

"*Ahalan* Nahari. May we come in?"

"Of course, come in," he said as he showed them inside the house.

Hassan, who counted on the ancient custom of respecting one's guests, entered fearlessly, and Asher followed. Nahari the eldest, whose head was covered by a bandage, sat on the couch and moved over to clear some room.

"Let's not waste time," Hassan began. Asher always admired his father's directness. The injured boy had three brothers, and Asher saw that they were all were staring at Hassan with wonder and anger. "My son made a mistake when he acted violently," Hassan continued. "But your son was also wrong. They were both wrong, though it was decreed from above that your son was injured and not Asher."

People cleared their throats, but Hassan didn't seem bothered. He continued to look around at each family member. They were all dark-skinned, much darker than him. The twins stood by each other at the entrance to the kitchen, and the youngest one, darker than all the others, with a black birthmark on his cheek, stood next to his father and looked on with wonder. He was Asher's age, and something in his dreamy eyes drew Hassan in, but he continued:

"Instead of looking for revenge and spilling blood, I brought Asher here. He's a talented boy, and he is learning carpentry and metalworking. I don't have any money, but you decide on the amount of the damage, and he'll work for you to atone for his deeds."

The room was silent. The logical, honest solution Hassan suggested softened the family's anger-filled hearts. Even the injured Nahari, who knew the truth of what had happened that day, realized that Asher wouldn't blame him.

"I pulled a knife out. He didn't have a choice," he whispered.

"And still, the boy will compensate you for the injury he caused," said Hassan. He didn't trust this family and was worried that if the debt wasn't repaid, they might change their minds.

"I have a few renovations in the other room," Nahari the father said. "Could he start tomorrow?"

"Deal," Hassan said, and shook the other father's hand.

"I'm sorry," Asher whispered to the injured boy.

"Yes. Me, too," he replied, in a voice heard only to Asher.

When Hamama heard where Hassan had gone, she beat him with her little fists.

"You're *majnun*! That's what you are! Going with the boy into the lions' lair?"

"It's over, Mother. It's over." Asher's words calmed her down.

A few days later, Nahari's youngest son showed up at their door.

"I told you it's not over," Hamama whispered to Hassan.

"Let the boy talk." Hassan silenced her, and turned to him: "Little Nahari, what do you want here?"

"My name is Aharon."

"Nice to meet you." Hassan shook his hand.

"I studied with Asher in Yeshurun," Nahari said, weighing his words carefully. "I know that he's not guilty."

"Thank you," Hassan said calmly, while Hamama eyed the boy suspiciously.

"I want to work for you, so that Asher won't work for Father for nothing."

"Does your father know that you came?"

"No. And he can't know."

"Then I don't think I should let you work for me."

"My father doesn't see this the way I do."

"Still, it won't be appropriate to take care of things behind your father's back."

"You're causing my father to sin," Aharon insisted. "I came so that our families can be even. Asher shouldn't have to work for him."

So that's what I saw in his eyes. The boy was an angel.

"I'm learning to be a gardener," Aharon continued.

An angel from heaven, Hassan thought. Hamama clicked her tongue, reading her husband's mind. She knew that for a while now he planned to uproot part of the orchard and plant strawberries. Of course, their sons were busy, uninterested in the yard work. She was worried they'd get in trouble because of these strawberries and this Nahari boy. Hassan turned to her as if waiting for an explanation.

"I don't trust him," she whispered.

"Well, I do."

"You're getting yourself into hot water," she warned.

Aharon Nahari started work shortly thereafter. And in time, the family got to know this boy, who had a heart of gold and the hands of an angel—or maybe it was the other way around? Hassan and Aharon Nahari worked a whole year to grow the strawberries, covering them with nets to protect the gentle fruits. The red and sweet produce filled them with pride, but after the joy of the first fruit, the field was overtaken by insects. These hungry, evil creatures spread and took control of most of the yard, and even killed some of the other fruit trees.

Aharon worked with the Vazif family for a whole year. Asher had long paid his debt, but Aharon, who grew fond of the family, became a regular member, so much so that Hamama herself offered to let him move in with the boys in the back room. She loved the boy and felt pangs in her heart every time she thought about his return to his house, to the drunken cacophony.

She talked with the boy's parents. They were both happy Aharon got to hone his gardening skills in Hassan's yard. Aharon himself was grateful for the invitation and worked even harder to justify the kindness he received.

Aharon planted a tree behind the house, next to the additional room Kokhava had helped her father build.

"All your trees bear fruit. This is an ornamental tree. A gift from me," he said to Hassan.

Hamama and Hassan weren't the only ones in the family who loved the boy. Rachamim, during his vacations from the Army, was often seen with him and Asher in the neighborhood, and even the younger kids were touched by Aharon's exciting and sometimes scary stories. Hamama threatened him more than once to stop scaring them, since Shira had already woken up crying two nights in a row. But of everyone, Kokhava loved him the most.

Kokhava had grown to be a tall and pretty girl, proud as her father, and with her mother's spunk. She nearly broke the hearts of all the boys in her neighborhood with her modest charm. Finally, Hamama decided to send her to a boarding school in Bnei Brak.

But this gray, closed institution was not to her taste, and the strict, submissive pedagogic style didn't fit her character, and the family life she sought. The simplicity of the love between her parents was the example she wished to follow, and she had closely watched the pair's relationship from the day she was born. Her father's great respect for her mother, and her mother's role in running the house and family— all these caught the girl's imagination and conflicted with the discipline and submissiveness from school. She loved coming home, finding comfort in the company of her younger siblings, and in Aharon's stories.

His presence brought up feelings of curiosity and pleasure in Kokhava. She loved watching him play with her siblings and helping her mother with the laundry. She especially adored the moments he worked in the yard, shirtless. His sweating, naked back glistened in the sun, as warm waves shot through her body. All the while, though, she felt Aharon was oblivious to her presence.

Of course, the boy wasn't blind to the beautiful Kokhava, who grew up beside him; he simply felt he didn't stand a chance.

Hamama noticed the tension between the two and hoped that his show of apathy would break Kokhava's heart and cause her to wake up from her dreams and concentrate on her studies.

While the love story between these two progressed slowly, without either being the wiser of the fact that it was mutual, another love story took center stage in the Vazif home. Rachamim, who had recently finished his military service, worked at Amidar, the state-owned housing company, and dreamed of opening a tour-guide business. Many had warned him that opening a private company was a dangerous, unstable move, but the young man continued to work hard in order to save money and realize his dream.

After the job at Amidar, he worked for the township and read water meters. In the evenings, he would let loose a bit with Asher, Aharon, and other friends from the neighborhood. They would sit together, boys and girls, and talk nothing and everything: politics, their strict parents, life in the army, the top ten songs on the radio—but they were careful not to appear to be flirting. Maybe a stolen glance, but that was all.

Nevertheless, many girls tried to win the attention of Asher, the boy who was tough on the outside but gentle on the inside, and with whom even the Army didn't want to mess. His anger and his time away had become part of aura, and he switched girlfriends like "pairs of underwear," as Hamama disapprovingly noted. Rachamim was more timid with the opposite sex and stayed close to Aharon, whose large birthmark scared all the girls off.

Rachamim was surprised that Aharon did not appear bothered by girls' indifference to him. He never suspected Aharon's secret love for his sister—not even for a second.

Every evening, representatives of the first generation of Yemenis in Israel sat on the fences and ate sunflower seeds, a long tradition that the second and third generations in the neighborhood would eventually adopt. And every once in a while, during a free evening from the boarding school, Kokhava would join the kids, and watch Rachamim, Asher, and Aharon turn from flirtatious—or almost flirtatious—to staid and protective.

One morning, while reading water meters, Rachamim passed by a small house across from the Yeshurun School. He noticed a pretty young woman taking out the trash. She met his eyes one long moment, and then she ran back inside. Rachamim recognized the woman. She was Shulamit, Masauda's daughter.

Everyone knew Masauda, and the smell of the fried *zalabiot* that emanated from her home every Friday morning. She would also prepare *Lahoh* and pass it out to the older residents of the neighborhood. The mother was friendly, and everyone loved her, while the daughter was much more introverted, and spent most of her time in the house. Shulamit didn't have a father, and her prospects were certainly not improved by Masauda's story that her daughter was the offspring of an argument she had with an evil spirit in Yemen.

"She was a tall evil spirit, five meters high," her mother would say. "And her breasts were long. So long that she would use them as a scarf. I told her 'give me a pregnancy.' She said, 'But then you'll give me whatever I ask for.' I wasn't so smart, so I agreed. And after the birth, she came and asked for the girl. I told her 'Fine, but wait until she's weaned, since your breasts aren't fit for feeding.' She said, 'Fine.' What did I do? I took the girl and ran off to the Land of Israel."

Rachamim walked by Masauda and her daughter's house often, and after noticing that the shy girl returned his smiles, he hurried to Hamama.

"I want to marry Shulamit," he declared.

Hamama froze. She was in the middle of washing the dishes, and she gently put down the cup to prevent it from slipping and breaking.

"Shulamit, of all girls?" she asked as she dried her hands.

"What's wrong with her?" Rachamim asked with a raised voice.

"What's good about her, that you want to marry her?" Hamama retorted, not impressed by her son's anger.

Rachamim didn't answer.

"After all, you know, they say she's not all there," Hamama continued, trying to open his eyes.

"And if not, so what? She doesn't deserve love?"

"But why should you be her savior?"

"Because I love her," Rachamim answered simply.

"If so, mazal tov," Hamama said with a heavy heart.

The wedding took place a few months later, in a little events hall in Pardes Hanna. The small hall barely contained the many people who came to celebrate with the couple. Hassan sat like a proud rooster at his son's wedding, and Hamama smiled at the sight. *Now it begins*, she thought as she looked around, examining her other kids, dancing and happy. *Who will be next? Asher and his current girlfriend?* Then she saw Aharon sitting at one end of the hall, looking at the other end, with a gaze of desire filled with sadness. Kokhava, who sat at the receiving end, also glanced at him occasionally while resting her head on Shira's shoulder, and little Shira, who had by now grown mature, caressed her hair. *Well, why not, actually?* After all, this business had been going on for more than two years already.

"What's the problem? Send them to pump water from the well," Miriam suggested a few days later.

"Very funny."

"It's actually very cute. They're both lovesick, certain that the other isn't interested. You should get Ahuva and tell her. This is better than an Indian film."

A year earlier, David had passed away of old age. He was eighty-five, and Ahuva, who was twenty years younger, remarried. The old man she married was very wealthy, but extremely stingy. He took control of her possessions and handled her accounts, and he never allowed her to go to movies more than once a month. Hamama, who was saddened by her father's passing, was saddened even more by Ahuva's fate.

"She married too quickly," she mumbled.

"Nobody wants to die alone," Miriam said.

The two sank into a sad silence for a moment, and then Miriam stood up:

"Ask Kokhava to take your place with the laundry. Tell you have a backache or something."

"Why? I feel fine."

"I'll make sure Aharon is there."

And so, it was. Kokhava went out with the basket of laundry, when she noticed Aharon waiting outside.

"You're hanging the laundry today?" he asked with surprise.

Kokhava wanted to bury her face in the ground. *He's disappointed that he has to work with me*, she thought in despair.

"Mother's back is hurting," she answered, "but you don't have to help me. I'll manage on my own."

I must be so repulsive to her that she doesn't even want help with chores, Aharon thought. *It's better that way.*

"In that case, fine. I'll be up there," he said, and left. Kokhava decided once and for all: she hated Aharon with all her heart.

When Hamama eventually returned from grocery shopping, she couldn't hide her disappointment at the sight of Aharon picking loquats in the garden out front while Kokhava was hanging laundry in the back.

"Why are you lifting all those bags?" Aharon asked. "I thought your back hurt too much."

"My back is fine. Aharon, I love you, but you're an idiot." She looked at her dear Aharon. "Listen, do you love my daughter?"

Aharon was so taken aback by the question, he dropped the bag of loquats. Hamama continued to stare at him, until he lowered his eyes with shame.

"Yes. With all my heart."

"So why don't you go to tell her? She's been in love with you for two years already."

She watched as Aharon's face lit up.

"Now go help her with the laundry."

Hamama wanted to watch the two from her bedroom window, but instead she brought the groceries to the kitchen, unpacked the heavy bags, and organized the food in the refrigerator. Her mechanical movements were not sufficient to calm the excitement that held her as she thought about the great love that was destined to bloom behind the house. She sat down with a sigh and waited.

Aharon silently made to help Kokhava with the laundry.

"What changed your mind?" Kokhava finally managed, struggling to remember her hatred.

"Your mother."

"Oh, she made you come?"

"No. She gave me permission to ask for your hand."

Kokhava froze in place. Aharon stepped through the hung laundry and stood beside her. She gazed into his brown, shining eyes. They returned all the love she had ever wanted. The slight moisture on her cheek made her realize she was crying.

"Kokhava Vazif, will you be my wife?"

"Yes!" she cried. She pulled him up, and together they walked toward the house, each quietly adjusting to the feeling of walking beside the other.

Hamama smiled when she saw the two holding hands. After she heard about their plans, she cleared her throat.

"First, ask Hassan. So, he doesn't hang me from a tree."

Aharon realized with a jolt that in his great love that he had forgotten this important formality. He wasted no time and immediately headed out to the Mishmarot Kibbutz on his bicycle.

Hassan felt Kokhava was still too young, but he knew that if he turned Aharon down he wouldn't hear the end of it from Hamama. He gave the couple his blessing.

On the wedding day, Hassan took Aharon to a new neighborhood in Neve Asher and showed him a one-and-a-half room apartment with a kitchen, shower, and small restroom.

"It's too expensive," Aharon mumbled.

"But do you like the place?"

"Well yes. Maybe we can find something similar, but less expensive."

"Here," Hassan said as he handed Aharon a large wad of cash.

"What's this?" Aharon asked in dismay.

"Did you really think I would let you work for me for free all these years? These are your wages."

Aharon was surprised by Hassan's generosity. He had helped out around the house and in the yard but felt that living with the family was more than he could ask in return.

Aharon and Kokhava bought the house and, after the wedding, moved in. A year later, the first grandchild—Etti—was born.

Asher, too, soon settled down, and came home with a bride. But although she was Yemenite, she was raised and educated on a secular socialist kibbutz. She was thus completely ignorant of all the customs, beliefs, and mannerisms that defined her fiancé's family. In fact, the soon-to-be wife wore the most immodest clothes Hamama had ever seen. Before Hassan could see the half-naked woman in their house, Hamama grabbed the woman's shirt and tore it, sending her to Shira's closet to change.

The girl burst into tears, but remained stubborn, and refused to heed the lesson. She returned three more times in immodest clothing, and all three times, Hamama tore the bride's clothes. Asher, who respected the tradition of his childhood home, felt stuck, and said nothing. But his beloved bride eventually gave in. She continued to wear the clothes that flattered her figure, but she learned to never wear them when she visited Asher's parents.

Hamama and Hassan were happy to marry off their children, but most of all they loved their first granddaughter. Etti was a dark, beautiful baby with big eyes and a wide smile. Everybody was crazy about her, played with her, spoiled her. Shira, the youngest of the siblings, was happy to have a niece, to finally have the chance to take care of someone younger than her. Aharon spent hours messing around with Etti, until even Hassan teased him about it.

"What kind of man are you, spending so much time around a little girl?!" he would say, laughing at the sight of the strange faces Aharon made for his baby daughter.

Hamama, who had just walked out onto the porch, admonished Hassan. "Said the man who walked out in the middle of a British attack to make porridge for his baby."

On the June 5, 1967, the Six Day War erupted, and Aharon, in his soldier's uniform, parted from his family. The lad was a gentle soul, and he insisted on parting from each person with a hug and a kiss. Hassan disapproved of this custom, but Aharon didn't give in, and hugged him, nevertheless. He then turned to Hamama.

"Hamama, promise me something."

"What?"

"If something happens to me, take care of my Etti."

"What are you talking nonsense for?" Hamama said, annoyed, "Come back and take care of her yourself."

"*Doda*, you never know. Just promise me. At least, I'll know that someone will be there to always take care of her."

Hamama didn't like his words at all, but still she promised. Aharon hugged her so tightly that she was about to faint. Kokhava walked him out, and Hamama watched them saying their goodbyes. She felt a pang in her heart, and immediately scolded herself. *Just because the lad is too sensitive, doesn't mean you have to give in to his worries, too. They all go, and they all return.* Hassan clicked his tongue with dissatisfaction and walked inside. Hamama looked at Kokhava, who entered with misery in her eyes.

"Go feed the girl," she told her daughter, knowing that the little one would surely cheer her up.

That week, two soldiers from the neighborhood fell. Tears and grief filled the houses, and Kokhava took Aharon's bicycle to comfort the mourners, as she attempted to extract bits of information about her husband from the friends.

Hamama put Etti to sleep in her bed and walked out to the porch. Looking out, she saw a military vehicle approaching. Her heart began to pound. Two soldiers came out, one an officer and the other a doctor, and they walked directly toward her. Hamama immediately understood and let out a shriek. Her legs gave out and she flailed about in a desperate attempt to grab a chair. The porch she sat at for years suddenly seemed foreign to her. Her emotions too felt foreign, as if the approaching guests had come for someone else. She realized she wanted to stay in this haze, to ignore reality for just one more second, but then the officer broke down in tears.

"Where's his girl? Show us the girl," he said.

Of course, he would like to see the living and breathing legacy of the dead.

Hamama walked to the back room and brought Etti, who opened her eyes, looking curiously but quietly at the action around her.

"He always talked about her."

Hamama sat with them. They didn't have to say another word. Tears welled up in her eyes, and her heart burnt from her dear daughter's torturous pain. When she saw Kokhava approaching on the path on her dead husband's bicycle, Hamama wiped her tears. Now she had to be strong for her.

"Mother! Mother! What happened?" Kokhava ran toward to porch and fell at her mother's feet.

"I'm sorry—" the doctor muttered with a shattered voice.

Kokhava immediately broke down in tears. Hamama, who had sworn to be strong for her, couldn't contain her tears over dear Aharon, and her daughter—a nineteen-year-old widow.

Hundreds came to pay their respects, but Hamama could only watch as Kokhava shut herself in her room. She wished to comfort her daughter, to erase the pain, just as she did when Kokhava was young:

"Nothing happened, *ya binti*, nothing happened."

Nothing happened, my daughter, except that your heart is broken, your dream is gone, and the air in your lungs refuses to continue on its path. That you will never again be whole, that grief will follow you throughout your life, that every bit of joy you find will not quench you, and that his face will appear at your every turn. Nothing happened.

Days after the *shiva,* Kokhava still kept to herself, barely managing to tend to Etti's care. At last Hassan came to his daughter's room.

"Kokhava?"

"Yes, Father."

"May I come in?"

"Yes."

Kokhava sat on her empty bed, her eyes red from all the weeping. Hassan sat down beside her.

"Kokhava is the Hebrew translation of Nadra, my mother's name."

"I know."

"My mother also lost my father far too soon. I was still very small."

Kokhava looked at her father sitting erect across from her. His eyes stared off, then shifted back to her. He never talked about his parents.

"Alone, with her baby, she continued on living. David, your grandfather, may he rest in peace, tried to convince her to return home, to him. But she wanted to stay close to her husband, close to the sea that he had loved so much. Maybe that's what killed her eventually. The grief. The loneliness."

Kokhava felt these words touch deep inside her. Her soul was an open wound, and she knew, watching her father, that this pain may never go away. Hassan stroked her hand.

"She was strong, like you. Worked hard and didn't turn down any job that would support us."

But the grief gnawed at her from the inside. She sat alone by the sea for many hours, crying.

"Kokhava, you have to be stronger than my mother," her father said. "Now it's too early, but for Etti, for yourself, you have to let your love go. Put him aside. Find a reason to live. A real reason."

"And if I can't find one?" Kokhava asked with a quiver.

"You'll find it. The Lord will help you find it." Hassan rested a hand on her back.

Kokhava took her father's advice and found work at a geriatric center. The busy routine improved her mood and took her mind away from the grief, but when she returned home to Etti, her daughter's dark face reminded her of Aharon, and she sank back into a deep sorrow. Afraid that she wouldn't manage to properly care for her daughter in all this sadness, Kokhava sold her empty house and returned to live with her parents.

Rachamim and Asher also brought children into the world, and Hamama, who didn't see herself as old enough to be a grandmother, found her house filled with barefooted toddlers every Shabbat. Ezra, Simcha, and Shira also married and left the house. More children were on the way.

Kokhava would isolate herself in the room behind the house, staring through the window at Aharon's tree standing in the yard. *Maybe, if she weren't so alone, in such pain, maybe we could've finally enjoyed the quiet*, Hamama thought, watching her husband study Torah. *But the quiet breaks my heart.*

Every evening, he would study. Every evening, she would sit across from him and ruminate on her family's past, and its future. There was always something and someone to worry about. Asher bought her a television set.

Shira had married partly out of love and partly out of her fear of being enlisted in the military. When she could no longer stand her in-laws' reprimands and her husband's beating, she demanded a divorce.

Hamama, who thought for a moment that her empty house was bound to be filled again, was disappointed to find out that the two sisters had decided to leave Pardes Hanna and move into an apartment together in Petach Tikvah. They took Etti with them, and the house once again stood bare.

A year later, the Yom Kippur War broke out. Hamama, who sat in the women's section in the synagogue, heard the noises in the middle of prayer. Suddenly, she saw a stream of men in white walking outside. She and Miriam quickly joined. Military jeeps stood outside.

"This can't be good," she whispered.

Rachamim saw her. "Mother!" he yelled. "Tell Shulamit I went off to war."

"You won't go part from her yourself?" Hamama scolded him.

She knew his marriage wasn't a happy one, as she had anticipated. He never said anything to anyone, but he would often visit after work and linger, to avoid going home. She knew this. But it was important that he treat his wife with the respect she deserved.

"We're leaving immediately!"

Simcha waved to her with half a smile, and Ezra skipped up the stairs toward the women's section and kissed her on the cheek.

"Pass this kiss on to Hadassa," he said.

Why didn't any of their wives attend services at the synagogue? Hamama thought angrily as she watched her sons climb onto the vehicles and head out to war.

Yechiel hugged Miriam and slid nonchalantly down the railing.

"Come on, man, let's go," Simcha said as he wrapped his arm around his friend's shoulders.

"They're just happy to get away from the services," Miriam tried to joke, but her pale face gave her away.

The war was difficult. It came unexpectedly and caught the Israeli Army off guard and unprepared. There were continuous reports of fallen soldiers. Hamama and Hassan sat tensely, waiting for news but not really wanting it. After two weeks of fighting, Rachamim and Ezra were discharged from duty. They first stopped by their parents' house, knowing that Hamama and Hassan were probably worried sick. The boys looked as if they had been buried alive, their uniforms drenched in mud and sweat.

"Shower here and then go home," Hamama ordered. "I'll call your wives and let them know you've arrived." Her heart shrank as she saw their filthy bodies, and she wanted to save this grief from their wives.

"I think I'd better go home," Ezra said and parted from the three.

"I don't mind staying here for a bit," Rachamim said as he took off his shirt. "Come by later, and we'll head into town," he told Ezra and hopped into the shower.

The war was nearly over, and Simcha had yet to return. Yechiel Ben Tzion also hadn't returned. Hamama and Miriam sat in their homes, tense and worried, their eyes staring into the horizon. They could feel each other tense at the sound of each automobile that went by, for fear that it was a military vehicle. Ezra, who was in the army professionally, tried to use his connections to get some information. When this failed, he set out to track down his brother's unit. He made it all the way up to the Golan Heights and walked around the fortifications. After five days of searching, he returned, crushed. Hamama embraced him and kissed him on the head.

"He'll return, Mother," Ezra said with confidence.

The winter beat down with all its might, and Hassan had to abandon his hut in the eucalyptus tree and come into the house. Hamama sat on the porch in silence. It was hard for him to see her like that, and even harder to be unable to help. At one time, he was the man who went out to fight. And until now, he had never really understood what Hamama had gone through every time he left. *I wish I didn't have to understand,* he thought. He looked at his wife. She still looked young, despite the wrinkles and white hairs that had started to peek out.

"Should we read Psalms?" he asked and sat down next to her, starting to recite by heart. "…Even when I walk in the valley of darkness, I will fear no evil for You are with me…"

Hamama shut her eyes and let Hassan's deep voice carry her away, praying in her own way to God Almighty.

That night Hamama heard noises outside the door.

"Hassan, wake up!" she said, and the two headed toward the porch.

Suddenly the door opened, and they stood face to face with a dark man they did not recognize. Hamama trembled and was about to scream, but to her surprise Hassan jumped onto the dark man with a strong embrace. It took Hamama a few more seconds to recognize Simcha.

"Mother?"

"Simcha?"

Hamama ran to her mud-covered son, wet from the rain and with dark, hollow eyes. She hugged him warmly until he gently pushed her away a bit.

"I need to take a shower."

Hamama hurried to the kitchen and started preparing food while Hassan stood and watched her with a frown on his face.

"You're not happy, *ya* Hassan?" she asked.

"I'm happy," he said and smiled at her.

Only then did she realize that something was not right. Simcha's eyes had tried to tell her, but in the excitement, she had missed it. After he showered, he stood across from his parents and sat down.

"We were five tanks in the Rama. We were attacked, and our tank blew up. Everything burned, and without weapons, we didn't have a chance. We hid in the trench for a few days until we were found by a military search party."

"A few days? No food?" Hamama asked.

"No."

"So, sit down and eat," she implored.

"No."

"Maybe you should rest first? It's the middle of the night. Where are you hurrying off to?" she asked.

"To town."

"To town?"

"Mother, I need to go to Miriam."

"What? No!" Hamama's breathing came to a halt. "Hold on. I'm coming with you."

The three walked up to Miriam and Ben Tzion's house. The pouring rain mixed with their tears. In the darkness of the night, it was easy to find their lit house. Miriam was sitting on the floor, her clothes torn. Ben Tzion sat at the other end of the room in bitter tears. Several soldiers sat between the two. The three sat down silently.

"Yechiel commanded the tank," one of the soldiers explained. "Yesha'ya and Mantsur were with him…"

Yechiel and both his cousins, too? Hamama was shaken.

"A shell hit the tank, and it blew up. They were inside."

"Did you see it?" Hamama whispered to Simcha.

"I saw everything," said Simcha. And Hamama realized that her son would never be the same.

She noticed Ben Tzion quivering. "Bring the boy back to me!" he suddenly screamed. The words came forward from somewhere deep inside him. "Bring the boy back to me!"

Hassan quickly went over to provide support for the aching father, just as Ben Tzion collapsed. Miriam broke down in tears beside him. Hamama sat down next to her and helped guide her head to lean on her shoulder. Simcha sat by the wall, wondering what he was supposed to do now.

Ben Tzion was adrift and bereft from the moment he heard of his son's passing and could not manage to find his way back to his old self. Miriam, who had to function for both of them, developed the skin of an elephant. Only rarely—alone or with her dear friend Hamama—did she permit herself to delve back into herself and cry.

Hamama was worried about her friend and kept close watch. After all, Miriam had been with her though so much hardship. She felt so helpless sometimes but tried to remember that simply being present for her friend could bring some peace.

She watched her son suffer, too. The war tore something within Simcha. Hamama watched as he withdrew and visited only rarely. He opened a local bakery, turning his mother's instruction from years ago into a business. His bakery flourished, and Hamama hoped it brought him some happiness.

All her children seemed to be occupied with their own struggles and routines and ambitions. Rachamim's marriage to Shulamit crashed into an iceberg and recovered. Shulamit, however, refused to sign divorce papers. He nonetheless married his new love and took care of two families. *Only Rachamim could carry the weight of two families on his back*, she would tell Hassan, partly with grief and partly with pride.

The irony was that Asher ceased to be a source of anxiety for Hamama. He directed his strength and frustrations toward the difficult labor at the orchards' packing warehouses. He would return home exhausted at the end of each day, ready only to love his wife and four children.

Kokhava, on the other hand, had a more difficult time finding her peace. She remarried and gave birth to two more children, but eventually ran away from her violent husband. She found an isolated corner in the north of the country, where she sat and yearned for Aharon. Hamama missed her terribly, and Ezra occasionally drove her to visit Kokhava.

One day Shira, the youngest daughter, returned from Petach Tikvah with a young man whose head was covered with curls and whose zest for life infected the entire family. After endless courting, she agreed to marry him, and she brought three girls into the world. I'm the third.

Hamama sighed when Hassan returned from the synagogue one Shabbat morning. Her hands already hurt from the kneading of the *jachnun* dough. She knew that this dough was the glue that bound her family together every Shabbat, and so she insisted on continuing to prepare it. *In an hour, the house will fill with my rambunctious grandkids,* she thought happily.

Hassan held her hand, as if reading her thoughts, and massaged them. Hamama smiled into her husband's eyes. Her childhood friend, the love of her life.

"Unfortunately, now that we've attained peace and quiet, we're already old," she told her husband.

"You're calling me old?"

Thinking about his habit of learning Torah in the hut he built into their eucalyptus tree, she answered with a smile, "You're right, what am I talking about? After all, you're still climbing trees like a monkey."

"At least I don't have a red bum like those monkeys, and I'm not chasing you around." Hassan laughed at the memory.

"Wait until I pinch you and run off," Hamama answered, and joined him in laughter.

2010

The girls are finally asleep, and I'm planning on heading to bed, too.

The phone rings. I curse the telemarketers but run to pick up the phone. I'm afraid the ringing phone will wake the girls after I worked so hard to put them to sleep. I reach for the phone, so I can slam it down.

But with typical clumsiness, the phone slips out of my hand, and I see the number from home.

A phone call from Pardes Hanna. It's five in the morning there, and right away it dawns on me. Grandpa has passed away.

THE END

Thank you for taking the time to read *Hamama*. If you enjoyed it, please consider telling your friends and posting a short review on the retail site where you purchased it. Word of mouth is an author's best friend and much appreciated. Again, thank you.

~ Sarit Gradwohl

ABOUT THE AUTHOR

Sarit Gradwohl studied social work and film and television at Tel Aviv University, obtaining BA degrees in 2004 and 2007. The Hebrew version of Hamama, titled *Saperi Tama Temima*, was published by Pardes Publishing House in 2014. She also authored several short stories, published in Hador and the Jewish Literary Journal. When not writing or parenting, she lectures on the topic of Yemenite Jewry.